DECEIVED BY THE GARGOYLES

LILLIAN LARK

Deceived by the Gargoyles

Editor: Ellie, My Brother's Editor
Proofreader: Rosa Sharon, My Brother's Editor
Cover Artist: Lillian Lark

Content Warning

***

Dear reader,
Deceived by the Gargoyles includes breeding without pregnancy, body shaming by the villain, stalking by the villain, family estrangement, lying, and deception within an open relationship.

Be kind to yourselves,
L. Lark

***

To my amazing husband.
I'm sorry/ not sorry that you now know what knotting is.

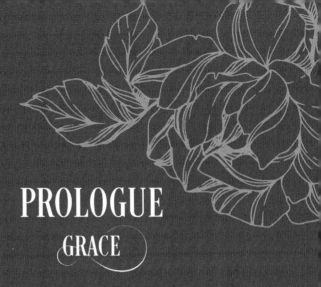

PROLOGUE
GRACE

I snicker at the storefront before me. This can't be the place. Of all the ways they could disguise a magical bathhouse, did they really choose a video rental location? It'd be a magnet to collectors or any nostalgic person, human and paranormal alike. I double-check the address and shake my head.

This is it, the Love Bathhouse. Behind the blinking Open sign and false exterior lies the premier place for paranormals of certain appetites to indulge in their sexual desires. But I'm not here for *that*.

I'm here for the matchmaker. The moment I walk through the glamoured doors, my plans and commitment will be put to the test. I'll be trusting the best matchmaker of this generation to select a partner for me, a match.

It's surrender, but my sanity is at stake.

I'm a witch with an obsession for planners and lists. I can break down any goal into actionable steps, but with how things have been going… the idea of outsourcing my dating decisions is a relief. If it weren't, I wouldn't be standing on this sidewalk, contemplating my goals.

All I need to do is walk through that door and keep the appointment I've scheduled. Nerves threaten to rise. Is it too much to hope that this works?

A prickle of awareness travels down my spine, as if I'm being watched. I turn in a circle. The street isn't empty. There's a popular café across the way, with big windows. Maybe that's why my senses are going haywire.

The red bodycon dress I wear is sexy and loud, the design skintight in a way that usually draws eyes to the width of my hips, my stomach, and rise of cleavage. I'd chosen the dress to boost my courage. Coming here is a step in getting the life I've always wanted. The family I've always wanted. I won't let stray eyeballs from strangers make me hesitate.

Come on, Grace! Do it!

I'm a badass witch who deserves love.

I draw in a breath and push the door open.

CHAPTER 1
GRACE

The sizzle of magic over my skin is slight in comparison to the view before me. The tiled floors to the vaulted mosaic ceilings are gorgeous and completely unexpected. A deep laugh sounds through the space, and I close my mouth with a blush. The familiar redheaded man sitting behind a giant front desk smiles at me.

"Lowell!" I exclaim. "I didn't know you were working here now."

The last time I'd seen the affable male witch had been at our school reunion. He'd been full of stories from his adventures backpacking and the way he'd worked his way around Europe doing odd jobs.

The click of my heels echoes on the tile as I approach the desk.

Lowell raises his chin at the beautiful decor with pride. "I decided I should stop running from the family business. I'm the bathhouse manager now."

"Really? That's wonderful," I say. "I'm sure Rose and Jared love you being around more often."

"Yeah." Lowell's face is soft. "I'm sure they'll get sick of me eventually, but it's been nice to be all together again."

The Love family has been a source of envy for me throughout my life. While interactions with my parents and cousins are always peppered with sneers at my wardrobe or snide comments about the hottest weight-loss trend, the Love siblings and their cousin Lowell have been tight knit since childhood. I'm still jealous of them.

I want a family like the Love family. That's why I'm here. Actionable goals.

"I have an appointment with Rose." I try to push down the embarrassment. It's hard to accept that I need help, but for as long as I've known this family, they've never been cruel to me. And in the society I come from, that's more valuable than gold.

Maybe having a family business built on acceptance and sex for all paranormal beings makes one less judgmental.

Lowell points me down a hallway. "Rose is expecting you."

I nod in thanks and head in that direction. A moan comes through a closed door that must lead to the main bathing area and my skin burns. My mother would be horrified by my presence in this establishment. That thought doesn't help with my red cheeks, but it does put a pep in my step that carries me to the open door of an office.

Rose sits behind another giant wooden desk, biting her lip as she types away at the laptop in front of her. Her red springy curls stir with a dismayed shake of her head.

I knock on the open door.

"I hope I'm not the project making you frown," I say, my cheer brittle.

Rose's face lights up. "Grace! You're here already!" She looks at the clock and coughs a laugh. "Right when you were supposed to be. Forgive me, I got distracted and lost track of the time."

A little of my stiffness melts away at the warm welcome. "It's no trouble."

"Come in!" Rose rises from her desk and rounds it. We hug and the rest of my stiffness leaves me. This had been the right decision. If anyone can help me, Rose can.

"Take a seat," Rose says while she closes the door.

The office is decorated in lush colors and patterns. A stunning, highly erotic piece of art hangs on one wall and the other has an impressive multicolor display of different types of stationary. Rose and my witch talents both gravitate toward paper, if quite different manifestations. Hers aids her in finding matches for people, while mine assists me in reading the history of documents and absorbing the details transcribed on them.

My office has aged parchment on display rather than colorful patterns, but I love what I do too much to regret that. I pull my chair closer to the desk to fill out the paperwork. My eye catches the carvings of copulating figures and flames and I hold in a laugh. Of course Rose has erotic images of copulating figures carved into her desk.

"You're still at the library, working on the Archive project? Right?" Rose asks.

"Yes, I am," I say.

Rose hums. "Did your mom ever come around?"

My smile is wry. "If by come around, you mean talk about how bored I must be by playing with crusty old things all day long, then, sure."

My mother had not come around. She'd rather I spend my time planning events for appropriate organizations and meeting bachelors with a similar pedigree to ours.

Rose rolls her eyes. "That woman makes handling magic history sound like watching paint dry."

I laugh. Why had it taken me so long to reach out to Rose? Why didn't I keep in touch?

The answer is clear. I wasn't ready.

There was a time in my life when the weight of my family's insufferableness nearly drowned me. The condescending comments had been slow but persistent, each one like a drop in a bucket adding to a weight around my neck. Being in the presence of Rose, the witch with a family that doesn't ignore or belittle each other, would have been too much.

I hadn't known the way to free myself would be by having others in my life. Others like Rose and her family.

The time of letting my familial connections tear me down is over.

"Yes, well, she's charming like that," I say.

Rose shakes her head with a sigh. "There's no helping who your family is."

"That's why I want to make my own," I blurt out without meaning to.

Silence.

I widen and drop my eyes to the desk. Rose's presence exudes comfort and trust. The waves of it had lulled me into speaking aloud the very personal reason I've suffered through all the failed dates.

"I-I shouldn't have said—" I start, but a freckled hand rests on my pale one on the desk. I raise my eyes to Rose's understanding smile.

"Yes, you should. Being honest and open will help me pick the best match for you. Your wants are valid."

My wants are valid.

The things I've meticulously listed out for my life are valid.

The simple statement softens me. "Thank you. I'm not expecting you to perform miracles if you can't find someone. I just can't go on another terrible date where I'm told I draw too much attention to myself by the way I dress."

"They do not! You look fabulous!" Rose exclaims.

I chuckle, feeling more like myself. I do look fabulous. It isn't so much that these dates are shaking my confidence in myself, but rather each one chips away at my hope that there's someone for me.

Someone who wants what I want and doesn't mind the way I dress or that my magic isn't the *right* kind of magic. Or—

I shake my head. "One guy said I'd have to lose twenty pounds before he'd take me to meet his family."

Rose's mouth drops open before a look of angry horror scrunches her brows.

"What. The. *Fuck*," she says.

I jump a little at the expletive, not expecting it. Even after so many years living outside of my mother's house, cursing is still a taboo action for women. *It's not ladylike.* I give a mental snort.

"Have they all been assholes?" Rose asks.

Her reaction is gratifying, even with how frustrating this whole endeavor has been.

"In different ways. There were a few that were just meh. The other issue with dating witches is the draw of my family name." I press my lips together before continuing. "Last week, my date spent the entire dinner scrolling through his phone and was astonished when I wasn't interested in a second date. Then he asked if I'd vouch for him with my father."

Rose's brows crease. "I could see how that could be a problem with how old the Starling line is. I didn't think you were that close to your dad."

"I'm not," I say with an arch of a brow that has Rose rolling her eyes at the audacity of these men.

I'm not as bendable as either of my parents wishes me to be. My father is practically a stranger to me and contact with my mother only occurs when she thinks I could be steered one direction or another.

The Starling name is full of pomp and prestige, and I don't want a single thing from it.

Rose picks up a pen and taps it on a pad of dark-emerald paper. "How do you feel about branching out and matching with non-witches?"

I blink. There isn't a stigma in the witch community at large for mating outside of the witch population, but some of the older families still have quiet beliefs about the topic. Beliefs that must have somehow made it into my psyche, because I hadn't even considered the option.

The possibility of not having my match clamor over my family name… it's tempting.

"I think I'd be open to that. The type of paranormal shouldn't matter," I say.

That should cast a wider net. I'd already filled out different questions for Rose over email, questions about my life and goals with more follow-up questions to come based on the availability of other to-be-matched applicants.

Rose writes a note to herself on the dark paper and the bright-gold ink shines.

My eyes follow each line she draws. "That color is my fav—Oh! You're casting!"

I feel silly, but Rose just flashes me a smile.

"Pretty paper is still one of my best tools," she says.

"Well, anything that works is fantastic."

Rose looks back down at the paper and makes a gold flourish to accompany my answer. Her concentration visible in the narrowing of her eyes.

"Are you open to being in a relationship with more than one person? Like a triad or larger?" Rose asks.

I sit back and think for a moment. "I don't think so."

My answer doesn't sound as sure as it should.

There'd been a couple of bad dates in my younger years that had graduated into bad relationships. Those relationships had been full of mind games, routines where I'd get the impression that I wasn't the only woman in the relationship, but it would be adamantly denied, and I'd doubt my instincts.

The infidelity would come to light and the relationships would end. It had taken twice for me to eschew the practice of dating until now.

Now I go with my gut. I don't let bad dates turn into bad relationships.

Being in a relationship that is more than two people? That sounds like more complication and jealousy than I'm okay with. Maybe it works for other people, but I can't fathom doing the same.

Still… some flicker of curiosity is hard to snuff out.

Rose makes a note, unaware of my internal thoughts.

"Have you thought about what you're looking for in a partner?" Rose asks.

I breathe out in relief, ready to go back to the things I'm sure about.

"Yes, I have a list."

CHAPTER 2
GRACE

"I can't believe you gave the woman a list." Emilia's mouth twists in some mix of consternation and amusement. Her dark shade of red lipstick a beautiful complement to her light-brown skin.

Note to self, ask Emilia what lipstick to wear with my green outfit. My best friend, fellow librarian extraordinaire, has an uncanny eye for color matching even if she keeps her own clothing choices monochromatic.

Emilia continues typing at her desk across from mine in our office, located off the main archives. Both of our positions would warrant our own offices, but we've been sharing since a pipe burst in Emilia's. It's worked out since both of us spend most of our time at workstations outside of our office. I have my own lab for cataloging and testing things of magic history, while Emilia's is devoted to restoring items of the non-magical variety.

What had originally been a temporary fix turned into a permanent solution when I'd glimpsed the personality hidden under Emilia's severe shyness. We'd bonded over a love of old books.

It's been nice having an office mate. I'd been hesitant to admit how isolating my dream job felt when I'd finally gotten the posting.

And anyway, Emilia had confessed that her old office had smelled like mold in a way that wax warmers couldn't compete with. I can't send her back there when her company finally makes this job what I want it to be.

Emilia has teased me more than once that I only put up with her because her mother makes the best mantecaditos. I always laugh and try to hide that the fact that her mother inviting me over for holiday dinners is more valuable than all the shortbread cookies in the world.

"What's so odd about a list? I have things I'm looking for in a partner," I say.

Emilia shakes her head and her dark curly hair bounces at the motion. "I don't know. It seems a little limiting. What if you meet the perfect person and he only fulfills one aspect?"

I scrunch my face. "Well, then he's not perfect. I'm not expecting that a person can be *everything* on the list. Half would be excellent."

Emilia looks up from her computer, her dark eyes assessing. "Maybe I'm too much of a romantic, but it's so clinical."

I scoff. "It's supposed to be. The list is something I wrote up so that I'm not swayed by pretty faces and romantic gestures."

I didn't lie to Rose. Many of the dates had been awful, but there had been a few that swept in with a strategy to woo. Those men had the intention of gaining valuable connections like the man who had sat through our date on his phone, but with a much better plan. Flowers, chocolates, manic calling afterward. The actions so robotic and over the top that I put them in the category of being solely business-minded.

Being connected to my family name? That's simply a good investment.

Some of those men had been very pretty, and very determined to romance me, but I have my list. The list itself may be generic and basic, but it's a physical item that I can use to guard my heart in a world of pretty faces and smooth lines.

Emilia rolls her eyes in disgust. "I can't even with some of your dates. Does every man in your sphere think that flower deliveries on the hour are a sign of devotion rather than rabidity?"

I laugh. "It seems that way. Which is why I went to someone."

"A matchmaker," Emilia considers. "Maybe I'll try it if I ever break down from my mom's pestering and start dating again. Though it probably costs an arm and leg." Emilia narrows her eyes before waving her hand. "We'll see how desperate I get. It'd probably be worth it to skip the online dating apps."

I wince. "It's more unconventional than that. I know you don't go in for all the woo-woo stuff."

I always try to keep it close to the truth with my human friend. I don't like lying. Rose could match Emilia easily, my friend is beautiful and talented, but the Love Bathhouse doesn't charge money for matching.

Matches are paid for through an exchange. If Rose does find me a match, I'll be paying in the form of spending a night with my match at the bathhouse. We'll make magic in the most natural way possible, sex. The bathhouse harvests that magic and sells it to warding companies and the like.

I hide large parts of my life from Emilia.

My best friend is human, and I am not.

The drag of the guilt is so familiar by now that I've gotten used to it.

It's not *absolutely* forbidden to tell humans about the existence of paranormal beings, but it's messy. I'd personally become responsible for every action of Emilia's, and the actions of anyone she tells for the rest of her life.

That isn't the reason I haven't told her though. For a human to know that the things that go bump in the night are real is uncomfortable. The things above a human on the food chain are vast. To face that with no magic at all...

I've done what I can without alarming her. She and her mom are listed as under my protection and a ward master has fit where they live with the appropriate spells to keep the worst out.

I make do with lying because the other option is to not be friends.

I can't lose Emilia.

She is my rock, my reality check, she brought me back to the surface during my worst moments and she'll probably never know it. It had been the small things that had done it. When I'd let situations with my family or past relationships slip, highly edited, it had been Emilia's shock and disgust that signaled how toxic it all was.

Without Emilia, I may have never been able to separate myself from my family. My trust fund coming in when it did helped, but being treated a certain way all my life made it hard to imagine that I didn't somehow deserve that.

Emilia saved me from my doubts, the parts of ugliness I'd absorbed without knowing, and I've been lying to her our whole friendship.

I try to ignore the guilt prodding the back of my mind.

"I'm sure your mother has a long line of suitors in mind if you ever let her," I say.

Emilia glares. "Don't encourage her. She's dropped the nagging about dating for now—"

Emilia breaks off at a knock on our office door. Agnes peeks in, her gray hair artfully arranged and sprayed within an inch of its life stays immobile.

"Hello ladies, I hope I'm not interrupting. I'm just dropping off a delivery for Grace before the director sees it." Agnes's voice is a combination of warmth and sternness, with the warmth always outshining the stern when it's us she's talking to. When it's the director, it's always steely.

The door swings open and reveals the large flower arrangement in her arms. Emilia and I share an alarmed look.

"I'm not expecting anything," I say as I round my desk.

Agnes's brow furrows. "There's a card."

The arrangement includes red and white roses. The hairs on the back of my neck rise. I don't tell my dates where I work. I've worked too hard at this job to have this place be somewhere inundated by excessive, shallow gifts. My doorman already gets enough of them.

Emilia raises her brows asking, *Maybe your matchmaker works quick?*

I shake my head. Rose would never tell a match all my details until I consented to it.

I carefully slide a white card from the holder and flip it open.

Grace,
> *I can't wait for our next date.*
> *–Theo Bradshaw III*

I blink. What in the gods' name? It takes me a moment to place the name. *Theo*. The phone-scrolling date that I've already told there won't be a second date. My annoyance and a small bit of fear must be clear on my face because Agnes's expression takes on her Mama Bear look. It's the same look she gets when an intern has a run-in with one of the many men that think a public library is the place for masturbating.

A look that heralds doom for a perpetrator and comfort for the ones she thinks of as hers.

"Am I correct in guessing these are unsolicited?" Agnes asks.

"Yes, but I'll deal with it." I shake my head, trying to figure out if I need to take the arrangement all the way out to the dumpster or if it would fit in a different trash can. The violation of my privacy has me paranoid about going out alone. *Stop it! You're overreacting, Grace.*

I force a smile. "It isn't your job to handle my bad dates."

Agnes huffs. "It's not your fault if a man sends you flowers that you didn't ask for."

She steps back with the arrangement. "Don't worry about this, I'll tell the director a donor sent them and make it something he has to deal with. I won't let anymore flowers make it past the front desk. I'd advise filing a complaint with the police for the record, but it's up to you what you want."

Just like that, the fear of overreaction for a flower arrangement disappears. Not for the first time, I want to hug this woman. "Thank you, Agnes."

"Of course, dearie. Remember what I said. There's no being too careful."

"I'll think about it," I say.

Agnes leaves with a nod.

"I love that woman," Emilia says. "I think my mom and her would be the perfect power couple."

I try and shake off the weird feeling from the flowers.

"Maybe you should do some matchmaking of your own," I tease.

Emilia narrows her eyes. "Maybe. Do you know how one of your dates found out where you work?"

I bite my lip. "I have an idea, but I should check before placing blame."

I open the drawer where I keep my purse and pull out my phone. There's a text from Theo who I'd changed the contact name to "scroller."

Scroller: I hope you like my surprise

I pause and itch to just block the number and ignore him, but I can't give this guy any reason to think that his attention is welcome. I text back.

Theo, I've already stated that I have no interest in us continuing to date each other. Kindly cease contact.

I hesitate for a moment before calling the person who I hope isn't the one to give out personal details but….

She picks up on the third ring. "Mary Starling speaking."

I roll my eyes. "You know it's me, Mother. That's the way cell phones work."

"Yes, but we still should begin our conversation properly."

I shake my head, getting away from myself. "It's your decision how to answer the phone—"

"It's the polite way to answer the phone."

I sit and look up at the ceiling. Emilia casts me a sympathetic look. She's never met my mother, but I've told her so many stories about the woman that she knows her enough.

"Yes, well, have you given out information about where I work to anyone."

"Oh! Did Theodore surprise you? He said that was the plan."

My heart falls at the confirmation. "Mother, Theo and I aren't dating. And I don't—"

"Whyever not? He seems like such a nice young man. His family and ours would make such a good connection and—"

"We aren't dating because our date didn't go well—"

"Interrupting me is rude, Elizabeth Grace."

I stop, trying to keep the frustration that always accompanies speaking to my mother from bleeding through.

"I apologize for interrupting." The words leave a bitter taste in my mouth. "But that doesn't change the fact that giving out my details to anyone who asks is impolite."

"Nonsense. I know his family, and that still counts for something."

I blink, not knowing how to even respond. There are too many things that can be said, but she won't listen.

"Mother, I'm kindly asking you not to do this kind of thing again. Please respect this boundary."

She sniffs. "I think you should give the man another chance."

"I'll think about it." I won't. "But he was rude during the date."

Mother makes a sound of dismay and I roll my eyes again. Me stating my disinterest in a man isn't enough to deter her, but rudeness is.

"That's a shame. I must be going now. I'm meeting Janice for lunch. You know, her son's divorce was just finalized, and he would—"

"No thanks, Mother. Have a good lunch." I hang up.

"Oof," Emilia says.

"Oof indeed."

"I've changed my mind about the list. You deserve to have every box checked. I'll send positive vibes to your matchmaker, woo-woo or not." Emilia's face is painfully serious.

I huff a laugh and my phone buzzes with an email from said matchmaker. I open it and scan the contents. Hope soars in my chest, even if there is a very real thread of wariness through it.

"Your positive vibes must be something else because I have a date," I say.

CHAPTER 3
GRACE

The hostess smiles at me, her eyes widening at my outfit. I mentally shrug. I might as well start off strong. I have a way I love to dress, and it doesn't blend in. Tonight, I'd gone all out with a glamour theme. The white fabric has a lovely shine to it and wraps my heavy breasts up like a present. The small dip of my waist appeared more prominent with the vast amount of dress that flares around my hips and over my stomach.

I'd styled my blonde hair in pin curls with makeup to match.

I look fantastic. Emilia had picked a red for my lipstick that perfectly speaks to the vintage feel of the dress and offsets my pale complexion.

The hostess's expression appears delighted with my ensemble, and I add this restaurant to my repeat list. It's a lovely new place. According to their website, the chef made the society pages with her promise of farm-to-table cuisine with locally sourced and seasonal ingredients.

And the waitstaff doesn't titter at my sense of style. Most of the restaurants that my dates pick don't make the repeat list.

This is promising.

The hostess brings me to a table with a man sitting pointed away from us. From behind I catalog the suit he wears as nicely fitted and his blond hair is rakishly mussed. I nod to the hostess and walk into this stranger's sight line.

"Are you Elliot?" I ask.

The man shoots to his feet with such force that he knocks the table. The silverware clatters and water glasses tip but with an uncanny speed, he keeps them from spilling.

"Oh shit, I'm so sorry—" His words stop as he takes me in. His cheeks pinken, his sharp jaw slackens for a beat. "Please say that you're Grace."

Elliot Bramblewick is a little taller than I am in my heels and the features of his face are fine with an aristocratic edge. My heart already picks up with nerves because this is no bottom-of-the-barrel match. There's something in the way he moves and the flash of his green eyes that quickens the flutters of butterflies in my stomach.

I smile and hold out my hand. "You're safe. I'm Grace Starling."

Elliot takes my hand and brings it up to his lips in a way that has my cheeks starting to burn. His eyes darken with teasing intensity.

"You look… I struggle for the words and words are my best talent." His voice is smooth and full of awe. "You're stunning."

Now the skin of my chest burns along with my cheeks.

I clear my throat. "You also look quite handsome."

He looks down and shrugs his shoulders in a way that communicates bashfulness and self-effacement before sliding around me and pulling out my chair.

"You're very kind, but I must admit that this isn't the way I really look. It's a glamour. Please sit, if I haven't scared you away," he says.

"Oh, I see." I sit. Rose didn't tell me much about Elliot other than his name. Many paranormal creatures don't talk about what kind of being they are to people they don't know. It's a safety measure as I understand it. A holdover from the time that being a rarer creature than a shifter or a witch was a cause of danger.

"Your true form is less human appearing?" I ask, skirting around asking something that would be considered highly impolite. *What are you, Elliot? Is that the reason my heart rate hasn't returned to normal? Are you putting a spell on me?*

That last one is ridiculous. I'd sense if anyone was trying to target me with a spell.

"Yes, can't have people running in the streets," Elliot says.

The conversation drops as the waitress approaches. She takes our drink orders and explains the special of the day. I mentally list this restaurant as one to revisit soon as my mouth waters at the description of New York steak with artichoke and horseradish crema. We both order the special and the waitress leaves us again.

I wait. This was usually the part of the date that it goes to the dogs. Too many men in the past start our interactions with commentary about what I eat. As if some passive-aggressive commentary is going to make me order a salad. I grew up with my mother. They're amateurs in comparison.

And I wait.

But Elliot smiles at me. "I'm so glad you agreed to meet. I only just applied to be matched."

"Me too!" I say, some tightness in my chest loosens. This could really work out. "I really like the place you've picked."

"I've never been. I hope you don't hold it against me if the food isn't as amazing as it sounds. I love trying new places and heard good things about this one."

He looks so eager that I laugh.

"I'll try not to hold it against you, but I'll be sad if it doesn't live up to expectation," I tease.

"That's understandable." Elliot's eyes gleam. "I'd have to beg your forgiveness and make it up to you by getting dessert from a tried-and-true place."

"Oh?" I ask.

He winks at me. "It's a surprise. So, my stunning movie star, why did you apply to a matchmaker? I can't imagine you have any shortage in suitors."

I hum and struggle how to answer. Talking to Elliot is easy, but I don't want the conversation to get too heavy too soon. I want to be the stunning woman Elliot called me without wearing vulnerabilities on my sleeve.

"I was having some trouble finding the right kind of suitors, if that makes sense. I've had some bad experiences lately, and I went to school with Rose. I figured she'd be able to find me someone; her reputation for matching is stellar."

The waitress comes back with a cocktail for each of us and I wipe my thumb on the condensation on the glass. I've worked hard not to be plagued with insecurities, but unlike the numerous dates I've been on before this, I want Elliot to like me.

Elliot raises his glass, the gleam in his eyes turning a little wicked. "To the right kind of suitors."

I bite my lip, keeping the bloom of my smile from taking over my face. I clink my glass to his.

"To the right kind of suitors."

***

The food is phenomenal, and this place gets mentally upgraded to one of my favorite food places. The conversation flows with an ease that I haven't experienced since getting to know Emilia.

It's a surprise how comfortable I am with Elliot, going along with my gut and Rose's assurance of compatibility, I talk about the specifics of my job and what library I work at.

Elliot is co-owner of a restoration firm that has been trying to convince the director to hire them to maintain the building.

The coincidence isn't unusual. The library is co-owned by the Council that governs all paranormal beings, since a good number of spells and histories are documented there before being sent to their final storage places. That a renovation company manned completely by paranormals would express interest in it fits.

"From what I've seen, Director Adder isn't known for his charming personality. I don't think there will be any influencing him without something becoming damaged first," I say.

"Well yes, my... clansmen tell me the same thing, but the building is so beautiful! I'd really hate for it to get to a state where the cost to renovate it is higher than the city or Council can afford," Elliot says.

Clan?

"I can see the wheels turning in your head. I shouldn't keep you guessing as to what type of creature I am, I know." Elliot's eyes crease in concern and he scratches the back of his head. "I guess I just wanted an opportunity to woo you before telling you."

His nerves about this start to spark worry. What if he's a creature I'm not attracted to?

"Are you worried I'm going to run screaming?" I ask.

Elliot considers it. "No, I don't think so. I can tell you're brave."

The words are almost a taunt even as his eyes crease in concern.

"Is…is it that you have slime?" I ask. Having slime like a slug might be my limit.

Elliot's head falls back on his guffaw. The restaurant stops at the loud sound before resuming. My date blushes.

"Uh-no, no slime," Elliot says. He drums his fingers on the table in a fidget before continuing. "Let's go, I'll tell you on our walk to dessert. That way you can gracefully bow out if it's too much."

We keep our conversation inconsequential as Elliot settles the bill. When we walk out into the brisk night, he offers me his elbow and I shiver. He frowns and takes off the suit coat, wrapping it around me. The action is so quick, I don't have time to react other than to soak in the warmth of the fabric and the lingering scent of granite and the night sky.

"Thank you," I say.

Elliot frowns at my heels. "The place I have in mind is just around the corner, but I can get my car if you need. I forget that ladies' shoes, however sexy, aren't made for walking."

I smirk. "I'll be fine, as long as the place is just around the corner and not, like, two miles away."

Elliot grins. "Perhaps this is how I trick you into being carried by me."

My eyes widen. "I think not. I'm not light."

"You are perfection." Elliot's smile takes on a salacious edge. "I'll lift and arrange you for all kinds of things if you'd allow me. I'm eager to provide you a demonstration if needed."

His brows move with suggestion and my mouth dries at the casual innuendo. That had been an innuendo, right? I shake my head.

"Don't distract me." I narrow my eyes and pull his suit coat tighter around me. "You were just about to tell me what you are."

I expect for him to pause dramatically but he doesn't.

"I'm a gargoyle," he says.

I almost trip at the abruptness of his words, but Elliot's elbow keeps me upright. The muscles of his arm are tight under my grip. I let the term roll around in my head. *Gargoyle, gargoyle, gargoyle.* I don't know anything about gargoyles. The only ones I'm familiar with are the ones on old buildings.

"So, no slime?"

His smile is so wide it almost looks like he has fangs for a moment. "No, Grace, no slime."

"Will—will you show me how you really look?"

He doesn't respond right away, his smile falling.

"Would you mind if we saved that for a different day? I kind of like the way you look at me now." Elliot wags his brows. "Um, my true form is shaped similar to this, I just have some extra attributes."

My curiosity catches on that. "Attributes?"

"Well, wings for one."

"You can fly?" I blurt out.

Elliot bites his lips, looking pleased with himself. "Yes, I can fly. Perhaps I'll take you sometime."

I stop myself mid-laugh and consider it. Elliot wouldn't drop me, and he said he'd *arrange* me for all kinds of things. *Flying.*

"Elliot Bramblewick, you are a terrible tease," I say.

He tilts his head.

"It's only a tease if I don't intend to pay up."

The idea of a moonlight flight sounds so fanciful. Maybe a time where I'm not wearing a dress.

"I'd like to do that sometime," I say.

"Your wish is my command." Elliot tips his head.

I frown and look at the suit coat I'm borrowing. "How do wings fit with your suit?"

"Oh, uh, the glamour that my clan and I purchase is very high level. It's costly, but necessary for working face-to-face with humans. I don't know how the magic works, but it's as if I'm walking around human. I don't feel my wings, or my tail, for that matter."

"You have a tail?!"

Elliot pulls me to the side of the walkway to muffle my exclamation with his body as some humans walk past. His chest shakes with silent laughter.

I tilt my head. Elliot's eyes are bright with mirth.

"Yes, I have a tail." The words are confirmation but there's some heat there. As if a tail means something suggestive. My exhale shudders out.

Elliot presses his front to mine, sliding his hands around my waist. The position would almost be casual if my breasts weren't pressed against him, his body heat sinking through my dress and into my skin. A different kind of heat lights in my belly. The lust that had been teasing at the edges of this encounter makes itself known.

"Does that turn you off, Grace?" His voice deepens and I press my thighs together at the thrill that it strikes in me.

"What do you think?" I ask. Elliot's fingers tighten and I want them to roam over me more. If he were touching me, I'd at least have a reason for my panting need.

He hums. "It would be fair to tell you that I have a fantastic sense of smell."

Why is he?—Oh! My face erupts in heat, but embarrassment only heightens my arousal.

Elliot lowers his face near my neck and inhales. This tiny tease has me on fire. That he can scent how wet I am only adds to the blaze. Who is this man? Gargoyle? He leans back, his pupils blown with lust.

Elliot strokes a finger over my heated cheek. "Don't be embarrassed, my star, your scent is delectable. I want to eat you up—" He blows out a breath. "But I think we should take this relationship slow."

I sigh in relief and a small part disappointment. "I think I'd like that. I'm very interested in making this work."

CHAPTER 4
ELLIOT

I pull into the covered parking, my body still frustrated at me for denying it a mating, but my heart is full of satisfaction. She's perfect. Elizabeth Grace Starling is going to be a member of the Bramblewick clan. I just need to finesse a few things. It's nothing a little strategy and charm can't solve.

A throb of guilt seizes my heart, but I breathe through it.

I'm not supposed to scheme anymore. My mates gave me very clear lines about manipulation. Mostly, they wrap me in their arms and tell me that I don't need to resort to underhanded actions to attain their love. They try to stifle the insecurities that lead to my masterminding.

But.

Grace is perfection. I can't risk letting her go.

The manor is as beautiful as ever; I walk into the entryway.

"I'm home," I call out.

No one responds. They don't need to. We all live separate lives, now more than ever. As if we are separate cogs in a persistent clock. We run a business together and time ticks forward, but the musical numbers are few and far between, only occurring when one of us notices the other's absence.

I get to the kitchen and find Eloise making a cup of tea.

"Oh, hello gorgeous," she says, her voice cracking a little with age. Her dark hair has more gray than when I'd first met her, but she's still one of the most beautiful women I've ever known, inside and out. I kiss her cheek.

"Right back at you," I say.

She's the heart of our clan and mothers us all.

Her mate, Graham, comes out of the pantry holding a tin of cookies. He almost never wears a glamour anymore. The old gargoyle could scare children with his craggy scars and horns.

Our last clan leader, Lachlan, started Bramblewick clan with his mates Graham and Eloise. It grew from there with their generous hearts taking in gargoyles no one else wanted.

"Are you two taking tea with Lachlan tonight?" I make myself ask.

Eloise's smile is warm, and she cups my cheek. "Yes, we miss him. I know you boys don't understand it, but talking to him, remembering him, helps us."

Graham comes up behind her and wraps his arms around his human mate, juggling the tin of cookies. "It's a good tradition."

His voice is gravelly, with the capacity to boom with no effort.

My throat tightens. "Tell him hello from me."

Eloise nods. "Of course. You should get Alasdair to try visiting sometime. That boy is too stressed, he needs some reflection time."

I swallow. It had been a year since our old clan leader had left us to his stone sleep, never to wake again. A year since Alasdair had taken up the mantel of clan leader, trying to replace the best gargoyle he'd ever known. The clan leader who had given a bunch of misfits a home.

It's taken me a year to realize how much our clan needs someone else in it.

"I'll mention it to him," I say.

Graham hums. "He isn't home yet."

I hold in my sigh and make a note to bring up Alasdair's work habits. It's been days since I've seen my mate at home. "Is Broderick in his studio?"

Eloise carefully picks up their mugs with a snicker. "Yes, he was mumbling to himself last I saw."

The couple moves past me and Graham freezes, inhaling. My heart drops into my stomach.

The old gargoyle frowns. "You smell like a woman."

Eloise gasps. "Elliot!"

My face heats. "You know neither of my mates mind me dating outside of the clan."

Graham grunts. "Foolish practice, but usually you discuss it with them first."

Eloise puts a hand on her mate's chest to stop him from judging. Our relationship seems unconventional to our clan elders, but when they started courting me, Broderick and Alasdair didn't want me to feel trapped. I'd been quite a free spirit when I'd come here.

I've tried dating outside of the clan a couple of times in the past, but it's never worked out. Before we lost Lachlan, our mating had been solid. We didn't need anything else. Now, our mating does need something. I didn't know what, until I saw Grace.

"Is that what this is?" Eloise asks me and even though she didn't raise me, I'll never lie to this woman.

"No," I concede. "But I have a plan. I just need a little time."

The couple frowns. Graham wraps a hand around the back of my neck and presses his forehead to mine, a sign of affection for our kind.

"Elliot... you are a son to me. Be careful with my other sons," Graham says.

I snort but absorb the fatherly love that I'd started life without. "I will. This will work out."

Eloise's smile is hesitant, but her words are stern. "Well, I hope to meet this woman soon."

"Soon, Clan Mother, I promise."

With that, the couple leaves to the turret, where their mate sleeps as a statue.

And I leave to wash the scent of Grace from my skin before anyone else in this house prematurely finds out my plans.

***

I'm scrubbing my skin with a loofa when the bathroom door opens. I smile but keep working the suds into my skin, a little remorseful to lose the traces of Grace so soon, but it's simpler this way, for now.

A larger warm body presses against my back and the loofa falls from my hand. The form and scent tell me which of my mates is ambushing me. Dark-gray clawed hands run over my soap-covered body and I place my palms against the tile, to keep from face planting.

"Broderick," I whisper as his fangs scrape over the back of my neck.

"You missed a spot," the wiliest of my mates says before his hands slide down and grip me. My hips buck into his grip. My moan echoes off the tile.

"Is showering as a human really that much more convenient?" Broderick's deep voice has my head falling forward.

Broderick almost never dons his glamour if he can help it.

"My wings always get cold. I can never dry them fast enough." And fitting one winged individual into my shower is hard enough, let alone two.

Broderick huffs a laugh, starting to stroke my quickly hardening cock. His heavy hardness already burning against my ass.

"I've missed you, my troublemaker," he says. Something brushes against my ankle before slithering up my leg. It touches every sensitive patch of skin, the back of my knee, the soft spot where my ass meets my thigh before sliding against my taint and asshole.

"Fuck…" I gasp. "Just been busy."

Broderick sighs. "Yes, we've all been busy lately. It feels like it's been ages since I've watched Alasdair destroy you."

I groan, precum leaking from me at the squeeze of his hand only to be washed away by the shower. It has been ages since we've all gotten into a bed together.

"You're already so close to spilling. Aren't you, troublemaker?" Broderick teases. "I guess I'm not the only one who's missed this."

"Broderick. I need you. Please. Fuck. I need this." The words fall out of my mouth. The tip of Broderick's tail massages against me before sliding in. I cry out. "You lubed your tail up? Gods, you're going to kill me."

"Of course, I lubed it up. I knew exactly what I was going to do to you." Broderick's words are broken only by his kisses on my neck. The tail twists and curls inside me, pressing against my prostate in a way that has a whine escaping my mouth.

"I'm close," I pant.

"Not yet." Broderick slides his tail from me and his heavy cock notches against me, leaking hot precum and already slicked with lube. "Will you take me, mate?"

I sob. "Please!"

I curse when he presses inside. It hurts, but we heal. The pain is second to the fiery pleasure of joining. Broderick's cock is large and the stretch of it burns, but I wouldn't have it any other way.

Broderick growls and snaps his hips against my ass, pushing farther inside me until the swell of his knot presses against my entrance. He groans against my ear, nipping my lobe.

"I'm sorry, sweetheart, I don't think I can wait long enough to coax you into taking my knot right now."

I babble something that sounds like a beg and break off on a cry as he fucks me into the grip of his hand.

It's messy and fast, but it's everything my heart needs as my climax rushes through me. My seed hits the tile wall and I clench on Broderick's cock in a way that has him cursing before filling my ass with his heat.

We gasp, our breaths in time with each other. Broderick's arms wrap around me, my head falling back against his shoulder.

"Gods, that was exactly what I needed," I say.

Broderick hums in agreement. "What we both needed."

I hiss as he slides from between my ass cheeks.

"I really do miss us being us. All of us," Broderick says, a thread of worry running through the words.

I hum, of course, Broderick, the artist, would sense the disruption. It's comforting that I'm not the only one to notice the dissonance.

"I think we're still trying to figure out our lives, our clan, without Lachlan," I murmur.

Broderick stiffens behind me before relaxing again.

"I suppose you're right. How do we even fix that? I thought with time—" Broderick's grief has him stopping.

I can't stop myself from saying something. From sharing the hope infecting me.

"I-I'm working on something." My whisper is hoarse. "But it's a secret."

Broderick nuzzles my cheek, his chuckle hesitant.

"Always strategizing. Should I be scared?" he asks.

Yes, Grace is going to shake up everything.

I swallow. "We'll be stronger for it."

I hope.

CHAPTER 5
GRACE

"So… it was good?" Emilia asks. She's still working on going through emails before going off to her current book restoration.

I bite my lip, gathering the paper forms for the items that I'll be handling today.

"It was more than good. It was the best first date I've ever been on. For dessert, he took me to this amazing little shop where hot chocolate made to order with fancy toppings is their specialty."

"He has good tastes." Her lips pull into an amused smile.

I lean against my desk, giddiness swirling in my chest.

"It wasn't just the food, I promise. The food was the best I've had that a date has planned, but it was him. We can just talk. He's a fantastic conversationalist."

"How is he in comparison to your checklist?" Emilia asks, her curiosity good natured, maybe finally coming around to the benefits of lists and planning. Or maybe humoring me.

I scrunch my nose. "He checks a good third of my list so far."

"A third is not half," Emilia says.

I scoff. "I know how fractions work."

"It's just an observation." Emilia's career deals with more science than mine, though she's never condescending about it. "Do you keep this list on your phone or something? Or do I need to worry about hiding a list titled 'Grace's Future Husband' if the director ever drops in?"

Emilia's teasing has a little concern bleeding through. She has more contact than I do with the director. Or as much contact as accepting tasks entails. I don't know if she's actually spoken to him.

"My list is on a paper," I say. "And I keep it in my bag. No need to explain it to Mr. Intense."

I'd checked the boxes after getting home last night to take my mind off the fact that the doorman had another worrisome flower arrangement from Theo the Scroller that I'd instructed him to throw out. This guy is more persistent than others have been.

I stand, everything collected to go to my workroom. My phone tucked in the pocket of my stylish wide-legged pants just in case I relent to the temptation to contact Elliot.

Am I a tiny bit concerned that he hadn't contacted me yet? We have each other's number. In a perfect world, he'd contact me first, then I'd know that I'm not the only one who enjoyed our meeting each other.

"Oh yeah, you with your love of paper," Emilia teases.

I shake my head. "Well, I'm all ready to start my day, handling my precious papers. Don't bleach anything on accident."

Emilia gasps as I leave the room. "I'd never!"

The tinge of guilt is only minor now. My love of paper is how I explain away some of my strangeness to Emilia. Paper and things in hard copy hold a significance because of my magic.

Each time I touch the paper that holds my perfect-partner list, it feels like the hopes of a bright future.

It's a new document, so it only gives me light impressions of the emotions I used to craft it. In time, it'll absorb more of my intention or the events that surround it. Each moment adding a drop to its essence until it's as heavy with emotion and significance as the documents I'm preparing to handle.

My workroom is in the basement. The walls are thick with wards to keep anything I handle from bleeding out of the room. I'd worry about missing any messages from Elliot if my phone didn't have improved reception. Magic and all that. I lock the room behind me.

Wood crates line one wall with an assortment of stamps ranging from local to exotic. Invoices and packing slips are stacked in a basket on my worktable. Each sheet is number coordinated to the content descriptions on the crates but acts as a key for what the crates actually contain.

Functioning under the notice of humans requires a lot of paperwork to subvert the real paperwork. Smoke and mirrors and safety spells. Each crate has its own containing charms to suppress any dangers hiding in an object or a book as a standard. Is great grandma's amulet as harmless as believed? We aren't taking any chances.

I heard a rumor that someone accidentally raised zombies out of the cemetery next door when this department began functioning.

The Archive project is an effort to document and safeguard every ancient magic item, spell book, or history

book about our world. Every item submitted gets sent
to my department first. I analyze it, perform some tests
to determine its risk level. Then I take whatever scans or
photos that are important to document the item before
shipping it to a specialist for study or a specific library for
storage.

I love getting to touch every single thing that comes
here.

Submitting items to the Archive is on a voluntary
basis. Sometimes collectors will submit sections of their
collections in exchange for other items to be evaluated to
be stored in their care.

The routine part of the job goes quickly. I don my work
apron and gloves, starting with a crate marked from Italy.
I take a gem charged with the specific counter ward over
the edges of the crate before prying it open. Dust kicks up
in the air and I sneeze before turning up the ventilation in
the room. I've only encountered magic dust once, but that
was enough for a lifetime.

Sneezing out flowers is not charming. It's also hard to
hide. I had to stay home a week before the spell subsided.
The magic had been too old to readily contact an expert to
reverse the effects.

I move the packing material to the side and slide a
folded letter out before lining the items in the crate on my
worktable. The letter is first, then a couple of leather tubes
with rolled documents inside, and the last to be placed on
the table is a carefully wrapped rectangle with the weight
of a book to it. The first impressions I pull from the items
aren't much to go on, the wrapping and containers are new
and the letter was only touched when drafted.

I open the letter.

To the librarian,

Please accept the donation of the enclosed spell book and map on the behalf of Mr. Kalos to the Archive. The blueprints are of interest to my employer, and if time allows, Mr. Kalos would appreciate the contents to be analyzed using your specific skills and returned.

Sincerely,

Ben Hanes

Excitement hums in my blood. Kalos is a renown collector. Every donation made from his collection adds to the history of paranormals everywhere. He is an immortal of an unknown type. I've wasted too much time contemplating how much of his collection is just from his old age, hoarding until an item is useful.

With the amount of goods I've handled from the immortal, there is a noticeable difference to the items compared to what others donate. The knowledge is never the type that reveals details about rare creatures.

I get to work, starting with the spell book. After checking it over for latent spells, I record the pertinent details on a laptop, warded to protect the hardware from the odd magic flare.

The spell book appears to be the record of a witch family. I spread the pages with careful wonder. Each page is heavy with meticulous ink drawings of plants with tight writing in a language that I don't know.

I remove my cotton gloves, cleaning my hands with some specialized solution to remove unseen dirt and grease. Carefully, I slide my fingers over the paper and the history of it fills my mind. The familial love hits me first and I gasp at the fierceness of it. This book had been passed down a line of matriarchs who worshiped the warmth of the sun, the damp of rich soil, and the tender sprouts of new life. The words may be indecipherable to me, but the essence of the paper tells me that these pages detail potion making, horticulture experiments, and the family tree.

Each matriarch faithfully detailing their own accounts at times when very few knew how to read and write. When it was dangerous to have such skills.

Every matriarch, until it ended abruptly, with sickness. My throat swells with borrowed grief. This story isn't a unique one, just one more thread of sadness to the history of the world.

Plague. It toppled many humans and paranormals alike. Witches are only slightly stronger and longer living than humans.

I sniff back the story and put the emotions in a box, donning the gloves again. I type my account as the item description before categorizing the book. There's a specialist in plant lore that requested to receive items of this nature. I set the book aside to make scans of later. The book description and select scans will be available to the paranormal community online.

I go to the blueprint next. My curiosity too much to put off anymore. I uncap the tube and slide out aged parchment. Not as old as the magically preserved spell book, but still old enough that I handle it with care.

I unroll the blueprint, and my brows pinch together as I try to decipher the design. The delicately scrawled drawing seems to be the layout of a citadel. Like many documents I handle, the language isn't English. I breeze through cataloging the item, this time for a report rather than to enter it in the Archive.

I prepare to touch the pages all over again and breathe out slowly before stroking a fingertip along the edge. The frenetic energy of the architect is soaked deep into this piece, stress and delight in equal parts with just a touch of strict budget concerns that must come from the handling of whoever approved the project.

It's rather mundane. A lot of thoughts about how much light the building needs. This isn't what I'd expect Kalos to want to know about. Until I hit a detail. Like a snag, a tapestry of information unravels.

A secret. A level hidden by magic. A spell intricately woven into the matter of the blueprints, distinguishable only to the most sensitive individuals. Or to someone with my skills. The spell is set to reveal with the utterance of a single word. I pinch the parchment and it rises to the surface.

"Manifesto," I say

Lighter sepia lines bleed into existence and I grab a camera and snap a few pictures before they disappear again. This is what the immortal wants.

I type up a report with the document history, the details of the spell, and activation word. I insert the photos I took of the piece before emailing the report to Mr. Hanes and printing a hard copy to send back with the blueprints.

A buzz from my pocket distracts me.

Elliot: I swear I fell asleep without meaning to last night and rushed out of the house this morning after sleeping through my alarm.

Elliot: I meant to message you how much I enjoyed our date. I hope you have a good day at work.

I sigh in relief and a giddy feeling has me smiling. I message back.

Me: So, you weren't planning to ghost me?

His response is instant.

Elliot: Never. I dare say you're going to have to deal with me from now on.

The words ease the worst of my worries.

Me: I like the idea of that.

Elliot: Do you like the idea of lunch?

Elliot: Like… in ten minutes?

The plan for my day rebels at the invitation. Ten minutes? That's hardly any notice. I love my plans and lists. I love having everything just so, but… spontaneity is on my list of things I want in a partner.

Exactly for the reason that I'm the opposite of spontaneous.

I debate with myself. Will going to lunch really burn down my day? Isn't this rush of excitement what I wanted?

I look fabulous with my chic wide-legged pants and my matching tight top that has a tiny bit of midriff peeking out at times. Why not spend lunch with my match?

I tap out my agreement instead of dithering. The more I get to know Elliot, the sooner I'll know if this can work out.

CHAPTER 6
GRACE

I see him before he sees me. Elliot has his head tilted back and turns in a slow circle near the front desk. His suit is a navy one, more casual than what he wore on our date, but not by much. This gargoyle is a smart dresser. Agnes gives me a smile with a raised eyebrow of approval that makes me duck my head in sudden shyness.

"You're going to get a sore neck that way," I say.

"It's not the only way I can get a sore neck," Elliot mutters before clearing his throat and blushing. "You look fit for the red carpet, my movie star."

Did he make a dirty joke? I lift my brows. "Thank you."

The hungry way Elliot's eyes move over me vanquishes any doubt in my heart that the compliment is being given out of kindness.

Elliot casts his gaze up again. The ceiling is stunning. A dusky mural of clouds and sky surrounded by gilded plaster beams and faux bois.

"The ceiling details are gorgeous." His words are wistful. "I really wish the director would hire us to fix that dipping corner before we'd lose any more of the original paneling."

I snicker. "Is that the real reason you wanted to take me to lunch? Am I just the lucky one here while you're working?"

Elliot's smile is wide, pulling his attention away from the crumbling panel. "Of course not. I'm tricky, but I'm not that tricky. I'd have to court the director for that and I'm not selfless enough for the task. No, your beaming countenance is the only reason for our date."

"Oh good, I'd hate to think you were here under false pretenses."

Elliot loses his smile for a split second before it brightens. "Shall we go? How do you feel about tacos?"

**

My comfort to do things with Elliot that I've never done before astounds me. Before Elliot, I'd never wanted to have a date the day after the first. Before Elliot, I hadn't told anyone I dated where I worked because as Theo the Scroller has proven, unsolicited gifts from dates gone awry are awful.

Being with Elliot is proving to be as illuminating as it is enjoyable. Shaking up my routine has already paid dividends. How did I not know about the wonderful tacos two blocks away from the library?

I do now, and Emilia and I are going to be coming here for lunch next time we go out. Elliot and I claim a booth, the savory scents of meat and cheese have me salivating when I notice an important detail.

"No napkins, I'll go get some," I say.

"I can do that," Elliot says, trying to cover his mouth as he chews.

I laugh. "I've got it, you're already compromised."

The trip is a quick one and I bring back a stack. Elliot nods in thanks, but he seems thoughtful.

The taco is as good as it smells, and I moan in delight. Elliot smirks and my cheeks burn at the wicked gleam in his eyes. I chew and swallow.

"It's fantastic," I say.

"Oh, it's glorious," he says, and I can't say for sure if he's talking about the taco.

I duck my head and we eat our lunch.

Sometime later, Elliot wipes his hands and his expression goes thoughtful again. "Grace, what do you want out of being matched? Like—in life."

The spell book comes to mind. The sense of family and community has my breath catching in my throat. Last night, I'd wanted to hide all my vulnerabilities, but now that our interactions have been so seamless and compatibility undeniable, it's time to be more open.

He should know what I'm looking for.

"I've never fit in with my family." I say. "I don't know how much you know about witches, but the Starling name is somewhat well known in higher witch society…. And I was raised to continue that line, make good connections and such…"

"Oh, one of those families," Elliot says, raising his pinkie as if sipping tea, and I laugh.

"Yes, one of those families. Or rather, not like a family. It's like being tossed in a piranha tank and being eaten alive one flaw at a time."

Elliot's brows shoot up. "That's not like a family at all."

It's a marvel how often we seem to be on the right page, with only the briefest of details. Is this what real compatibility is?

I suck in my breath and continue. "Yes. What I want is my own family. One that isn't like that."

Saying the statement out loud, while on a date no less, is like cracking open my very heart. The practice is so revealing that I drop my gaze. I pick an imaginary piece of lint off my pants but a sound from my date's throat has me looking up again.

Elliot leans in, his eyes darkening. "You're wanting lots of babies?"

The look on his face lights a fire in my middle. It's as if I only need to say the word and he'd be happy to spread my legs and give me—*whoa Grace! Out of the gutter!*

I cough. "Maybe one or two."

Elliot's eyes are still dark. His smile easy but whispering all the thoughts from before. I adjust in my seat, it's as if all he would need to do is crook his finger at me and I'd slide into his lap—

"If the lady desires lots of babies, the lady should have lots of babies," he says.

I throw my napkin at him, trying to hide my red cheeks. Elliot laughs, but his cheer eases until his eyes crinkle in warmth. He slides his fingers through mine.

"So, making a family is on the table, but what about joining one? Being a part of a group of love and support," he says.

I swallow. Oh, this is the feeling I'm looking for. "Yes."

Elliot brings my hand up to his mouth, and he kisses it. "Well then, I'd say we want the same things."

The warmth of his breath over my skin, his promises. It's all almost too much to bear.

The gargoyle hums, the vibration plucking something low in me.

"And I'd be happy to breed—"

"I really should be getting back!" I say louder than I mean to.

Elliot breaks into a laugh but gives me a look that tells me this isn't the last I'll hear his salacious words.

"I'll walk you back, and try to control my tongue," he says.

We've walked a block in comfortable silence before my blush recedes enough for something to occur to me.

"It's daytime, I know nothing about gargoyles, but do you guys turn to stone?"

Elliot's smile is sad. "Sometimes, it helps us heal if we need it… And other times, it's permanent."

"What?"

"When we get to an age, we know the end is near and it just… happens. It's our final rest. It's tradition to caretake the statues of our elders. The old clans have castles full of them."

"That's kind of a beautiful thought. Is your clan old?"

"Oh no, not at all. Let's see, my clan isn't considered a proper one. None of us are related by blood and there are only six—" Elliot breaks off, expression pained. "Sorry, five of us. We lost our last clan leader a year ago."

I thread my fingers through his in offering.

"I'm sorry for your loss," I say.

That sad smile is back again. "Thank you. It's been hard to adjust. Lachlan started our clan with his mates. The thing about gargoyle communities is that well…" Elliot sighs. "Most of them are archaic and care more about blood purity than an orphaned kid."

I gasp.

"Okay, that sounds worse than it is," Elliot allows. "Most clans will foster a gargoyle until they're eighteen. Some… not so much. Eighteen is considered the age of maturity but young gargoyles need a clan structure, the hierarchy. Or they get into trouble."

Elliot's shoulders come up at that.

"You were the one who got into trouble?" I ask.

"Uh, yes, that was me. But it's easier to get all the details right if I go chronologically. The first young gargoyle Lachlan took in was Alasdair, at fifteen. He's actually full-blooded, but his home situation was shit, and his dad threw him out."

I shake my head. "Um, will they mind you telling me this?"

Elliot smiles. "I'll keep it brief, but it's old history."

I pay close attention. This is a family group I'm probably going to meet, and if things go well, join.

"I think Alasdair was the luckiest, he's been in Bramblewick the longest of us 'boys.' Next was Broderick, he was orphaned and his clan didn't want to keep him past his eighteenth birthday. His mother was human," Elliot says as if to explain. "They're a little older than I am. I came along later. Absolute and total trouble."

I bark a laugh. "You couldn't have been that bad."

Elliot's face softens. "That's very kind of you to say, but… I was pretty bad. If I wasn't running a con, I was stealing or cheating. I lived my whole life without a clan. Lachlan came across me when I was twenty-one and didn't take no for an answer. I was a mess."

My laughter is a distant memory.

"Your whole life?" I ask.

"I mentioned that some clans will reject orphans. I wasn't technically orphaned, but my mother wasn't ever around to care for me, no one knew who my father was. They sent me to a home. The ones that will take in paranormal kids that can't mesh in society without glamour."

"H-how old were you?" I almost don't want to ask, but I need to know.

"Ten, I think." He shrugs. "It's not like I know my birthday, to say for sure."

My sadness moves over for my outrage.

"Elliot, that's just… how—that's awful."

He wraps an arm around my waist. "It wasn't great. When you talk about wanting a family, a home, I get it."

My cheeks burn. "My reasoning seems mild in comparison—"

"Stop."

We stop walking now and I let Elliot step into my space.

"We don't need to compare hardships. There is no need for a hierarchy of suffering between us." Elliot puts a knuckle under my chin to tilt my face up. "All that matters is that we want the same things. I'm looking forward to discovering every want we share and building that family you desire."

Words stop in my throat, unable to work their way past the swell of emotion in my chest. Elliot leans in, and my lips part in anticipation. His breath brushes them and my cheeks before he kisses my forehead.

Elliot takes a step back and I blink. Slow. We are taking this slow, being careful.

Even if I want to entwine my body with his or take him up on whatever wicked words he says, slow is the best course of action.

Right?

CHAPTER 7
ℰLLIOT

I'm fresh out of the shower, still contemplating the list I'd found in Grace's purse. I'd memorized it on sight and the more I think about it, the surer I am of my plan.

The Perfect Partner
~~Funny~~
Thoughtful
~~Spontaneous~~
Protective
Wants children
Passionate about something
Book lover
~~Sexually compatible~~

The crossed-off items make me smile. Of course the sexy librarian has a list of desired attributes for her mate. Soon, I'm going to need to make the argument that the best solution to get all those neat items crossed off is to expand her thinking… a little wider.

Soon. It's already difficult enough to go slow. To not cross any more physical boundaries until I tell my mates about Grace, and Grace about my intentions.

The deception and manipulation I'm plotting needs to be forgivable.

What if it isn't? What if, as soon as I tell Grace, I lose her? I shake my head at the thoughts and pull on some sweatpants.

I leave my room in search of anyone else in the house. In the face of my doubts, loneliness creeps into my heart. I get to a lit-up office first and that loneliness turns to delight.

"You're home," I say.

Alasdair looks up from his laptop and gives me a tired smile. He sits in the very sturdy custom-made office chair, resplendent in his true form. Shirtless, his full-blooded coloring is beautiful. Gargoyles all tended to be a variation of gray, but Alasdair's skin has a mottling pattern that is textured with blues and teals.

We work together, I see my mates all the time at the office and on our building sites, but when we're at work, we are our roles in the company we started together.

When we're home, we're our triad.

"And before nightfall. Is it a holiday?" I tease.

"I missed my clan," he says. His voice is deep and soothes something fundamental in my soul.

I raise a brow at the laptop in front of him. "So, you thought you'd get some work done instead of see us? You know the rules."

No work in the manor. Lachlan had made the ruling when we started Bramblewick Renovations and after some mild disagreements, it stuck. Broderick had his art studio, but that's his passion. Alasdair can't make the argument that his spreadsheets are the same.

His cheeks flare a ruddy color as he closes his computer. "I got a little distracted."

Alasdair leans back and the chair creaks ominously. My eyes travel down his bare chest to the kilt-like garment our kind favors. My mate is a wide and muscled behemoth, and I don't get the opportunity to trace the pattern on his skin with my tongue near often enough.

I tut. "It wouldn't do for the clan leader to break the rules."

Alasdair winces. The title is still an uncomfortable one for him even after a year.

He frowns at me and pats one of his thick thighs. I purse my lips at the office chair and shrug, if it breaks, it will still be worth the cuddle. I take a seat and his arms enfold me. Some tightness in my chest, the worry that something is unfixable in our home, eases.

Alasdair rests his forehead against my hair and the texture of his horns on my scalp has goose bumps raising on my human skin.

"You've been staying in your glamour more often, is everything alright?" Alasdair asks, his brows crease in concern.

The question strikes at my very core. This is my mate. The quiet observer who supports with small touches and inner strength. I've barely seen this facet of him since he's become clan leader.

He sees me.

"It's—you know that sometimes it's more comfortable for me," I say, looking down where my glamoured fingers thread through Alasdair's clawed ones.

"I know, my heart." His words are soft, but the consistent love beneath them is strong.

I don't deny that growing up in a home of others who couldn't mix with the human world left some marks on my soul. Some wounds that only a snug glamour around my skin suppresses.

I swallow. "And here I was going to ask you if you're okay."

"Me?" Alasdair asks.

His puzzlement makes me want to roll my eyes and I push my own vulnerabilities down deeper.

"Alasdair, this is the first time I've seen you home before dark in a month. We own the same business, I know there aren't any projects burning down, what's going on?"

He shakes his big head back and forth. "I've just been busy with work—"

I make a noise. "Alasdair..."

I hear him swallow. "Nothing is burning down. The company supports our clan. I'm trying to take all the steps and precautions possible to set our family up for success."

The warmth of our cuddle unwinds my tongue to voice inconvenient truths.

"You are an amazing business owner," I say. "But I think you're using it as a crutch."

"Ouch." Alasdair's reaction lacks energy, and a thoughtful look overtakes his features.

"You're clan leader, my mate," I say. "You should be here with us."

He sighs. "I know. It—it feels like a lot of pressure sometimes. I don't want to disappoint the elders, or dishonor Lachlan's memory."

"Eloise thinks you should spend some time talking to him." I poke his muscle-bound middle and he jumps.

Alasdair's smile is heartfelt. "Maybe I should. The woman is much wiser than I am." He sighs and massages the bridge of his nose. "Perhaps I have been overworking myself. Everything at the company is going so much better than when we started and instead of it alleviating my stress, I've just been worrying more."

We sit in silence for a moment, not making any promises, just absorbing each other's presence. This is home. This is what Grace is looking for. She'd fit between us so well. Her presence could cinch the tie of our family.

I can't help but ask. "Have you thought about adding another to the clan?"

Alasdair frowns. "You want to foster? I didn't think anyone had the time to spare for that."

I make a sound of dismay. "I mean, I wouldn't say no to offering a home to another gargoyle in need, but I don't think it would be for the best right now. Not with this… disruption."

"Disruption?" Alasdair asks.

I rub my chest. "Something feels off."

Alasdair tilts his head before nodding. "I think I know what you mean. We feel… unsettled."

I breathe out in relief. We are all on the same page. Broderick and I may have noticed it before Alasdair, but it's there.

"I'm talking about maybe adding another to… us," I say.

My mate clears his throat and blood rushes to his face, darkening the blue tone of his skin. He shakes his head even as his mouth stretches in amusement.

"Elliot." Alasdair's chuckle warms me through. "A mating isn't just something you can throw another person into to patch the gaps."

"I know." I cast my eyes away so Alasdair can't read my lie for what it is. I'd normally agree with him if I didn't already know that there is a Grace-shaped hole in our mating.

This may take more strategy than I intended.

Alasdair's chest still shakes with some mirth and his face buries into my neck. His breath tickling and reassuring all at once. He stills and breathes me in.

"You smell like roses," Alasdair says and inhales again.

I freeze. Grace smells like roses. I made sure to scrub her scent off my skin, but Alasdair is the strongest of us. How quickly would he be able to spot my duplicity if he wasn't overworking himself?

"It's nice," he says, nuzzling his face into the crook of my neck.

I relax into the embrace with a hum.

All the lying will be worth it in the end.

Grace belongs here.

CHAPTER 8

GRACE

Hot kisses cover my skin. My fingers clutch the darkness as whimpers fall from my lips.

"My star," he growls.

Then I wake up. The sheets twist around me in a way that could impress a bondage amateur, my skin damp with a need denied.

A dream. A horny hot dream of a certain gargoyle.

Dreams that are nowhere close to being a reality.

The light fills my apartment and I untangle myself from the bedcovers. Sitting up, I stretch, letting the light from the sun catcher hanging next to the door of my balcony decorate my bare arms with flares of dancing color. The sexual frustration winding my body tight releases me with each motion of the little lights.

I let my arms fall and sigh. Today is going to be a good day. A weekend day should always be a good day. Elliot is going to the flea market with me to look for treasured old books and then we'll get lunch at someplace he's been wanting to try. It will all be perfect.

So, why does it feel off?

I bite my lips and start to make coffee. Caffeine will make everything better. I'm sitting out on the balcony, enjoying the morning caress of air against my cheeks and the hot mug of coffee warming my hands when I break.

This requires outside advice.

Me: How slow is too slow?

I take a deep breath and sip from my drink. I'm not used to asking anyone else for help. Thankfully, I don't need to wait long.

Emilia_The_Great: Slower than you want = too slow
Emilia_The_Great: It's only been a week, hasn't it?
Me: But we haven't even kissed.

My phone lights up with a call and I answer it. "Yes?"

"I feel like you should have mentioned this sooner." Emilia's voice is sleepy, and I hear a voice on her side of the call. "Mom says hi by the way."

I snort. I appreciate the idea of Emilia having this conversation in front of her mom comfortably. I could never be so relaxed to talk about this around my mother.

"Tell her hi back. And I haven't been keeping it from you on purpose per se… I guess I thought that he was going to at least kiss me last night."

Emilia clears her throat. "You and he have been seeing each other almost every day, right? And he hasn't kissed you… I'd say it's a little weird."

"He gets close and then… stops. Like, I can tell he wants to." The heated looks he gives me, the extended casual touching, the hungry way he smiles. Elliot is interested.

"Maybe he's shy? Maybe he wants you to make the first move, and he's letting you pick the pace?" Emilia asks.

I bite my lip. "So, I should just jump him?"

There's a distant cackle.

"How loud is your phone?" I ask.

Emilia laughs. "It's nothing worse than she's heard me say. She'll live. If you want to jump him, jump him. But you could start with a conversation first. Communication and all that."

I hum in thought.

The kissing matter is kind of the tip of the iceberg.

"What are you really worried about?" Emilia asks, as if she can see all my inner turmoil.

I sigh and look up at the clouds.

"It's going to sound stupid."

"Oh, come on, Grace. If you can't sound stupid to me, who can you sound stupid to?" Emilia teases and it breaks my hesitance.

I smile. *Absolutely no one.*

"He's super close to his… family." Using the term clan would inspire too many questions. "They all live together, multi-generation style and everything. He talks about them a lot."

"Annnnd?"

"Well, is it stupid that it feels like he's hiding me from them? Gah! It's only been a week. I know I need to relax."

Emilia doesn't respond for a minute, and I wince.

"It's not stupid. You both went to the matchmaker because you're wanting to find someone to marry, right?"

"Yes."

"And this guy seems crazy about you. Agnes says you two are so cute she could cry, and I've seen the way he looks at you… If you feel like you want to meet his family, especially since they all live together, you should talk about it with him. I wouldn't assume he's hiding you until he makes excuses about you meeting them."

Is it funny that Emilia, the one who is the shyest around strangers, is always the one to remind me when I need to be bold? Yes, but she's always been right.

"So, I just need to talk to him instead of hiding everything?" I ask, my smile small. Habits built over a lifetime are hard to break.

"Exactly! That conceal don't feel isn't going to work here. Hey, is that one loser still sending you flowers?"

I scrunch my face in discomfort. "Um, yes. It's weird. Usually, they'd stop by now. My doorman suggested I start refusing the deliveries altogether, so that's what I've been doing."

"Have you given any thought to filing a report? This is concerning. You've blocked his number, sent back the gifts, what is wrong with this guy?"

I shake my head and sip my coffee.

"I think it just has to do with wanting a meeting with my father. Business reasons."

"It's fucking weird."

I smile at the scolding of Emilia's mom over the phone and stifle my instinctual wince at the expletive. Eventually, I'm going to unlearn my response to swearing. It's one of the last holdouts from my childhood. A holdout that isn't going to go away until I make it.

"It's… *fucking* weird," I say.

Emilia laughs. "Did that hurt to say?"

"It was awful!"

We both laugh.

"Talk to your man," Emilia says. "Maaaybe file a report about the weird guy and enjoy your Saturday."

"You are the wisest of the wise."

CHAPTER 9

ALASDAIR

Elliot taps out a text on his phone and smiles.

"Good news?" I ask.

"Huh? Uh, yeah. Something I've been waiting for has come in." Elliot beams to top off what would have been a convincing lie to anyone else and drops his eyes to his coffee.

Broderick and I share a look. Something has been going on with our resident troublemaker.

"I'm going to check in with the guys about the chapel project after my errands today. Are either of you planning on being there?" Elliot asks.

Broderick frowns. "I have some projects I've been wanting to get to here."

I want to lift a brow at Broderick, that wasn't a negative answer, but there is a glint in his eyes that has me shelving the response.

I shake my head. "I'm heading to the office today."

Elliot makes a face. "But it's Saturday!"

My face heats. "It's a small thing that I want to get out of the way."

Elliot sighs and leaves the table, putting his coffee mug in the sink. "You're a big boy, I won't mother you."

"Yes," Eloise calls from her place at the table with Graham with the newspaper. "Leave the mothering to me. Alasdair, don't overwork yourself."

I smile. "Yes, Clan Mother."

"Well then, I'm off, I'll see you all later for dinner." Elliot says, giving Broderick a kiss before bestowing one on me. His lips hold a warmth that infects me as usual, rousing the part of me that wants to hold him close. Protect this troublemaker from whatever bear he's undoubtedly poking.

The faint scent of roses that clings to him brushes me and eases something in my soul.

I nod.

A dinner all together as a clan. It's been a while since we've planned one, but I'd taken Elliot's words to heart. Not the addition of a mate, that seems like an extreme step for our situation. But I'm clan leader, I should be more in tune with what our clan needs rather than burying myself in the company that supports it. There are needs to be addressed, such as Elliot's lying.

The door snicks shut as Elliot leaves, and I glance at Broderick.

"What do you think he's up to?" I ask.

Broderick shrugs. "I have no idea, but it's something. He's been different. I was starting to get worried about him, but now he's been humming and smiling to himself. He's got some sort of project going and we'll find out what it is soon…I don't think it's going to be anything illegal."

Guilt twists in my chest. How had I not been the one to notice that Elliot was off? But I know the answer. I've been hiding from my responsibility to my clan.

It stops now.

"You didn't answer his question about the building site today," I say.

Broderick ducks his head in self-deprecation. "Well, knowing that we'll find out what he's hiding doesn't mean I'm not curious why he asked if I'd be there today. It's probably nothing."

I arch my brow, the situation is a curious one, but Broderick is right, it's probably nothing.

CHAPTER 10
GRACE

I moan at the bite of pasta Elliot feeds me from his plate. The rich cheese and bacon mixture melts on my tongue until I swallow and sigh.

"I think you made the better choice," I say. "The red sauce in my pasta is marvelous, but that carbonara is transcendent."

Elliot grins. "If I was more of a gentleman, I'd offer to trade."

The restaurant is another successful selection of Elliot's after spending a wonderful morning at the flea market. I'd found a book of knitting patterns with heavy annotations on the pages that sang of cozy feelings and a vintage cocktail recipe pamphlet, but failed to bring up any of my concerns. Things between the two of us have a fragility to them, as if it will shatter as soon as I bring up my demands.

Or maybe that's just what my mind says will happen. What has happened in past relationships.

"But you're not a gentleman?" I ask.

The light hits the fork in his hand and illuminates something hungry in his face before it disappears with a smile.

"Oh, Grace, not on your life. I'm enjoying feeding you from my plate too much. If we switched, then I wouldn't be able to claim any of those happy sighs or the way your whole face lights up in delight. Not to mention the moaning."

I cast my eyes down at Elliot's napkin-covered lap and bite my lips. I've never felt the physical need to be with someone as poignantly as I do with this gargoyle. This gargoyle who has yet to show me what his true form looks like or delve into any physical intimacy except for a kiss to my cheek.

Elliot's hand cups my face, his thumb pulling my lower lip from my teeth. His eyes darken as if he knows my thoughts. Knows how much I want him. With his enhanced sense of smell, maybe he does.

This is it. The moment he'll finally kiss me.

Elliot's eyes are hot, wanting.

But instead of consummating anything, instead of being drawn in closer and sealing our match with the kiss I've been aching for, Elliot clears his throat and sits back. His hand drops from my face and disappointment has me blinking.

Elliot goes back to his lunch, as if nothing happened between us. Because nothing has.

I want this relationship to last, I can't afford to let myself be timid about my wants.

"Have you considered that we should schedule our session at the bathhouse?" I ask.

Elliot chokes on his food.

"Session at the bathhouse?" he asks once he clears his throat and swallows.

Worry starts to seep through my temporary bravery.

"You know." I gesture with my fork. "Being intimate at the bathhouse in exchange for our successful match."

"Uh." Elliot doesn't continue. There's a small amount of panic on his face.

Doesn't he want this? Me?

My heart falls into my stomach as if it's become detached from where it beats in my chest a thread at a time, descending lower and lower before the last one snaps. Maybe we aren't compatible. Maybe Elliot is just a brilliant actor. Scratch that, I let Elliot barter over the knitting pattern book for me. He is an excellent actor.

"Unless sharing heated glances is all that we are going to do for the rest of our relationship?" I ask.

Elliot makes a sound in the back of his throat.

"My star, I just…" He struggles to say anything, and I bite my lips for a different reason. I blink my eyes to keep them from watering uselessly.

"You've told me so much about your family, but haven't mentioned when I'll get to meet them. You say salacious things, but won't even kiss me." I laugh, but it sounds a little broken. "I'm starting to wonder if you're even attracted to me."

Elliot looks horrified. I shake my head; I'm working myself up. Nearby tables have gone quiet and the voice in my head telling me not to make a scene has the blood rushing to my cheeks.

I need a moment. I need to just take a minute to breathe through the utter disappointment carving out my heart and reassess.

I slide my chair back and stand. "I-I'll be right back."

"Please, Grace, give me a moment."

I grab my purse, not meeting Elliot's gaze. I should have brought this up sooner. I should have been clearer. I should have communicated.

Elliot's body meets mine so suddenly that I look up in surprise, ready to make an excuse, some reason I can give to gather my composure. Every excuse in my mind flies out the window when he kisses me.

The first moment his lips touch mine has a frantic edge, flavored with my own recent distress, but it all fades as Elliot coaxes the kiss on. His lips are warm and sure, stoking the hot look we'd shared earlier to flames.

When his lips leave mine, I sigh. Elliot cradles my cheek and wraps an arm around my waist to bring us flush together.

"Just one more," Elliot whispers and kisses me again. This one is hungry. My skin heats as I groan into his mouth. I grip his arm, not wanting it to end, but it does. Elliot brings the kiss back down slowly, nipping my lip as a parting gift.

I gasp as he breaks the kiss.

"I need to confess something," he says, breathless

"Uh?" I ask. The sound of guilt in Elliot's voice is bringing me down from the kiss.

"I haven't introduced you to my clan yet because I haven't told them about you," he says.

That drops me. "What? But—"

"It's not for any bad reason, I swear. Things are just in a rocky place right now, and I don't want to cause more strife than I need to."

"That's not comforting," I say, but the disappointment from moments before doesn't rage to the surface.

Elliot's smile is sad. "And I haven't wanted to advance our relationship without you meeting my clan first."

"Oh." That makes sense.

"I've also just been enjoying this time between the two of us, maybe it's been making me hesitate more than I should. I never meant to make you feel unwanted, Grace."

"Will you tell me what's so rocky about your family? Are you and your brothers fighting?"

Elliot winces. "It's not that we're fighting, and we aren't brothers, Grace."

I roll my eyes. "I remember. If it's not that—"

He kisses me again. It's brief but takes my breath away all the same.

"Just give me a little bit more time," he says.

I hum. "If you keep doing that to distract me, we are going to have words."

Some of the urgency in Elliot's face fades and his teasing grin returns.

"Is that so? What kind of words will we have, my star? Will they be your whispered fantasies in my ear?"

"Elliot!"

My gargoyle smiles. "I did have a surprise if you're interested."

I tilt my head, curious.

"I thought I might take you over to our current project and show you what we do. It's turning out beautifully."

To see the company that Elliot speaks about with such pride up close? To get to know more about this gargoyle through his and his brothers' works?

"I'd love that," I say.

CHAPTER 11
GRACE

Elliot reaches behind my seat and pulls out a pristine hard hat for me. It's pink.

"Oh, you prepared for this. You brought protection and everything." I rattle the hat.

Elliot looks struck dumb at my silly joke before he laughs.

"I've been wanting to show you this project, it's just passed the ugly state of the renovation."

"What's special about this project?" I ask.

Elliot beams at me. "You'll see."

We get out of the car, and I get my first glimpse at the building. There's a stone wall blocking my view, but I see a spire. Elliot snags my hand and pulls me to a wrought iron gate that opens with a rusty creak.

There are some trees and bushes, but everything clears as we get farther down the path.

"Oh," I say. It's a stone chapel, and it looks sad. Boarded-up windows and crumbling parts.

Elliot huffs a laugh. "Hold your judgments, my star."

The doorway is a pointed arch and stands open. The sound of a saw rents the air. Elliot leads me through, and a lean figure makes a hand gesture.

"Idiot on site!" comes a call, and the saw ceases, letting the stone and wood around us fall silent.

I stop at the words and the lean figure freezes. "Oh, not you, pretty lady, the bosss. I'd take off my hat and bow but that would be a sssafety concern." He taps on his own hard hat. "Elliot didn't say anything about bringing company."

"Thanks for that," Elliot says. "Here I am trying to make a good impression and show off the window you just installed—"

"It isss a beaut!" The speaker comes closer, and I make out scales. I straighten, as what can only be described as a lizard man grins at me with all his teeth. His coloring is green, and form is similar enough to a human that at a distance I didn't make out the otherness of him.

I don't know the type of paranormal this man is, but that isn't a surprise. There are so many varieties and mixes of creatures that horde details about their kinds to themselves as a safety measure. He could be a type of dragon, a wyvern or anything else with scales. The possibilities are endless.

"Grace, this is Alex. One of our best when he's not insulting me." Elliot's tone is warm. "Alex, this is Grace… my date."

I mark the hesitation. The renovation company Elliot and his brothers run is a small operation. And if the way he acts with Alex is any judge, a tight-knit one. Elliot said he hasn't told his family about our relationship yet, but he probably will have to now.

Alex's brows shoot up. "Oh?"

The floor creaks and a huge man peeks through a doorway. "You're placing Alex above me? Really?"

Ogre. I'd seen some on a trip to the countryside. Usually, they live away from human cities in their own groups, so I've never been able to speak to one.

The ogre gives me a smile. "I'm Barry. I'm much better than Alex."

Alex scowls at that, but his mouth twitches. "If you're so much better than I am, you should definitely be the one to finish the stairsss."

Barry sniffs at the lizard man. "I still think you should do it. It gives you a chance to practice."

Alex's scoff has the same sibilant hiss to it that his words do.

Elliot snickers.

"You don't have to worry about being out of glamours?" I ask.

Alex's smile is warm. "The Bramblewicks understand how uncomfortable holding a glamour is, they have wards around the building that repels humans."

"Don't get sappy. Happy workers do good work," Elliot says, but there is an edge of satisfaction to his words. As if providing comfort to their workers is something they especially take pride in.

Elliot presses a hand to my lower back. "If you'll excuse us, I want to give Grace the tour."

Barry salutes. "Sure thing, boss."

As we walk away, Elliot drops his voice. "I'd like to point out that they work on projects on a volunteer basis over the weekend, we aren't slave drivers. They're living in the rectory while we renovate this place to keep an eye out, so they tend to put in more hours. Alasdair will account for it in their bonuses. I promise."

"Do you hire rarer species specifically?" I ask.

Elliot tilts his head. "It isn't on purpose, but with our own histories, we always make room to hire the people who need a place, a community. Some leave after getting the work experience they need, while others become permanent. They show up for holidays and say the only reason they stay at our small company is because Eloise and I cook too well to leave."

"Oh." *Community.*

We enter the main chapel, and I gasp. The sun shines through a large stained-glass window. Shapes of purple and reds transition to the fires of yellows and oranges with accents of blue. The light doesn't dance, but creates an absolute stillness. The manifestation of meditation.

The sounds of Barry and Alex seem to disappear. Elliot's hand grips mine and we stand in the still calm.

"It's beautiful," I whisper. The word doesn't encapsulate the awe but it's the only one I can think of. The leaded pattern is geometric; circles that radiate outward like flares of sunlight.

"It was exactly what was needed to make this place whole," Elliot whispers as well, but he isn't looking at the window, he's looking at me.

The clearing of a throat startles both of us.

"Sorry boss," Alex says. "That mantle got here from Ace. If you could approve it before you go, we'll be able to install it."

Elliot turns to me. "Do you mind? I should only be a minute."

Alex scoffs. "Don't lie to the pretty lady, the paperwork you need to sign is thick."

Elliot rolls his eyes. "Okay, like five minutes. Is that okay? This place is safe to poke around if you want to explore."

"I don't mind exploring. I'd like to see what the second level looks like," I say, a spiral staircase calling my name.

Elliot nods and kisses my cheek in casual affection. I'm left in the stillness.

The stairs creak under my feet.

Old places soak in histories privy only to my touch. It's not as potent as paper, but the artistry of every carving holds its own faint sensations. Wood is easier for me to read than stone and I let my hand run over each thing I find as I walk along the second story balusters.

I stop as a vibrant sensation hits me. I lift my hand from the carved wall panel and see where new wood has been attached to the original piece. I stroke over one of the new figures in the repair and get the same sensation of humor and satisfaction. The figure has wings and a tail.

A demon? This is an old chapel after all, but that doesn't match what I'm picking up. My finger follows the whip of the creature's tail when the answer arises in my mind.

A gargoyle.

A nearby clatter startles me. The sounds continue from the doorway of the next room. I pull my hand from the carving and curiosity has me peering inside before it occurs to me to be wary.

I blink at the living version of the carved figure. Fear roots my feet to the floor. The creature is large, an expanse of gray skin save for a dark kilt-like garment he wears on his hips. This isn't some human-shaped creature with scales. This is something I've never seen before.

He mutters to himself as he pokes through tools in the box at his feet. Or rather, the raptor-like legs that end in claws that act as feet. Membranous wings spread from his back with clasping talons at the bend, one holds a chisel. Slowly, the instinctual fear leaves me. This isn't some terrifying being getting ready to eat my heart.

This is one of Elliot's brothers.

I breathe out and the race of my heart changes as I take in my first sight of a gargoyle. His muscles ripple as he works, and his face that frightened me a moment ago creases in concentration.

Now that I'm calmer, the features of his face don't appear as demonic as my fear whispered to me. The jut of his brow, the angular nature of his jaw and nose, seems sharper and more exaggerated than what a witch or man would have. There's the lash of something behind him, a tail.

I hesitate at the doorway, torn between wanting to introduce myself and something else. Unexpected heat warms me the longer I let my eyes wander over the gargoyle in front of me. I should go.

The gargoyle's gaze snaps up and his golden eyes have another ripple of fear stabbing through me.

"Oh, hello," he purrs.

I take a step back on reflex and faster than I can track, his sinuous tail lashes out and wraps around my waist, pulling me into the room and closer to him.

"Careful, the railings haven't been checked." The gargoyle's voice is jovial and teasing at the same time.

I blink up at him and some of the cheer on his face fades into something else. Something that looks like hunger.

"What's a delightful little witch like you doing sneaking around this site?" The words aren't accusatory, and I don't feel unsafe no matter that the sight of him had roused fear in me just moments before.

It snaps me out of my reverie. I scoff. "I don't think any man has called me little in a very long time."

His grin is pure wickedness. "I meant it as an endearment, though compared to me or my mates you are on the smaller side." and his gaze falls to swell of my cleavage. "Though parts of you are deliciously noticeable."

The burn of my cheeks chokes my laugh, and I press against his bare chest. My nerves distract me from an odd detail. Elliot hadn't said any of his brothers had mates. "You are being very familiar with a woman you just met. And I'm not sneaking. I'm here with Elliot… so maybe you should give me some space."

There's a pause. My eyes defy my self-control and wander over the gray skin. This close, I can see the purple undertones to his coloring. His skin appears thicker than mine.

Stop checking out your boyfriend's brother, Grace!

The creature inhales as if I'm a chocolate chip cookie. "You do smell of him. You must be the secret he's been hiding. What a wonderful surprise."

The tail doesn't loosen.

I drop my gaze and focus on my pale fingers flat on his chest. "He said he hadn't told you yet, but I guess the cat's out of the bag now. And since I'm dating your brother, you should—um, let me go."

The gargoyle makes an odd choking sound in his throat and his tail slides from me. I force down the pang of disappointment at the absence.

"Grace?" Elliot's voice echoes and a pang of guilt strikes in my heart at my body's interest. I take a step back from the gargoyle and run a hand over my arm awkwardly. Elliot stops in the doorframe.

"Broderick! I didn't know you were here," Elliot says, his voice matching the widening of his eyes.

"Oh, you're Broderick, it's good to meet you. I'm Grace." I hold out my hand to shake as if I hadn't just been in his arms.

There's some dark undercurrent to Broderick's expression as he clasps my hand and brings it up to his mouth. It's not anger. The feel of lips to the back of my hand has a deviant shiver running up my spine.

"It's good to meet you, Grace. I see why Elliot has been hiding you away." Broderick's voice has lost all mirth and is pure sin now.

"Uh, Grace, could you wait for me downstairs? Broderick and I need to talk." Elliot shuffles his feet in discomfort.

"Sure," I say, needing a reprieve from the tension in the room.

I nod to Broderick and move to the door.

"You are in so much trouble, *brother*," Broderick taunts.

I flee, my own guilt giving my feet wings.

CHAPTER 12
ELLIOT

I cringe. "Don't call me that."

Broderick lifts a brow. "It's what that delectable witch thinks."

"I've told her we aren't related," I say as if that excuses any of my trespasses.

"But you left out the part where we are mates. If I was a more insecure gargoyle, I'd be wounded."

"I thought you said you weren't going to be here today."

Broderick raises his brows. "I said I had projects at home, never that I wasn't going to come here today."

I open my mouth and close it. Sneaky gargoyle. "Why?"

Broderick tilts his head and makes a gesture to where Grace had just been. "You've been acting shady. I wanted to know why, and now I do."

Broderick leans against the worktable he set up, this room acting as his workroom for this location. Here he does talented carvings and repair work. The beautiful details.

"So, she's the mystery project you've been working on," Broderick says. It's not a question but I answer anyway.

"Yes." I lean against the doorway with a sigh.

"You think that you're going to solve all of our issues by bringing in a woman."

"It's not—it's not just that."

"Tell me." Broderick's face is open, free of judgment or scorn. In this moment he is the artist, asking me to show him the world the way I see it.

"I don't know how to describe it." I duck my head, embarrassed. "I love our relationship. Even if I'm afraid we're drifting a part, even if I seem to spend more time missing you two than with you, but when I saw her it's as if something yanked on my heart and suddenly, I could see exactly how we'd fit together. I didn't even know her name, but I just knew, knew she belonged with *us*."

Broderick's lips curve. "Not just with you?"

That startles me and I shake my head.

"No, of course not. I've been working toward the idea of bringing her into our clan."

My mate nods, thoughtful.

I narrow my eyes. "You're taking this much better than I expected."

"You're my troublemaker. You are meant to cause trouble," he says.

My cheeks burn.

"And I'll admit I'm curious. She isn't what I'd expect to want in a mate, but I can see why you're so taken with her."

I grin. "It's not just because she's gorgeous."

Broderick grins. "I can see past a pretty exterior too, Elliot. There's something about her that calls to me, but you're going about this wrong."

The part of my heart that had eased at Broderick's easy acceptance aches.

"You're right," I say. "I thought this deception was going to be a small thing, and it isn't anymore. Every time I prepare myself to tell her, I freeze."

Broderick approaches and wraps me in his arms. The hug helps dispel the worst of my fears. He leans back and tilts my face to meet his, the kiss a simple thing that spans the seconds.

Broderick breaks it on a hum. "I like the taste of her on your lips."

My face burns and arousal zings through me.

My mate presses his forehead to mine. "Be brave, troublemaker. We call you a mastermind for a reason."

I swallow. "I'll tell her."

Broderick releases me. "You better get going. Barry probably called Alasdair to approve the mantle before you got here. It wouldn't do for your witch to run into our clan leader before you can explain everything."

The blood drains from my face.

"*Fuck!*"

CHAPTER 13
GRACE

I'm careful as I go down the stairs. My cheeks hot and my guilt throbbing in time with my heart. I need to figure out my issues before I meet anymore of Elliot's family. I'm with Elliot, I can't let myself be affected by Broderick.

I want to groan.

They all have an enhanced sense of smell. Literally everyone in the room will know the way my body reacts to either Elliot or Broderick. How awkward.

"Hey, Grace, you doin' okay?" Barry asks. His face creased in concern. The ogre and his lizard-man companion seem to be strategizing about the wall in front of them.

I force myself to smile. "Yep. I met Broderick."

Barry's face eases. "Broderick's a good guy. He's our master carver."

My smile feels more real now. "Was that his addition to a panel upstairs?"

Alex's laugh is a cackle. "Alasdair wasn't pleased about the signature, said it might make the place harder to sell."

"It looks great. The style looks just like the rest of the carving. I'm sure a buyer won't even notice." I frown. "Is Elliot's other brother that… intense?"

Alex and Barry both freeze and share a look. A sense travels up my spine. A sense that they know something I don't know.

"Um, they aren't brothers," Barry says.

As Elliot has said. I should make an effort to stop calling them that. What if I'm trampling over some past trauma? All of them have had past issues with their families or clans, calling them brothers might hit on a sensitive topic.

"I mean, I know they aren't related," I say.

If anything, the ogre's eyes get wider, and he looks to Alex, who adjusts his stance, uneasy. It pricks something, suspicion tickles my nerves. What don't I know?

What is Elliot not telling me?

I take a step backward. "I-I think I need some fresh air."

I turn to flee once more but run into a wall.

A wall in a suit, emanating body heat, that grabs my arms to keep me from falling backward. I look up into a face that can only be described as distinctive. Heavy brows over bright-teal eyes, a shade I've never seen before, with sharp features lined with stress.

But I know this isn't the man's real face. Because this can't be just a man. Something about the energy, the size, or just the forceful presence of him as he grasps my arms informs me he must be wearing a glamour. This is a gargoyle. Another of Elliot's clan.

A rabbit in the clutches of a falcon would have done better than me. I freeze.

"Roses." The giant man's voice is deep with a commanding edge that flows over my consciousness and demands I stand at attention. The single word comes out on a breath and his brows crease in confusion.

There's a sound from behind us and I turn my head.

"Alasdair, I can explain." Elliot halts from the direction of the stairs, his eyes wide in panic.

Alasdair steps away from me and releases my arms.

"You can explain why your scent is all over this woman?" he asks. The words aren't sharp, but there's a pain in them that levels me.

It's a pain that I'm familiar with, one that speaks of betrayal and *love*.

My frozen state shatters and I suck in a breath.

Oh.

Not brothers at all. *Lovers.*

And I'm the one that doesn't belong.

The outsider.

Just like always.

CHAPTER 14
ELLIOT

Alasdair's pain is like a lance to my heart and the small sound Grace makes is another. I have officially run out of time to strategize this meeting.

Alasdair's and Grace's gazes are on me and the guilt I've been harboring rises to meet them.

"It's not what it looks like," I say.

Alasdair straightens and tucks in the betrayal that had been evident on his face. He's always been the epitome of *still waters run deep.*

"You're allowed to date outside of the clan." *If you communicate about it.* Alasdair doesn't say the last part, but the terms of our relationship are clear.

"Alasdair," I say, but my stubborn mate shakes his head. He doesn't want to talk about this here. Now. In front of Grace.

My beautiful Grace, who knows.

Her eyes water and she shakes her head. "I-I need to go."

She pushes past Alasdair, and he lets her.

"Grace!" I call out, but I'm torn. My prospective mate and my mate are both hurting.

I grip Alasdair's sleeves. "I need to go after her. I promise this isn't what it looks like. Please, just give me some time."

Alasdair's expression doesn't change, and Broderick's voice calls from behind me. "You're out of time, Elliot. I'll talk to Alasdair; you see if your witch will even speak to you now."

I nod to Broderick, not looking at Alasdair's face because if I see him in pain, I'll never be able to go after Grace.

I run.

Grace stands next to my car, facing away. Her hand comes up and her head ducks, wiping away tears.

"Grace," I say.

She doesn't turn toward me. "I need my purse. Unlock your car."

"I will. Let me drive you back to your place."

"No," she says, the word is sharp, cutting.

"Okay." I fumble for my keys. "Please, Grace, let me explain."

I unlock the car and she snatches her purse, replacing its presence with her construction hat.

"What is there to explain?" she asks, but sounds calmer. She pulls out her phone, probably putting in a request with a rideshare app. "I'm just the woman you conned into liking you while you stepped out on your mates."

"Grace, I have permission to date—"

"Not from me!" She glares at me, her eyes red. "I didn't consent to date someone who was already in a relationship."

"And we never said that we were exclusive." My words are soft, but Grace looks like I've slapped her. I shake my head. "You're right. I lied. I misled you. Please let me explain."

Grace shakes her head. The underlying pain surfacing. Her anger is just and I can steel myself against it, weather the much-deserved fury. But her pain? Her pain is a fiery lash, searing and excruciating. I'll do anything to stop it, but the truth is all I have to offer.

"I don't know what you can possibly say to make this better," she says.

"How long until your ride is here?" I ask.

Grace shakes her head. "Ten minutes."

"Give me that long. Give me ten minutes, and if you still don't—" The pain of the possibility is almost too much to speak. "If you don't want me to court you, I'll stop. You'll never have to see me again."

Grace's exhale is shaky, and she looks up at the sky, determined.

"Just ten minutes," I implore.

"Nine," she says.

I stop myself from cheering because I don't have the time.

"We are the family you're looking for," I say.

Grace whips her face to me. "What?"

"Separately, we're all pretty great, but together we are everything you want in a mate."

"What are you talking about?" Grace asks, but her glower is aimed at me this time instead of the ground or her phone.

"I'm funny and good in social situations. Alasdair is serious and the best protector you could ask for. Broderick is empathetic and passionate—" I stop at the look on her face.

She blinks, confusion and incredulity fighting for supremacy.

"How do you know about my list?" Grace asks.

Shit.

"I… may have peeked into your purse," I say.

Grace throws her hands up.

"Because why not add to it," she mutters.

"We need you, Grace." The honesty of the words reverberates between us, and she stills. I've snared her attention. Grace doesn't respond

"Something happened when our last clan leader passed on, we've always fit together so well, but now it's as if there's a gap that has never been there before," I say. "When I met you, I just knew. I lied because I didn't want you to reject the idea of multiple mates before you got to know us."

"You shouldn't have hidden it from your mates," she says.

I pull up at that. It hadn't occurred to me that she was angry on Alasdair's and Broderick's behalf. A thrill of giddiness hits me at how perfect she is, but her scowl has me tamping the sensation down.

"I-I shouldn't have. You're right. I'll go through everything with them, they deserve my apology. They're used to my masterminding, but I've never gone this far before. But, Grace, will you please consider being courted by us? You're exactly what our clan needs, give us a chance to show you how good we can be together."

A car I don't recognize pulls up to the curb with a screech and my heart drops. Grace mutters something about speeding and the driver, the quiet Emilia from the library, glares daggers at me.

"Grace?" My voice is hoarse, my throat tight at the possibility that she'll deny me.

"I'll think about it," she says.

Grace gets into the car and leaves. She doesn't look back.

I hang my head, trying to suppress the panic raging in my soul.

I turn to repair the damage I've done to my triad.

CHAPTER 15

ALASDAIR

"And the troublemaker returns," Broderick mutters.

I blow out a breath as Elliot swings the gate open. The courtyard in this place is a little overgrown, but in better condition than the chapel had been when we'd purchased this project. Every so often I stop here on my way back to the office and let the birdsong and creaking of branches center me.

It's not enough to quiet the storm of emotions in my chest now.

Broderick had started trying to talk to me about Elliot's plan, but I didn't want to hear the explanation from anyone else. Not even from him. It's clear that Broderick had only just met the witch. An encounter that Elliot hadn't planned on.

My wayward mate approaches us, his face full of distress.

"Elliot—" I clear my throat, trying to combat the raw emotion in it. "What have you done?"

My mate's brows furrow with intention. "I found a solution."

There is no regret in his voice. I want him to regret causing us this pain, causing me this pain, but Elliot has always been one for strategy.

"You've manipulated a woman that you care for," I say, and the distress returns to my mate's face. "You let this woman think we were brothers."

"I told her we weren't brothers," he mutters.

Broderick rolls his eyes but lets this play out between the two of us.

"You didn't tell this woman you're courting that we are lovers, mates. My heart—" I break off, trying to reel in the wounded ache in my chest. "You hid our relationship and didn't tell us you were dating someone. We established rules about dating outside of our mating and you dishonored them."

"Alasdair—" Elliot starts.

"Are you looking to leave our clan?" The question my heart fears the most leaves me in a rush.

Elliot blanches. "What? No! Never! Grace belongs with us."

Grace... the name fits her elegant scent.

Elliot shakes his head, eyes watering and I want to pull him into my arms. To comfort him even as my own pain persists.

"Alasdair." Broderick breaks in, ever ready to be a mediator. "Perhaps we should listen to him. I only just met this woman and... I'm intrigued by what our troublemaker has planned."

Intrigued. Under the pain of Elliot's deception lives an emotion similar to that. The way the woman's very scent has eased my stress when I'd catch hints of it over the past week.

"Elliot, can you explain?" I ask.

My mate straightens, steeling himself for something. "Our relationship changed when you became clan leader. We changed when we lost Lachlan."

I flinch, even though he's only speaking the truth we all know.

Elliot continues. "We've stagnated and I fear our connection can't weather much more without something else. Someone else."

"She deserves more than to be used as glue for our problems," I say.

Elliot's mind for the larger picture always tends to trample over the little things, like people's emotions.

"I'm not using her as glue. I never even planned to meet her… but I did, and we could be so good together."

They'd made a pretty picture. Grace with her pretty features and Elliot's sharp sense of fashion. There's something else there, some other truth that Elliot isn't baring, but I let him keep it. There is enough truth in the air that it's a challenge not to choke on it.

"Have we—I not been enough? I know I've been struggling with my position in the clan, but have you felt neglected?" I ask.

Elliot's eyes are clear and full of an answer I don't want to hear but must.

"In the beginning, we were all grieving." Elliot casts his eyes to the decorative stone under our feet. "It was difficult to tell which direction was up, let alone to notice the distance we'd all put between each other. By the time I'd realized it… the gap seemed unbreachable. But, Alasdair, I'm ready to move past our pain. We need to change something, and I think having Grace in our clan, in our mating, feels right."

I nod. Elliot hadn't said it, but the truth is that I pulled away. I'd thrown myself into our business to keep from dwelling on the new weight on my shoulders. I had done this.

"You need her," I say.

"We need her—"

"Do not presume that you speak for me, my mate," I snap. There are more emotions in me than whether I need the presence of this witch, but I'm not the only one in this relationship. "I'll admit that I've failed you, and I'm open to this woman being in our relationship, but I have yet to even get to know her. I won't make any decision on whether she and I will have a relationship until I do."

Elliot breathes a sigh of relief, as does Broderick. I lift a brow to him, and he shrugs with a sheepish grin.

"I've only now started to notice the cracks in our relationship. I want to spend time with her," Broderick says.

"We will not treat Grace as glue," I reiterate. "If any or all of us court her, she deserves to be treated as more than a solution."

Elliot winces and nods.

"That is, if she is still interested in being courted," I say.

CHAPTER 16
GRACE

"Wow," Emilia says, and I sniff. We're parked at my place. Emilia won't come up because she needs to pick her mom up soon, but demanded I recount everything that upset me. So, with some edits to make the story mundane, I told it.

I really didn't have to change much.

"Exactly," I say.

"That's not cool. And weird. Do you think he went to a matchmaker to find someone like you?" Emilia asks.

"Like me?"

"Wonderful and open."

My cheeks glow a little at that. "I don't know why he wouldn't just tell the matchmaker that he was in a group relationship."

Emilia barks a laugh. "What kind of matchmaker did you go to? I know you move in some rarified circles, but you didn't tell me they were kinky ones."

I wave away her words and stumble over my response, trying to not lie. "Well, I guess that could be a reason he didn't say anything before."

Poly relationships in the paranormal community are relatively common, even if the traditional witch community sticks its nose up at them.

"So, this guy was totally out of line with not telling you before, buuuuut are you into it?" Emilia asks.

I give a mental sigh of relief that she's moved past the matchmaker before sticking on the question.

"Into… being with multiple men?" I ask.

Emilia nods. "Who are also with each other."

She makes pointing gestures to signify some sort of triangular shape, before pausing and adding another corner to it.

"I—I didn't sign up for it." More than one mate. I didn't even think I'd find one that would work out. And now Elliot is asking for me to accept two more who he's already in love with…. The idea of coming late to the party for a mated unit causes a stab of discomfort between my shoulder blades. It's sharp and fraught with all the ways an arrangement like this could go poorly.

But, he said they needed me.

"You don't see any problems with it?" I ask, giving myself time to figure out my answer.

Emilia shrugs. "I don't think I could personally do it, but I don't think it's morally wrong or anything. Like I said, what Elliot did wasn't cool. It sounds like he broke rules. You're the only one who can say if what he did is forgivable, or if being with them is even something you're open to."

We sit in silence for a minute until Emilia snorts.

"What?" I ask.

"Him not kissing you suddenly makes sense."

I narrow my eyes. "Clever. He said he was waiting until I met his family."

Emilia bites her lips and shakes her head. "You say the word and we'll plan a whole breakup date. Ice cream, movies, and cuss him out."

Silence reigns again as she waits for me to figure out my feelings.

I lean my head back against the headrest. "I like Elliot…"

Stupid feelings.

"What about Broderick? You spent a little time with him before running into the other one. Did he pique your interest?" Emilia asks.

My mouth goes dry.

Her brows rise. "Oh, the look on your face says yes."

I cover my face with my hands and groan. "It's confusing. I felt so guilty for reacting to him at all. I thought they were like brothers!"

Emilia laughs. "Well, you don't have to be guilty anymore."

"What do I do?"

My friend's face goes serious.

"You like him."

I sigh. "Yes."

"And what about his boyfriends?"

I stop at the question. *Boyfriend* seems like such a friendly word for both Broderick and Alasdair. They emanated a certain energy. A car ride and rant later and I can admit that they are all compelling. Even Alasdair, who I barely met. I shiver at the memory of his voice, his touch.

"Am I nuts? I've been cheated on before, I didn't want to worry about jealousy or anything like that."

"One, does it feel like cheating?"

"The first moment I found out… a little bit, but Elliot isn't like the guys who cheated on me. He… cares deeply about his family and wants me to be a part of it. I can't even say he's just interested in sex because he's been wildly wooing me this entire week."

Elliot had spent quality time with me, courted me with different cuisines and seductive touches. I had been ready to jump him by the end of the first date, but he courted me instead and talked about sharing a future and wanting the same things.

I shake my head. "That's one, what's two?"

"Are you jealous?" Emilia asks.

I gnaw on my lip. *Am I jealous?*

The men who'd be courting me are lovers. If I agree to date them, it's with the knowledge that they will be with each other in bed rather than with only me.

My face burns at the mental image of the large form of Alasdair intertwined with Elliot.

Emilia laughs again. "You look intrigued."

I scrunch my nose. "What do I do?"

"If you're interested, you talk terms. Lay down your boundaries, ask for theirs. You have your own wants, see if you guys even want the same thing." Emilia taps on the steering wheel. "If you have any big asks… you might want to start with that before lust addles your mind."

Big asks. I could think of a couple.

The world stills and just like that, I can see a way forward. I have options to deliberate.

"What would I ever do without your guidance?" I smile at Emilia.

"Hope we never find out." Her smile is lopsided. "Now, get. I have a mom to pick up."

***

I spin my phone on the counter, trying to make a decision.

I told Rose that I didn't want to be in a relationship with multiple partners because of my dating history but being cheated on is different than dating multiple people. And those options feel different than a mated unit. Is being in that kind of a relationship something I don't want… or something I've told myself I couldn't have?

Something about Elliot makes me want to try. Something about all of them piques a curiosity I didn't know I had. Something makes me want to be brave.

Separately, my mind catches on another detail over and over again.

We need you, Grace.

No one has ever needed me before.

I call Elliot and he picks up on the first ring.

"Grace?" His voice is so hopeful it almost hurts.

"I'm not saying no to being in a relationship with you all."

"That's… gods, let me sit down. That makes me so happy."

"I need to officially meet them. I won't be in a relationship with someone I don't know."

Elliot hums. "That can be arranged. What about dinner next week?"

"Today," I say, and wince. "Or tomorrow… I can't draw this out. I need to know if this is going to work."

There's a pause. "Let me ask. I'm sure we're both aware that I shouldn't be making plans on everyone's behalf without their say."

"Okay, I'll let you do that. And, Elliot?"

"Yes?"

"I'd like everyone to be in their true forms. No more glamour between us," I say.

There's a pause, a hesitation that I don't understand.

"I won't argue a lady's choice."

CHAPTER 17
GRACE

I drive to dinner. I can't expect Emilia to be able to bail me out twice in one day if this all goes south. I don't want to plan for the worst, but I'm so far in uncharted waters here that a life raft of any kind is prudent.

Is this a mistake?

I won't know until I try.

When I pull up the gravel driveway my GPS leads me to, I blink. *This is their home?*

The Victorian mansion is beautiful with rose-colored brick and white and blue accenting the architectural details.

I'm sure my family has similar property holdings, but none of them emanate a warmth, a homecoming, like the building in front of me. The crunch of the gravel under my feet surprises me. I've parked my car and am approaching the building with the awed motions of a bee to honey.

"It's even more impressive inside."

I jump at the voice and see the gargoyle lounging on the wraparound porch. Broderick's grin is smug and cheerful at the same time. I look back to the gate. There are bushes and trees surrounding the property, but someone could still see the house from the sidewalk if they tried.

Broderick chuckles. "We have wards. Humans see what they expect to see, which isn't a gargoyle."

"Oh," I say, embarrassed.

"But your concern is touching."

"I am the one who asked everyone to be in their true forms." Something that causes an underlying hum of nerves and excitement. I won't be seeing Elliot as the man I've gotten to know. The man who wears a sharp suit like it's a second skin.

Will I still be attracted to this person I've come to care for?

"That isn't an issue for me," Broderick says, spreading his arms. "I'm glad to show you any part of me you desire."

My cheeks burn and I duck my head. "Are there any of you that aren't going to make salacious commentary?"

Broderick throws his head back on a laugh. "Oh, Elliot has been busy."

I climb the steps of the porch with a shake of my head. "I think saying things that make me blush is one of his favorite activities, and here I find out it's a trait you all share in."

Broderick's smile softens, but the tail behind him whips with an energy that belies his ease. He's like a prowling tom cat, preening in the presence of prey to hide its feral nature.

"You won't have to worry about that from Alasdair. He's more private. Elliot and I are more scandalous, but if we go out in public together, he'll keep us in line," he says.

"Are you going to tell me all the secrets?" I tease.

Broderick raises his brows. "Just enough secrets to keep you from running away in fright."

"I am a little nervous about this," I admit.

Something about Broderick calms me. Elliot is easy to talk to, his social acuity is bright and engaging, but Broderick's presence is casual. The fire that you curl up to at the end of the day, hot, wild, but comforting.

"Aw, don't be nervous, Gracie. Elliot has enough nerves to spare for everyone else."

I scrunch my nose. "Gracie? I've never been called that."

Broderick tilts his head, considering me. "Do you hate it? I'll stop if you want me to."

"I don't hate it." The nickname bestows an intimacy that I've only ever experienced with Elliot before this. Could I be compatible with all of them? On first look, it seems so.

"Where is everyone else?" I ask.

Broderick hums. "Elliot is panicking in the kitchen and Alasdair is probably trying to sneak in some work task he isn't supposed to. Both of them have their own coping mechanism."

Blood rushes to my cheeks. "I didn't mean to stress Elliot out about dinner. Pizza would have been fine."

Broderick makes a sharp motion with his hand. "Don't say such things in front of him. Elliot is trying to show off. Food is his love language."

Somehow that helps with the nerves. That Elliot clearly wants this to work out. That he cares about me.

I make a zipping motion over my mouth.

Broderick looks down. "And you are definitely dressed for fine dining rather than pizza. You look spectacular."

He grasps my hand and twirls me in front of him. The swing dress and added petticoats flare with the motion. The burgundy fabric is off the shoulder and dips just right for my cleavage. The shape and color of the dress is sexy, while the stiffness of the fabric gives it the sophisticated air I wanted.

"Can I tell you a secret?" I whisper.

Broderick's eyes shine with delight, and he tugs me close to him, dropping a kiss to my cheek. The motion brings with it his body heat and the scent of cedar and sawdust.

"I hope you do." His voice vibrates along my skin, and I take a step closer, letting myself appreciate this gargoyle in a way that I hadn't before, when I'd thought he was off-limits.

"It's my coping mechanism," I say. "If I nitpick my outfit, it keeps me from spending time dwelling on my nerves."

Broderick pulls back and his eyes trace the line of my dress where it stops, and my breasts rise above with the aid of a structurally sound bra. His perusal goes on so long that my skin heats. I know my cheeks are red and I'm not bold enough to see if my blush has traveled down my chest.

"A distraction and armor all at once," he says.

Armor. I haven't thought about what I wear as armor in a long time, the joy of adulthood is that you don't have to stay in situations that feel like emotional warfare, but he's right.

Broderick makes a sound in his throat. "Oh, dear Gracie, I fear you and Elliot have the most generous coping mechanisms. A delicious meal with a delicious vision to feast on. I feel sorry for both of you that Alasdair's and mine are much less beneficial."

"I'm sure they aren't that bad." If Alasdair is even half as smooth talking as Broderick, my fears of compatibility can freely be cast into the wind no matter what coping mechanisms they have.

Broderick only hums and we both turn as the front door swings open.

"Broderick, you're hogging your date. Where are your manners?" An older woman glides from the door toward us and Broderick takes a polite step back. Her black beaded dress catches the light and sparkles with each move. An older grizzled man follows her, wrapping a shawl around her shoulders with care.

"What manners?" Broderick teases but turns to me. "Grace, this is Eloise Bramblewick and her mate Graham. Elders—" He bows his head in respect. "This is Grace Starling."

Eloise grabs both of my hands. "Oh, you're so lovely! And Elliot says you're a librarian. I'd love to spend some time together when these boys stop falling all over themselves."

The exuberance of the woman is only part of the reason I'm so surprised. Eloise is human. The complete lack of witch blood obvious as soon as our hands touch. There aren't many humans who live immersed in our world.

The man behind her nods to me. He gives me the distinct impression of wearing a glamour with how his energy is similar to the rest of his clan. A human and a gargoyle, how ever did that happen?

"Uh, that sounds nice." I recover from the stunning effect of her friendliness and smile.

"They are fleeing our dinner while they still can." Broderick sighs.

Eloise makes a sharp flicking gesture at Broderick. "The best sort of courting is a private affair. And now

Graham has a reason to take me to the ballet that he's promised me."

The glamoured gargoyle behind her rolls his eyes with affection. "I took you to the opera last week."

"The opera was lovely, but it isn't the ballet."

"It isn't? The seats are uncomfortable for both."

Their exchange has me smiling. "Well, I hope you enjoy it."

Eloise's skin crinkles around her eyes. "And I hope you enjoy your night. Or at the very least, that Elliot doesn't keel over in my kitchen."

Broderick makes a sound. "We should go pull him away before he gets it in his head that we need another course of appetizers or something."

The older couple give a parting chuckle and wave as they walk to the covered parking arm in arm.

"Courses?" I ask.

"I talked him down to two," Broderick says. "Shall we?"

He offers an arm, and I thread my hand around it, allowing this devil to escort me into their home.

CHAPTER 18
GRACE

The savory smells of cooking have my mouth watering with the first step we take into the mansion. Even as my nose wants to take me toward the kitchen, my eyes don't know where to look.

The ceilings are high with an antique-style chandelier in the entryway. The doorways and the edges of the ceiling have wood panels with intricate details. Some designs look fitting with the original period the house was built, while others are unique.

Just like the outside, this place hums with the warmth of *love*. There are few places I've experienced that feel like this. The last time had been dinner with Emilia and her mom at their place. Every tea cozy and photo frame had an ache settling in my chest. It would be easy to blame my best friend for this want of a family where love is freely given, but it's a regular thing to want.

"Have you been seduced by Bramblewick Manor?" Broderick asks and I realize that I've stopped in the entryway. "I'd say that method of seduction is easy but this house was not an easy thing to renovate."

"It's stunning," I breathe, ignoring his commentary about seduction for now. "You guys worked on this?"

Broderick's smile is warm but sad. "Did Elliot tell you about our last clan leader, Lachlan?"

I nod.

"Well, he got this place with Eloise and Graham with it falling down around their ears. They needed a place for a clan to grow into but lacked the funding a traditional clan has. They made it livable with all the grit in their souls and worked on projects over the years to bring parts of it to the former glory. When Alasdair and I came along, we were a bundle of young energy that needed an outlet and a way to keep our hands busy. They helped us refine our skills, and we were finally able to complete a full renovation. This manor is how our business was born."

"That's beautiful."

Broderick's eyes meet mine. "It is. Our clan is a small one, smaller than Lachlan had planned, but our loyalty is unquestionable."

The pang in my heart is wistful.

Broderick frowns. "What's that look for?"

I swallow, it's a hard thing to confess. "I just—I love that you have this family, clan, but I don't see where I fit. You already have each other."

Broderick's hand is warm at the small of my back. The gargoyle is practically a furnace and when he takes a step closer, I'm drawn in more.

"What I was trying to say is that our clan was always meant to expand. Elliot believes that you'd be a good fit to join our clan, not just our mating. And, for what it's worth… I think he's right."

"We've only just met!" I blink in disbelief.

Broderick playfully tugs on the fabric of my dress. "Don't let conventional thinking get in the way of finding your place with us. We are the epitome of unconventional. You've met Eloise. Lachlan and Graham were ostracized from their clan for mating with a human. Elliot and I were both abandoned because of blood-purity beliefs."

The same anger that rose when Elliot had detailed their backgrounds rises again.

"I'm glad you don't have to put up with those kinds of clans anymore. They don't deserve you," I say.

Broderick dramatically gasps. "Oh, Grace, we've only just met!"

Him throwing my words back at me has the burning edge of anger cracking and I can't help the laugh that escapes me.

Broderick's face softens. "Calm yourself, witch. As much as it delights me to see your anger on our behalf, it has no place in our night together."

I take a breath. "No one deserves to be rejected based on lineage."

"I agree," someone else says. The deep voice strikes me to my core, and I straighten.

The gargoyle that rounds the corner from what appears to be a sitting room is massive. His wings are folded, clasping his shoulders like Broderick's. His coloring is nothing like the gargoyle next to me though. His gray skin has a dappled texture of cool colors of light teal and indigo. His black hair is long and held in a low ponytail.

"Grace." He nods his head. "We didn't have the opportunity for proper introductions before. I'm Alasdair, the clan leader of this rag-tag bunch."

I press my thighs together and Broderick hums in a pleased way that I don't understand.

"It's good to meet you. Properly." My voice is hushed and the heat in my face may be permanent after this night. Neither of us moves to action, this gargoyle doesn't glide forward and kiss my hand or press his formidable body into my space. The absence of motion has an awkwardness blossoming.

I didn't think I'd miss the seduction I've become accustomed to with the pair of gargoyles I've already met. Is Alasdair not interested in me that way?

Alasdair tilts his head and the nerves that had receded rise to the surface again.

Broderick clears his throat. "Shall we continue to the kitchen? Elliot is probably going to be done soon."

I nod and Broderick pushes me along. I try not to look back at the gargoyle that follows us.

The kitchen is bright and airy. Its mesh of modern appliances and antique cupboards somehow works for the space. The positive vibes embedded in every surface of this room proclaim the importance it has as the heart of this clan and I relax in it.

The gargoyle at the stove is not relaxed at all.

"Elliot?" I ask.

"Grace!" The creature whips around so fast that his wing tips over the stool pulled up to the counter.

Elliot's true form is similar in size to Broderick but slenderer. He's still larger than he is in his glamoured form. His gray coloring has undertones of green and his hair is pulled back in a stark white bun.

His features aren't harsh and distinctive like Broderick and Alasdair, but instead, almost look delicate.

He's just as pretty as a gargoyle as he is when he wears a human face and suit. The last thread of nerves in me knits itself back and my heart beats faster in something other than apprehension.

Elliot's brow creases in concern and I approach, leaving Broderick behind.

"Hey, you," I say, quiet and low.

Elliot ducks his head to look at the floor, his feet shuffle, the talons on his feet clack against the tile of the kitchen. His movements are awkward, as if he's uncomfortable in his own skin. "You look stunning, my star."

I step until my front presses against his, my cleavage in his sight line.

"So, this is you?" I ask.

The greenish hue of Elliot's skin darkens across his cheekbones and pointed ears. He spreads his arms and smiles weakly. "In all my naked glory."

I want to roll my eyes, but lean back and take in the kilt-like garment he wears instead. His chest is bare and demarcated with grooves of lean muscle.

I pout my lips in a moue of dismay. "Not quite naked."

Elliot gives a surprised laugh. "It wouldn't do to cook naked. I didn't want to scare you off before dinner even began."

Discomfort mixes with his words. *Is he truly uncomfortable as a gargoyle, or does he really expect me to dislike it?*

"I'm not running off, Elliot. Not from your true form." *Maybe because you lied to me.* I keep that detail to myself.

"You don't find this horrifying?" Elliot gestures down to himself.

Broderick snorts behind me. "Troublemaker, can't you scent her? Or have you destroyed that sense with caramelizing onions again? She's far from horrified."

It takes me a moment to realize what he's saying, and my ever-present blush deepens. They can scent me. The way my body heated at Alasdair's words, Broderick's touches, and the sight of Elliot.

There's a sound from Alasdair and Broderick looks away, as if remorseful, but not without winking at me first.

"I think it's rude to bring that up. Can we make a rule against commenting on my scent?" I ask.

Elliot's laugh is full of relief. "I'm sure we can behave."

He leans down as if to kiss me, but freezes, indecision flashing across his expression. I grip his face and kiss him before he can retreat. His lips are similar in this form even if his skin has a sturdier texture. It's a simple kiss, not one inviting him to lay me flat on the counter for him and his clan to sample. I tamp down that thought before my scent can expose me any more than it already has.

The kiss may be simple but it's significant. This courting is for more than sex. It's for a future together and it can't start without getting through any of the awkwardness any of us bring to this arrangement.

"No," I say once I break the kiss. "I don't find your true form horrifying. I like it."

Elliot hums, it's a little broken, a little unsure, as if he isn't convinced.

"I'm glad," he says. "Now, let's feed you."

CHAPTER 19
ℰLLIOT

Everyone makes sounds of enjoyment through bites of food and the stress that's been churning my stomach since the upset this afternoon eases. We're trying this. Grace is open to trying a relationship with both my mates. She's open to being a part of our clan and my mates are open to courting her.

Now if only Alasdair wasn't being so stiff.

He's always been one to hold his cards close, especially upon meeting someone new, but his silence is communicating a message to our guest that he may not intend.

The longer Alasdair doesn't speak, the jitterier it makes Grace. The slower she is to laugh at Broderick's quips and my teasing. The more she distances herself.

Dinner continues without the input of our clan leader. I want to shake the gargoyle but he's massive and I've caused him enough hurt feelings today. I don't know what's going on inside his head, but there are some things I can interpret from the years Alasdair and I have been together.

He likes Grace.

It's in the watchful way his eyes linger and the flare of his nostrils.

And despite Broderick's crack about my sense of smell, Grace likes him too. Every time her gaze catches our clan leader's, the captivating scent of her interest swells. None of us comment on it after she teased about it being rude.

"This is delicious, Elliot. I almost don't forgive you for not cooking for me before this," Grace says.

"What did you two do for dates?" Alasdair asks.

I want to kick him, the first thing he says, and it borders on sounding jealous.

"Oh, um, Elliot has been picking food places mostly. He's wonderfully informed. Each place has been a discovery that I haven't heard of before," Grace says.

Alasdair nods, thoughtful.

Broderick jumps in. "What kind of dates do you like to go on?" he asks.

Grace tilts her head in thought.

"Uh, well, I haven't really considered that. I haven't been on that many dates except for lately. I dated while in school but those were the college things. Hanging out rather than going out." She shrugs. "And the dates I went on before Elliot and I were matched were all the same sort of affair at one of two restaurants thought to be respectable."

"Matched?" Alasdair asks.

My heart drops. *Shit.* That's a detail I haven't explained to my mates. It requires another confession that I haven't come clean about. One that paints me in a worse light.

Grace blinks and the room gets a little more uncomfortable. "Well, yes. I went to the Love Bathhouse to be matched and was matched with Elliot the day after."

Alasdair looks at me and I want to slide under the table. This disconnect between us sparks. It's plain on his face. He wants to ask why I went to a matchmaker, but he must see the hesitance on my face.

"Tell us about yourself, Grace," Alasdair says.

Grace adjusts in her seat while our clan leader stares at her. Having been on the receiving end of one of Alasdair's stares, I'm very aware of how penetrating it is.

Broderick and I share a look. Alasdair Bramblewick is terrible at courting. He doesn't have *any* game, none at all. It's a belated observation, but it's one I've never had to make. When we came together, it was because I instigated it. I'd taunted him with words and looks. I'm pretty sure I'd walked down the hall naked after a shower with a silly excuse about forgetting a towel.

I'd driven him crazy.

Until, with a snarl, he'd claimed me.

Fuck.

That isn't going to work with Grace. She's a respectable witch from a traditional family, more communication than a snarl is needed.

"Well, what do you want to know? I work at the library for the Council's Archive project." Grace's stiff posture starts to loosen. She enjoys talking about her work.

"What about your family?" Alasdair asks.

Grace stiffens. I have an urge to stuff something in Alasdair's mouth. Not something fun either, something like a sock.

"My family are… we don't really get along. My mother likes to wax poetic about how I should abandon my boring career with dusty papers." Grace laughs, trying for a teasing self-deprecation.

"From what you've told me about your job at the library, I can't imagine that it's boring at all," I interject.

Alasdair frowns. "Why don't you get along with your family?"

I squeeze my fork. With Alasdair's position at the head of the table, he's too far away to kick. Broderick could reach him, but waits for Grace's answer with interest, unaware of the extent of this prickly subject.

Grace's brows crease at the direct question, but my star isn't a coward. "My family is more worried about status than my happiness. They'd rather I marry a witch from another well-known family and start popping out children."

"And you don't want children?" Alasdair asks, as if disregarding the rest of the statement. I freeze, too many possible actions pop in my mind, begging me to steer this conversation better. Any other topic would be better to bring up, but I flounder.

Broderick shakes his head in slow motion. It's like watching a train wreck.

"I don't want to be in a loveless marriage where my only importance is the lineage I bring. I don't live my life in accordance with what my parents want." Grace's tone gets colder, more definite.

"Alasdair—" I start, wanting to avoid the impending collision.

He interrupts, his brows winging downward. "Family is important—"

"And so is my happiness," Grace says. "I'd like children, but I want them to grow up in a family unlike the one I was raised in."

"We also want children," Broderick cuts in.

"But if your family disapproves of your career—"
Alasdair starts.

Grace sets her silverware down and the noise cuts him off.

"You don't know how toxic my family is. You actually don't know anything about me." Grace's cheeks redden.

"I know that I put the well-being of my family above everything else in my life." Alasdair says. His words strong and final.

My eyes widen.

Broderick clears his throat. "Hey, um, Alasdair doesn't mean to sound like he's critiquing your choices—"

Alasdair makes a sound as if he's about to smack the lifeline Broderick is throwing his way.

Grace stands and the room stills as if something has shattered.

My heart falls in my chest, her cheeks are red with anger and hurt. Her body stiffens as if she didn't mean to jump from her chair, but it doesn't stop her from continuing, eyes laser-focused on our clan leader.

"I've separated from my family because they are bad for my mental health. Maybe you don't understand what it's like to be treated like an asset that can be wielded for profit or to be torn down for every single thing you enjoy, but I do. I'm glad you have a family full of love, that isn't the type of family I have."

Alasdair doesn't say anything back. His posture freezes, as if he's only now realized how oblivious he's been.

Grace blinks in the same panicked way she did in the restaurant when she'd confronted me about physical intimacy. The way that screams, *I need to escape*, heartbreak clear on her face.

I stand. "Grace—"

"I think I need to go. I'm—" she makes a gesture but doesn't say anything, flustered. "Dinner was lovely, Elliot. It was nice to see you again, Broderick."

The overwhelmed vulnerability on her face speaks the words before she does.

"I-I'm sorry," she says.

I want to wrap my arms around her and coax her back down from whatever emotional land mine she's been pushed on by Alasdair, but she stumbles back.

Broderick stands. "I'll walk you out."

It's a quick affair and I turn to Alasdair.

"What was that?" I hiss.

CHAPTER 20
ALASDAIR

"I…" I can't continue. I have no valid excuse for what just happened.

"You…" Elliot motions for me to continue, and when I don't, he casts his eyes to the ceiling. "If I didn't know you better, I'd accuse you of trying to chase her off."

"I didn't do it on purpose." I lean back and the chair creaks. My words sound weak even to my own ears.

"I know, but did you even hear yourself? What if she had asked you why you never went back to your birth family after your father threw you out?"

I flinch.

"I didn't mean for it to come off that way. I just—when she said she'd rebelled against what her family wanted for her…" I'd gotten protective. My mind had narrowed to the fact that she'd caused a disruption for her family because of her wants and my clan-oriented mind had reared.

"You should be able to empathize with being treated poorly by family," Elliot says. His cheeks are ruddy from anger instead of the adorable awkwardness from earlier.

"Yes, but in our clans and families, we were thrown out when the clan found us lacking, not kept and abused," I try and reason.

Not for long. Elliot is right. I, more than most, can empathize with being in a toxic family. I had been banished well before adulthood, but that was because I would not break, because my father had feared the day I'd become stronger than he. My mother and the clan at large had let it happen.

"I'm sorry, Elliot," I say.

"And the rest of it?" he asks. "Are you jealous?"

"No." That I can answer without deliberation.

Grace provides something to Elliot that I can't, and I understand his infatuation. She's vivacious, a mix of shyness and boldness that draws me in. The way her face flushed with hurt had my instincts rearing to protect her. To be her champion, even if I was the one who'd caused the damage.

I'm not jealous, but I am curious about how many strings Elliot has pulled behind the scenes for this to happen. I am protective and concerned that his scheming is going to end up shattering this fragile setup.

"You went to a matchmaker." I raise a brow.

Elliot's eyes widen. "That's not what we're talking about right now."

I narrow my eyes, but he is correct. "I regret my reaction. I regret not truly listening to her words. I don't have any excuses except that… it's as if I can't find the right words to say to her."

"You've never dated, have you? I never asked," Elliot says. The anger drains from his form.

I swallow, my cheeks now heating under his scrutiny. "I-no, I never dated. Broderick and I would work our frustrations out every so often. I didn't feel a desire to court others. I didn't feel a draw to be in a real relationship rather than what Broderick and I had until you joined the clan."

Elliot sighs, dragging a hand down his face. "You're kind of adorable."

I rear back, disgruntled. "I'm at a disadvantage and have offended Grace. I don't know what you find endearing about that."

"You'll have to apologize. This is new for you, tell her that. She's an understanding person. She's delightful when she isn't being interrogated about her life choices."

I wince and stand.

"Where are you going?" Elliot asks, looking from me to the food on my plate.

"I need to apologize. I need to settle this between us."

Elliot arches a brow. "You can't apologize over the phone and finish the dinner I made?"

I freeze and he rolls his eyes. "Fine, I'll put it in the fridge."

"It was wonderful, Elliot. You're skilled."

He preens with the compliment before nodding. "You just can't eat when upset. I know. It wouldn't be a bad idea if you took some time in the air to figure out what you're going to say to her. She probably needs some time to cool down as well."

***

Elliot was right. I needed this. The full moon and the bright city lights illuminate fluffy clouds, the stars are a distant thing tonight. The chill wind skims over my skin and untangles the emotions in me. My muscles and lungs burn at the exertion of flying. Thoughts swirl in my mind along with the beat of my heart. Being up in the air always has a way of distilling things.

Grace belongs with us.

I hadn't been sure at first. I'd only had Elliot's assurances and the scent of Grace to work from. Now that I've seen her in our home, see the way that she can settle Elliot with a wry phrase and attract Broderick's ever-wandering focus with a look, Elliot is right. Grace fits in the clan.

I need to figure out how our own courtship will go. I need to not ruin things with my floundering.

The witch intrigues me. I want to wrap her in my wings and seduce her as aptly as Broderick or Elliot can, but I'm just not wired the same way. I'm not as open with my emotions as they are. I've never been with a woman.

I only hope that she's as intrigued as I am. That she's willing to be patient with me.

I bank and soar in the direction of the apartment building Elliot shared with me. I wear the ring for my glamour on a chain around my throat. I'll communicate with Grace through her doorman as a witch courting her would.

Landing uninvited on her balcony would be rude and it's undoubtedly warded.

I know the building on sight, we'd done some renovation work on the neighboring structure last year.

I start my descent when a sound reaches me and wraps tight around my heart.

Grace's scream.

CHAPTER 21
GRACE
Earlier

My emotions are a riot. It's as if Alasdair has kicked a hive of wasps, completely disrupting my equilibrium, and leaving the sting of disapproval in his wake.

Broderick is quiet, the hand against the small of my back comforting as he escorts me to my car. When we walk out the front door, I inhale the night air with a sniff.

I shouldn't be fleeing. I should stay, talk through my emotions, my disappointment.

Trying to walk over the gravel in heels with only the light from the front porch is a good distraction.

Broderick makes a sound. "Here, let me."

"Wha—whoa!" I'm cut off when Broderick picks me up.

I flail in surprise but stop at Broderick's apologetic face. I'm safely in a bridal carry, and he isn't going to drop me. He isn't even struggling with my weight at all.

"I guess I should have asked," he says.

"You just surprised me." My voice is thick, and I sniff again. Broderick's warmth soaks into me. The comfort of him, his arms around me, cracks the wall I put up around my emotions.

"Oh, Gracie, it's going to be okay," Broderick says. His voice soft as he walks toward my car.

"I don't think it is. The first disagreement and I'm running away. I-I can't go back in there and talk about that. He assumed that I'd made those kinds of decisions lightly—"

"You're regrouping," Broderick says.

"He doesn't like me," I say. That's the crux of it. I want Alasdair to like me. There's something about him that makes me lean in. Something that has some primal part of my brain shivering in delight.

That's why his disapproval hurts so much.

"He does. I promise you he does. Alasdair isn't a social butterfly. His communication skills are rusty. I don't think he's actually been on a single date." Broderick gets to my car but doesn't put me down yet. "Don't give up on us, Grace."

I swallow and realize how close our faces are. We share breath for a moment before the corner of his mouth rises.

"Don't look at me like that," he says.

"Like what?" I ask.

"Like you want a good-night kiss. I want our first kiss to be one of the happiest moments of your life."

Unbelievably, my lips twitch. "Conceited much?"

"You'll see. It will be worth waiting for, just like it will when Alasdair figures out how to tell you how much he likes you instead of stumbling over things that upset you."

"I'm still angry." I'm not lying. The giant gargoyle had judged me without knowing any of the details. Anger and undeniable hurt lodge in my throat and make it hard to even think of the words Alasdair had said.

Broderick clucks. "Be angry. Fight with us. Take the time you need with your emotions, but don't shut us out. Don't give up on us."

"I'm not making any promises," I say.

Broderick sets me down on my feet.

"Someday I'll convince you to make some promises," he teases. "Drive safe, Gracie."

* * *

The burning anger and panic in my chest are slow to leave, but they do. The drive back to my place is uneventful and lets me mull over the interactions of tonight. Alasdair had stumbled on the worst topic for me, I'm sure of it. If he were to bring up any other topic, I'd have easily navigated, but he had wanted to talk about the wounds I still carry. The shame. The doubt.

Could I have done more?

I hadn't thought I needed to work through the drama of my family, but maybe I do. With distance from the conversation, I can understand that Alasdair brought up family because it's the most important thing to him. He lives for his clan. He is clan leader first and foremost, maybe even to the detriment of his relationships.

According to Elliot, the issues in their relationship started when they lost their last clan leader. It isn't much of a stretch to assume that Alasdair's rise to that role had consequences for them all.

Is he as much of an asshole as he sounded, or did I react poorly? Is it a bit of both?

Can I really give him that much of a benefit of the doubt?

Ugh. I wave to my doorman, a friendly troll named Stan, and enter the elevator with my thoughts.

I have two reasons to try and work through this, Elliot and Broderick. There's something there. The connection with those two had been instant. Can I be a part of a clan with the three of them if I'm only romantic with two?

I don't think I can. I'm attracted to Alasdair. His rumbly voice makes my knees go weak when the words he speaks don't cause my temper to rise, or for me to pull away in hurt. That attraction would make it uncomfortable to continue a relationship with only Elliot and Broderick.

It's all or nothing with the three. I shake my head at my reflection in the elevator door. What a predicament to be in. Three males when I'd only been looking for one.

The elevator dings and I exit, making my way to my apartment. I get to the door and pull out my key.

I freeze.

It doesn't feel right. The buzz of my personal wards is missing. I turn the knob of my door and it swings open, unlocked. Fear seizes my lungs. I didn't forget to lock it, did I?

That doesn't explain how my wards are down.

I pull out my phone, my hands shake as I bring up the number for the front desk and call. This building houses many witches and has standard wards in place for the structure itself. Those had hummed at me as usual when I'd walked in. It's only the wards for my apartment that don't.

"Ms. Starling?" Stan asks. With how often I get deliveries, the front desk has my number in their system.

"The wards on my apartment are down."

"I'm on my way. Stay in the hall." The phone clicks with the disconnect.

I squeeze my hands. Stan helps run the wards for the building and has a fierce true form, but I'm not helpless. I have a stun charm on my key ring. I may not have the capabilities of most witches, but I can handle myself.

This is my sanctuary that's been violated.

I enter my apartment.

The lights are on and fear lodges in my throat, but the place feels empty.

Disturbed, but empty.

I walk into my living room and gasp. A white circle is drawn on the wood floor with geometric lines and symbols I don't recognize. The circle alone would be hair raising, there's an air coming off it that fills the room with an eerie sensation, but it's not the most disturbing part.

There's a pile of dead doves in the center. Tiny white feathers litter the floor, waiting for the barest hint of a breeze to spread throughout the space and infect it with this violence. The snowy white bodies have bloody rings around their necks and five silver bowls placed around the circle appear to be filled with blood.

I'm unfamiliar with this type of magic, but it feels wrong. The kind of magic that uses blood is common enough but doesn't have to be for malicious intentions. This feels malicious.

My breaths come quick as I move over the room, checking for anything else out of place. The carefully coordinated decor that sparked joy every time I'd touch a throw pillow or straighten a frame now feels different. The accents of velvet and lace are frivolous, indefensible. This space doesn't reverberate with positivity and safety anymore.

I step forward and something moves. I stop and turn my head. The doves explode into motion, scattering with morbid half flaps.

I scream.

Little bodies that have ceased to breathe fling themselves around the room. My hands come up over my head as the reanimated birds make ugly swoops and dives. They smack into walls and photo frames. A vase breaks.

A giant crash comes from behind me, and Alasdair stands in the destruction of what had been my balcony doors.

"Grace! What the—"

I throw my arms around him, and the pelting of birds stops as his wings wrap around me. His body is tense and there are impacts against the membrane of the protective shield of his wings.

"What is this?" he asks.

"I don't know," I say, squeezing my arms around him tighter.

It doesn't matter that I'd been too upset to stay on our date earlier, or that I barely know this gargoyle. His presence means safety.

He is a harbor.

"Ms. Starling!" Stan's voice shouts.

"She's here," Alasdair says.

Stan mutters some incantation and all at once, things thud to the ground and the apartment drops into silence.

Alasdair moves his wings so I can peek at what's happening. My doorman's frown is mighty on his green-patterned face. He's a formidable being, similar in size to Alasdair.

Without the wings around me, the warmth of safety dissipates. The scent of mint and old books lessens and the smell of blood rises. Every surface the birds had hit has a spattering of blood. My arms and dress are no exception.

I start to shake, and I don't know if it's from adrenaline, fear, or anger.

"Are you injured, Ms. Starling?" Stan asks.

I shake my head. Alasdair squeezes my shoulder and I realize his arms are wrapped around me.

Alasdair clears his throat. "Grace, he needs a verbal confirmation and perhaps to be told that I'm not some monster accosting you."

"Oh," I say, noticing the tension in the room. Stan holds himself at the ready, eyes narrowed. "I'm not injured. This is Alasdair, he's—well, I don't know what he's doing here."

"This witch is being courted by my clan," Alasdair says.

Clan. I'm being courted by his clan, not him. I should let go, take a step away, but the press of his bare skin is what is keeping my panic at bay. Someone violated my place.

Stan sighs in relief. "The Bramblewick clan, correct?"

Alasdair's mouth twitches. "We are the only gargoyles in the area."

Stan shrugs. "It's not something I stay up to date on. I remember you guys worked on the bank last year."

I cut in. "Alasdair, what are you doing here?"

Alasdair looks at me, the blue tone of his skin over his cheekbones darkening. "I was coming to see you. I heard you scream." He casts his gaze to the shards of wood of the door he'd busted through. "I didn't spare a thought about the wards."

Stan sniffs. "If you had meant her ill, the building's wards would have stopped you."

"Really? It doesn't seem that way by the looks of it." Alasdair's brows crease in anger at the mess of the room.

Stan's face darkens in an anger of his own as he narrows his eyes at the room. "The wards are somehow undisturbed. We'll figure out how this was done, Ms. Starling. Did you see anyone or notice anything missing?"

I shake my head and finally convince my body to loosen my grip around Alasdair. I pull away and take a step into the disaster that is my home.

I blink to keep from crying, but something catches my eye. "Those aren't supposed to be here."

I point to a vase of roses on the dining table in the next room that have somehow remained intact in the commotion.

Stan approaches the bouquet with careful focus. He pulls a note from the roses and looks to me for permission. I nod and he opens the note. The anger on his face darkens. He rounds the circle on the floor and hands me the note instead of reading it out loud.

I appreciate it. I don't want to hear the words in the air of my home.

We could be so good together, call me.
You'll regret it if you don't
–Theo

"What on earth," I breathe.

"What is this, Grace?" Alasdair's voice isn't full of accusation or suspicion. He sounds worried.

Still, guilt squeezes my heart. Had I caused this?

No. This is not my fault.

"A-a guy that I went on a date with before meeting Elliot. I told him I wasn't interested, but he keeps sending flowers. I had to block his number."

Stan's upper lip curls in disgust. "It would seem as if this guy has moved to scare tactics. Do you know why he's targeted you?"

"I assume that the guys that send stuff want to be connected to my family, but they've never done something like this. That he's sent stuff for so long has been concerning. I was hoping he'd get tired of it."

Stan grunts. "We've rejected all his previous deliveries, that he's moved to this isn't good. I'll file this with the Council until you can give your testimony."

"I—" I really don't want to go on the record about a man who won't stop sending me things. Though this is something else entirely, I still can't shake the feeling that I somehow asked for this. "It's just embarrassing."

Alasdair slides a claw over my cheek, tucking strands of hair behind my ear. "This man wants you to isolate yourself. He wants you to feel ashamed for not accepting his overtures. It's how he gains power over you. This is dangerous and there is no shame in treating it like it is."

The soft rumbly words have me inhaling a shuddering breath. Shame and guilt are swept away. Alasdair is taking this seriously. Stan has been dealing with deliveries all week and he thinks this is concerning.

The small voice in my mind that's telling me not to make a big deal about this, to not make a scene, isn't my voice. It's merely just one more poisonous thought.

I nod. "Okay."

Alasdair nods back to me.

Stan grunts in relief. "I'll have a team come in and clear out the magics and clean up the blood. You can stay here if you want, but I'd recommend staying somewhere else. We won't know if there's some sort of hidden magics in here until the team can do a total overhaul, and that could take a day."

"She'll be staying with us," Alasdair says.

"What?" I ask. My voice louder than I meant for it to be.

Stan's brows rise. "I'm going to check over the rest of the apartment, if that's alright with you, Ms. Starling?"

"Yes," I say, and the troll moves to the other room. I glare at Alasdair. "What do you mean, I'm staying with you?"

Alasdair's face freezes, as if now that he needs to discuss something with me instead of dealing with a larger danger, he's speechless. He shakes his head. "Elliot will worry if you try to stay here."

I bite my lip. Unsure why him saying that stings.

"Would you stay at the manor tonight?" he asks. "We have a guest room and I'd appreciate knowing you're safe."

"You would?" I ask.

Alasdair swallows, his discomfort clear. "I came to apologize for my words at dinner. What I said was thoughtless. I'm no stranger to being mistreated by blood relations. I have no excuse for the way I reacted. I didn't want the unpleasantness between us to flourish while courting."

He flew to see me in person just to apologize.

"I thought your clan was courting me, not you," I say.

Alasdair blinks. "I am a part of my clan. If you'll allow me, I wish to court you. If not, we'll still want to have you stay with us. We're—I'm protective of you."

He's protective of me.

Somehow that one confession is a bright spot in this terrible situation. My knee-jerk reaction to refuse his offer, of being independent and figuring out my own accommodations, eases. If I want to be a part of their clan, shouldn't I let them take care of me?

"I'll stay the night. Let me pack a bag and" —I look down at my ruined dress, the streaks of blood on my skin and feathers in my hair— "take a shower. I'll head over after."

"I'll stay. I can fly you home with me."

My brain taps on the brakes. "I'd like to have my own vehicle."

Alasdair considers me and nods. "I'll still stay while you get ready. I'd rather you not be here alone before your doorman can get that team in."

I nod. It's a compromise I'm more than willing to make.

CHAPTER 22

GRACE

The shower is hot and quick. I scour my skin with my favorite body wash, letting the fragrance of roses destroy the memory of feathers and blood. I do a quick blow-dry of my hair and pack some essentials. At least it's Sunday tomorrow and I don't need to figure out a work outfit as my adrenaline drops off.

When I walk back into the living room in my comfiest sweat set, I find two gargoyles instead of one. Broderick and Alasdair stare at me for so long that my cheeks begin to heat. The sage sweats and matching long sleeve are a long way from any outfit that they've seen me in, and my face is makeup-free.

I clear my throat. "I can't be stunning all of the time."

Broderick's face splits in a grin. "You're gorgeous no matter what you wear. I'm just fighting the temptation to cuddle you with how cozy you look."

I cast a look at Alasdair. "I didn't think you'd call in the cavalry."

Alasdair makes a chuffing sound. "The cavalry is Elliot. I called Broderick to board up your door. We'll fix it tomorrow."

"We were just fighting over who would drive you back to our place," Broderick says. "We don't like the idea of you driving over alone but he's" —Broderick points a finger at Alasdair— "not going to fit in your car no matter if he wears a glamour."

I look Alasdair up and down. "You could fit, but it'd be tight." I shake my head. "But neither of you need to ride with me."

Broderick makes that strange purr he does and slides my bag from my shoulder to his. "Let us take care of you, Gracie. It's our privilege as the ones courting you."

I hesitate but my shoulders drop, do I really want to drive all alone across the city?

"Okay," I say.

Broderick lifts his brows. "How about you let me drive your car? It's getting late and you've had a bad night."

My mouth twitches. "Now you're pushing it."

"Nonsense," he says and drops a kiss on my cheek.

Alasdair makes a sound. "Stan has put in the call. He thinks he can get the place cleared by noon tomorrow. I'll board up the door on my way out and meet you two at home."

"Thank you," I say.

Alasdair's eyes glint. "This is a part of being in a clan. It's our pleasure to take care of you."

* * *

I yawn when we pull up to the manor.

Broderick looks over at me, from the driver's seat, of course. "Rough night?"

It hadn't taken much for Broderick to convince me to let him drive. After the adrenaline drop and hot shower, my legs are noodly and I'm ready to pass out in a bed.

Broderick donned a glamour to take the wheel and most of the drive I'd squinted at this version of him. His human form is similar enough to the gargoyle one I've grown used to, but different. He retains his bad-boy appeal in this form with narrow hips made to swagger and sharp brows. His hair stayed the short curls that look tousled. I almost miss the sight of the horns.

"It's been a little stressful," I say.

"Right." Broderick hesitates. "Elliot might freak out a little bit. Alasdair didn't tell him when he called me, otherwise you would have had three gargoyles in your living room. But he'll know now since Alasdair made it back before us."

"Freak out?" I ask.

"He'll try to smother you with affection and snacks."

I blink. "He's going to mother me?"

Broderick shakes his head. "He's going to care for you in the way he knows how. It might be overwhelming. Say the word and I'll text Alasdair to distract him for the night."

"That would be cowardly," I say.

Broderick grunts. "With the amount of energy he has, it would be prudent."

I tilt my head. "I… I want to see him."

"Oh?" His brows rise.

"With how I left dinner, I just…" I don't even know what to say or really what is causing this need to see Elliot after the night I've had.

"You don't need to explain anything to me." Broderick grins knowingly.

We get out of the car and are almost at the porch when the front door bursts open.

"Grace!" Elliot says before pulling me into his arms. His human-appearing arms. He's wearing his glamour again. Alasdair follows him, the stiffness from our dinner date missing. It's as if the clan leader has come to some decision that had been up in the air.

"Told you." Broderick mutters before raising his voice. "Where's my welcome home? Am I to be left out in the cold because your girlfriend is over?"

Elliot breathes me in and squeezes tighter, lifting one hand to flip off Broderick.

"I'm so glad you're here," Elliot says. "Alasdair made me promise that I wouldn't go overboard, but do you need a snack? Or some alcohol?"

I laugh. Broderick grumbles and pulls Elliot away from me and into his arms, kissing him.

Oh.

The kiss isn't a chaste thing. It's the first time I've seen any of them be with another, and I'm surprised how quickly my body heats. Elliot relaxes into the kiss, and a hint of fang flashes from Broderick.

Broderick breaks the kiss. "That's for making me jealous."

"Uh?" Elliot says blearily.

"Welcoming Grace home and not me."

Elliot stills, his mouth drops open. "Good gods, are you really jealous?"

Broderick hums. "Maybe I'm just letting our witch have a breather from you."

Elliot's brow creases in concern.

Broderick taps his nose. "I'm not jealous. I just missed you."

Alasdair watches the couple with a glint in his eyes that does nothing to suppress the tight warmth in my core. Wasn't I just ready to fall into bed?

His gaze turns to me and I try and push down the arousal singing in my veins.

"Welcome back to Bramblewick Manor," Alasdair says. "I'll try not to be insufferable again."

CHAPTER 23
ELLIOT

I hum, drying a pan that Broderick hands me. Usually, he and Alasdair would do the dishes when I cook, but the incident with Grace has thrown off the rhythm. I'd rather Alasdair be showing Grace to her room than doing the dishes.

Alasdair is the strongest and most protective gargoyle of us. If Grace can take a small measure of comfort in him giving her a tour of our space, I want that.

"You're happy she's here," Broderick says.

I avoid my mate's gaze and hang the pan in the rack. Broderick's stare continues.

I sigh. "Yes, I'm not happy about the circumstances, but I'm happy that the night for us all didn't end with the dinner."

Broderick hums and tugs the towel out of my hands right when Alasdair appears in the doorway.

"She's settled in the room you prepared, next to Broderick's," Alasdair says.

Broderick raises his brows at me. All our rooms are on the same level, but the guest room right next to

Broderick's had been a strategic choice. I want Grace close. I want Grace as a part of our mating.

"You need to ease up on the strategizing. You can't force this," Broderick says.

I narrow my eyes at him.

Alasdair's tired voice interrupts what I'm sure would have been a spirited debate. "I'm heading to bed, unless you two need anything else."

He leaves without giving me a chance to speak and my heart falls into my stomach.

"Go." Broderick gestures. "I'll finish off here. You two need to *talk*."

My mate gives the word a wicked emphasis, but he isn't wrong. I deceived everyone and Alasdair and I haven't had a moment to clear the air. To reconnect after my betrayal.

I kiss Broderick and follow Alasdair. I don't catch up to him until I get to his room. He sits on the large custom-made bed, removing the chain he keeps his glamour ring on from around his neck, dodging his horns with care. I swallow, leaning against the doorframe.

"What are you doing here, Elliot?" Alasdair asks without looking up.

"Am I no longer invited?" I wait to see if he'll say he's too tired, for him to come up with an excuse to send me away tonight. Once upon a time, I'd be the solution for a stressed Alasdair. Within the last year, sex stopped being his go-to. *How had I let that happen?*

"I don't think I'd be able to go easy on you tonight," Alasdair says.

My mouth dries. "Maybe I need for you not to go easy on me."

Alasdair's brows rise.

I correct myself. "I'd still need to be worked up to it."

His stature isn't the only massive part of Alasdair. My blush is hot and though we've done this countless times, a surge of awkwardness hits me.

Alasdair's mouth crooks. "I'm conflicted."

He wants me to stay but…

"I lied to everyone," I say.

My clan leader nods.

"You did. We'll be working through that with words soon. We need to." Alasdair looks down. "It's not only that. I'm your mate and you didn't confide in me. Instead, you found a workaround."

"I-I didn't notice how bad it had gotten until I saw her." My voice is a small thing.

Alasdair's bright-blue eyes snare me, guilt lines them. I'm drawn to him, emotionally and physically. My approach is slow.

"I should have realized something was off," Alasdair says.

"You take too much on yourself. I didn't want you to know yet. Not until I'd convinced both of you that we needed to add to our mating. Not until I told her I'd courted her while being mated."

"I should have been more suspicious." Alasdair stands. "At the same time, I'm glad you found her."

"You are?" My eyes widen.

Alasdair rolls his eyes. "Don't act so surprised. You predicted the whole thing."

"I didn't want to hope for too much. You told me to not speak for your needs."

"I was hurt. Still am hurt," he says.

I press my dress shirt to my clan leader's bare chest. "I'm sorry, Alasdair."

My lips brush the skin of his throat, and he grips my arms.

"And I'm sorry I'm failing as a mate, so sorry," he says.

I choke on the emotions in my throat. "No more than I have. I made the decision to deceive you."

"That you did…. A matchmaker, Elliot?"

That has me stiffening. "Um."

Confessing that part feels like something I should talk to Grace about first. A matchmaker indicates intention and planning. More planning than I've done. And with the situation that has her staying with us… the way I'd behaved may not be well received.

"You need to tell her everything," Alasdair says against my forehead, speaking my conscience aloud. "Anything else you have hiding up your sleeve. I don't want your strategy messing up our chances with her."

Success! Alasdair is already treating Grace as a part of our mating.

I wince with dread all the same. "I will. Does that mean I can't stay?"

"I didn't say that. Am I seducing you in this form?" Alasdair's question is slow. Steady.

My face burns, I forgot that I'd donned my glamour. We've done the deed while in my human form before, but tonight… tonight I need to be bare with my clan leader. Tonight, I can't hide behind a handsome human face.

"Oh, um, let me take off my clothes," I say.

Unlike Alasdair's and Broderick's glamours, mine doesn't come with human-style clothing. I liked variety and fashion too much to be contained to one outfit.

Alasdair's eyes darken as he leans back, waiting.

I unbutton my shirt, each second that ticks, each breath and rasp of fabric against skin has my nerves pulsing to attention. My skin heats with anticipation.

Alasdair stands motionless as I fold my clothing and set it aside. I swallow my silly nerves, Alasdair has seen my true form many times, but it doesn't help my personal feelings about it. I wiggle the glamour ring off and set it on the stack of clothes.

My wings stretch and I suppress the hiss of discomfort from my other traits being bound by magic. It's a familiar sensation.

Alasdair steps toward me. The lust on his face helps ease the self-consciousness that plagues me when I take my true form. Alasdair is slow to be pulled into games of bed play, but when he gets going, it's a powerful thing.

He's still clothed so I don't get to feast my eyes on his entirety, but he can see me in mine. To be bare like this makes my breath catch. Arousal is a low thing in my belly. Arousal at the vulnerability of standing before him, of the impending connection, and the idea that the rest of my mates are just down the hall.

I can't call Grace my mate yet.

My heart knows what she is, even if polite society requires a courtship.

"When was the last time you were taken?" Alasdair asks, taking my mind off the ache of glamour and thoughts of courting.

My blush reaches my ears. Alasdair always starts like this. Speaking softly, in euphemism. It makes the moments he speaks explicit words later hit harder.

I clear my throat. "A week ago."

Alasdair blinks in surprise. Our relationship may have lulled into one where sex between us occurs sparingly, but Broderick and I are usually more active.

He tilts my chin up with a knuckle. "Explain, my heart."

I could say many things and they would be truthful, but they wouldn't be the truth. I could say that we've all been busy, that Broderick has been working himself to exhaustion on his current project and I've been preoccupied with Grace, but I don't.

"It didn't feel right," I whisper.

"You were already deceiving her," Alasdair says somehow pinpointing exactly what I meant, but misses the other parts.

"Not just to her." I bite my lip. "It felt like cheating on you two if I touched her and cheating on her if I was with either of you."

Alasdair strokes my cheek.

"Oh, my heart, you must be wound so tight." The gravel of his voice hits low in my gut and my erection bobs. My knot already beginning to swell.

I groan as his hand wraps around me, the practiced stroke has me raising to my toes, rocking my hips into his grip.

"You've been waiting for this," Alasdair says, and we both know he's not talking about sex.

I need his commanding hand.

Soft kisses fall on my cheeks, my lips, my eyelids when they fall shut as he strokes me again.

"Alasdair, *please*."

He hums. "It's going to take a lot for you to take my knot."

I almost cry. I don't want something quick. My heart is a tangled mess and I need the careful hand of Alasdair's dominance to wash me clean, to absolve me. To shorten this between us because of something like preparation feels like a rejection.

At that thought, I choke on a sob.

"Shh, my heart." Alasdair's clawed hand clasps my hair, and the tug creates a cascade of relief in me. When he utters his next words, my knees almost give out. "Lie on the bed."

He releases my hair and I stumble to do as he's requested. I pull back the blankets and lie on the sheets. I want to press my face into the fabric that bears his scent but resist. That may very well still happen tonight, and I'll be patient for it.

Alasdair flicks on the lamp beside the bed and turns the lights off. Something tense in me relaxes at the warm ambience. Light and shadow lovingly caress our bodies. His hands go to his kilt. He doesn't rush the motions of removing it and each moment heightens the delicious sensation of waiting.

When Alasdair's body is revealed, I whimper. My massive mate's smile is wry. He goes to the nightstand, removing a bottle of lube and the butt plug we use when we plan on me taking his knot.

My hips rock up, and embarrassment sings through me when he laughs softly.

"So eager," he says as he approaches me with the lube.

I set my head back on the sheets when the snick of the bottle has my cock jerking.

"*Fuck*," I whisper. He hasn't even touched me yet except for a few chaste kisses. Coming early isn't an option. I need to take him, all of him, my heart and soul require it.

Alasdair's tail whips around and my mate slides his lube-slicked hand over it. My breath comes out in pants and anticipation ratchets up the tension in my core. Alasdair raises a brow at me, and I place my feet on the bed before gripping my thighs and pulling them to me.

The tail slides between my cheeks and my puckered hole. Flicking against my balls. The soft way he strokes me there a tease.

Alasdair stares at me there, watching the tip of his tail press inside me. I grunt as the small invasion grows.

Alasdair growls, his tail slides away from me and my heart stops when he drops to his knees, his large hands press the backs of my thighs higher to me. I cry out when his tongue runs over me and presses there until I give. I moan as he rims me. I'm so hard, precum paints my stomach, so out of my mind that I don't catch him grabbing and lubing up the plug. I don't even notice until his tongue is replaced with the round hardness pressing into me.

"Oh!" I grunt.

"Relax, you can take it." Alasdair's voice is dark, hungry.

I breathe in through my nose, trying to push out on the exhale. It takes a few breaths and Alasdair's patient pushing in and out, but when the plug slides in we both moan. The full stretch is nothing compared to what's to come, but it's been such a long time since we've done this.

The physical give of me has mental and emotional walls coming down.

"I never meant for it to go so far," I say. "To lie for so long."

Alasdair lets my feet fall back to the bed and he softly kisses the inside of my thigh. Silent in the face of my words.

"I swear," I gasp, emotions rising with a vengeance. "I planned to tell her right when we met, but the chances of her rejecting us stopped me. I was afraid of losing her right after finding her. I was afraid it would mean the end of us. That our relationship would continue to deteriorate. That I'd lose the only family I'd ever had."

My voice is thick with tears and Alasdair presses his hand against my heart, rubbing, soothing the tension with the heavy weight.

"Hush, Elliot."

I gasp in a shuddering breath. "Please say I didn't ruin everything."

It's my deepest worry. That no matter how strategic I've been, no matter how much I care about everyone involved, my actions will single-handedly ruin what was possible.

Alasdair tilts his head. "You didn't ruin it. Elliot, you've shined a light on the cracks in our relationship. You may have behaved regrettably, but your family is still here for you. I'm still here for you. I'll love you in the face of every underhanded thing you do because your intention is never to hurt us."

I swallow and wipe away the tears, adjusting to the stretch of the plug. All that's left in the lull of us is the intimacy we share.

"Kiss me?" I ask.

"Oh, my heart, always."

Alasdair climbs over me. When his lips meet mine, the kiss starts slow, gentle. My body rocks against his and our kisses take on a breathless nature, staying controlled. His hard cock presses against mine and pulses when I make a helpless sound.

Alasdair breaks the kiss, his eyes dark. He drags his fangs against my neck, catching on the mating mark he'd left on me years ago. He continues kissing down my body, interspersing nips with licks.

"No no no," I say when he gets lower, guessing his destination.

Alasdair arches a brow. "No?"

The tone is taunting, the playful side I don't see from this gargoyle as often as I should.

"I-I can't keep from coming if you give me head," I say. My cheeks are so flushed the heat of them almost hurt.

Alasdair's smile is unmerciful. "If you want to take all of me tonight, you'll keep from coming."

I squirm and squeeze around the plug with a gasp when he takes my cock into his mouth. Careful of his fangs, he licks over me and sucks me in deeper. Each action is so methodical, so measured, I could weep. Alasdair rings his fingers around me, squeezing right above the swell of my knot as a tease.

For either of us to reach orgasm, our knots need a clamping squeeze to them. Both of my mates are talented in knowing just how to grip mine manually. Alasdair's other hand reaches under me and grips the plug, moving it in time to his mouth.

It hurts not to come. I'm a breath away from becoming a rutting mess, wishing that Grace or Broderick were here to fill.

I must wish so hard I get a whiff of her scent, but it's gone again, and I whimper in need.

Alasdair finally pulls the plug from me and flips me over on the bed. His patience running out as his lube-covered cock presses against me.

I groan and try to relax enough to take him. It's a process, accepting the beast Alasdair is equipped with.

"Oh fuck," I moan.

"So beautiful. Take me, Elliot."

I hiss when the head of him slips past the ring of muscle and groan deep in my chest in time with his. The rest of him follows in slow pulses that I feel from the ends of my hair to my toes, until his fleshy knot presses against me.

Alasdair starts to fuck in and out of me, the motions slow.

"My heart, you fit me so well, I can't wait to see my seed dripping out of you," he says.

I can't help tightening on his unforgiving thickness and he moans. He thrusts inside me, hitting every sensitive perfect place.

I curse and groan at each impact. Pleading sounds start to fall from me, my body so tight and needy for completion. My claws dig into his sheets and I want to grip my cock but I crave Alasdair's dominance too much to give in.

"That's it," Alasdair says. "Are you going to take my knot?"

"Yes!" I sob.

Alasdair presses hard, and the stretch has my eyes rolling back in my head before it slides in, and I shout. Alasdair snarls and throbs, painting my insides with him.

My words are lost and gibberish by the time Alasdair grips my knot tightly and my body arches in release. My face digging hard in the sheets I cover.

The climax shatters me. My guilt, my worries, break in physical release and pleasure. The throb of my body in time to Alasdair's the homecoming I craved.

He kisses my neck and I melt at each murmured word of praise.

"My heart, my love, my beautiful mate. I will always forgive you."

CHAPTER 24
GRACE

I'm barely in the comfortable guest bed when I'm out of it again. The room is beautifully decorated, and I packed as many things as I could to put myself at ease, but I'm still alone in an unfamiliar room, an unfamiliar house. My mind won't let me cuddle in the sheets yet. I pull on my silk robe, it covers my favorite short frilly nightdress.

I hadn't lied to Broderick earlier tonight. Fashion and pretty things are my coping mechanisms. Each of my favorite clothing items were custom-tailored and required time and lists with my favorite seamstress. Each list and exacting detail fill me with calm.

This nightdress is vintage in design and practically transparent, the abundance of gauzy fabric falls from my breasts and hips, the lace edging hitting mid-thigh. It's gorgeous and makes me feel like a starlet, but it's not something I can wear without the robe for a trip to the kitchen.

Water, a glass of water, will help me relax in this new setting. I peek into the hallway to find it empty if not dark. The door to the room Alasdair had pointed out as his is cracked open and light spills from there. I scurry away, not wanting to be tempted to bother the protective gargoyle.

I descend the dark stairs with care until I find my way to the kitchen. The light in the entryway is still on and the cozy ambience of the kitchen, the years of heartfelt moments and tasks of love, help slow the racing of my heart. Some sips of water later, and I'm on my way back to my room.

As much as I enjoy the comfort of the kitchen, once my jitters calm, I become more aware that anyone could discover me walking around the house in my robe. It's not exactly polite.

The hallway is how I left it, but after the context of the cheery kitchen, the shadows wrap around me in welcome. The light from Alasdair's door is still the sole illumination and I tap down the temptation to ask him if he also has trouble sleeping.

I shake my head and turn toward my guest bedroom when I hear it.

The moan is distant, soft.

I freeze at the door to my borrowed room and my heartbeat quickens. Something has me walking down the hall instead of returning to my bed for the night. Later I might lie to myself that I was only checking on a sound, not that curiosity and lust drew me.

The moan sounded like Elliot.

And it came from Alasdair's room. Light spilling from the door's opening acts like a beacon. A deeper groan seizes control of my body. I shouldn't look... but as if in a trance, I do. A reading lamp nearby reveals two gray bodies moving on a bed. Alasdair's form dwarfs Elliot's, but it doesn't stop me from seeing what's happening.

Elliot arches his back against the pillows, Alasdair's head between his spread legs, moving in an unmistakable rhythm. Elliot makes a sound as the bigger gargoyle fiddles with something under him.

I should go.

"I keep finding you in doorways." The whisper has me jumping, but a hand clasps over my mouth to keep me quiet. Heat and the scent of sawdust wraps around me, I relax as the familiarity of it clicks.

Broderick chuckles softly, more of a movement of his chest against my back than a sound. He removes his hand slowly, his claw dragging over my cheek in a way that has a shiver tickling my spine.

"We wouldn't want to interrupt them; this has been a long time coming." Broderick keeps his whisper low.

I swallow and my face burns. "I should go, you probably want to join them."

There's a hardness against my back that has me wanting to shift my hips. It's been so long since I've been with anyone and now I've been thrown into courting three males at once. It's a miracle my brain hasn't short-circuited.

Broderick presses his large hand against my belly, keeping me where I stand.

"No, they both need this. Elliot hurt our clan leader with his deception, this is their time to work through that."

"Through sex?" I raise a brow.

"You say that as if pain can't be worked through with intimacy. As if Elliot giving himself over to be stretched until Alasdair can thrust his cock inside him isn't something significant and beautiful."

Heat consumes me and I press my thighs together. It won't hide anything. I'm bare under my nightdress and robe. Already my thighs are slick at the moving bodies on the bed.

"Th-this is private," I whisper.

"Ah, but you've had your need stoked. What will you do, little Gracie? Go back and toss and turn in your bed until the fire under your skin cools?"

Broderick's hand slides down the silky material of my robe, pulling on the tie. The knot gives, and the robe falls open, exposing the thin nightdress to the cool air of the hallway. The warm glow catches on the white fabric, revealing the lines of my body beneath it. The contrast with Broderick's gray hand sliding ever lower has the breath shuddering from my lips.

"So pretty, like the prettiest pastry. Or maybe you won't suffer, maybe you plan on going to your bed and thinking all sorts of naughty thoughts. Touching yourself until you can do away with the need. Did you happen to bring a vibrator?"

My words catch in my throat. I shake my head. No, I brought a number of things, my favorite nightdress, sweats, a robe, a small set of cosmetics, and even a pillowcase. I did not bring a vibrator.

"Ah, well, that means I can't just let you suffer. That would make me a terrible host." Broderick presses his fingers against my mons through the fabric and I tense my thighs together to keep from groaning. Broderick stops, his other hand curling a strand of my hair around a claw. "Tell me to stop, Grace. Tell me you don't want me helping you alleviate the ache between your legs."

I breathe out. I should tell him to stop.

Broderick's voice deepens. "Tell me that you wouldn't welcome my tongue licking away that wetness."

The words have my pussy weeping. I don't think I've ever been so wet.

"W-we barely know each other," I say.

"Oh, I know you, Gracie. I know the scent of you makes my mouth water and I recognize the feelings you have for Elliot, no matter that you try to hide it. But this doesn't have to be about that. We can be two strangers in the dark, satisfying curiosity as well as feeding a craving."

His claws reach the lacy trim of the nightdress and start to pull it higher. In the bedroom, Alasdair puts something on the nightstand and flips Elliot on the bed. I whimper.

Broderick groans in my hair.

"Shh. Do you want this?" he asks.

Alasdair's hips start working against Elliot, who muffles his face in the sheets.

My lips fall open. "Please—"

Broderick turns me to press my back against the wall, I've lost sight of the two gargoyles, but his hands come up to squeeze my breasts and the heat melting my insides blazes into an inferno.

A sound escapes Broderick's mouth. "Later I'm going to lavish these with attention, but now I get my dessert."

He kneels before me, his wings silently spread before the talons at the hinge wrap around my wrists, lifting and pinning them above my head.

I gasp and Broderick freezes. "Say the word, Grace, and I stop… say nothing and you get to find out what a gargoyle's tongue feels like."

My brain does short-circuit at that. A gargoyle's… tongue.

I say nothing.

Broderick's grin hits me, a sharp spark in my belly. He pushes up the nightdress and stops.

"Oh, you look as pretty as a picture. All pink and juicy," he says.

His breath hits my wetness, chilling it. I can hardly help that my legs spread for his examination. He leans in and heat strokes through me. I gasp, discovering just what he meant about his tongue.

Broderick's tongue is long, thick, and strong. The first lick up through my pussy has me biting my lip to the point of pain to keep quiet.

All gods above save me. Or make this moment never end. There is no in-between that I'd be satisfied with.

Broderick grips my nightdress in fists.

His eyes are dilated when he leans back. "Fuck, Gracie, your taste is my new favorite meal."

"I need my hands," I say so softly that I'm surprised he hears, but he does. The talons on his wings release my wrists and I press my hands against my mouth to muffle myself.

Broderick's grin is so broad the light catches on his fangs.

Okay? He mouths to me.

I nod and the gargoyle destroys me.

I thought I'd experienced being eaten out before. I'd experienced *nothing* compared to how Broderick eats me. His tongue slides over my slick folds, varying the pressure from hard to soft in a way that has my hips rocking against him. Broderick wraps a hand around the back of my knee and hooks my leg up over his shoulder, pressing me harder against the wall in a way that *oofs* the air out of my lungs.

He's everywhere at once. Enthusiastic and skilled.

I'm desperate to come when Broderick slides his tongue inside me. He moves it in and out, penetrating me with the slick thickness of it, tasting every inch of me.

Elliot shouts from the room and Alasdair growls with what must be his release. Broderick's tongue slides from me and sucks on my clit, forcing the pleasure he must have been stoking to come to a head with my climax.

My body arches, and I muffle as much sound as I can, but the wave of sensation has my ears ringing, and a sob makes it past my hand.

Holy gods. I don't think I've ever come so hard.

Broderick laps me as I come down, slurping up my juices like they are his favorite dessert. I pant and whimper, sensitive to the touch. The gargoyle stops tonguing me but doesn't move from nuzzling his new favorite place. His shoulders shake in what must be a silent laugh.

Why is he laughing?

I frown and Broderick taps the side of my thigh. Like tapping out in a wrestling match. With horror, I release the grip of my thighs around his head, and he places the leg that had been on his shoulder to the ground.

My nerves at having nearly suffocated the gargoyle before me dissipate at his salacious grin. *Oh, well, he doesn't seem to mind.*

I breathe out a sigh of relief and just like that, the tension and strength holding my body up disappears. Falling asleep won't be difficult at all now.

Broderick rises, and with a grip at my waist, moves us away from the cracked door as if to give his cohorts privacy as they murmur to each other.

I don't realize our destination until he stops at the room I've been given. I widen my eyes. *Should I invite him in?* This gargoyle gave me an orgasm, surely he must want me to return the favor.

I open my mouth but snap it closed when he kisses my forehead, his lips still damp with my own essence.

"Sleep well, Gracie."

"You don't want to…" I trail off as my eyes drop to the bulging hardness pushing against the kilt he wears.

He smiles. "Oh, I do, but it's not the right time for that. We won't be strangers exploring in the dark when we come together."

My mouth twitches. "Is this like waiting for the perfect moment for us to kiss?"

"Every first between us is something I plan on savoring. I may not be as patient as Alasdair or as strategic as Elliot, but I can ensure that every first we have is sinfully memorable."

With that, Broderick leaves me and walks into the room next to mine.

I stand there for a moment after he leaves.

Where did the air go? Something tells me that the way I consider sex and the way it's treated in this house is very different, or maybe I've just never been with people who care so much about my pleasure.

Sex has always been something that's a given in the relationships I've been in. If I'm dating someone, we're having sex. If I'm not, I'm soloing it.

But the way Broderick spoke about Elliot and Alasdair coming together… he'd called it beautiful. An ache wells in my chest.

I'm yearning for something I've never known was possible in real life.

Intimacy.

CHAPTER 25

ALASDAIR

I'm reading the news on my phone when Broderick breezes into the kitchen. Elliot plates the French toast he's been preparing, an apron over his human glamour and dress shirt and pants. It's concerning how often Elliot is hiding behind his glamour of late.

It's usually a sign that he's stressed, but now with his feelings for Grace… I foresee discussions about his self-consciousness. The glamours aren't meant to be worn so often. They aren't comfortable.

"Thank you, Elliot. You seem nice and relaxed this morning. Is our houseguest still sleeping?" Broderick asks, his eyes full of mirth.

Elliot blushes and a glow of happiness distracts me for a moment.

"Grace is still asleep. She did have a stressful day yesterday." Elliot says. His blush morphing to a look of discomfort as he turns back toward the stove.

I arch a brow at Broderick, whose smile widens.

"I scented something quite interesting outside my door this morning," I say. The fragrance of Grace and Broderick's arousal had been faint, but present. Roses and cedar with the tang of musk. It had my mouth watering and Broderick and I rarely come together like that.

Elliot didn't scent it, but my sense of smell is stronger.

Broderick's smile is pure wickedness now. "Did you? I was just escorting our *guest* back to bed."

I snort. "In the hallway?"

Broderick's grin starts to fall. "Neither of you mind, do you?"

We haven't had to navigate courting the same individual in a long time. Broderick and I don't consider ourselves each other's mate. We're physically intimate at times, but Elliot has always sparked different wants in us. We're both mated to the same male and at the beginning, had to navigate the feelings that came with.

Elliot turns and stills. "You and she…?"

Now Broderick clears his throat, uncomfortable. "Yes, we were intimate. After we both caught sight of you and Alasdair."

Elliot's brow creases and it's hard to decipher the expression there, but his scent is tinged with jealousy. And then he blushes.

"Oh, you both saw that?"

I roll my lips to keep from laughing at him. The stress that's been dogging my steps is gone. The intimacy Elliot and I had shared last night destroyed it.

Elliot purses his lips. "Broderick, we're wanting more than to seduce her, and you two just barely met."

Broderick lifts his hands. "I don't need a week with her to know these things, but Elliot, you courted her a week and didn't touch her. She was practically vibrating with tension."

I hum as Elliot frowns, looking away.

"I was trying to honor our mating."

Broderick nods. "And Grace probably knows that, but you can't leave such a lively woman wanting."

"I won't," Elliot says and then winces. "I have to talk to her about something she might not like."

"What?" Broderick asks.

Elliot shakes his head. "She should be the first to know."

Broderick shrugs and turns to me. "Are we good?"

"About the spying or—"

Broderick's grunt interrupts. "I'm not stepping on your toes? Leaving her scent everywhere?"

I sip my cup of coffee before answering.

"No. Grace is her own person. Honestly, I'm a little jealous with how easy your interactions have been. I don't seem to be able to say anything without it going poorly."

Broderick gives me a sad smile. "In time, I think you'll figure out how to talk to her."

"I just have so many emotions and then say the wrong thing," I confess.

Elliot tilts his head. "Maybe you need to take time going through the emotions on your own. She'd make a list and write it down. I think you two are similar in that way."

A sound has us all freezing guiltily.

We don't want Grace to think we're gossiping about her. Even though we are.

Eloise and Graham enter the kitchen and we all breathe a sigh of relief.

"Good morning," Elliot sings.

"Morning, sweetheart. Anything you want me to help with?" Eloise asks.

Elliot scrunches his nose and points at the seats at the counter. "I'm on breakfast duty, don't you dare try and take over."

Eloise laughs and takes a seat gingerly on the stool next to me. I make a note to get better stools for them. Graham remains standing.

"How was the opera?" I ask.

Graham grumbles and Eloise jabs an elbow at him.

"Ballet," Eloise corrects me. "It was wonderful, Alasdair." There was an awe in her voice and her face was dreamy in a way I haven't seen in a while.

She continues. "The seats were wonderful—"

Graham scoffs. "I got stuck!"

"They were wonderfully placed in respect to the stage," Eloise puts in. Her eyes are bright with humor, but she turns back to me. "You spoil us."

I can't fight the smile on my face. "I spoil you. Graham is just spoiled by proxy."

The elder gargoyle narrows his eyes at me, but we both know he wouldn't let her go alone. He's the only mate she has left. It's his honor and responsibility to be her escort.

Eloise folds her hands politely. "But surely the expense—"

"Clan Mother," I cut in with utmost reverence. "You gave us the roof over our head, the family we needed, and have worked to provide for our every need. Let us spoil you."

Eloise's eyes water, but she sniffs and is back to the no-nonsense woman that took in an over large teenage gargoyle no one wanted.

"I suppose it's alright for you three to spoil us," she says, and Graham wraps an arm around her shoulder.

There's a sound on the stairs and we all stop talking as Grace walks in.

She's wearing a dress. I know almost nothing about fashion, but this one is more casual than the red one she'd worn last night. I'd almost gaped at that dress and the way it had lovingly cradled her tits. It had been a challenge to keep my eyes on her face throughout the night. This dress is pretty, but thankfully makes the concept of speaking words not as difficult.

She freezes in the doorway under our stares. "Um, good morning."

Her gaze touches on Broderick and her cheeks erupt in a blush.

That Grace had her needs met by our master carpenter soothes something in my soul.

"Grace," Elliot says, placing a plate down for her, next to Broderick.

I sip more coffee to hide my smile. It's difficult to get Elliot to stop scheming. It's a compulsion that has persisted in the years we've been together. How quickly he can get over momentary jealousy if it means that she might forgive him for whatever trespass he needs to confess.

I hope it's something Grace can accept, whatever his confession may be.

CHAPTER 26
GRACE

The silence in the kitchen when I entered had been alarming.

Four gargoyles and a human stared at me. I'd had the urge to turn tail and run. Then Broderick had smiled at me and everything we'd done in the hallway had come to mind in vivid detail.

Now, I'm sitting at the counter next to the gargoyle that had tongued me in the dark, focusing on not thinking about that. They'd be able to scent my arousal. Think family-friendly thoughts. No thoughts about gargoyles' tongues, or how I'd last seen Elliot and Alasdair.

Avoiding thinking about those details is more difficult than I'd ever imagine with the lull in conversation I've inspired.

"It's so nice that you're staying with us, Grace," Eloise says. "If Elliot ever lets me handle dinner, I'll need to make something special. Really welcome you to the family."

Elliot rolls his eyes and mutters something about Eloise being able to do whatever she pleased.

I'm so grateful for the diversion of topics, I smile at her even as Broderick's thigh bumps mine under the counter.

"That sounds wonderful! I'm pretty sure I'll be back in my apartment in no time, though. I'd be interested in a family dinner all together sometime."

Alasdair frowns. "You want to stay at your apartment while the situation is unsettled?"

"Well, yes," I say. "They'll have it cleaned out today, and after filing a report with the Council, there isn't much that can be done about the situation. I can't just move in here—"

"Let's not rush anything," Elliot says.

Alasdair closes his mouth on whatever he was going to say, but his disapproval chafes. I can't let one stalker witch uproot my entire life.

"A family dinner sounds delightful," Eloise says. She picks up her plate and Graham's. "We'll let you all have some privacy; we've been wanting to spend some time on the patio and the weather is beautiful outside."

Eloise winks at me as if I'm planning on doing scandalous things with these gargoyles on the breakfast counter. My face burns as Broderick chuckles.

"I don't know what she expects is going to happen over breakfast," I say after the elder members of the clan leave.

Broderick bumps his shoulder to mine. "She's just giving us as much of an advantage as she can. I don't know whether to be offended that she thinks we need it, or grateful."

Elliot smiles, but it's a little weak. It brightens when he looks at the French toast. "Tell me what you think of my recipe."

I blink. *Feeding people is his love language*. Elliot and I are still in an awkward place after the revelation of his clan, but I want to try for this. Now that I've seen a little of how they interact with each other, had more than a minute conversation with each, I'd like for this to work out.

I take a bite of French toast and my eyes fall closed on a moan. It's fluffy and spicy, the sweet of the syrup mixes perfectly with cinnamon, nutmeg, and something else. Cloves. It's warm, comforting, and perfect.

I open my eyes to compliment Elliot and still. They are all staring at me. It's not the alarmed stare from before, this is like a predator sighting a mouse. Their eyes are dark, hungry. I continue chewing and the gargoyles all seem to realize their reaction at once.

Broderick smiles at himself as he starts eating his own toast and Alasdair drops his gaze entirely, frowning. I glance to Elliot, and he stares the longest. The hunger and hope alive on his face as he waits for my response.

"It's the best French toast I've ever had," I say, and Elliot grins, plating the last pieces for himself. Taking a spot at the counter across from everyone, choosing to eat standing.

"How did you sleep?" Elliot asks, and I almost choke.

Broderick snorts and I elbow him. The gargoyle freezes as if considering something.

"I told them that we spent time in the hallway. I'm not used to hiding anything. If you'd rather we not disclose details to each other while we're all courting, I'll respect that."

"Oh." My blush is fierce, but I fight down the passing embarrassment. "I'm okay with you talking about it. It doesn't seem right to keep secrets like that if we're all courting."

I almost choke on my next words, but I force it out. "I'm sorry for spying on you two."

Instead of being upset, Elliot laughs.

"I thought I'd caught your scent, but told myself it was wishful thinking."

Wishful thinking.

"Um." I swallow, my sensibilities keeping me from boldly talking about this.

Alasdair of all people puts down his coffee and considers me. "You are always invited, so please don't feel bad about catching us in the act. Elliot is quite vocal. Neither of us are shy."

Now, Elliot's blushing and I take comfort in the fact that I'm not the only one embarrassed.

Always invited. "I think I need a little more time getting to know you all before being included in… group activities."

Alasdair's mouth may twitch at that, but it's gone so quickly that I almost convince myself that I'd imagined it. With the nod from the clan leader, we lapse into comfortable silence as we eat the French toast.

I push my plate away when I'm done. "Thank you, Elliot."

"You're welcome." Elliot beams at me. "We all take turns cooking, but I admit I enjoy it the most."

"Um, is ordering takeout cheating? Because I've never been a good cook, though I've been trying to learn—" I stop because just like that I'm inserting myself in this clan. It's an odd thing that within a single day, I can see myself living here with these gargoyles.

Tap the brakes! I don't even know if I'm going to be compatible with this way of life or these gargoyles. They could decide that I'm not a good fit for their clan and all these visions I have of cozy teas with Eloise and wicked moments with Broderick would be for nothing.

"I'd love to help you learn if you'd like," Elliot says eagerly, with no concept of my own inner thoughts.

"That sounds like fun," I say, my smile brittle.

Elliot beams, but his expression falters. "I have something to tell you, Grace. Something you should know."

I lift my brows, curious but dreading whatever has put the wince on Elliot's face.

"I think…" Elliot starts. "That I should tell everyone at the same time, but if you'd rather I tell you first, I will."

"What is it?" I ask, glancing at Alasdair and Broderick. Both appear concerned. "You're going to tell them too anyway. Might as well just tell us all together."

"Um, about the matchmaker…" Elliot scratches his scalp in discomfort. *Why is he wearing his human glamour?* "I saw you before we were matched."

"Oh?" I frown, trying to remember back.

"I saw you in front of the bathhouse and was entranced." Elliot doesn't quite meet my gaze. "I followed you in and asked Lowell about you—"

My heart sinks and ice takes its place as his words start to make sense.

"We weren't matched by Rose?" I ask.

I can hardly believe my words come out clearly. My thoughts are spiraling. The way we met had all been a setup.

"We were!" Elliot replies hastily. "When Lowell said that you were visiting with the matchmaker, I made an appointment right after… and went through your notes."

"How?" I ask, as if with more details I'm not going to stumble over the fact that Elliot followed me. As if any detail will silence all the doubts that are coming screaming to the surface.

"I may have capitalized on a disagreement happening in the main bathing room that left me alone in her office." Elliot's nerves flavor the air. "I didn't hack her computer or anything, but she had some handwritten notes that I knew had to be you. I saw that you were looking for a single mate…"

That detail falls into the puzzle with a resounding thud.

"And that's what you told Rose you were." I shake my head in disbelief. "Did you match us up?"

I'd gone to a matchmaker because I needed to, and Elliot played the system.

"No! I figured that if we were matched, then it was meant to be, and we are! The matchmaker rated us as compatible—"

"But you lied to her, you followed me." The thought of being followed, especially with Theo's activities, sends a chill up my spine. I stand. "All to trick me into dating you."

"Grace." Elliot's face falls. "If we weren't compatible—"

"We wouldn't have been matched if you hadn't lied!" I shake my head, trying to keep the doubts from welling in my soul. *What else could he have lied about? How compatible are we really?*

Broderick and Alasdair are both frowning, but this is probably an easier chain of events to follow than Elliot going through the motions of meeting a matchmaker without them.

But I never belonged in this beautiful life that I've gotten a taste of.

"I only lied about being single. I promise," Elliot says.

I shake my head, reeling. "I don't know if I believe you."

Elliot's expression morphs into devastation, but I try and wall off my heart from caring.

"I'm already packed. I'm going home," I say.

"Grace, please don't go—" Elliot starts.

Alasdair interrupts. "It may not be safe—"

"Gracie—" Broderick says but I make a cutting motion in the air, and it all falls silent.

"My place is being cleared out today. I need to think about things."

"What about the stalker?" Alasdair asks.

"I'm not going to hide the rest of my life until the stalker is handled, and I don't want to stay here when Elliot acted similarly."

Elliot makes a sound as if I've hit him.

"What he did is different," Broderick says, coming close, but keeping himself from wrapping his arms around me. "I know you're upset, and you should take whatever time you need, but lashing out at Elliot isn't going to make you feel better. He didn't violate your home."

I shake my head. I need space to dispel the growing panic, the realization that I like them too much, that I like being here too much.

When it all can come tumbling down from a faulty foundation of lies.

A sob hiccups from my chest, and I turn from the trio. I need to get my stuff.

No one stops me from leaving.

CHAPTER 27
GRACE

Hours later, I look up at my building and draw in a deep breath. It would be ridiculous to be leery of going back to my apartment. This is my home, not some manor full of gargoyles that whip my emotions and body into a frenzy with hardly any effort.

Ridiculous.

Deep breaths. Maybe stroke the pages of the book I'd treated myself to at the rare bookshop. The aged pages of my find are full of calming thoughts and love. The book itself is a collection of stories used as bedtime stories over the years.

It didn't help my ache for a family, but the paper signature did succeed in slowing my heart rate. Being calmer helped me mull over Elliot's confession.

I'd been upset. At this point, it's hard to identify exactly why. Was it that he lied to Rose for the express purpose of matching with me? Or that he'd followed me and manipulated everything at the same time I'm dealing with the ugly situation of Theo? Is it because I don't trust my judgment now?

Or is it a combination or any of those things?

Why did his confession upset me more than if he had gone to Rose first?

We are compatible. I don't think he'd lie about that. He saw me, he wanted me, and he engineered this whole situation. My trust in him may be tarnished… but I still like him.

Maybe it's that if this match hasn't been ordained by Rose, then the chances of it failing, of the group of males courting me losing interest, are higher. I have no guarantee, no choice but to trust myself, and I've already proven lacking in relationships.

The dates before Elliot had been terrible, but the relationships I've been in had also been terrible. I settled with people who said they wanted to date me and then made every excuse until infidelity forced me to end things.

It had all coalesced in my mind. Broderick, speaking about sex and intimacy in a way I've never heard before, opened my eyes to how shallow those past relationships had been.

I want the intimacy they share. I don't want these hiccups to define our relationship.

I deserve what the Bramblewicks are offering.

With that, I dial Elliot.

"Grace—"

"I'm sorry," I say.

Elliot makes a sound. "You don't have anything to be—"

"I shouldn't have blown up at you."

"I did lie," he says.

There's a pause and I bite my lip. "I don't want this to go up in flames, but I think I've been waiting for you to reject me."

"Grace." Elliot's voice is sharp. "I'm not going to reject you. I've been a devious bastard to try and manipulate you into our clan. I ache at your absence."

I swallow.

Elliot's sigh is pained. "I'm going to ask for your forgiveness when I see you again in person. In the meantime, I want you to allow yourself to believe this will really work out. I have every belief that we can do this."

I'm a badass witch who deserves love.

"Okay. I'm sorry my baggage—"

"Don't finish that thought. We all have baggage. I'm just glad my baggage hasn't chased you away." Elliot's whisper hits my heart.

We say our goodbyes and I'm left in my car, relieved and hopeful.

Nothing can move forward until I figure out my apartment. I muster my courage and head inside.

Stan smiles at me. "Ms. Starling, it's good to see you."

"It's good to see you too, Stan."

The troll had called me to tell me that the apartment is clear. All that's needed is for me to resurrect my wards. I'd gotten more supplies for them while out.

"Did you manage to get in contact with a Council enforcer?" he asks.

I sigh. "Yes."

The enforcer had seemed bored with the details until I'd listed my full name for the report. The idea that they had been much more responsive after that makes me cringe, but it's hardly unusual.

"Did they already tell you that there isn't enough evidence?" I ask.

Accusing a fellow witch of violating my apartment is a big deal. Our only evidence that Theo is involved are the flowers and a message just vague enough to be waved away as a coincidence. The spell he'd used in my apartment had been precise and wiped clean of any signature that would lead to a user.

Stan's expression darkens. "They did. We've scaled up our surveillance of the building. At least having a report will give us more ground to stand on if other incidents occur."

It's as if Stan is reciting the silver lining in the situation but I still appreciate it.

"Did you find out how he got past the wards?" I ask.

Stan winces. "One of the residents let in someone claiming to be locked out near the back of the building. We've adjusted the wards."

I nod. A resident of the building gave permission. They probably thought they were being nice. "Would they be able to give a description?"

Stan shakes his head. "It was Pamela."

My shoulders drop. "Oh"

Pamela was a lovely elderly witch who badly needed vision assistance… and was convinced she didn't.

Stan brightens. "Your gargoyle is here."

I blink. "What?"

Stan stills, as if unsure. "One of the Bramblewicks."

"What is he doing here?" I ask.

"He's fixing the door. Did they not clear that with you first?" Stan's green tone starts to redden.

"Oh, I guess that's fine." Alasdair did say something about that and it's not as if a bunch of strangers haven't already been through my place already.

But now I have a gargoyle I need to deal with.

CHAPTER 28
BRODERICK

I whistle as I work. This job shouldn't take long, and I feel torn about whether I want Grace to come home while I'm still here or not. I don't want her to feel crowded, but I also don't want to give her too much space and question my affection.

The door I've brought to replace Grace's has some custom carvings that I worked on after she'd stormed out this morning. It had been meditative. I'd let my memory of what her apartment felt like guide my claws and Dremel. The delicate vintage-inspired scrolls turned out beautifully.

The bumps in our relationship are occurring much quicker than I figured. Carving helped calm my mind after Elliot's confession, but my instincts are still screaming to touch base with our witch.

I decide I want her to catch me at her place. Even if it annoys her.

The sound of the key in the lock startles me and I put down the drill. The door swings open and Grace walks in, her sundress swaying, as cheerful as it had been this morning. She has her bag slung around her shoulder and a sack with dried herbs in one arm with what appears to be a wrapped book in the other.

"Let me help you." I approach and take the herbs from her without hesitation.

Grace gives me a wry look. "I didn't expect you to be here."

"Do you want me to leave? I'm almost done." I look back at the door, all that's left is to clean up the dust from the drill. I'd finished the wood of the door with the help of some magic products and the stain color goes well with the frames on the wall.

"No." Grace looks tired. She shakes her head. "I'm… glad you're here."

I hum. "I'm glad to be here."

And just like that, she blushes.

I give a cursory sniff of the herbs. "Are these for the wards?"

"Yes, I'll put them in my workroom."

"I can do that," I offer. "Take a seat, relax."

Miraculously, Grace does what I suggest. She drops her bag on the ground and curls up on a comfortable-looking sofa, holding the wrapped book to her chest. Her eyes run over the surfaces of her apartment. The working and blood smears are gone, but by the sadness in her eyes I'd guess the space doesn't feel as it should yet.

I pause. "Where is your workroom? I'd hate to end up riffling through your panties."

I waggle my brows and Grace laughs. The sound brings a peace to the space that I hadn't known was missing.

"Down the hall to the left," she says.

I follow her directions deeper into the apartment. It's a nice place, but not ostentatious. Grace comes from old money, but her separation from her family probably means she lives off her own funds.

I wonder if she realizes how opposite our upbringings were. Will she care that we're a group of rejects?

I try to shake off the jab in my heart. It's a ridiculous insecurity. One left from my teen years. Gargoyle bloodline beliefs left me without a clan once I'd reached an age old enough that the clan leader didn't feel guilty about kicking me out.

Grace doesn't live her life separate like the people with money that we've done work for. She works a job, her apartment is lovely but not giant, and she'd looked at the work we'd done on Bramblewick Manor with adoration.

I find her workroom and stand in the doorway for a moment, marveling. Each wall is covered in shelves of books, scrolls, and paper sculptures. The room is humidity controlled and the books aren't the kind you'd get new from a trip to the bookstore. These are old, with leather spines and gold lettering. A glass case holds a few books that must require extra temperature control.

It's very orderly, and I spot an inventory list on the side of each bookcase.

Grace does appear to love order.

I set the dried herbs on the desk, sure to keep it far away from any of Grace's treasures.

I turn a slow circle and jump at the sight of her in the doorway.

Grace's mouth twitches in a reluctant smile. She holds up the wrapped book. "Sorry for startling you, but I need to add to my collection."

I watch her go through what must be a standard routine of unwrapping the book, an old collection of stories. She grabs one of the inventory lists and takes down the information, gathering details from the front inside of the book. She turns back to the shelf and slides the addition into its new home.

The glow of satisfaction has me leaning in. I won't kiss her yet, but it's easy to forget that when she's so stunning. Grace's chin tilts and her eyelashes lower. The vibe of sexual tension is quick and lingers. My lips form a smile and I shake my head in a message. *Not yet*.

Instead of being annoyed, her pert mouth smiles.

"Will you allow me to show off my work to you?" I ask, needing to get out of this small room before I forget about saving our first kiss.

Grace allows me to lead her out and soon enough she's bending over to get a better look at the carvings I'd added to the replacement door.

I clear my throat. "I'll just get the vacuum."

I turn from the sight of her luscious ass to give myself some time to cool down. Everything about this beautiful librarian pushes my buttons. Last night, I'd nearly come just from the muffled sounds she made and her taste.

Someday I'm going to put her between Elliot and me and fuck her senseless. *That thought is not helping*.

"It's in the coat closet next to the entryway," Grace calls to me.

By the time I take care of the mess of wood shavings, Grace is no longer bent over. She stands to the side with her arms wrapped around herself.

"Are you cold?" I ask, going to grab a fluffy blanket from the couch.

"No, this is just… I don't know how to thank you. It's added something to this place that it needed after everything… I don't know what it is, but when I look at it, it makes me feel safe."

My chest swells with pride. I'm a talented bastard, and I love hearing it. But Grace being the one to compliment me, and that it helps her feel safe, is like the last stroke of a paintbrush or when Eloise gave me the first hug I'd received in two years.

It's elated acceptance.

To be seen by the woman my clan and I are courting inspires a warmth in my chest that won't dissipate.

I blush. "Well, Alasdair did break down the last one—"

"That one didn't have artisan-level carvings on it. It's so beautiful, Broderick."

The breathy way she says my name has me at half-mast, swinging from heart feelings to kilt feelings with the pout of her lips.

"I can get out of your hair now if you want," I say, trying to force myself to give her space after all her nice words.

"Oh, of course, you'll probably be wanting to get back."

There's a trace of disappointment in the air that has me halting.

"Gracie, I want to give you whatever time and space you need to process having us all in your life."

She bites her lip, shy. "What if I don't want time and space right now?"

I step in front of her. The shyness and touch of arousal of her scent is heady. "I'd love to spend time with you. You only need to ask."

"Oh, do you want to stay for pizza?" she asks.

I place a hand on her waist, pulling her against me. "I thought you'd never ask."

CHAPTER 29
GRACE

Broderick Bramblewick is smooth. He's a wonderful craftsman—er craftsgargoyle? He'd gone to the trouble of custom carving something for me, and the personal touch has my apartment starting to feel *right* again. As if it needed the touch of this passionate gargoyle.

What if there was also a touch from Elliot and Alasdair, would it feel even more like home? I shake away the insidious thought.

We stuff our faces with pizza and Broderick tells me about the current projects he's working on and the commissions he's picked up on the side. Our late lunch is done in no time and a pang of disappointment has me dragging my feet until Broderick catches sight of my horror movie stash and begs for us to watch one.

"No one will watch them with me! It's a travesty. Lachlan was the only one—" Broderick breaks off.

The grief in this clan runs deep. Every single detail I glean about their past clan leader adds to this picture in my head. The gargoyle, Lachlan, was larger than life and I don't know how someone like that could have existed. It's no wonder that they feel his loss so greatly.

So, we watched a bloody horror movie, jumping and cackling at all the right parts, even though I'm sure we've both seen the classic before.

Slowly, and from the point of Broderick installing the door, my home becomes mine again. If it feels a little emptier now that I've experienced the bustle of Bramblewick Manor, there's nothing to help that.

I'm curled up next to Broderick on the couch, his heat and scent of cedar lulling me into contentment as the credits to the movie run.

Broderick squeezes me to him, and the simple gesture breaks me.

I press away to take in his face. The coziness of our cuddle changes with each shared breath. Broderick's eyes hood and he doesn't try to hide his hunger. His lips part as if he's going to say that he should be going, as if he's going to flee this intimacy.

I make my move before I can convince myself otherwise.

I kiss my gargoyle. My lips touch his, chaste at first and full of nervous want until Broderick responds. Chaste turns to heated with each press of our lips. A flick of my tongue and his taste is everything. A large hand grips the back of my neck, holding me firm as he tastes me back.

When I moan, he pulls me to straddle his lap, his thighs forcing my own wide. The position isn't entirely comfortable, but Broderick's mouth devouring me blows every stray thought out of the water.

Broderick pulls back. "Tricky, tricky witch, getting me to kiss you before I planned to."

"You make me needy, Broderick," I say. He moans and pulls me in again.

The strong tongue from last night strokes into my mouth with care, bringing the heat in me to a blaze. He grips my hips and grinds the needy place between my legs to his, and I gasp. The friction feels fantastic even through the clothes. My pussy is already achy with the taste of him, but each rock of our bodies has me hitting something… different. I pull away drowsily.

"What?" I look down and see the imprint of his hardness through his kilt, with an unusual bulge at the base. I tilt my head.

"Gracie, have you been missing out on our best features?" Broderick asks with a gleam in his eyes. "I'm surprised you didn't catch a view of Alasdair and Elliot the other night."

"Is your tongue not your best feature?" I ask, the memories of Alasdair and Elliot's bodies moving together have me wanting to slide my hand to where I'm wet.

He smiles smugly. "It's one of them."

I tilt my head the other way, the curiosity in my blood making me bolder than I usually am. "Can I see?"

A purr comes from Broderick's chest and his hands fall to the fasteners of his kilt. I slide off his lap and kneel on the floor between his legs. I must look a mess, my lips swollen and hair a mess, but Broderick's dark gaze heightens the arousal flowing in me.

"You want to research gargoyles by using my body?" Broderick asks, pulling the kilt open to expose himself.

"Be my guest," he says with a flair that I'd laugh at if my attention wasn't captivated.

The cock on this gargoyle isn't what I expected. The shaft and head are similar in shape to a human, but larger and a slightly darker gray color than the rest of his skin. The lack of pubic hair makes each difference more noticeable. I trace the form of it with my eyes and as I reach the base, my lips part. That's new.

Near the base of Broderick's shaft is a bulbous shape that flares wider than the shaft. Almost like a…

"Is that a knot?" I ask.

"Oh, naughty Gracie, have you been reading fanfiction?" Broderick teases. "But very good. Yeah, we have knots."

My blush is almost painful. I bite my lip but need has me speaking.

"S-so that would go inside me?" I can't believe I'm asking something like this.

"Only if you want it. The stretch takes work, but I think you'd like it. We can come just fine if it's gripped hard enough." Broderick strokes a hand up and down his shaft until he grips the bulge in demonstration. "Like that, but harder."

My eyes are glued to the motion. My panties are positively ruined.

"And then we'd be stuck together?" My mouth can still speak.

Broderick nods. "It varies from minutes to a half an hour."

"What varies it?" I'm getting too specific here, but if I talk about details, my brain won't combust with talking about such a subject out loud.

"Is my Gracie shy?" Broderick croons.

I squirm again. It's as if Broderick has turned my embarrassment into one more way to get me wet. This gargoyle doesn't need any more ways.

"I-I'm not used to talking about such things," I say.

Broderick hums, his cock jumps a little and I jump along with it, startled. His eyes glitter, as if enjoying this game.

"You don't want to explore how it feels?" Broderick blinks his eyes innocently, even as a drop of precum beads on his tip.

I press my thighs together at the sight.

"Are you offering?" I ask. My voice is coy in a way I've never heard it before.

"Oh, Gracie, I may start begging soon." He gives me a lazy smile. The tip of his finger appears to run over the dip of my cleavage but I don't feel it, he doesn't allow the contact. "You wouldn't even have to use your hands."

I snort. "You're the worst."

Broderick lifts a brow. "You're a librarian who has knowledge sitting before you. I'd think you'd… jump on the opportunity to explore."

I try not to reward him with a smile, because even with how out of my depth I am, he's right. I want to explore. I crave to learn every throbbing vein of his length and analyze how much that knot of his gives under my grip.

I push down the scandalized part of my consciousness and reach out. I touch the shaft of the thick cock and Broderick moans. His skin is soft here, as if made to slide in my grip, a softness over a turgid stiffness. I slide my hand up his shaft, not applying any real pressure at all, tracing the hot veins under the skin.

Broderick moves his hips as if trying to keep from thrusting into my grip. I apply a little more pressure and pull the foreskin of him down to reveal the glands and head.

I lean forward at another bead of precum and follow my body's demand to taste. I flick my tongue out, catching the fluid. Broderick's warm scent is stronger here with more musk. The taste of him is salty with a bitter tang that has my mouth watering as if in preparation to taste more.

"*Fuck!*"

The hissed expletive startles me, and I pull away abruptly.

Broderick's core tenses and he moans. His brows drop in concern at my actions. "Is everything okay?"

"Um, yes." Real embarrassment flares. Not the type that had coaxed me into this position, and he can somehow tell.

Broderick frowns and caresses my cheek soothingly. "If I did anything to make you uncomfortable—"

I roll my eyes. "It's stupid."

His mouth twitches. "Now I'm very curious. You are many things, Gracie, stupid is not one of them."

I scrunch my nose, but I don't think any of the males courting me would tease me maliciously for it.

"I'm not used to *that* kind of cursing," I say.

"You're not used to the word *fuck*?"

I purse my lips and nod.

"Does it bother you?" he asks, tangling a curl of my hair in his claws.

I think about it. "No… it's like, I can't help physically reacting. It just feels like a shock. I don't say it because it was forbidden in my parents' house, and I guess I just haven't gotten used to hearing it."

Broderick hums. "And what about using the word *cunt*?"

He puts extra emphasis on the word and a wave of heat flows through me, right to that specific area.

Broderick's grin is devious. "Oh, Gracie, the way your eyes just dilated at that... I think we're going to have fun with this."

He grows serious. "Unless you say it's your boundary. No matter how silly you consider it or how embarrassing it may be, I'd rather you say when you don't like something than for you to be uncomfortable in a bad way."

"It's not a bad way," I say and decide at the same time. The use of *fuck* has always been jarring, but it's never flared heat in my belly like when Broderick says it. The other word... I should just remove my panties at this point, but I'm too focused on the stiff length in front of me.

"Can I keep going?" I whisper.

The heat in Broderick's eyes flare. "If you want me to beg, just let me know, sweet Gracie."

I hum and continue my exploration, sliding my hand up his hardness and pressing my thighs together at the same time. I don't know if I want him to beg, but I do know I want to taste him again.

I've given head, but those times feel different compared to this. It takes me a moment to realize it's because those times had been rushed and done because my partners wanted it, not because I couldn't help my mouth gravitating toward the cock in my hand.

The way Broderick watches my every move as I run my hand over him is spellbinding and erotic.

"I think you're curious about something else, Gracie." He arches a brow and I bite my lip. "Feel me how you want, little witch. I can't wait until you let me do the same."

I let my other hand touch the part so different to what I've experienced before. Broderick's knot swells, and I stroke over the skin before grasping it. He grunts, groaning when I quickly release him. The knot feels fleshy when I apply pressure, it's hard but with more give than the shaft of his cock, I can only imagine the way it would hit me inside.

I lick the head of him again and moan, wetting my lips before sucking him into my mouth.

"Just like that, Gracie. Fuck my cock into your mouth like you can't get enough of it."

I moan helplessly and try to suck more of him inside my mouth. He's larger than I've ever done this with before. *Will he even fit in other places?*

"Shh, relax your jaw, sweetheart. You can do it, you're trying too hard, let yourself sink it deeper, don't try to force it, unless you like gagging," Broderick says.

I pull off him and he makes a sound of distress that stops when he realizes I'm laughing.

"What?" he asks. His cock pulsing in my grip still.

My shoulders shake. "I just realized you're the first male I've been with that has the experience to give pointers."

"Hell yeah, I have the experience. I can even suck down Alasdair if I have a mind to."

I stop, surprised. "For some reason, I didn't think you and Alasdair were together like that."

The thought kindles another spark of heat, adding to the inferno of arousal inside me.

"Very observant. We aren't most times. Ours is a love that is closer to friendship than mates, but from time to time we give each other a hand, or a mouth." Broderick grins. "It's a nice exchange and drives Elliot wild."

My dress feels entirely too tight as he speaks. I can't seem to get comfortable, my skin flushed and body more aroused than I've ever experienced, other than that short time in the hallway.

"Oh, sweet Gracie, you look a little uncomfortable. You smell delightful, if you're tired of being on your knees for me, I'd love to lick your cunt until you scream."

I whimper and Broderick's eyes glow with satisfaction.

I don't want to just be licked again. I want this gargoyle in a way I haven't been had in too long.

"Don't you want to try and fit your knot inside me?" I ask.

Broderick stills, his cock jerking in my grip with more precum appearing at the tip. The gargoyle shakes his head as if trying to focus.

He frowns. "I plan on courting you, Grace. I didn't think you'd want our first time together to be on a couch."

I try and stop my huff, to not whine about everyone's attempts to woo me.

"You've all been so careful with me, but Broderick, this ache *hurts*. I don't need flowers or candlelight dinners. The hallway last night was the hottest thing I've ever experienced, and I feel greedy asking for more but—" I stop as Broderick makes a sound in his throat.

"But you're hungry, and we've been treating you like spun glass. I'm not good at holding back my impulses, sweet witch. I won't make you beg much."

I straighten, hopeful. "You'll be with me that way?"

Broderick picks me up from the floor and stands with ease. "If you want this, I'll never be able to deny you, but I require a bed. I want to take my time with you."

I scoff, even as my body sings with joy. "That's not what you said about kissing me."

He laughs. "I'm going to be ungentlemanly and say my drive to fuck you into the sheets until you scream is greater than to kiss you."

CHAPTER 30

GRACE

I shiver at the expletive and snicker at the same time.

Broderick's face has lost the tension that had lined it when he let me explore him. He walks through my apartment, all naked swagger and hungry edges. He purrs when he finds my bedroom.

The presence of the fierce, devilish gargoyle in this feminine space should be incongruous, but it's not. It's a perfect meld of soft and hard, feminine and masculine.

"I love how much this room smells of you," he says, pulling the blankets back on the bed and setting me on the sheets. "Gargoyles don't carry sexual diseases, but would you like us to use protection?"

I hum. "You've hidden condoms that fit you in your pockets?"

I cast my gaze down to his proud, bare erection.

Broderick freezes. "Well, no."

"I have my amulet," I say. It's tradition in witch families for girls to be gifted the charmed jewelry that wards against pregnancy and sexual diseases when they reach a certain age. My mother had sent me off with the housekeeper to pick one out.

My chosen charm is delicate in design and something I always wear. As much as I want to make a family, I'd like to do that with a spouse, or perhaps, if all goes well, with mates I know and love.

"Oh, good." Broderick sighs in relief. "I didn't want to stop to fly home for supplies. You look too good spread out and the scent of your arousal is stealing away my sanity. I can't wait to see you stretched around my knot."

The sound that comes from the back of my throat is a mix of arousal and impatience.

"But all in good time," Broderick says. "Show me those pretty nipples, Gracie. I caught sight of them through your sleep dress last night and they've haunted me ever since."

I bite my lip. I'm not self-conscious about my body most of the time. It took a lot of work and time to wash away the toxic feelings my mother and cousins had piled on in regard to the way I look.

I like my body and love dressing to emphasize it, but I haven't been naked in front of someone else in a long time. It's easier to be confident in my curves when I'm not bare before a partner.

"Shy, Gracie?" Broderick asks when I don't jump into motion. "Or do you know that seeing you naked is going to test my control not to sink in the sweet depths of your cunt?"

The nerves stilling me dissolve with my laugh. "Has anyone told you that you're a bit overdramatic?"

"Constantly. I'm an artist. It comes with the territory, but that" —Broderick shakes his head— "that wasn't me being dramatic at all. Show me your body, Grace. Spread your legs for me and let me see every rosy, lush part of you."

The breath is long gone from my lungs, and I don't know if it will ever return. If doubt comes with breath, I never want it to. I unzip the side of the sun dress and pull down the straps, revealing a nude bra that I paid too much for. Broderick's breathing goes shallow, and I shimmy the dress the rest of the way off, over my soft stomach and the swell of my hips. The panties match, almost transparent with how wet they are.

"More," he growls, and my pussy clenches at the sound.

I swallow and undo the clasp of the bra, sighing in relief at the release and the caress of cool air against sensitive skin. I throw the bra toward my dresser and suddenly Broderick is in front of me. He kneels on the bed, his hands going to my exposed chest, each move reverberating with awe.

"Oh, Grace, it's a crime to hide these," Broderick says. His breath caresses the pale skin and my nipples, making them pucker. His hands cradle the weight of them, squeezing in a way that has my hips rocking. Each touch and pinch grows the need inside of me.

"Well, it's a crime to walk around naked—" I cry out when Broderick takes one peak into his hot mouth. His strong tongue lashing as he sucks.

I moan at the cascade of heat flowing through me and pooling arousal between my legs.

His shoulders are hard with muscle where I grip them, and I don't think I'd have the strength to push him away even if I wanted to.

Broderick switches to the other breast, letting a clawed hand squeeze the one he'd abandoned. The damp skin chills in the air even as the heat from his mouth on the other has my core clenching.

"Oh gods," I whisper.

Broderick releases my nipple with a pop and grins at me. "Praise the gods indeed. I could stay like this all night, but it doesn't get me any closer to fucking your perfect cunt."

I gasp and arch at the filthy words, and the gargoyle laughs. He presses my breasts together and his long tongue traces designs on their swells.

"One day I'm going to fuck these," he says idly.

I move my hips. The ache almost extends past hurt with how empty I feel. "Please, Broderick."

He curses. "When you say my name like that, it makes me not want to take my time."

"Then don't," I say.

Broderick chuckles. "You've felt my knot. If you want that fitting inside you, I need to work you up to it."

I hiss when I clench on emptiness at the words. Frustration swelling in time with need and pricking my eyes with tears.

"I need—" I start but break off.

Broderick hums. "What do you need, sweet witch?"

A claw slips under the edge of my panties, tugging them down.

"I need you inside me," I say.

"My tongue?" he teases.

"You!"

"My shy librarian can do better than that."

"Your cock, your knot, your tongue. Please, Broderick!"

My words move Broderick to action, and he slides down, kneeling on the floor, dragging my panties all the way off. My knees fall open, the chill of the room hitting my wet pussy.

I hesitate.

Broderick stills and groans, his gaze taking in my completely exposed body.

"Oh, Gracie, you are so fucking beautiful," he says. It's in a different way than how he speaks to incite me, as if the mere sight of me is what brought him to his knees.

Affection swells in my chest, but my body is still on fire.

"Broderick," I whisper.

His fingers dig into the flesh of my hips and he pulls me in, I cry out and fall backward as his mouth descends on my pussy. My gargoyle doesn't start off with just his tongue this time. His whole mouth sucks on me and my hands grip his curly hair.

Contrary to his teasing, Broderick doesn't take his time. His tongue thrusts inside me and I groan at the thick slide of it.

"Please," I beg along with other words I don't even know I'm saying at this point.

Broderick spans his hand over my mons and lower belly, working the pad of his thumb in circles over my clit. I moan when his tongue leaves me.

"Be a good girl and come on my tongue, Gracie. Then I'll give what this little cunt is begging for," he says.

The frustration from before is still high. "I can't just come on command!"

Broderick laughs into my thighs, dropping a kiss to the skin there. "I know, sweet witch. We're just barely getting to know each other's bodies. Give me a little time to get you there."

"But I want you there now." My face burns after I say it, but it doesn't make it any less true.

He hums against my sensitive flesh. "Soon, my pretty witch."

His tongue slides inside again and something else slithers up my body, wrapping its narrow tip around my nipple and tugging. I squeak and gasp. I'd forgotten about his tail.

Broderick works his mouth, thumb, and tail in tandem.

"Oh god, oh gods, oh gods," I chant as if really asking for deliverance.

Broderick slides his thumb away and sucks on my clit and I come. My body tenses around nothing and I gasp helplessly until the surge of pleasure begins to fade.

Broderick rises above me with a growl. "Someday I'm going to take you on your hands and knees, hold you there with my teeth and fuck into you like the beast I am, but this first time, I want to see your face."

And then the thick cock I'd playfully licked earlier starts to push into me. It's a slow thing. The resistance of my body to Broderick's requires finessing.

I gasp as he circles his hips and I make a sharp sound of disappointment when it still doesn't make any headway.

Is it going to fit?

"Fuck, you're going to kill me. I'm going to get inside this cunt, and die from bliss," Broderick says, almost as if he's talking to himself. He leans back as if to reassess.

"No!" I reach out to keep him from leaving. "It can fit!"

Broderick chuckles. "Don't worry, sweetness, I'm not going anywhere. I was just being greedy. I wanted to taste your release on my lips and now I need to work you up to my cock."

Even though I'd already climaxed, the hunger hasn't abated. Broderick holds my legs apart and a string of saliva falls on my pussy, I groan at the drip of it hitting my sensitive flesh and jump when something touches me there. I push myself up to my elbows and watch as he slides his tail through my folds.

And then it slides inside me.

"Oh!" I exclaim.

The tail twists some way that has me jolting in surprise. It's as if it's stretching me.

"I'll need to get some toys just for spreading you out. The downside of my pretty nails." Broderick wiggles his talons, his tone casual, as if a part of him isn't surging and twisting inside of me.

I try and relax and let his tail stretch me. It feels good, an oscillation of a tickle and pressure. I clamp on it experimentally and we both moan.

"Broderick," I say.

"You don't need to ask again, sweet witch." His tail slides from me and I watch as it spirals up my gargoyle's cock, slicking my arousal up his length.

He climbs over me again, spreading my thighs wide. This time when the head of his cock presses against me, it slips in, and I gasp at the stretch.

"More?" he asks.

"Yes!"

Broderick groans and sinks into me. My body gives to his with pulsing little thrusts. I breathe out in bliss when his knot hits my entrance.

"Gracie," he whispers, stroking the tip of his nose up my cheek. "I don't have the words to describe how you feel. So hot, so wet—"

I squeeze around him, and Broderick breaks off on a moan. His hips drag out his cock and snap to thrust into me again.

I gasp. "More—"

Broderick complies, thrusting into me, hollowing out my body. Each thrust presses his knot against me and the swell of it feels good against my clit. I'm so wet it's a wonder that it doesn't slip in. Each movement inside my body sparks sensations that drive my arousal higher.

My gargoyle's body starts to tighten, he growls, and his motions get sharper, wilder. I wrap my ankles at the small of his back and the small change of angle has me crying out.

"Need you," I say, in a haze of heat.

"Take all of me, precious, that's it, almost."

I don't even realize what he's saying or what's happening until the swell of the knot is almost halfway.

"Whoa!" I say and hiss at the stretch.

Broderick's thrusting is now a gentle rocking that is working the knot against me, into me.

"Too much?" he asks, panting.

"J-just give me a moment. It feels bigger than I thought." I take a deep breath, trying to relax against the new girth.

Broderick seems to be trying to match my slowed breathing.

"You can take it, Gracie. Your cunt has been so greedy, so perfect. You'll take all of me and then I'll rut my seed into you."

I moan. Each word from his lips causing a surge of heat.

"You like that, don't you? Like the thought that this knot will keep my seed deep inside you," Broderick says, a vicious, aroused smile on his face. "Push out, sweetness, let me claim you."

I do what he says and as my body relaxes, his knot slides all the way in. I cry out at the fullness and Broderick snarls. Heat and pressure spill into me and the sensation has pleasure crashing over me in a climax.

Broderick continues rocking inside me, rutting me just as he said. It takes time before the words he's whispering my hair start to make sense.

"Gracie, Gracie, Gracie. My sweet mate, perfection. So glad we found you. You belong with us."

The words are like the sun, so bright and warm but too much to stare at head-on. I start to stiffen but tell myself that he's just in the after waves of orgasm. He doesn't mean what he's saying and soon enough he moves to peppering my neck and face with tender kisses instead of speaking.

"You okay?" Broderick asks.

And I blink, shaking what he'd said away. I take inventory of my body, squeezing on the fleshy knot still swollen inside me with a gasp.

He grunts. "If you keep doing that, this will last longer."

"How long can it last?" I ask. My body sings with the pleasure he's just wrung out of me but the way we're stuck together, with my legs tilted up, is going to be tiring.

"Five to twenty minutes. If you keep tightening on me, it might start another round and that could be up to an hour. Am I squishing you?"

An hour?

"Not at all." I'm enjoying the feel of Broderick's skin against my own. "But my legs are getting tired." I squeeze my heels into his lower back as an emphasis.

"Hm, let me try something," he says. An arm slides under my back with the other under my butt, then he lifts me from the bed with ease. My arms wrap tight around his neck. I don't know if I'm ever going to get used to him picking me up with no warning.

"I won't drop you," Broderick says. His wings move and I twist my head back to the bed to figure out what he's doing.

The talons on his wings act like hands and are currently arranging my collection of pillows against my headboard before Broderick slides onto the bed, folding his legs behind my body and resting my back on the incline of pillows he built. It's like a relaxed interpretation of the lotus position that I'd seen in a Kama Sutra book once.

"How is that?" he asks.

I wiggle, pulling at the knot and making us both gasp.

"This is good," I say, my voice breathy with arousal.

Broderick fluffs up the pillows behind me, and I relax my legs over his.

A purr comes from Broderick's chest. "I like this."

He smooths a hand up my body, the gray against my skin has my breath catching. I'm practically spread out before him as a sacrifice. He strokes designs over my skin. Goose bumps rise and I shiver. The rise of my breasts and stomach shakes with the motion.

A stab of insecurity has me speaking without meaning to. "This is hardly flattering."

Broderick lifts a brow. "Oh Gracie, I beg to differ."

He leans back some and I realize he can see *everything*. "If you could see this the way I do, you'd be as entranced as I am. Seeing your soft cunt stretched around my knot is what fantasies are made of. I'd knot you all day long just to be able to see you spread like the gift you are."

My chest rises on my inhale and my cheeks burn.

Broderick's other hand caressing against a breast.

"You have the prettiest tits," he says. "And when you blush, the skin here gets so flushed."

Broderick drops a kiss to the sensitive skin at the center of my chest. The tickle would have me moving if I wasn't filled to the brim with him. The wet of his release starts to drip out no matter that I'm tight around his knot still.

"That's not making either of us think unsexy thoughts," I say.

Broderick's mouth stretches into a smile. "And why would we try and do that?"

He's acting as if he wants to do this for another hour. Maybe he does.

I widen my eyes in alarm. "I don't think I can go again."

In an instant, Broderick stops his teasing strokes and his hands start moving in soothing motions, dropping to massage the muscles of my hips.

"Did I hurt you?" he asks.

"I'm good. It's nothing some salve won't fix. I just underestimated how big you are."

Broderick makes that trilling purr and I relax into his massage. It feels wonderful and my eyelashes start to fall closed sleepily. A moment later he tilts his hips some and I gasp when his knot leaves me with an easy wet slide.

I tense, but Broderick kisses me until I relax back into the pillows.

"Shh, sweetness, let me clean us up. Do you have any salve here?"

I hum, letting my gargoyle take over the work with surprising ease. "I have some generic stuff that will do the trick. It should be in the first drawer in the bathroom."

I rise as if to show him, but Broderick presses me back with a chuckle.

"Relax. I'm not helpless. I can find it. You wouldn't want to drip on your pretty rugs anyway."

I scrunch my nose at that. "Well, when you put it that way…"

Broderick kisses me and leaves the bed. He returns with supplies, and I let the gargoyle work. He runs a warm wet cloth over me, cleaning up our mess with a gentle stroke. I wince at the raw, used feeling of my pussy.

He kisses my inner knee. "The hamper okay?"

I hum in agreement, and Broderick tosses the washcloth into the hamper. Next, he opens the jar of salve. I move to take it from him, to apply it myself but he holds it away from me and makes a sound.

"Let me?" he asks.

Normally, I'd say it wasn't necessary, that I could do it, but something about Broderick has me giving in to this pampering. I lie back down, and my gargoyle makes another purr of pleasure.

"You're the only one I've heard purr," I say.

Broderick smiles but his cheeks get a little darker in a fascinating way. "There is a little diversity in gargoyle clans. Some have different traits depending on where they are located. The gargoyles of the clan that hosted me until I was eighteen, the ones that my father hailed from, purr. I think it's the only clan that does."

"It's nice," I say.

"I'm glad you like it," Broderick says as he applies some salve to his tail. This salve has healing magic in it, but the scent is medicinal. I make a note to get some specific salve. If I'm going to have three males courting me, all with knots and sized proportional to their body, it would be a worthwhile investment.

Am I going to continue with this?

Yes. I want this. I want moments just like this and if it means having to face whatever issues I've been dragging around, whatever wounds that have gone unhealed in my soul, to keep this, I will.

CHAPTER 31
ℬRODERICK

Grace gasps when I slide my salve-covered tail inside her, but her body relaxes in an instant. The salve already working its magic. I'm familiar with the product. A more specific salve would work better, and I make a mental note.

"I should have warned you," I say.

She squirms deliciously as my tail coats her inside walls with the salve. "Mm, yes, you should have."

Grace sighs and some of the tension in my own body leaves. This after part of sex is one of my favorites. Ensuring that she's taken care of. Usually, it's Elliot I spoil. I'm a little more demanding with him because he likes it and can physically take it. I'm sure that Grace and I will get to know each other's limits in time.

I pull my tail from her and press the pads of my fingers to the soft folds of her. Her pretty opening does look a little redder and swollen than it should, but the tension falls from Grace's body with each touch.

"That feel better?" I ask.

Grace blinks slowly at me, looking dazed.

"Hm, yes." She shakes her head. "I need to get up before I fall asleep. You wore me out."

I laugh. "We wore each other out."

It isn't a lie, going slow and working myself inside her tightness had taken energy and willpower. I could do with a bath, a cuddle, and a nap, in that order. But Grace needs some time and I need to be getting back.

Elliot is going to be worried about our little witch. This morning had upset him even if Grace said she and he spoke.

But Elliot isn't my only responsibility now.

"Do you want me to stay?" I ask.

I have a sense of Grace enough to know how she's going to answer, but she could surprise me. I kind of wish she would. To sleep with her in my arms would be delightful.

Grace freezes and I keep from sighing in disappointment.

"It's not that I don't want you to," she says, somehow seeing my disappointment anyway. "It's just everything has been happening so fast and I need" —she makes some hand gestures trying to find the words— "to take some time to think about why I reacted so poorly this morning."

I run my claws through her hair and her lashes fall in bliss.

"Sweet witch, I'll give you all the time you need. I'll pack up." I drop a kiss to her forehead.

I'm in the living room, dressing, finished packing away the tools I'd brought for the door when Grace comes out in the robe she'd worn last night in the hallway. The beast in me wants to rip it off her and see if she's wearing another nightdress that makes her look like a treat, but I push the need down.

Her brow is furrowed, her eyes sad.

"Hey," I say, cradling her cheeks in my hands. "What's this?"

Grace shakes her head. "I feel bad for kicking you out."

I laugh, no doubt that's part of it, but the distress tastes different.

"Don't," I say. "You've been through a lot lately. You found out the gargoyle you're dating comes with two other mates, you met our ugly mugs, and had to deal with the fucker who broke into your place."

She looks around at the apartment and it clicks.

"If you want me to stay tonight so you don't feel alone, I can just sleep on the couch." I want her to feel safe.

Grace straightens and squares her shoulders.

"No. I need to resurrect my wards. This is my home. I need to be able to stay here alone," she says.

Ah, the independent streak making an appearance. It's hard to lean on others if you're used to handling things yourself. Everyone in our clan has had to go through the same transition at some point in their life.

I drop a kiss to her lips. "Call us if you need anything. I mean it. Alasdair, Elliot, and I are all more than willing to make a flight over here just to check under the bed if need be."

Grace's shoulders fall. "I—thank you. For everything. I'll call if I need anything."

And if we make some flight checks during the night…

Grace is a Bramblewick, and Bramblewicks take care of their own.

Even if she doesn't know it yet.

***

I'm putting my tools away in the garage storage when Elliot finds me. His blond human hair sticking up all over the place like he's run his hands through it.

"How is she?" he asks.

I frown. "Have you been this stressed all day?"

"No. Yes. No. Alasdair has kept me busy, he even played cards with me. It was easier when I knew you were there with her."

Elliot is a terrible cheat when it comes to cards. Alasdair must have been concerned to voluntarily play with him.

I clip the last storage container closed. "She'll be fine. A little nervous to be alone at her place right now, but determined to be independent. I already plan on swinging by to do a visual check during the night."

"You don't think she'll consider that like the stalking?" Elliot asks.

I tilt my head. The anxiety coming off Elliot isn't like him.

"I thought you two spoke?" I ask.

Elliot blushes. "Yes, I think she'll even forgive me. I just… worry."

"I believe she will. Take heart, Elliot. She belongs with us."

Elliot comes closer to greet me and stills. His eyes dilate as he picks up my scent, even in the glamour he wears.

"You and her?" he asks.

There's a tone in his question and it takes me a moment to place it. Oh, jealous Elliot. My talented, beautiful mate is jealous that I've had sex with Grace.

My mouth twitches. "Does it drive you crazy that she welcomed physical attention from me?"

Elliot's brow creases as if he didn't notice the reaction until I pointed it out. He blows out a breath.

"I-I deserve it. I'm the one who lied," he says.

I nod. "How fast we get her into bed isn't a competition."

Elliot's jaw clenches. "I know. I just—I feel out of control."

I hum and pull my mate into my arms. Everyone has their own scars to work through, and being in a mating is understanding the parts that still hurt when pressed. I don't get angry at Elliot's manipulations. The compulsions he struggles with served him well for most of his life when survival trumped everything else.

My place is to support him as he deals with them and the issues they cause.

Elliot burrows his nose in the crook of my neck. "Fuck, you smell so good."

The sensation of being worn out flees my senses and arousal rushes through my blood. "I'm sure you wouldn't mind licking the taste of her off me."

Elliot gives a needy moan.

"I've missed you, troublemaker," I say.

Elliot's human tongue licks over my neck. "I've missed you too. I've missed us."

I press his body against mine.

"I can't wait until she accepts her place here, and we can take her together," I say on a moan as I grind the swell of my knot against him. "Can you imagine stretching her out to be taken by Alasdair."

A throttled sound falls from Elliot's mouth. It softens my heart when he surrenders to me.

"Let's take this inside, troublemaker. We don't need to give Eloise or Graham an eyeful."

Elliot's cheeks pinken. Just a dash of humiliation to quicken his heart.

"And if you do everything I say, I'll tell you something you can give Grace," I tease.

Elliot's face lights up. My troublemaker is such a giver.

CHAPTER 32
GRACE

"Jesus Christ, Grace! Why didn't you call me?" Emilia asks, her brows furrowing in concern.

I'd show the same concern if she'd told me the guy who has been sending me flowers broke into my place and vandalized it. Why didn't I call Emilia?

Was it because I'd have to lie? Tell her half-truths like I am now?

"It was fine," I say. "I've filed a report and stayed with the guys that I'm dating. They've been really great about it."

Emilia blows out a breath. "Well, that makes me feel better. Are you going to stay with them until they catch this guy, or do you want to stay with Mom and me?"

I swallow at her fervent questions. I'm a terrible friend.

"We only just met and there isn't really a 'catch this guy' plan."

Emilia's eyes bug and I rush to explain.

"I have no proof that it's him doing this. The authorities are really just waiting to catch him in the act," I say.

Emilia's brows furrow in frustration and worry. "You're not staying in your apartment by yourself, are you?"

I blink at her. "Um, yes, I am. I'm an adult. My building has security, a doorman."

Emilia shakes the tension out of her shoulders, and I know I have a debate on my hands.

"Everything you've said is true," she says. "But are you honestly comfortable staying there alone?"

Am I fine staying there alone... I slept terrible last night. Every sound from the whistle of wind to the refrigerator had me jumping even after setting up the wards. It's not comfortable. I tried to focus on the ache in my body to keep my mind off my fears. The generic salve isn't going to cut it. Broderick is sizable even without his knot and I expect Elliot and Alasdair to all be comparable.

I shouldn't be thinking about this right now.

Emilia's brows rise. I clear my throat.

"It's fine—" The lie croaks from me only to be interrupted.

"Grace!"

"Okay! I'm a little freaked out," I capitulate. "But I don't want to bring trouble to you and your mom's doorstep. The guys want me to stay with them, but I'm scared I'm getting too attached."

Emilia considers that. She's always good at looking objectively at my reasonings.

"We'd love to have you, but I could see how if anything happened, you'd feel awful. Mom's fierce, but three hunky guys are probably a safer bet with a stalker."

My breath leaves me in a relieved sigh.

Emilia starts again. "These guys... aren't you dating to settle down? Like to get married, have babies, the whole shebang? I thought you and Elliot already talked about it."

I bite my lip before answering. "Yes."

Emilia tilts her head. "It sounds like everyone is already set to start getting attached. It's an untraditional situation, but your timetable is really only dependent on finding out how compatible you all are."

Timetable. Something about the technical word soothes me about the whole conversation. *Did she do that on purpose?*

"Here's what I propose," Emilia says. "Stay with them. You'll get to know them quicker. It will advance your life goals. If you're the right person for them and they are for you, you'll know sooner and talk about painting a nursery or something."

My mouth drops open.

Emilia nods at her own words. "Aaand, I don't have to worry about a guy being a creeper and catching you unawares."

"I hardly know them," I say. I know Elliot the most, but I still need to go through things with him to see if he fudged any details.

Emilia rolls her eyes at me. "There's only one way to fix that. Think about this as a trial run."

A trial run for operating as a unit. I don't hate the idea.

"If they decide you don't fit, then they are fucking idiots," she says.

"Emilia!"

My friend laughs at my scandalized tone.

"We are at *work*," I say.

"It's not going to matter the number of times you lecture me; I have a sailor's mouth and it isn't going to change. It's why I don't work at the front desk," she says.

That, and she freezes up around strangers. I shake my head.

A trial run.

It's a sound idea. The Bramblewicks have the space, they issued the invitation, and living with them would immerse me in their clan. I like Elliot, I miss him, but trust is something different.

What if you end up brokenhearted?

Then I end up brokenhearted. I already care for them all in some way. Am I really worried about getting attached or am I worried they won't like me once they get to know me?

There's a soft knock on our office door that has both of us jumping with a start. Elliot pokes his head in.

"Hello ladies, how are you on this fine day?"

Emilia's eyes are wide. She's met Elliot a time before and reacted similarly. This time she clears her throat and looks down, muttering something about how she's good.

I take mercy on my friend who gives the sagest wisdom and suffers the strongest social anxiety of anyone I know.

"It's been fine," I say. "I wasn't expecting you."

Elliot ducks his head with a blush. "I'm just stopping by and was hoping to catch you in your office. Agnes was quite kind to direct me here."

"I'll give you two privacy. I need to head to my lab anyway," Emilia says almost too quiet to hear, but she winks at me and closes the door behind her.

Elliot locks the door before coming toward me. I stand and meet him around the desk. It's an action I don't question. I'm drawn to him.

I might more than like him.

My brows rise at the locked door.

"For privacy," he says.

I scoff and Elliot's smile is sharp, but it shifts quickly to repentance. Mysterious, mysterious gargoyle.

"Grace." He takes my hand, and the warmth of his skin sinks into mine. "I'm sorry. I'm so sorry about following you to the matchmaker. I'm sorry if any of my actions have made you feel unsafe."

I frown. "You seem to strategize a lot."

Elliot winces. "I don't know if Broderick has been telling all of my secrets, but it's a habit of mine. I fixate and arrange."

"Is there anything else you're hiding from me?" I ask.

His face is so earnest a stab of pain hits my heart.

"No. You know everything else. I'll give you any details you ask of me. I'll do whatever you need to grow the trust between us. You're *it* for us, Grace. Nothing is worth losing you."

Elliot's words wiggle their way past the defenses I'd built of barbed wires of doubts around my soul. He's a master manipulator, but my heart sings for him. His clan trusts him. I trust Broderick. I want to be able to trust Elliot, and I won't know if it's a mistake until too late.

But this is worth the risk. This thing between us, fostered over the week of courtship he'd done under false pretenses, it's worth it.

I need to close my eyes and jump, trusting he's going to be the one to catch me.

I grip his hand in mine.

I'm a badass witch who deserves love.

"I forgive you."

Elliot looks as if some heavy weight has been taken from him. I did that. My regard weighed on him so much that three little words from me pulled him up.

His quicksilver emotions go from profound relief to wickedness in a blink.

"I'll even detail every single moment I licked the taste of you off Broderick's cock—"

I slap my hand over his mouth, and he laughs into it, his eyes still showing a shine of awe. The moment is broken but something new is between us. This thing is what we make it.

And right now, Elliot is making my skin flush *all* over.

"*Elliot!*" I hiss, trying not to envision exactly what he described.

Elliot's laugh subsides and he kisses the palm of my hand. The teasing look on his face gaining heat. He pulls my palm from my mouth and leans in. I take a step back and my ass hits my desk.

"Tell me, my star, do we have real privacy here? Will someone be knocking down the door to get to you to sign a form or look at a book?"

"No one comes here," I breathe, my chest tight with the heat he's spread to me.

"I have a gift for you, and it would mean a lot if you'd let me help you apply it," he says.

"What—"

"But first—" Elliot breaks off and kisses me. The move is such a surprise that I don't react to his lips on mine, but slowly he coaxes my alarm to defrost, and I kiss him back. Elliot moans as he tastes me, but he doesn't push the kiss to the point we're ripping off each other's clothes. Each move he makes is slow and I relax into it, letting him pick the pace until I break away out of breath.

Elliot's pupils are blown. Are my lips as kiss swollen as his?

"I missed that," he says.

"Me too," I gasp.

Elliot leans back and pulls a small jar from his pocket.

"Your gift," he says.

I reach out, but he pulls it away with a tease.

"Will you let me apply it?"

The jar of healing salve, and the context, click and my face burns in arousal and shock.

"I'm at work. You can't be putting that *there* right now!"

"You said we have privacy." Elliot's thumb rubs over my fingers. "I happen to know a little bit about the cause of your aches and pains. I think it's safe to say that you'll work better once you get some salve."

I blink, still shocked, still scandalized, and ridiculously tempted. *Could I really?* It is time for my lunch break and Emilia won't be back for at least an hour.

I swallow against nerves.

I would be able to focus better without the ache of having stretched to fit Broderick. Elliot is being helpful.

The hunger that hits my pussy is insistent. My body wants this, Elliot wants this, *I* want this.

"H-how?" I ask.

Elliot's eyes light. "Lean back, my glamorous treat."

He presses his body against mine and I place my hands on the desk behind me. He kisses the skin of my collarbone before sinking to his knees in front of me. Elliot's face is pure trouble as his hands slide up my tights.

He's lucky I wore a dress and thigh highs today. Elliot's hand hits the lace at the top of my stocking and his expression goes intense with want. A spike of arousal has me tensing. Elliot slowly lifts my dress to see the stockings, with garter belt.

"*Fuck*, that's hot," he says.

I bite my lip to keep a whimper from escaping.

His hands continue their journey up my thighs. "I was going to take these off," he says as he slips a finger under the fabric of my panties. "But they're just so pretty that I think I'll keep them on."

Elliot stands and I squeeze my legs together where his hand is. "Uh, uh, uh, I need you to keep your legs spread. Can you do that for me?"

These males are going to be the death of me.

Elliot lifts a brow.

"Yes," I whisper.

Elliot grins victorious. "Good."

His hand slides away and he gathers my dress up so it's held at my waist. "Now hold this, I need to be able to see what I'm doing."

I almost forgot what he's supposed to be doing. I grasp the fabric bunch with a hand and Elliot takes the jar out. I catch sight of the label and my brows shoot up. That is some special custom-made salve.

He unscrews the jar. "Now let me know if you want a different scent. And Grace."

"What?"

"You will never be the one to get this salve. It's our place as your clan to provide for you. This is a gift I vow to always fill. This is a courtship gift."

I swallow.

"And you're going to need it with how often we're going to want to squeeze into your tiny pussy. Especially once you want to try to start having children. You probably won't even be able to leave the house without one of us filling you up, trying to get our seed to take."

The heat flowing through my body straight to my pussy is unmerciful.

"But the knots," I say. The salve he's gifting me is the best there is, but constantly being knotted…

Elliot chuckles. "We don't need to knot you every time. Quickies aren't quickies if you end up knotted for twenty minutes."

"Oh."

Elliot's face becomes serious. "And Grace, if you ever don't want to take a knot, you don't need to. We will always respect your boundaries."

He kisses my forehead and I melt.

I somehow miss him getting the salve until his thumb tugs my panties aside and two fingers press into me. I tense up at the smooth slide and hiss at the ache.

"Shh, let it work," Elliot says. His fingers are gentle in his movements and the amount of salve he must have taken from the jar is generous because he spreads it deeper. Warmth blooms with each slide and sinks into my aches. The lightest scent of citrus and roses permeates the air.

I moan and Elliot slides his fingers even farther in, massaging in strong strokes.

"That's it, my star. You're so beautiful like this." Elliot wraps an arm around my waist and I relax into the hold at the same time as my core starts to tighten. As the coil of arousal winds in me, I start to squeeze my thighs together.

Elliot tuts. "No, you don't. Keep your legs spread, my star."

I whimper but do as he says. My legs shake with the need to clamp around something. Elliot's thumb starts to circle my clit and I gasp.

"I want to see my beautiful movie star melt for me. I want to feel your climax around my fingers. Someday, when you welcome me into your body, I'll be between your legs, giving you everything you ask for."

"Elliot," I gasp.

"That's it. Your little pussy is feeling much better, isn't it?"

I try and slow my breathing, but calming breaths aren't helping with the wave of release I can feel approaching under my skin. Each deep thrust of his fingers has my hips rocking to meet them and the promise of climax comes as waves.

"Elliot, *please*," I beg.

His face looks fierce and entranced. "You beg so pretty. I think I may grow addicted. I'll wake you up every morning with my head between your legs trying to get my fix of your soft panting words."

My body tightens around his fingers and the knuckles that hold up my dress are white. I am an overdrawn string, waiting to snap. The sound that comes from my throat is desperate and needy.

Elliot does something inside me, it's a twist and a different kind of stimulation. I groan at the full sensation. I might scream.

With a couple more circles to my clit, I snap. Elliot crashes his mouth to mine to muffle my cry and I hardly notice anything past the white spots in my vision and the rush of pleasure.

The kiss sweetens the comedown and I pull away to pant.

Elliot's face is soft and full of emotion, his fingers are back to soft movements until my body relaxes. He slides his fingers from me, and I sigh, gasping when he licks them clean with a euphoric expression.

"You're just how I imagined, perfection." Elliot presses his forehead to mine and I recognize the gesture of affection among his kind. "Thank you, Grace."

We stay like that for a moment, sharing breaths. I sink into this intimacy, my body in a state of bliss. Elliot sighs and drops a chaste kiss to my lips, the taste of me, the salve, and him a mix on his lips. His cock throbs against me and my awkwardness comes back all at once.

"Oh, did you need me to… return the favor?" I ask, trying not to wince at the awkward question.

Elliot lifts my chin with a knuckle. "Shh, Grace, relax. It's not that I don't want whatever you'd offer me, but I haven't earned it yet. Let me woo you a little more."

I frown. "Affection isn't something that you earn, it's what I choose to give you."

Elliot's smile is all trouble. "Ah, but we're talking about a little more than affection."

Elliot readjusts my panties and takes the fabric of my dress from my grip, spreading it, trying to smooth out the wrinkles.

I let him adjust my clothes. The bliss of my release still ringing through me, relaxing my mind and body.

"So, this was just an afternoon delight?" I ask dreamily.

"This is me touching base with you—"

I snort. "Touching, indeed."

Elliot's eyes glint with humor. "This was also an opportunity to give you your first courtship gift as one of my clan."

I think back to the different types of food we sampled together. Our relationship is in a different place now. Those times had been Elliot dating me as if he were a fellow witch.

"What exactly does courting entail?" I ask. "I thought it was just a fancy word for dating, but the way you guys use it is making me start to wonder."

Elliot tilts his head. "Courting would be similar to dating, but we are making it a clear intention that our endgame is for you to be mated to us, to join our clan. Perhaps it's closer to being engaged or approaching that. Our goal is to prove to you that we can provide you with a loving place in our clan. That we can satisfy you sexually, financially, and have the capability to give you all the babies you wish."

He waggles his brows at the last and I poke him.

"I'm starting to regret telling you I want kids," I say to let my mind go over those details. *Approaching an engagement.* Emilia was right about everyone setting up to get attached.

"Oh, but the way your body reacts whenever I mention it, it doesn't lie," Elliot croons, but he becomes serious. "Though, if children through natural means of conception aren't possible, I do hope that you'd be open to foster other gargoyle young."

He looks nervous and I want to wipe away the worries.

"Of course. I want to build the loving family I didn't have. Families don't come just from blood. Your clan is proof of that."

"Yeah." Elliot's face softens. "The Bramblewicks really saved us. Even me, though they brought me in older than the others."

I stroke a finger down his human cheek. "I'm glad."

Elliot sighs and pulls away, placing the jar of salve in my hand. "I should really get going, do you want one of us to come over to your place tonight and keep you company? I still don't like you being there alone."

I squeeze my hand around the thoughtful gift.

"Um, actually, I was wondering if it would be okay to stay with you guys. You've offered before—"

"Really?! Of course, we'd love to have you stay at the manor. I thought I was going to have to work to convince you to stay with us again."

I narrow my eyes at him, and Elliot blushes. That certainly sounds like scheming. "Well, Emilia kind of convinced me of it…" I admit.

"We'll definitely have to have Emilia over sometime. To get to know her, if not just to thank her for bringing you around to the idea."

"Uh—" I blink, uncomfortable. "She doesn't know about the whole gargoyle… or witch thing."

If I were telling this to any of my family or the witches they associated with, they'd nod. The act of revealing our world to a human is a rare one. I don't know anyone who has human friends.

Then I'd met Eloise Bramblewick.

Elliot frowns. "I know she's human, but isn't she your best friend?"

I rub the back of my neck. "I haven't felt ready to tell her everything."

Elliot cradles my face in his hands, making me look at him. "It's, of course, your decision. Telling a human about our world is undoubtedly an uncomfortable thing for both parties, but I happen to know that lies have a way of spiraling out of control, no matter if the intention was good or ill."

Elliot's green eyes hold a world of understanding.

"I'll work on it. I don't want to hide everything from her. She really is my best friend and I should treat her like it."

Elliot nods. "She deserves honesty."

He kisses me and we make plans for when I'll show up at the manor tonight before saying our goodbyes. The whole time, his words reverberate in my soul.

She deserves honesty.

Elliot and I both know firsthand, and recently, about the damage of dishonesty. He's right. Emilia deserves honesty. Now, how to bring up in a conversation that magic is real and I'm a witch being courted by a clan of gargoyles?

CHAPTER 33

ALASDAIR

The numbers of the report start to blur, and I rub my eyes. Though Elliot cuddled up to me after he'd enthusiastically welcomed Broderick home, I did not rest easy last night. I sit back in the custom office chair with a creak, arranging my wings in a more comfortable way.

Broderick had taken a few flights to check on Grace's place from a distance, but I could not fall asleep with the prospective member of our clan facing danger. I'll need to get used to it. I won't allow myself to suffocate Grace with my overprotective tendencies.

"Alasdair." There's a knock on the doorjamb of my office. The goblin office manager's bright-pink skin never fails to momentarily alarm me.

"I'm heading out for lunch. Same thing as always?" Susan asks.

"Yes, thank you."

Susan scrunches her neon nose. "You look like you need a break, maybe even a vacation."

I lift a brow.

"Thank you, Susan." I roll my eyes. "My clan has made the edict that I need to stop overworking myself. No need to worry about me."

The older goblin brightens. "Oh good. I was wondering if they were going to start demanding you go home before sundown. Does this have anything to do with the woman Elliot has been seeing?"

I blink at her. "How did you know about Grace?"

She blinks back. "Alasdair Bramblewick, there is not a thing about this business I don't know."

With that, the goblin leaves.

Years ago, Eloise had started in the role, demanding that we needed to take better care of ourselves, and she would mother us in the meantime until we could learn moderation. We still struggled with moderation, but after Lachlan met his final sleep, we'd convinced Eloise to retire. She and Graham needed more time together to find their footing in being a mating of two instead of three.

Eloise had met Susan at some card game for women in the paranormal community and hired her for the position. It was a good hire. Susan kept the company running better than I can on my own and never misses a detail.

She gives more thought to our physical office than I do and each improvement she makes to the space echoes through all the employees. Susan mothers everyone in the office and most of our employees need it. We have a habit of drawing in beings who are outcasts from their own community in one way or another.

The Bramblewick Renovation building has a showroom for clients and the odd human to wander in, but these back rooms were meant for nonhumans. It would be maddening to spend all day in a human glamour.

Elliot is head of sales and communicates directly with people the most. Usually he's out and about, checking in on different jobsites or touching base with future clients. His job is an ambiguous one, but new jobs always come in. I don't question his methods, even if the expense reports make me roll my eyes.

Elliot knows many people in the community and he's someone that can keep the types of details about each being separate. It could be a holdover from his days of running cons, but it works for him.

By the sounds of it, his courting of Grace started like that, and I can't fault his methods even if he'd acted alone.

The buzz of my cell phone pulls me from pondering that and I answer the call from Elliot.

"Grace wants to stay with us!"

I pull the phone away with a wince, but quickly recover. "She does? Is she okay?"

"I think she didn't sleep well last night, but she forgives me and is going to stay with us." Elliot sounds elated.

"That's… great." I'm also elated, but all the hope comes with the knowledge that I'm the only one not to have a relationship with this witch brewing. I want one, but I'm struggling with making it happen.

"Alasdair." My mate sounds like he's smiling. "You two will work it out. We'll court the pants off her, or the dress."

I nod and Elliot laughs at my nonanswer. He can be ecstatic for both of us.

He sighs. "You've built up our business by pure will alone. I have no doubt Grace will fall for you."

"That wasn't just me—" I start.

"And it won't be just you now," he says, his words gentle and reassuring. "I've got to go, I can't leave Ace waiting."

"No, you can't. I love you."

"Love you too!"

I stare at the phone after we hang up.

How will I court Grace? I'm interested in being mated to her. There's something about her that pulls me in. But when the others in the mating would be Broderick and Elliot, what use could she possibly have for a male who can't even express himself around her without it going awry?

Maybe you need to take time going through the emotions on your own. She'd make a list and write it down. Elliot's words from yesterday come to mind.

I look back at the report. I should take a break. If I write down what I'd say to this witch, maybe I won't offend her every time I speak.

I pull out some paper and the best pen for the size of my hand and concentrate.

Dear Grace,

I freeze and cross it out. That sounds too formal.

To Grace,

I cross it out again, too curt.

I put the pen down, clenching and flexing my hands before picking it up again. She will never see this. No one will ever see this. I'll take it home or maybe burn it like some witches do with wishes. This letter is only to help organize my thoughts.

I start again.

To the witch who has entranced my mate,

It's a ridiculous start, but it helps shake the tension from my shoulders and releases the tightness in my chest that's binding and tangling my emotions.

I take a breath and continue, my pen scratching paper, filling the page with every frustration, hope, and desire that rises out of the muck of worry burying it. Each truth reverberates as I put it to words. Finally, ending with:

Your ineloquent gargoyle,
Alasdair

Something settles and I breathe out, relieved. The words are cramped and almost nonsensical, but the dread circling me about courting a woman for the first time is a little lighter.

Maybe I should write another.

CHAPTER 34
GRACE

This time when I drive up to Bramblewick Manor, I'm not stunned or exhausted. I'm hopeful. None of the guys are on the porch. Did Elliot tell anyone else that I'm moving in? Awkwardness starts to build in my mind until I step out of my car.

"There she is!" Eloise comes from the front door and her overwhelming warmth settles the scurrying worry scratching at me.

Graham's voice reaches me right as Eloise wraps me in an embrace.

"Try not to smother her, love. She's going to be living here. Let the poor girl breathe." Graham winks at me. "Any luggage?"

"I can—" I start.

"I insist," the older gargoyle says. "El wants you to have tea with her and it's already all set out."

"Hush, you. You're ruining all my surprises." She narrows her eyes at her mate before turning back to me. "Is that okay? I want some time with you to myself before any of the boys come and monopolize all of it."

My nerves make my smile over wide. The woman who had a hand in raising Broderick and Alasdair wants to have tea with me. She'd said as much before, but the world I come from is heavy on saying things as pleasantries without the intention of doing them.

"Yes, that sounds great," I say.

"Oh, don't look so scared. I just want to get to know the newest member of our family."

I widen my eyes. *Our family.* As if my place with them is already a done thing.

Eloise flicks away a piece of lint from her sweater, the fidget broadcasting nerves.

Somehow that helps.

This woman is nervous about me, a stranger coming in to join the mating of the males that she's protective of. I'm not some harridan, but she doesn't know that.

"I'd love to take tea with you," I say.

The nerves flee Eloise's bright smile.

***

The tea isn't some grandiose affair that my mother would have hosted full of hoity-toity women making snide comments masquerading as wittiness. Instead of being in a parlor with delicate china and finger sandwiches, we settle on the back porch with heavy mugs of spicy tea and a plate of shortbread cookies.

I sip the tasty brew, the steam warming my cheeks and chasing away the stress of the day. Eloise's gaze takes in the view of the backyard and gardens. The moment between us full of calm and contentment.

This time of year, most of the garden has begun to rest for winter but there are still some hedges and plants that retain their green far past the time of summer.

"You aren't too cold, are you?" Eloise asks.

"No, not at all," I say.

"Oh, good. Winter is going to be here before we know it and I want to spend as much time outside while we still can. There are some lovely rooms in the house, but this porch is one of my favorite places."

"It's beautiful out here."

Eloise's face goes soft. "Graham and Lachlan planned the garden for me in our third year of mating. They knew I missed the garden my mother grew. I lost her the year before I met them."

"I'm so sorry for your loss." I look over at the sleeping plant beds and the way they were arranged around the dry fountain in the middle. "They did a wonderful job."

Eloise laughs. "They did a terrible job. They tried to surprise me, but they knew a lot about building things, not as much about growing them. When I'd stumbled on the plans, I thanked them, but changed everything about it."

My laugh is silent. "Well, at least you got exactly what you wanted. It's the thought that counts, right?"

"Right." Eloise smiles into her mug. "So, how was your day at work?"

I open my mouth to deliver what should have been a standard reply before snapping it shut. Today had been a different type of day with Elliot's visit. I blush and push forward. "It was good. I processed a spell book from the Caribbean today."

The scent of salt and coconuts had taken awhile to leave my senses.

"And Elliot visited me," I say.

Eloise laughs. "Oh, that's the reason for your red cheeks."

My cheeks burn hotter at that.

"You two talked things out?" Eloise asks. "I heard there was a disagreement."

"Uh, yes, we talked it out. I didn't react the best way to something he'd done."

Eloise snorts. "I have no doubt your reaction was warranted. Elliot has a devious streak a mile wide. A good heart, but—" She shakes her head. "He doesn't know how to just let things happen."

"Well, if he had, I wouldn't have met any of them." I shrug.

"That's looking on the bright side, but I think you don't give fate enough credit," Eloise says kindly.

I blink. As a witch, it would be silly of me to reject the concept of fate, but it's also something I don't spend time thinking about. I have lists and organization, things don't happen for me unless I make them happen.

"Oh, you're not convinced," she says.

"I guess I don't see fate having much influence in my life," I say into my tea. Fate didn't get me out of my family's toxic environment and fate didn't get me into my beloved career. I did that.

Eloise nods. "You and Elliot share that in common. I did as well when I met my mates. It wasn't until we started giving a home to young gargoyles that it became apparent. We're all so different. Each time we took in a gargoyle, it had been by chance. They needed a place to go, and we provided them with one. Somehow, they were exactly what the clan had needed. Alasdair, Broderick, and Elliot were all a piece of a puzzle until the clan felt whole. I have no other explanation to how our family came to be and chance hardly strikes three times."

Instead of poking a hole in Eloise's story, that *she* was also a common factor, that their actions and the way they treated the gargoyles fostered the clan they have today, I focus on something else.

"You think I'm fated to be here?" I ask.

The concept of that, like the idea of being matched by Rose, is pretty. Untouched by anything I could have messily done.

"I think that your kind and beautiful soul would have found its place here, with or without Elliot lying to everyone."

That has me smiling. "Then I don't have a bright side for his deception."

"Ah, but forgiveness is forgiveness. Wouldn't you still make the decision to forgive him without a silver lining? If you'd have come to this place anyway, would you still choose to forgive him?"

"Yes," I say. No doubts plaguing the word.

"See?" Eloise grabs a cookie.

I squint at her. "I thought this tea would be you interrogating me, making sure I was good enough for your boys."

Eloise laughs. "I'm sorry to disappoint. I trust that you belong here, Grace. I want to make sure you feel welcome and get to know you. And having another woman around sounds lovely."

"Oh, you've been the only one since the start?"

Eloise scrunches her nose. "Yes, and as much as I love every single gargoyle in this clan, I'm glad to have someone else like me. They can all forget that they are strong and have different senses than I do."

"A sense of smell, for one," I blurt out without meaning to, but Eloise just nods.

"Yes! They will always know when your time of the month is. They can even sniff out when you are angry. It's a little unfair when we can't do the same, but—" She shrugs. "There are bound to be differences."

I'm glad she doesn't bring anything up about arousal. Eloise is easy to talk to, but I'm still shy about certain topics. I didn't know they could scent anger.

Eloise hesitates. "I should warn you of something though. They'll end up building something for you."

I knit my brows together. "But I just got here."

"It's a gargoyle culture thing. Males outnumber females, so clans are generally made up of multiple couplings. To entice a female, a group of males will show their capability to provide within their clan by giving gifts."

"Courtship gifts," I say, thinking back to the healing salve.

"Exactly. With their skill set, I'm anticipating that they are going to end up building you something. Since you seem nervous about your place here, I just thought I should warn you so you aren't shocked."

"But what if this doesn't work out?" My voice is small.

Eloise places a hand warm from holding her mug on mine. Love and comfort in her gaze.

"But what if it does?"

CHAPTER 35

GRACE

But what if it does?

The question reverberates through the rest of the tea with Eloise. We switch to lighter topics and even with my own mental turmoil, I spend the time laughing with the older woman.

How will I know if this can work if I don't go into it with the correct mindset?

I'm a badass witch who deserves love.

This will be my clan and Eloise is going to be basically my mother-in-law. I'd been nervous at the idea. The relationship between my mother and I is hardly one I want to repeat, but every second I spend in Eloise's company chases those fears away.

We swap stories back and forth. Eloise talks more than I do, telling me how she'd been, quite literally swept off her feet by Lachlan when he'd snatched her out of the way of a car and then he'd ruined a perfectly amazing meet-cute by lecturing her for not looking where she was going.

"He looked human, didn't he?" I ask.

"Oh yes, he looked like the biggest man I'd ever seen, and he was worriedly telling me what my mother would think if she'd known I'd almost been hit by a car."

"No…" I say, horrified.

"Yes! That's when I burst into tears. I had been in the spacey part of grief. Going through the motions, wanting to forget that I'd lost her, and here was this stranger, lecturing me."

"How on earth did he come back from that?" I ask.

Eloise laughs. "Well, his horrified face when I said that she'd died helped. And then Graham walked up to see what the fuss was about, and he used his words in ways that Lachlan always struggled to. I found myself allowing these two men to take me to lunch."

She smiles, thoughtful.

"Looking back, I don't know how they did it. It goes against all common sense to go to lunch with *two* men… I don't know what I had been thinking, other than it was the first time I'd felt seen since I'd lost her. We'd lost my dad when I was younger, and her family hadn't been involved with our family growing up, so it'd just been me."

"Lachlan confessed that he knew he wanted me as a mate when we first met, but our dating was a slow thing. There would be dates to the movies, calls to check that I'd gotten home from work, it almost felt like a friendship, but I liked them more than that. I think they were waiting for me to find a balance in my life before upsetting it."

"They didn't tell you about being gargoyles for a long time?" I ask, my mind straying to Emilia without meaning to.

"No. That revelation had been a bumpy one. They were right to wait," Eloise says.

"Do you regret finding out?" I squeeze the mug in my hands and shake my head when I hear how that sounds. "I mean, if it wasn't to be with your mates, would you have still wanted to know about witches and gargoyles and everything else?"

Eloise's eyes focus on me, too perceptive by half. "No, I don't regret finding out. The conditions of it and what happened after were rough, but I don't regret having my understanding of the world opened up. It brought me to this family and all the friends I've met since then. I've seen fantastical things I never would have if I'd lived my life in ignorance."

"What happened after?" I ask.

"Well, they had figured that eventually they'd be able to convince their clan to accept a human, but that turned out not to be the case. They didn't want to mate and not be able to provide…" Eloise looks sad before smiling at me with determination. "And I told them that we were a team, and we'd figure out our own clan together."

My smile comes unbidden at the thought of this small woman lecturing the gargoyles she'd been dating. I glance over to the French doors to the manor. "Broderick said that you guys renovated Bramblewick Manor to be the clan home."

"Yes, that boy is proud of their work, as he should be." Eloise beams in pride.

"The love in it reverberates in the very walls," I say without thinking. My eyes going a little misty.

Eloise frowns at me and I explain.

"I pick up emotions from certain materials, mostly paper. It's what I do at the library."

Her face lights up. "Oh!"

And I tell Eloise all about the spell book I processed today, and the story embedded in the paper.

A knock interrupts us. Elliot, in his human form, smiles as he stands at the door.

"You two look cozy," he says.

Eloise's smile is teasing. "We're just gossiping about you, don't mind us."

Elliot's hand goes over his heart. "You wound me!"

I laugh and his eyes catch mine.

"I was going to start on dinner… and I was wondering if you wanted to join me?" Elliot asks me, shyly. "If you still want to learn. You can unwind before dinner if you'd rather. No pressure."

"I'd love to." I look down at my work clothes. "Let me change into something else."

"I do have an apron." His smile looks sharp at that.

"I'd rather not risk it." I adore my clothing too much to hazard cooking stains.

"I'll be waiting," he says.

CHAPTER 36
ELLIOT

I'm pulling ingredients out and setting them on the counter when Grace comes into the kitchen, having swapped the stylish dress hiding the prize of lace stockings for comfy-looking sweatpants and a thin T-shirt that stretches tight over her chest. I stumble. Something about the new silhouette makes me want to run my hands over her and weigh the feel of her tits in my hands.

Or maybe it's the ache of leaving her this afternoon. It had been the right thing to do, but my cock may never forgive me. The squeeze of her pussy around my fingers had almost been enough to spill in my pants. It would have been uncomfortable, but I might have been able to pull my eyes away from her bouncy chest now.

Doubtful.

"Elliot," she says.

"Uh?"

"My eyes are up here."

I raise my gaze to find Grace grinning at me.

"I'd say I'm sorry, but I'm not." I give her the smile that usually gets me out of trouble.

She laughs. "So, what are we making?"

"I thought it would be fun to make sausage ravioli in a red sauce."

"Oh!"

"Have you ever made them?"

Now she blushes and I want to pull her shirt down at the collar to see if it spreads down her chest. *Down, Elliot! Behave!*

"My family had a cook while I was growing up. I've only started learning how to make food now so I don't need to survive on takeout."

I whistle. "I know you said your family name was a big deal, but I guess I didn't figure the money that meant."

Grace winces.

"Hey." I soften my voice. "I don't have to mention it if it bothers you."

Grace shakes her head. "It's a fact. Just because I'm not used to talking about it doesn't mean it doesn't affect everything in my life."

Grace turns to the sink to wash her hands and I resist the need to readjust my half-hard cock. It won't do any good. Some of the discomfort that spreads through my body is from wearing the glamour, but I shake it off. I need to focus on wooing my mate now.

Wooing her and not thinking of bending her over the kitchen table. The counter would be too high, but if Alasdair were here… *Gods damn it. Focus!*

Grace turns back to me. "Well, boss, how do you want me."

I bite my lip to keep from groaning.

***

Grace takes direction tantalizingly well. She mixes up the dough and kneads while I start the sauce to simmer. Our conversation moves easily, just as it had on our dates. This witch is a delight to have around.

I've only let myself make her blush once when I asked how the rest of her day went after I left. The reddening of her cheeks is a rush. It's the same type of rush as when I make her laugh, or when I scandalize her speechless. But I'm not doing that last one tonight.

I'm behaving.

It's when it comes to putting the dough in the pasta roller that I break.

Grace is shorter than I am, so we set it up at the kitchen table. The table of perfect height. She bends over and suddenly I'm behind her like a moth to a flame, my hips pressing against her ass as I cradle my hands around hers, as if she needs instruction on how to feed the dough through the roller. The heat of her body against mine has an uncharacteristic itch forming in my chest. Almost like a hungry growl, but I don't growl in this form.

She stills for a moment at the contact before the corner of her mouth ticks up and she leans her head to the side. The expanse of her neck, a little damp from the heat of the kitchen, draws me in and I brush my lips over it.

Grace sighs at the touch and I open my mouth, inhaling her delicate scent. The scent of the salve still mixed with it. There's no way that she misses my erection pressing against her and instead of scowling at me and calling me a hound dog, her body softens.

The air in the kitchen is heavy, or is that the tension between me and this witch?

I scrape my teeth along her neck and a small sound escapes her mouth. I want to hear it again. My hips rock against the curve of her ass and we both groan. She doesn't say anything. I should say something. Woo her like I said I would.

"You feel so good," I say, the words rough, but better than grinding against her in silence.

"Elliot," she breathes, and I grind my cock against her harder with a moan.

My tongue licks over the skin I'd run my teeth over before and she gasps.

"My star, I should stop," I say.

"Don't you dare," she says.

I hum. "In the kitchen? Really? Where anyone can come in and interrupt?"

Instead of that snapping her out of the lust winding around us, Grace's eyelashes lower and the scent of her arousal increases.

"Is that something you like? The risk of being caught?" I ask, as if I hadn't already guessed. "Is that why you enjoyed the interlude in your office so much? Why you came so hard around my fingers?"

I direct her to place the dough back in the bowl and cup her tits, squeezing.

Grace gasps. "Do you think someone would catch us?"

"All they'd have to do is walk in," I say instead of answering her. No, I don't think anyone is going to interrupt us. They all know I'm having a cooking date with our witch. They all know I need to have some alone time with Grace to attempt to mend the rift I've made with my past deceptions.

They wouldn't put a kitchen seduction past me.

"I was trying to be on my best behavior," I say, nipping the skin higher on her neck. "But you just had to bend over. I can't think of anything but how tight you were today, how wet."

She whimpers and pushes back into me. I really should stop. Our first time together should be a measured affair, not a quickie in the kitchen. I bet Broderick had taken his time, but Broderick is patient. Alasdair would be patient with Grace too. I'm not patient.

"Please, Elliot," she whispers.

I slide my hand down her body before sneaking it under the fabric of her shirt and touching the skin of her stomach. Grace shivers like I've tickled her, and I smile. The warmth of her skin keeps me from seeing how much I can make her shiver. I want to make her moan. I slide my hand under the tight band of her bra until I'm gripping her breast.

The itch to growl starts up again right as my body rocks into hers again, as if my instincts want me to claim Grace against the table like this, gripping her to keep her in place. The thought has me massaging her breasts.

She tilts her head back, and I press against her back with my chest. Grace bends for me, letting her head fall forward instead. The submission has a roar of lust surging in me, and I don't hesitate.

CHAPTER 37
GRACE

Elliot pulls off my shirt and expertly undoes my bra. When the cozy air of the kitchen hits the bare skin of my breasts, I freeze. Are we really going to do this here? My body wants to, but I don't want to scandalize any of the rest of the house.

Elliot must sense some of my trepidation because he nips the lobe of my ear, making the heat at my core liquid.

"What's wrong, my star? Too risky?"

I blink. "Eloise was very nice. I want her to like me... not get an eyeful of me."

Elliot laughs. "Luckily, she's only gotten an eyeful of me once. When I was younger and dumber."

I twist my body, my hand coming to cover my breasts. I raise my brows.

"And what about now?" I ask.

"No one is really going to interrupt us, Grace. Tonight, the kitchen is ours until we tell them it's time for dinner."

"But you said—"

"I exaggerated to heighten the moment," he says. His mouth quirks in amusement. "Trust me, my star, I wouldn't sacrifice your comfort around our clan for a quickie."

I want to narrow my eyes at him, exaggeration is just a different sort of *lying*, but I'm distracted by his use of *our clan*. Then he rocks his hips against me and my indecision crumbles at the swell of need burning in my core.

No one is going to walk in. I let my hands fall from my chest, the smears of flour left behind looking messy and erotic. Elliot must agree because his groan is rough and his hands come up, gripping and massaging like he'd done under my shirt.

The touches spark waves of heat that flow through me, the stiffness of my body gives. Elliot can make me feel good, he'd proven that in my office already when he'd made me keep my legs spread and shattered my mind at the same time.

"That's it, my star." His voice sounds deeper, like it's scraping the bottom of the barrel of his borrowed human appearance. "You're so beautiful, I want to spend hours worshiping your tits—"

I make a sound, cutting him off. This feels wonderful but I'm not patient enough for *hours*. Elliot laughs, as if he knows exactly what I'm thinking. As if he knows that I want him to grip me tight and possess my body with his. To see if I can fit his knot—

I turn my head and frown.

"Why are you wearing your glamour?" I ask.

The motions of his hands falter and the look of lust on his face changes to one of alarm.

"Uh." Discomfort lines his eyes. "Is it okay if I keep it on?"

I try to keep the confusion from my face. I'd thought he'd kept wearing his glamour because he didn't want to scare me away.

"If that's what you want…" I trail off.

Elliot buries his face into my hair, as if he's scenting it, but his breathing is even. Is he embarrassed?

"Elliot," I say softly, wanting to ensure my meaning is clear. "I'm a fan of either form you wear. I'm just saying that you don't need to appear human for my sake. I was with Broderick. I know what to expect."

"I'm more... comfortable like this right now."

"Okay," I say. Some of the tension winding around us has loosened. Elliot's hands cradle my breasts but his movements are soft as he breathes into my hair.

I'm starting to wonder if the moment of heat has passed and if we should continue making dinner when Elliot drags his teeth against my shoulder.

"I need you, Grace." His words have the tension returning to my body, like the stretch of a rubber band needing to be snapped. "Will you let me have you?"

There's something starved about Elliot's tone. Something with sharp edges that stabs into my skin and makes me want to surrender.

"Yes," I breathe.

A growl that doesn't belong in this human appearance breaks from my gargoyle and he releases one breast to yank down my sweatpants and soaked panties. The scent of sex and healing salve increases the sticky arousal between my legs.

"Fuck, you smell divine," he says.

I jolt a little at the curse, but this darker, hungrier version of Elliot doesn't notice. Something about this exchange has me bending over. My hands flatten against the flour-dusted wood surface of the table and Elliot's breathing goes shallow at the move.

"You'll let me take you like this, my star? You'll give me exactly what I want?" Elliot asks.

"Yes." It comes out with a whimper. I want this so badly. This gargoyle that hid so much from me now revealing the instincts driving him.

He groans behind me. "I don't usually do this."

I snort. "You don't usually have sex in the kitchen?"

"I don't usually make demands. I give. I thought I'd be on my knees for you, begging for forgiveness, among other things." Elliot's fingers stroke through my wet folds and I sigh when he slides two inside me.

I blink and something makes sense. With Broderick and Alasdair, Elliot submits. With me… he wants something else. With how slick I am, I want the same thing.

"Take me, Elliot," I say.

Elliot releases my breast and the sound of his belt echoes in the kitchen. The head of his cock presses against my opening and I sink lower against the table. The primal part of my brain knows what my body needs. It knows what he needs.

I gasp at the first vicious thrust of Elliot inside me. The stretch is bright and intense, but my body accepts him and his cock slides deep, human shaped even there.

Elliot's hand grips my shoulder, keeping me in place. He grunts on his second thrust and a cry falls from my lips.

This isn't like the way he fingered me in my office. This is desperate and necessary. This is every heated look exchanged since the beginning of our relationship. This is the worry that I'd leave when I discovered the truth.

This is Elliot pounding into me with his apology.

I forget to be quiet. I forget that we're in a kitchen and that flour smears against my front. I don't worry about how I fit into this relationship or the stalker that sent me to this house.

I'm only heat and flesh. A body burning out of control. His mate meant to be claimed. Each slap of our bodies has a keening cry building in my throat. Each thrust of his cock invading my senses and mind until I'm clawing at the table.

Elliot snarls behind me and his thrusts lose rhythm. Another inhuman growl sounds from his chest, and he gushes inside me. His cock kicking with each spurt.

The kitchen falls into stillness except for our gasping breaths and the simmering of the sauce on the stove. Elliot releasing my shoulder to lean over me and kiss my neck.

"Grace, my beautiful Grace. I'm… I want to say I'm sorry."

"But you're not." I almost giggle but I don't have the breath for it.

"I'm not, but I shouldn't have come first," he pants and his hand slides between my legs. His fingers stroke my clit, massaging me as his release trickles out of me. I moan.

"Come on my cock, sweet mate. Let me feel you squeeze around me, gush my seed from your body if you can."

Sweet mate.

Oh gods, heat sweeps through me and Elliot's talented fingers and the thick cock that hasn't softened yet pushes me to climax. My cry is hoarse, and I pulse around Elliot. My cheeks heat at the feel of his seed dripping from me.

Elliot leans away, sliding from me, but pressing his fingers to me to keep his release inside.

"I may not have a knot right now, but I still like the idea of keeping this all inside you." His tone is almost casual.

I straighten, a little wobbly, gasping and used.

"You are all going to be the death of me," I say.

CHAPTER 38
GRACE

"The food is delicious," Broderick says. His grin and the glint in his eye have me wanting to sink in my chair. It's as if he knows what Elliot and I did in the kitchen, even after I showered off the flour and the smears of Elliot's release while he'd finished dinner. With a gargoyle's sense of smell, he probably does. The way Elliot beams in the clothes he wore during our activities solves that mystery.

It's as if he's proudly wearing my scent on him.

Which means all the gargoyles at this table know. Yes, I'd like to disappear now.

"The food *is* wonderful. You two make such a good team in the kitchen," Eloise says. Graham sits next to her, his stoic face ruined by the twitching of his lips.

Kill me now.

Alasdair's reaction is different. Instead of teasing, the way he looks at me is warm. Approval. It tingles over my skin.

Alasdair's face goes serious. "How is the situation with the man who broke into your apartment? Did the Council take care of it?"

The change of topics is jarring.

"Um," I start, realizing I haven't shared all the details with them. "There's no proof that it's Theo. I filed a report, but without evidence, the Council won't take action."

There's a cascade of reactions around the table at that ranging from dismay to frustration. I sink a little in my chair.

"They couldn't read the magic?" Elliot asks from my side.

I clear my throat. "It was clear of signatures."

Elliot's brows furrow. That detail is a disquieting one. The fact that Theo moved to scare tactics and was careful enough to plan it in a way that wouldn't lead back to him… that's calculated.

"I don't know why he won't just let it go," I say. "We only went on one date."

Broderick shrugs. "Some guys react poorly to rejection. This is weird though. I don't like it."

"Neither do I." Alasdair's dark voice has a sensual shiver running up my spine. This gargoyle exudes protection, and my body wants what his voice is offering. There's a part that wants to be bundled up and coddled.

Alasdair taps his talons against the table. "We should hire someone, a third party. I've heard that's the best course of action when the Council won't step in."

There are multiple nods around the table.

"To do what?" I ask. "We have a witch who, for some reason, wants me to date him."

"And is willing to scare you into it if he has to." Alasdair's words are almost a growl. "This is not an average occurrence. We don't know this witch."

"I know someone who can get information for us," Elliot says.

Alasdair raises a brow. "Someone on this side of the law?"

Elliot clears his throat and blushes. "Yeah, Mace is the best in the business."

Alasdair frowns and takes Elliot's hand, squeezing it. "I'm sorry for assuming otherwise, my heart."

Elliot shrugs. "I know someone who could take him out too so it's not like you're wrong. I figure that one is a worst-case scenario."

My eyes widen and Broderick's head falls into his hands. Eloise sips from her glass as if selectively hearing this conversation. No one at the table looks surprised at Elliot's statement, maybe slightly disgruntled.

Elliot looks around. "What? I didn't suggest that be our first option. Not that I don't want to."

"Are you saying you'd kill him?" I ask, my voice squeaking.

Elliot's eyes laser to mine. "If it meant keeping you safe, in a heartbeat."

"Funny how you hide the fact you have multiple mates but are willing to set out that you'll commit murder for her." Broderick shakes his head and smiles at me apologetically. "Elliot's upbringing was a little rough around the edges. If you haven't already realized, his moral compass is… wonky."

"If it means protecting Grace—" Elliot starts, frowning.

"Just hold on. Give me a minute," I say.

Alasdair looks like he's trying to keep from rolling his eyes at Elliot. "We start with information."

"I-I can handle that," I say, trying to tamp down the reflex to refuse this clan swooping in and saving me. "You all shouldn't need to be involving the clan in this."

This sparks a bigger reaction than Elliot's blasé statement that he'd find someone to murder the man. Everyone starts talking at once. Even Graham.

"Now, Grace—"

"You're clan—"

"Don't overwhelm her." This from Broderick.

Alasdair raises his hand, and the table falls silent. The skin on the back of my neck prickles. This is the first time I've witnessed Alasdair flexing his position as clan leader.

He turns his gaze to me and it's as if he sees into my soul.

"I understand it's hard to go from having to handle all of this yourself to suddenly being in a clan, but, Grace, we handle our problems together."

"But I'm not a part of this clan," I say.

The room erupts in noise and Alasdair makes a sound that ceases all arguments.

"You are being courted by us. By gargoyle law, that makes you an honorary member until you decide to commit to mating or accept a permanent position here."

I shake my head, confused. "A permanent position? I could be a part of the clan without mating?"

Alasdair gentles his face. "Yes. If this were a traditional clan, you'd join before we'd court you. Since we aren't, we didn't want to put undue stress on you to join."

"I don't want to burden the clan," I say, choosing to skip that little detail. "Or to get anyone in trouble with the Council, for, say, hiring a hit man for a troublesome ex."

"You aren't burdening us. We take care of our own, and while we court, that means you." Alasdair pauses. "And Elliot won't get into trouble with the Council because he isn't going to be hiring a hit man."

Alasdair's gaze is on Elliot, unwavering until Elliot drops his gaze to his food.

"I won't hire a hit man. We're only looking for information," Elliot says begrudgingly. "But I want to put out there, so that we are all on the same page" —he looks at me— "this is not for a troublesome ex. This is a man who has violated your space and harassed you. This is a serious risk that shouldn't be trivialized."

Alasdair nods at that and my cheeks burn. The urge to not make a scene is still a physical aversion, but…

"You're right," I say. "I'll be careful. I just don't know what we're going to do with what information we would get."

"Let me handle it," Elliot says, and everyone makes an exasperated noise. "That wasn't what I meant!"

Something about the exchange and the stress of the situation has a laugh escaping me. The sound has the tension in the room receding.

"Grace," Alasdair says. "We can physically protect you while you're at the manor, but unless you're willing for one of us to join you at work, or to take time off, you'll be left vulnerable there."

For the first time in this conversation, anger flares.

"I'm not taking time off." I've been embarrassed and worried at being a burden, but I'm not going to let Theo rearrange my life and ruin everything I've worked for. I shake my head. "We don't know how long this will be. I have responsibilities. And I don't need a guard. Nothing is going to happen to me while I'm at the library. It's a public place with security."

Alasdair pauses and everyone seems to be waiting for his response. If I'm an honorary member of the clan, does that mean I need to defer to him? The days of letting someone else run my life are over. I hesitate.

I want to be in this clan, but what would I be giving up?

Alasdair nods. "If you change your mind, let any of us know. We can shift around our business and have someone go to work with you."

I nod back and swallow, struggling with a new question in my mind.

Can I have my autonomy and still be a part of the family I want?

CHAPTER 39

ALASDAIR

Grace is quiet through the rest of dinner and it's as if the rest of the clan doesn't pick up on whatever wheels are spinning in her head. Wheels that I've started. I've tried to curb my overbearing tendencies, but when it comes to safety, they make an appearance.

Maybe I'm worrying too much about my part in the thoughts the pretty witch sifts through. Maybe it's Elliot's statement about getting a hit man that is causing her this pause.

That hadn't helped, but that's Elliot. He'll be able to smooth over things with her. He'll explain that he may have run with rougher crowds while his soul searched for its place in this world, but that he's reformed now. Save for a few manipulations here and there.

The more I ponder it, the surer I am.

I've distressed Grace again.

There's a lull after dinner and Broderick takes over the dishes. When I raise my brows, he tilts his head in the direction that Grace had gone, saying she was planning to unwind and read.

I'm not the only one who notices the tension she's carrying.

I have a suspicion of where she'll be, but that I'm correct surprises me.

In the summer, the back sitting room gets all the evening sunlight. Now that the days are getting shorter, the light isn't as ideal, but still carries an atmosphere of comfort and retreat. It's the best place to read in the house. Hence the bookcases lining the walls featuring the interests of two generations.

Grace is curled up on one side of a couch, most of our furniture is made larger to account for gargoyle anatomy and she looks cozy in the cushions. Cozy and occupied, but not by the book lying open in her lap.

Her face is achingly pretty. I didn't know what that meant until seeing her stare off into space, deep in thought. The reading lamp and crackling fireplace casting shadows over her skin and licks of gold in her hair.

She's like a painting, all warmth and seduction and distraction. The rightness of seeing her in the manor, at dinner next to Elliot, blossoms in my chest now. Grace is where she is supposed to be.

"May I join you?" I ask.

Grace jumps. "Oh! I'm sorry. I didn't hear you come in."

Or notice me staring at her like a lovesick fool. Small favors. I lift my brows and Grace shakes her head, realizing she hasn't responded to my question.

"Of course you can join me. I can leave if you want privacy, it's your house," she says, a blush racing over her cheeks.

Our house. I hold back the sentiment. Don't need to go scaring her off.

"No, I'd like you to stay. I used to read to take my mind off work…" An uncharacteristic nervousness makes me want to fidget. "I'm out of the habit now. So, if you don't mind, I'd like to join you."

Grace looks at the couch. "Oh."

I try to not wince at her hesitation. We don't know each other well and our interactions didn't start off the best.

"Sorry, I'm a little in my head tonight, but if you want to join me, that'd be nice." Grace avoids my gaze, but it's more from shyness than discomfort. I open the drawer in the side table and pick up my e-reader.

I sit on the opposite side of the couch, wanting to give her the space she needs.

"I didn't expect you to be an e-reader person," she says.

I lift my brows. "Why is that?"

"I don't know. I guess it's a silly thing to say, I hardly know you."

"It's okay to say I seem traditional," I tease. "I did try and lecture you about family and have been told by a few people that I don't know how to have fun."

Her lips twitch. "Only a few?"

I grunt. "Maybe more."

Grace laughs and the bright sound makes me want to pull her to my side. I swallow down the urge.

"And you're not an e-reader person?" I ask. I don't understand the feud between those who only read books rather than e-books, but if Grace wants to talk to me about it, I'll listen.

"Oh." She looks down at the book in her lap. "I actually have to use an e-reader if I want to focus on the book."

I tilt my head and she blushes prettily.

"That's right," I say. "Elliot said something about you picking up things from paper as a part of your magic."

The structural diagram in the book on her lap catches my eye and I recognize it. The book is from these shelves. It's an old textbook I'd gotten to study for a building certification. I'd poured through it with Broderick every moment we could.

"You were looking for some light reading?" I ask. Delight fills my chest. The witch we're courting picked something of mine to use her magic on.

Grace looks up, eyes wide. "I guess this looks pretty incriminating."

"If you want to learn about me, you only have to ask."

Grace runs a finger up the edge of a page on trusses.

"I didn't mean to spy. I was just looking for something comforting and this one called to me."

I bark a laugh. "That is not the book to pick for comfort. I think I passed that test on stress and lack of sleep alone."

"It's not the stress that called to me." Grace swallows. "It's there, but under the stress, there's this vibrant loyalty and purpose. The love for your clan and the need to be able to do what's best for them."

The words stop in my throat and my cheeks burn in a blush that I hope doesn't show up on my skin.

"Did it help?" I ask.

Her eyes widen.

"Did it help with whatever is distressing you?" I ask.

Grace drops her eyes. Her nod is tiny. "I haven't had a family in a long time, and I've never had a real one. One that supports each other."

I nod because I know what that's like.

She continues, "I've had to be independent to get what I wanted in life…"

"And you don't want to lose that," I say. It's a conundrum that I haven't had to face. I was accepted into this clan when I was a teen with nowhere to go. Broderick had to basically raise himself to adulthood and Elliot… Elliot had to survive.

"I had so much of my life controlled by others growing up." Grace turns the page. "I know you're the clan leader and I expect that I'll need to defer to you if I'm to be in this clan."

"I—" I break off, trying to pick the words that won't push this witch away. "I want to say that you don't need to worry about that. That we aren't *that* sort of traditional."

Grace's blue eyes raise to meet mine. She knows the direction of this conversation. "But?"

"But the clan has a hierarchy. It's not to control its members. It's to make sure our family is taken care of. If I make a call about safety, I need my clan to follow it."

I need you to follow it. I don't add the mental thought.

"I welcome debate and discussion, but my say is final," I say.

Grace looks down and bites her lip.

I place my hand on hers, the softness of her skin under my palm before I can talk myself out of it.

"That is as clan leader. As a prospective mate and in matters regarding our possible relationship, you can tell me to go fuck myself whenever you need."

Grace sputters out a laugh. When it subsides, she turns the hand under mine until our fingers intertwine. She squeezes, the action soft and full of understanding.

"It did help," she says.

I furrow my brow in confusion. "What?"

"You asked if the book helped with what was distressing me. It did." Her eyes capture mine again, the flicker of the fire adding to their shine. "I needed to know if I would be okay with deferring to you."

My body tightens at her words, and I grit my jaw, trying to push down certain urges. She's talking about deferring to me as clan leader. Not in the ways of bed play.

Grace's lips curve in a smile that has me questioning exactly what she means.

"And?" I ask. My mouth goes dry.

"If you come to feel even a fraction of loyalty and love for me as you do to the rest of your clan, I think I'm safe deferring to your judgment."

It shouldn't sound sensual, but it does.

"We can take our time," I say, not sure if I'm the one talking about bed play rather than clan business now. My words are deep and Grace shivers.

"I'd like that," she says.

We hold each other's gaze for a moment. I'd like to take our time. I'd like to get to know Grace in a way that I'm not blurting out things that come off as offensive.

"Would you like to read with me?" I ask.

"What?" Her brow creases.

I hold up the e-reader. "If you need one of these to read because of your abilities, I'm happy to share... I'd like to spend time with you."

Grace sets the book down on the table and slides to my side of the couch. Her eyes bright with a teasing light. Her thigh presses against mine and her scent fills my lungs, tinged with Elliot's.

"How will this work?" she asks.

Her proximity is intoxicating. It takes me a moment to understand what she means.

"You pick something, and we can read it together or aloud," I offer.

She takes the e-reader and taps through the different books already downloaded. As she does, she leans against me. I don't question the urge to wrap my arm around her. Golden hair tickles my nose.

"This one?" she asks, selecting a murder mystery I'd had on my reading list for a couple of years.

I clear my throat and nod.

"Can you read to me?" Grace asks. She pulls away enough for me to see her blush.

"Of course." I pull her against me again and she rests her head against my chest as I start.

The soft press of her cheek sweet and enticing. As I read, the actions of my claws stroking through her hair soothes me.

She likes my voice. I have something going for me in this courtship.

CHAPTER 40
GRACE

If anyone had told me a week ago that two gargoyles would be fighting over me, I'd have laughed in their face.

"Her scent is all over you, Elliot. It's time to share," Broderick says, pulling me toward him.

"But I want to cuddle with her tonight. We should let Grace pick who sleeps in the same bed as her."

I open my mouth to object. I don't want to make anyone feel left out.

"Elliot, when have Alasdair or I made you pick between us?" Broderick asks patiently.

Elliot's mouth snaps shut.

"That puts undue pressure on her—" Broderick starts

"You two are being ridiculous." Alasdair's voice echoes down the hallway and we all freeze.

I suppress the urge to fidget in my robe and nightdress. I thought I'd be sleeping alone tonight but two gargoyles showed up to steal me from my bed.

"You are both mated, why can't you both sleep with her, if she wants that?" Alasdair adds with a frown.

There's a pause.

"Neither of our beds are big enough," Broderick says.

Alasdair lifts his brows. "Then use mine."

Elliot beams. "That's an excellent idea."

"I don't want to kick you out of your bed," I squeak.

Alasdair's smile is warm. "It's temporary until we get a bed better equipped for multiple gargoyles. I'll just steal Elliot's."

"Y-you could join us," I say before my brain catches up with my words and stalls.

Alasdair walks down the hall, and the air disappears. I'd temporarily forgotten how imposing he is. He wears authority like a second skin, and my toes curl at the thought of him commanding me.

He lifts my chin with a knuckle and there's lust in his face when my eyes catch his. Lust with something dark threaded through it that reminds me of the way his eyes had darkened when I'd talked about *deferring* to him. Each interaction between us adds another thread to the tapestry that is Alasdair Bramblewick.

I've never been with someone so dominant, that could light my body on fire with one small touch, one look.

"Little witch," he starts. "All of our relationships with you will happen at a different pace. We'll get to that part of our relationship when the time is right. Until then, I'll enjoy the thought of you in my bed, carrying my scent."

A weak sound escapes my mouth and Alasdair smiles at me. It's a satisfied smile that melts my insides into a pool of liquid. The towering gargoyle leans down. *Is he going to kiss me?*

My body trembles in anticipation and I almost pout when he presses his lips to my forehead.

Alasdair pulls away with a chuckle. "Good night, Grace."

Just like that, he's gone.

Elliot moans. "Fuck me, I'm no slouch, but I'm going to enjoy the way he ramped you up."

"Like the best sort of dessert," Broderick says and pulls me into Alasdair's room. He sets me on the sheets of the giant bed and a sharp inhale gives me Alasdair's scent. I recognize it from the time we spent reading, old books with a touch of mint. I want to wrap the blankets around me and imagine he's here too, taking care of the arousal he sparked.

The males shuck off their clothing. Elliot is still in his human form and takes longer compared to Broderick's kilt.

"I thought we were just sleeping," I say, a little breathless.

"We were," Elliot says as he's unbuttoning his pants. "But you're in need, Grace. Something to take the edge off. And I'd be remiss if I didn't reapply the salve."

I squirm on the bed.

Broderick groans and smooths a hand up my bare thigh. "She likes that idea. Look at that blush."

Blushing seems to be the default around these males. Broderick slides a claw under the robe's tie, pulling the knot in an artful gesture like he's unwrapping a present. Each measured motion makes it harder to keep from shifting my hips.

Last week I'd been celibate, and now the tease of something more has me panting with need.

Elliot pulls a jar from his pocket before dropping his pants to the floor.

"Is that another jar of salve?" I ask.

Elliot grins. "I believe in being prepared. Now pull up that dress. Broderick wants to taste you."

I don't question how Elliot could possibly know that. The memory of Broderick's tongue in the hallway when I'd watched Alasdair take Elliot is enough to convince me. I lean back and pull up the nightdress, baring my pussy to the room.

Broderick doesn't give me a moment to feel self-conscious, his mouth descends to my wet folds. I cry out at the stroke of it, and he moans.

Elliot climbs onto the bed and kisses me, pushing first the robe off my shoulders and then the nightdress. Each touch of his lips sparks heat in my core that Broderick licks to life and soon I'm a writhing mess under the ministrations.

Elliot pulls back and marvels at my breasts. "I regret not giving these the attention they deserve during our time in the kitchen. I rushed us."

I huff a laugh. "We were kind of in a rush."

My laugh breaks into a moan as Broderick slides his tongue inside me.

"That's never an excuse, but I'll take it. So pretty," Elliot whispers before he nips the skin just under my collarbone, continuing down with little bites and sucks until he engulfs my nipple with his mouth.

I'm lost in the hard draws of Elliot's mouth on my flesh, but start at the brush of the pad of Broderick's finger on my back hole.

"Shh," Broderick says. "Do you want me to stop?"

"I-I've just never." My blush has spread to my ears now. Embarrassment and tantalizing fear rush through me in time to my rapid heartbeat.

Broderick hums against my pussy, and I gasp at the vibration. Elliot squeezes a breast and releases my nipple with a pop.

"Fuck," Elliot breathes. "I'd love to take the time to tease you until you're begging for one of us to fill you there."

Broderick licks through me again and raises his head. "Slowly, Elliot. We'll get there." His eyes glint as they meet mine. "This isn't a tonight thing, so relax, sweet witch. I'm just playing with you a little. Perhaps one day you'll be brave enough to try and take both of us at once."

I whimper at the thought. Broderick grins, his fangs flashing. "But I've missed you, and Elliot wearing your scent like a badge of honor has made me hungry."

I moan as he uses his tongue on me again. The length and strength of it has me moving without meaning to, and Broderick grips my hips, his fingers digging into me as he holds me still.

"Please," I beg.

Elliot's hand slides over my stomach to circle my clit and hums. "What are you asking for, Grace?"

A lock of hair falls across Elliot's human visage. He's handsome as a human, it was the first thing I'd noticed and tried to dismiss. I didn't want to get attached to an appearance that was a glamour. But now that I've seen him in his true form, I know that this version is the watered-down, generic one.

I stroke a finger up his cheek and flick the hair out of his face. His eyes focus on mine.

"I want to be with you, how you truly are," I whisper.

Elliot freezes and Broderick's movements slow, as if keeping watch.

This is significant. Elliot had said he was more comfortable in his human form in the kitchen and he's beautiful either way... but I can't help but want that part of him. Is that selfish?

I'm flayed by my emotions for these males, and I want nothing between us, not even a seamless glamour.

Elliot clears his throat. "Okay." The word sounds rough, like I've pulled on something visceral with my simple request.

Broderick releases my hip to squeeze Elliot's thigh in reassurance. Elliot looks down with a wince and I begin to regret asking him to do something that puts the stressed look around his eyes, but he removes the ring that holds his glamour and the pink of his skin morphs into gray green.

There's a moment of bliss on Elliot's face when the glamour leaves him and his wings move as if wanting to stretch. The bliss disappears as Elliot's eyes open, and he widens them at me in hesitation. The green of them brighter now.

Broderick kisses my inner thigh before sitting up and taking the ring in his talons. "Let me, love," he says, dropping a kiss to Elliot's palm before setting the spelled object carefully on the side table.

"Now, weren't you going to give this witch some more salve?" Broderick asks.

That seems to snap Elliot out of whatever has halted his motions. Wickedness takes the place of hesitation.

"Do you want that, my star?" Elliot asks.

"Yes." I swallow, knowing what I need to ask for. "And I want your knot."

Broderick purrs and Elliot's eyes widen even more. Surprise and delight chipping away at whatever ugly emotions keep him from living in this form. I crave that moment of intimacy I shared with Broderick. I want Elliot.

"You want my knot to stretch that sweet pussy? Did you get a taste for it with Broderick?"

I tuck my chin, but my gargoyle doesn't let me get shy now. Elliot kisses me. It's a soft gesture and the nerves start to recede. When the kiss breaks, I blink my eyes open, a little dazed.

My breath ghosts over my lips. "Yes... nothing has ever felt like a knot, and I want to feel you in that way, with us close."

Elliot's talons barely touch my cheek. "Careful, Grace, you keep saying things like that and I'll start to think that you've caught feelings for me."

I glare at him and spread my legs. Of course I've caught feelings for him, but I don't want to face that quite yet. Not in the face of this erotic moment. I trail my hand down to my weeping center to stroke myself. Elliot's teasing falls away and is replaced with hunger. A growl comes from him that has me tensing.

"My star wants a knot. I'll give her a knot." Elliot pulls me farther on the giant bed and I squeak at the quick motion before he throws himself over me. "I'll knot her until she can't do anything but drip for her mates."

Broderick's pleased purr has me shivering in anticipation.

"That sounds like the prettiest of pictures," Broderick says. He leans over and kisses Elliot. "And I can fuck your knot into our sweet witch."

It takes a moment for the words to sink in but when they do, I may faint. Blood rushes in my ears and my skin goes from prickling to ultrasensitive in the space of a breath.

Elliot makes a desperate sound that I hardly recognize except the night I'd spied on him with Alasdair. Broderick goes to the side table and my eyes meet Elliot's.

"Are you okay with that, Grace?" he asks. The desire and frenzy layering his words has me licking my lips.

I nod enthusiastically before pausing. "But… I've never done anything like this. If I do something wrong, you'll need to tell me."

Elliot's smile widens. "We'll have to make it memorable."

Broderick snorts. "Don't worry about doing something wrong, Gracie. Just enjoy yourself." He comes up behind Elliot and kisses his neck. Elliot arches his back and bares his neck in submission. The movement is graceful, practiced. Elliot's wings grab onto the sheet on either side of my body, supporting his weight as he rocks his hips against the cradle of mine.

The hard flesh of his cock is similar to his human one, the knot and coloring the main difference. The swell of his knot rubs against my wet clit and I moan, rocking my hips to increase the friction. Elliot's knot isn't as large as Broderick's and the fear that I won't be able to take this part of him dissipates with each slide of our bodies.

Elliot makes a sound and something moves between him and Broderick. Broderick's tail strokes inside the male on top of me and the stimulation has him gasping and grinding against me.

"Uh, uh, uh, don't forget what your task is, troublemaker," Broderick says.

Elliot shakes his head. "*Shit*. It feels so good."

I nod, and Broderick laughs. "The two of you are losing your heads before the fun part even begins." The claws on

Broderick's wings sort through the sheets before finding the small jar Elliot had dropped.

"You need to apply the salve to Gracie," he says.

"But-but—" I don't want the slow slide of the salve, I want Elliot.

"Peace, sweet witch, you'll get what you want." Broderick's smile has me biting my lip in anticipation. Broderick unscrews the jar and scoops out a generous portion of the salve before gripping Elliot's girth.

Elliot moans, his head falling back against Broderick's shoulder.

Oh gods. I thought watching one of them stroke themselves was erotic, it doesn't compare to watching the merciless grip of Broderick taking hold of Elliot and spreading the salve over his hard cock.

I rock my hips up without meaning to.

Broderick winks at me. "Now, give our witch her medicine."

Elliot's cock presses against my pussy and the glide of salve on my soaked flesh is erotically easy. I gasp at the stretch, but his cock just slides deeper and deeper.

Broderick grunts. "That's it. You're so good at taking him, Gracie. Like you were made for him. We'll get you to the point that you can take Alasdair one day."

I make a sound at the tease. Alasdair's scent makes it impossible not to consider what it would be like. Could I take the giant gargoyle?

The snap of Elliot's hips brings me back, and my hands come to his thick shoulders.

"Grace, you feel so good." Elliot's words slur a little.

Elliot's cock goes in deep, spreading the salve over every inside inch. The ache of him almost makes him feel bigger.

Broderick fists Elliot's hair and Elliot's whole body stiffens. Elliot lets out a guttural cry as Broderick grips his hip with his other hand and slides into him. The move has Elliot thrusting forward, his knot smacking against my pussy.

I whimper, and Elliot's tense face grimaces in dismay.

"*Fuck*. Are you okay, Grace?"

I squirm. "Yes, please do it again."

Both males grunt at that, and Elliot thrusts into me with a groan.

"Our little witch likes her cunt smacked by your knot. I wonder if I fuck you hard enough, if it will slip it inside her."

I gasp and tense at Broderick's words and Elliot moans. "Oh fuck, the way you squeeze my cock is going to put me into a rut."

Broderick's hips slap against Elliot's and the gargoyle between us cries out.

Elliot's eyes focus on my face, I must be a sight because he moves into me like he can't help it. "Oh, you like dirty talk? We're going to have so much fun with this. You grip my cock like your pussy was made for me. It almost hurts not to knot you."

Elliot presses the swell against my opening as if in demonstration and it slides in a little. I moan. "Yes, oh please, Elliot."

The eroticism of stretching to fit his knot has my body on the edge. I whimper when Elliot slides out, but he thrusts again and rocks his knot against me. Again and again Elliot teases me with the press of his knot until I'm a pleading mess.

Until finally, Elliot groans, as helpless as I am.

With a pop, the knot slides inside me. I scream. The stretch, the pressure of it against places inside me, and the splash of Elliot's release throws me into climax.

I soar, each rock of Elliot's knot from Broderick's snarling thrusts extends the pleasure rushing through my veins. The sounds that are coming from Elliot are all of pleasure and need.

Broderick suddenly snarls and presses his body hard against Elliot, and Elliot's body surges into mine, throwing me back into climax at his pleading cry. Broderick moans, and Elliot tenses, filling me again. I feel the excess of it leave me on a gush each time he tries to get deeper inside me.

Elliot falls onto my body, his face pressing against the crook of my neck.

"Oh fuck," Broderick gasps, straightening. "I lost my head there. Sound off, is everyone okay?"

Elliot mumbles something against my skin that is unintelligible, but he's still alive.

"Gracie?" Broderick asks.

It takes me a moment to form words. "I—" I pant out. "I'm something. I don't think I can feel my fingers."

Elliot moves to rise on a mumble. "Squishing you—" is all I can make out.

"No," I gasp when his movement pulls on the knot inside me. "You're not squishing me."

Elliot sighs and lays his head back down, kissing my neck. Before lifting to kiss my lips. The kiss is lazy and intimate as the sweat on our bodies cools.

I hum into the kiss. "How's being on the inside of the sandwich?"

Elliot clears his throat but the look on his face is dreamy as Broderick runs his hand over Elliot's wings, stroking the muscles.

"Heaven. You'll like it," he says.

I cough a laugh. "I don't know if I can take a knot in my ass as well as you can."

Elliot's smile is sweet and sexy at the same time. "It takes some practice, but you don't have to be knotted. The first few times we won't even try, even if you beg for it."

I open my mouth to say I won't beg for *that*, but snap it shut. I already begged for a knot. I'm not going to lie and say I'd never beg for a knot there. The sex brain asks for all kinds of things.

Elliot must see the mental gymnastics because he just smiles. "It's a someday thing, don't worry about it now."

Broderick grins, a little abashed. "I'll be much more careful with you, sweet witch. It will take time for us to learn how rough you like things."

My cheeks burn. "I liked this a lot. The salve is genius."

Elliot sighs. "That's all Broderick. I liked the idea of using my human fingers again, making you keep your thighs wide. The idea already had me half hard."

Broderick chuckles. "We aren't only going to do your fantasies, brat."

He smacks Elliot's ass lightly and Elliot hums. I giggle at the exchange.

We lay like that, connected and teasing each other until Broderick's knot goes down and he slides free from Elliot.

It's much later, after the gargoyles handled cleanup, Broderick cleaning Elliot while he and I were locked together and then later Elliot running a warm washcloth over my sensitive bits, when my mind goes to the way

Elliot's eyes had shone with vulnerability. Broderick is snoring next to us, his wing curled around my body.

I run a finger over Elliot's scalp, enjoying the way he sighs in bliss.

"Elliot," I whisper. "Will you tell me why you don't like to be in this form?"

Elliot blows out in discomfort. "It's… well, it's not really complicated, I guess. Being glamoured isn't the most comfortable thing, it makes my body ache where my wings want to burst free, but… I feel safer as a human."

I keep softly touching my gargoyle and he nuzzles my wrist before continuing.

He swallows.

"I've told you before that I was raised in a home for beings that don't have a natural way of fitting into the human world. It wasn't great. The glamours available were the cheapest kind and didn't hold up to touch or even close distances.

"It would have been different if it were somewhere secluded, but with whatever zoning the Council used and the resources available, it wasn't. It was in the middle of a city of humans. We couldn't go out, ever."

Elliot tangles his fingers with mine. The differences in our skin tones obvious even in the low light.

"Bored kids with burgeoning magic abilities don't make a good mix. Violence became the expectation because then at least that was something to do."

Elliot swallows. "It got… it got bad, and I couldn't stay there anymore. I thought, if only I could live out in the real world, I wouldn't have to be there. I wouldn't have to be trapped. I stole a cheap glamour and left. I survived and got better glamours."

"Oh, Elliot." I don't even have the words. My heart bleeds.

Elliot places my hand against his cheek. "Walking around glamoured means acceptance, *freedom*. I've gotten better at not compulsively wearing the glamour but sometimes the itch to wear it gets the better of me."

"I love you like this," I whisper, and my tongue freezes. I just said the *L* word. I didn't necessarily mean it in the way of confessing undying love, but my heart is heading that direction. If I didn't have my brain wanting to tap on the brakes and make a million lists, maybe I would have already come to terms with my feelings.

Elliot's face softens in the moonlight, and I release the worries besieging my heart.

"Thank you, Grace," he says. "I'll try and work on loving myself like this too. It's just hard when other things come up."

"Then I'll tell you every day," I say. It's a promise. More of a promise than I've given this clan. The worry that I've invested more than they have squeezes at my heart, but I force it away.

I'm a badass witch who deserves love.

And that means putting my heart out there.

CHAPTER 41
GRACE

"I'm taking a vacation after this," Emilia gripes from her desk as she straightens a stack of forms to take to her lab. I've barely seen her this past week. The director has her on a special project involving restoring a crate of books that need to be ready to ship to their destinations pronto.

"You'll deserve it," I say. "The director is lucky that you can even accomplish this kind of turnaround time."

"You're right. I'm a gem." Emilia leans against her desk and blows her bangs out of her face. Chagrin and satisfaction war with the stress that's been plaguing her.

"We need to do lunch sometime." She points at me with a stern look on her face. "I want to hear all about your new digs and relationships. It's been a week! I'm sure you have some updates on that front."

My tongue sticks to the roof of my mouth. I have many things to talk about. The past week has been idyllic. Most days, I have tea with Eloise when I get home. The older woman is quickly gaining a spot in my heart. If I'm being honest with myself, they all are in different ways.

Eloise and my conversations are delightful. Graham talks about different local news with me over coffee, he's familiar with the underbelly of squabbling politics between magic beings and humans from the years he'd spent working in this city.

Bramblewick manor is starting to feel like home and that's without mentioning the gargoyles courting me.

Elliot is the most vocal, and most nights we make dinner together. Broderick likes his solitude but once he's done in his studio for the night, he's been pulling Elliot and I into Alasdair's bed. Sometimes it's for mind-blowing sex, but most times we chat until falling asleep. Alasdair reads with me every night and I've grown addicted to the rumble of his voice. It strokes something in me that both comforts and arouses.

And I haven't had to think about the business with Theo at all.

According to Stan, the flower deliveries stopped. I've been back in my apartment a couple times to check things over and pick up items I needed and there haven't been any other break-in occurrences.

"Yes, there is a lot I'd like to talk about with you," I say. Only part of it is about what's happening in my life.

As my friendship with Eloise grows, I realize I need to tell Emilia the truth. About all of it. Eloise's happiness about being human in our world settles the worry that I'll be ruining Emilia's life with the knowledge that the world is different than it appears.

I may be afraid of Emilia looking at me differently once she finds out, but that's a selfish worry. It's the worry of a love-starved witch experiencing her first friend. Keeping a whole world from Emilia isn't fair to her. I don't want to lose my friend over my lies.

Now if only we could have a moment for me to explain.

"Oh, with that look on your face, I can't wait to live vicariously through you." Emilia picks up her papers and tablet, getting ready to leave for the lab once again.

My cheeks burn hotter, and I laugh awkwardly. "I don't know if you'll believe me, but it should be a good time."

Emilia's snort is interrupted by the door swinging open. Agnes looks flustered.

"Oh, Grace! Your car!"

***

My car, indeed. It isn't an especially nice car, but it was my first big purchase after becoming independent from my parents.

And now it's looking worse for wear.

The tires are slashed, and I assume there are some nefarious spells added to it with the way my skin itches.

In broad daylight.

The cherry on top? The part that has my heart dropping into my stomach and the blood draining from my face? The spray-painted words marring the finish and windows.

Slut. Whore. And as if to add flavor, *Monster Fucker.*

My stomach twists. Am I going to be sick?

"This is fucking awful!" Emilia spits out. "It has to be that creep that's been bothering you. It's too much of a coincidence for it to be some other asshole sticking their nose in relationships that don't concern them."

I open my mouth and close it. Oh, Emilia's talking about the polyamory. I guess that would make sense to her.

"Hey." Emilia gentles her voice and turns me away from the vibrant declaration of my bedmate choices of late. "You should call one of your guys. This is some serious stuff."

"I—" I break off on a sniff.

Why does this feel so personal? This has to be Theo with the involvement of magic, but what if it's one of those groups that targets people who mate with others not of their kind?

It's so ugly.

"Give me your phone," Emilia says.

"What?" I ask.

"Do you want me to call security?" Agnes asks, having led us out here to show us the damage.

"I think we're past the point security would be helpful," Emilia says and compresses her lips with annoyance. "How did this even happen?"

Agnes's brows furrow. "There's a library event at one of our satellite locations that required most of the security to cover. It was only going to be today."

The hair raises on the back of my neck. It's as if Theo or whoever he hired to do this had known. What else does he know about?

Why won't he just leave me alone?

I thought he'd finally moved on.

Emilia pulls my phone out of my coat pocket and hands it to me.

I unlock it and stare at the device blankly.

Emilia sighs and takes it from me. I don't fight her and instead focus on keeping my breath even.

"U-uh yeah, t-this is Emilia, Grace's friend."

I widen my eyes. Who did she call?

My eyes well without my permission. Emilia stutters more over the phone about my car and that someone should come and be with me. My friend with extreme social anxiety is talking to someone she doesn't know, for me.

I sniff and she hangs up.

"You're the best," I say wetly.

Emilia blushes. "It's a little easier when it's for someone else. It's the small steps, ya know? Oh, don't cry! He said he'd be here in a few minutes."

I hug Emilia, not even asking who. It doesn't matter. Any of the gargoyles would be welcome right now.

"What is going on here?" The voice of the director breaks through the moment, and Emilia freezes.

I pull away and wipe away my tears, trying to put on a brave face.

Director Adder is an intimidating person on a good day and this isn't a good day.

"My vehicle has been vandalized," I say, glad that my voice doesn't crack.

The director's sharp suit could cut, but it's his tongue that has the reputation for that. His uncanny gold eyes look over at my vehicle and he frowns. I'm not sure if he's human or some other being, but as the director to the library, he's well aware of the organization's dual purpose.

He knows what being called a monster fucker means.

There's a sickening pang in my stomach. I've lived the past week in a happy cloud. I haven't had to deal with the ugliness that may exist in the paranormal world toward those that engage in mixed matings. It didn't really occur to me to worry about how other people would react.

I'd already figured my parents would be horrified, but other than that… I can't lose my job for this, can I?

The director's face remains placid rather than twisting in disgust. There's a trace of something there I didn't expect though. *Concern.*

Perhaps he isn't as bad as everyone has said. He looks to Emilia. I turn to her.

"You should get back to work," I say. "Whoever you called will be here soon."

Emilia looks like she'd argue but casts a glance back to the director and nods. When she scurries away, I face the boss I almost have no contact with.

"You should take a couple weeks off," he says.

"What?" I gasp.

His brows crease. "It will be paid, of course."

As if that's my main argument. It should be, but the idea that I won't be able to do my job because of some asshole burns. The director's eyes focus on my face.

"It's not personal, Ms. Starling. I'm sorry that you're experiencing this, but we house precious items. We can't let our patrons think those things are in danger."

I fight back anger. "Maybe you should be looking into the security of the building then."

The director raises a brow. "Oh, I will."

The cool tone settles something. My boss is unforgiving and brutal to everyone. He's right. This isn't personal.

If I keep coming to work with a target on my back, who's to say what else will be hit with collateral damage. Or who.

Emilia, Agnes, even the director. Anyone could be hurt from this.

"Okay," I whisper.

"Grace!" We both turn to Alasdair and the director stiffens.

"Mr. Bramblewick," the director says.

"Director Adder, isn't it?" Alasdair sounds… dangerous.

Exasperation crosses the director's face, and he takes a step away from me. Alasdair's shoulders relax and I can't help the snort that escapes me.

"You know each other?" I ask.

"Yes," Adder says. "I'm well aware of the Bramblewicks. Your mate is rather… determined."

I frown, thinking he's talking about me.

Alasdair huffs. "Elliot is that."

I blink. Did everyone know about the Bramblewicks but me?

Alasdair catches sight of my car and snarls.

"Alasdair," I whisper, looking around to make sure there aren't any unsuspecting humans around.

Alasdair pulls me into his arms, and I let him. The warmth seeping through me even through his human suit is comforting. "Oh, Grace. I'm so sorry."

"I'll leave you to it," Adder says. "Please keep me informed about the situation, Ms. Starling."

I sigh. "I will."

Alasdair frowns down at me.

"It looks like I'm taking a vacation," I say weakly.

CHAPTER 42
ᴃRODERICK

Alasdair sent out the text as a group message. Grace's car was targeted while she was at work. The slimeball hexed and defaced it in broad daylight. It's a bad sign. An escalation that has worry tightening the muscles in my back.

The only good part about this is that we'll get to spend more time with her. Until this is settled, I don't see how we're going to be able to let her out of our sights.

Elliot blows out a breath and loosens his tie. "My informant is on his way. He has news."

"That's good, isn't it?" Eloise asks from her spot on the couch.

We're all in the main living area, the room filled with comfy seats that we use for movie night, waiting for Alasdair and Grace to get home for a clan meeting.

Elliot shrugs. "It's something."

The sound of the front door opening has a sigh of relief escaping me.

"We're home," Alasdair calls out. The strong voice of our clan leader has the rest of the clan relaxing. We're all together. We'll figure this out.

They make it to the room and my heart breaks at the sight of Grace's pale face. Elliot gets to her first, pulling her into his arms. She buries her face in his chest and grips him in a hug so hard that her knuckles turn white.

The doorbell rings and Elliot pulls away.

"I'll get it. It's my informant."

Grace's face meets mine and then she's in my arms. I nuzzle her hair. Even after a week of sleeping next to the sweet witch, the wave of her scent and the feel of her in my arms is just as special as the first time.

"I'm not going anywhere, Broderick," she teases.

"Stop hogging her!" Eloise exclaims and steals away my mate.

The sting of having her stolen subsides when Grace's face lights up in happiness.

"Oh Grace, we were worried," Eloise says. Graham pulls both the women into a hug using his wings. I narrow my eyes and the older gargoyle winks at me as if he knows about the surge of jealousy at the action.

They release Grace, and Alasdair places his hands on her shoulders. A purr escapes my throat at the sight. Slowly but surely, our clan leader and sweet witch are finding their footing with one another. It's a comforting thing. I've never doubted that Grace would stay with us, but expecting it and experiencing the pieces falling into place is something entirely different.

"It looks like my timing is as impeccable as always." The room tenses at the unfamiliar speaker, a man with a nonchalant tone and relaxed stature. I can't identify what he is on sight. He just looks like any other man with dark hair and eyes.

"Mace Reynolds," he introduces himself to Alasdair, somehow sensing the hierarchy of the room.

Elliot is behind him. "Mace is a professional. The best at what he does. I've worked with him a time or two."

Alasdair nods. "Elliot says that you have information for us."

"Yes, regarding the situation with Theodore Bradshaw III–"

"We don't exactly have proof." Grace's voice is small as she interrupts Mace.

Mace just smiles at her. "That's where you're wrong. We have enough proof that this man is causing you trouble, just not enough proof for the Council to act. I've come into some interesting information about Charming Theo."

"What do you know?" I ask, needing this informant to get on with it.

Mace shrugs. "He needs money, and lots of it. He's up to his eyeballs in gambling debt."

"But why is he targeting me? I've been cut off from my parents' money," Grace says.

"Ah, yes. The wonderful Starlings." Mace's tone is flat. "I've been told by a person who would rather not be identified that your father and Theo have had meetings. Meetings about certain business mergers and merging of families."

Grace's eyes bug. "What does that mean?"

Mace makes a careless gesture with his hands, but his eyes are dark. "There may have been an implication that should you and Theo marry, his company merger would go through, as well as him gaining access to a substantial amount of funds."

"Why would they do that?" Grace asks.

Now Mace looks apologetic. "There may have been words about how the Starling daughter is having a rebellious phase and when that's done, they'd like to have the two witch families connected. I take it your parents don't know about your mates?"

Alasdair shifts. "She hasn't agreed to be our mate yet."

The skin around Mace's eyes crinkles with concern. "I'd advise figuring out that situation soon since mates have special protections by law."

"We will not rush Grace because of an underhanded witch who wants to intimidate her into marriage," Alasdair says, but Grace looks down.

If this could all be solved by us mating with Grace… would that be so bad?

Mace sighs. "I can respect that. And the Starlings are the sort that may not even consider it legitimate. Even soul bonds can be severed. Oh, your kind don't do those, do they?"

Graham speaks. "We don't. It's something that can be considered if necessary, but the risks of a soul bond usually outweigh what's gained."

Eloise puts a hand on Graham's shoulder.

Mace just shrugs it off. He doesn't need to know about the intricacies of gargoyle culture. Grace frowns, and I foresee a discussion in our future.

"Is there anything else you can tell us?" Elliot asks.

"The entities that Theo owes are dangerous. This guy could get desperate. I can work at figuring out a way to have them… decide to treat him as an example instead of paying them back. They might prefer that if it becomes clear that he isn't going to be able to get his hands on Starling money."

He makes the suggestion offhandedly. It's a casual way to bring up having a man killed, but with this guy threatening our mate…

Grace's face is sheet white. "I-I don't know. I'm going to call my parents. Maybe if they rescind whatever gross offers they've been making, then this guy won't be our problem anymore."

If that works, it'd be ideal.

But that would require this guy to have the mind to be logical, and I doubt he does.

Mace winces, as if he's thinking the same as me, but he nods. "I'll keep some tabs on it. This guy is bad news. Elliot told me about your car. I'm glad you have a safe place to go."

I puff my chest up at that.

We are Grace's safe place.

***

Grace excuses herself after Mace leaves to call her parents.

Alasdair pulls Elliot into a hug. It's comforting and affectionate and I itch to do the same.

"Don't even think about it," Alasdair says to our mate, and I bark a laugh at Elliot's narrowed eyes.

"I don't know what you mean," Elliot says.

Alasdair makes an annoyed sound in his throat. "There will be no hiring a hit man or doing any actions that are going to come back and haunt us. Grace has a say in how we handle this. Don't scheme your way around her."

I stifle my grin. Alasdair knows Elliot well. I may have followed the same line of thinking if I weren't obsessed with knowing how Grace is doing right now.

Elliot sighs. "Fine. I'm just worried."

"We handle this together, my heart," Alasdair says.

"We should remind Grace of that," I say. My hand itching to pull her in a similar hug.

Elliot winks at me. "No one is stopping you."

I roll my eyes but move toward the patio.

I find her there, staring off at the gardens, her phone clutched in her hand.

"It didn't go well?" I ask.

The pain in Grace's eyes has me pulling her into my arms, surrounding her with my wings. She sighs and a small amount of her tension eases away.

"Breathe, Gracie. We'll figure this out."

Her breath comes out on a shudder, and she turns in my arms, pressing her face to my chest.

I tangle my claws in her hair and massage her scalp.

"It didn't go well," she whispers, and I want to soar to wherever Grace's parents live and kick down their door. Force them to apologize to our sweet mate. But the instinct isn't a logical one. One forced apology won't take the pain from Grace's eyes.

She needs a distraction and I need to work out my frustration.

I kiss her head. "Come and spend time in my studio."

CHAPTER 43
GRACE

If this man is targeting you, it isn't anything we've done. Don't be so dramatic.

I don't know why you're making this such a big deal. You should count yourself lucky to catch the attention of someone like him.

Someone. Like. Him.

That last one had hit the nail into the coffin. The callousness of saying that after I'd detailed the crimes of this man against me, anger and sadness swirl in my chest in time to the shirring sounds of Broderick's carving.

The repetitive sounds and motions combined with the way the wood is shaping into something else is mesmerizing and helps. It distances me from the hurt, little by little. Somehow, this is exactly what I needed.

"Do you want to talk about it?" he asks, not looking away from his project.

I swallow. "My mother denied that they were involved, so we can't have them just call off the guy."

Has my mother ever cared about me?

Being around the accepting Bramblewicks softened me. I'd started to think that maybe I could be on better terms with my parents. Surrounded with love and affection, I'd thought that maybe I'd hardened myself too much to the people who raised me in an effort to gain my independence.

There will be no making amends with my blood relations.

Instead, I have a best friend and a new clan. If they claim me. I shake my head. I know they're going to claim me. All our relationships are progressing. Alasdair is the only one I haven't been intimate with yet, but with Broderick and Elliot it's like breathing air.

It's easy. Attraction to seduction.

Alasdair's proximity is a tease… I hope it won't be much longer before I can find out if he'll so effortlessly command the room in bed.

Broderick hums. "If it makes you feel better, I don't think it would make a difference if your parents did call it off. The type of offender we're looking at wouldn't stop. This is personal now."

Monster fucker.

The sick lurch of my stomach returns with a vengeance and snuffs out thoughts about intimacy. Something occurs to me, and the nausea grows.

"I'm not putting anyone at risk here, am I?" I ask.

Eloise's face flashes in my mind, but Broderick shakes his head.

"We have spells and wards aplenty on this space. Graham guards the residence and is a capable gargoyle. Our skin has some magic resistance and we're much stronger than witches. Nothing will happen to Eloise."

I sigh in relief. "Good, I'm glad."

I look around at his studio. His projects are spread about in different stages of progress. There are some larger boards he covered with a drop cloth when we'd come in. I've only been in here once before to get him for dinner. I'd almost gotten lost on the way.

"You know, I haven't seen the whole house yet." Though I suppose I'll be spending much more time here since I can't go to work.

"Do you want a tour?" Broderick's delighted question pulls a smile from me.

He continues, "I'd love to give you a tour."

"That sounds nice."

***

Bramblewick Manor is impressive, but what's more impressive is the amount of care and attention to detail that went into each and every project. I could spend hours going over every carved surface. It ranges from geometric patterns in the younger gargoyle's area to flowery vines in Eloise's and Graham's space. Some of the carvings depict visual stories of gargoyles and castles, with a few words carved here or there to identify them.

All the details are starting to make my head spin. Each room is beautifully crafted, even the ones that stand empty, to be filled with future clan members. The nursery space takes me by surprise, the purpose undeniable with the height and storybook design of the carvings in that room. Broderick had only shrugged, sheepish, and said children of some sort had always been desired here.

We get to a door carved with cascades of roses, but Broderick pulls me past it.

"What about that—"

"That's a room we haven't finished yet. We'll be done with it soon." He flashes me a quick smile.

I scrunch my brow to ask something else, but the sight of the spiral staircase stops me. "Where does that go to."

Broderick's face is soft. "That's the turret. It's special to the clan. It's where clan members rest."

I don't know what to say and Broderick seems to understand. He pulls me up the stairs to a door and once he opens it, I blink in wonder.

The turret is hexagonal, with an arcing roof and railings making up the "walls" that are open to the outside. I distantly remember seeing the towerlike structure when I'd first driven up. The evening wind whistles over the surrounding roof, and I shiver. There are planters and shrubs decorating the edges and a stone bench in the center of the space.

"We'll close off the space for the winter soon. We try and keep it open as long as we can. Fall was Lachlan's favorite season."

Broderick moves and I catch sight of a statue. It's the size and shape of a gargoyle with its wings clasped across its body so they drape like a cloak. The face of the statue shows an old gargoyle with craggy features carved in almost lifelike detail. Or not carved.

Rest.

It takes me a moment to understand what I'm seeing, but when I do, emotions war in me.

I drop my eyes to the engraved stone beneath the figure.

Lachlan Bramblewick

Clan Leader, Caring Mate, and Father

"It's… it's him?" I ask in a whisper.

Broderick's smile is sad. "That's him. If this were an old clan, the grounds would be full of our past clan members, and we'd care for each statue until it finally crumbled away to dust, returning to the earth."

"Elliot told me that you turn to stone when you die," I say, trying not to think of the morbid thought of crumbling statues that were once alive. I guess it's not so different than the idea that humans eventually decompose. It's probably not such a strange thing to the clan.

Broderick nods. "And when we're injured or worn out. It's a healing thing for us… until we don't wake up."

I bite my lips. "Was it a surprise?"

Broderick shakes his head and pulls me closer to the space. There are multiple pedestals and they make me wary, thinking of any of my males taking a place on them and becoming stone. Broderick sits on the bench and pulls me onto his lap.

"Lachlan knew his time was coming," Broderick says. "He was older than Graham and Eloise. He'd known that this rest would be his final one."

We sit in silence for a moment before Broderick clears his throat and begins to speak, but not to me.

"Hey, Lachlan, this is Grace. We're courting her to make her clan. If there are ever little ones that use you like a climbing gym, it's because she took pity on us and accepted."

"Broderick!" I whisper. The idea of children playing in a space that is starting to gain a measure of sacredness is shocking to me. The idea of them being *our* children… he must be trying to get a rise out of me.

But Broderick's face is a little serene, and I let his happiness chase away the strangeness of talking to their past clan leader's remains.

Broderick inhales. "It's our belief that the ones who are gone remain with us. Eloise and Graham spend a lot of time here, talking to Lachlan. They say it helps with how much they miss him… and I think they may be right."

I nod in understanding.

We fall into silence. It's comfortable and spreads a calm feeling through me. I look up at the face of Lachlan.

"It's good to meet you," I say. "You've made a great clan. You must be so proud."

Broderick's arms squeeze around me and I turn from Lachlan, embracing my gargoyle as he breathes through whatever emotions make him cling to me.

"Elliot says you want children," Broderick says.

"Elliot has a big mouth."

Broderick grins. "We all want kids, but I bring it up because when Mace brought up soul bonds, you looked unsure."

I bite my lip. "Witches don't always soul bond, I only have known a few. Probably because many of the witches I know are more interested in picking marriages for social climbing than love matches."

Broderick nods and tucks a strand of my hair behind my ear.

His eyes get that far-off look, considering. "Gargoyles don't usually soul bond because in the most stable family units there are multiple adults, and if one were to meet their final rest, it could take the rest with them. If that happens, the young are left undefended."

"Is that what happened to your parents?" I ask slowly. Elliot had said that Broderick had been orphaned.

"Yes. I only had two parents, and they were desperately in love. They were already untraditional because my mother was human. My father had to leave the local clan to be with her and when she died in a car accident, he went with her. His clan accepted his statue on their grounds and raised me until I was eighteen."

"I'm so sorry, Broderick."

He nods to accept my condolences.

"It may be possible in the future," he says. "I think Graham and Eloise have spoken about being soul bonded, but they don't want to leave the rest of the clan without the two of them if we need them."

I blow out a breath full of emotion.

"I don't need soul bonds. The logistics around it don't make sense," I say.

Something occurs to me and I frown.

"How do you make matings official then?" I ask.

Broderick smiles. "Vows at sunset and a big party. The 'official' part is more of a private affair, bites to mark some in the mating, but it's a little more painful when the partner isn't a gargoyle. Our saliva has healing qualities to set the scar."

"I don't hate the idea of a bite," I say, surprised. "I didn't notice any bites on you guys."

"Elliot has two bites. They signal to other gargoyles that he's taken."

"But you and Alasdair don't?"

Broderick blushes a little. "It's a signal of dominance too."

"That seems like a very personal thing to broadcast."

Oh gods. How many bite marks would I end up with?

My face must show my thoughts because Broderick bursts out laughing.

Count me as thoroughly distracted.

CHAPTER 44
GRACE

I turn the pages of Alasdair's old textbook and try not to sigh in frustration.

I'm in a terrible mood.

I've run errands with Elliot, baked cookies with Eloise, and made headway through my considerable reading list with Alasdair.

And I'm going stir crazy.

It's only been a couple of days so I'm trying not to be dramatic. I can practically hear Emilia's eyes roll through our text messages. I'm living with a bunch of wonderful men that want me to have their babies. Boo hoo. Which of course makes me laugh.

Emilia doesn't bring up the worry on both of our minds of my harassing "admirer."

She's good at making me laugh. And every time she takes my mind off things, I make a mental promise that I'll tell her everything when I can see her in person again.

Soon. Emilia deserves the truth.

We just need to figure out how to deal with Theo and his threats. There haven't been any more flowers or messages.

Elliot has Mace gathering what info he can on where Theo is. The Council has elevated the threat Theodore Bradshaw III poses to the paranormal community and they are looking to apprehend him. A public display of magic in the middle of the day.... Apparently, they don't need the amount of proof that they'd wanted for my apartment to nail him to the wall.

But the Council can't find him.

So I'm here, indefinitely, or at least it feels that way.

Not being able to do the job I love is wearing me down. It's the uncertainty about it all. Until we can figure out a way to settle the situation with Theo the stalker, there's no end in sight.

Maybe I need to go back to my apartment and spend some time in my workroom. That may help. Have something to keep my hands busy. I can only bake so much, even if Eloise is wonderful company.

I run a finger over the textbook page again, biting my lip at the swell of devotion and loyalty. Alasdair left such a strong signature on this book. The stress is there, but it's easy to brush away the stress to find the overwhelming reasons for it underneath.

"Grace." At Alasdair's voice I snap the book closed and put it on the side table, like that will make it less obvious that I'm sneaking impressions about him from it again. He doesn't comment on my getting caught but his lips may have twitched too fast for me to be sure.

"Yes?" I ask.

"We have something we want to show you."

"You and the mouse in your pocket?" I tease, trying to keep my humor even if my mood is foul.

Alasdair comes up next to where I'm seated on the couch, and I tilt my head back and swallow. The breadth of this gargoyle and his bearing are daunting.

"Don't look at me with eyes like that, little witch." His deep voice inspires thoughts of growly sex. "I'll forget what I came here for, and our afternoon will be very different."

"I think you're just teasing me. When does that get to happen, Alasdair?"

He tilts his head in question.

Frustration and eagerness make me brave. "Every night we read together, and every night you kiss my forehead and send me off with Broderick and Elliot and tell me to sleep well."

And almost every night I end up screaming in his sheets from pleasure. I don't say that out loud, but with the sexual tension in the air, it's as if I have.

Alasdair lifts a brow. "I won't be rushed, little witch."

"I'm going to start teasing you back if you keep stretching this out," I warn.

Alasdair smiles. "I'd like that."

I blink. Huh.

Alasdair puts his hand in front of me. "Now, will you come with me?"

I put my hand in his and let him pull me up, my body presses against his more than necessary and he flashes a good-natured fang. Did all I need was permission? Some block in my mind, determined to be patient and to get to know Alasdair first, melts.

This scary gargoyle wants me for more than just a clanmate. I had started to doubt.

We go up the stairs and my heartbeat begins to pick up. Are we going to a bedroom? But, no, we continue up to the next landing. I start to think that we're on our way to the turret, but Broderick and Elliot are in the hall, beaming. They stand in front of the room I haven't yet seen.

The one with the carved roses in it.

"What's this?" I ask.

"Close your eyes, Grace," Alasdair rumbles.

I follow the command without hesitation and his laugh sparks heat in my blood.

Alasdair takes my hand and leads me forward. Broderick takes my other hand. His calluses are rougher than the others. That leaves Elliot, the grip on my waist from behind. Figures.

I laugh. "You guys are going to make me trip."

"Almost there," Broderick says and drops my hand. "Alright, open your eyes."

I open my eyes and blink and keep blinking as soon as my mind makes sense of what I'm seeing. I cover my mouth.

They'll end up building something for you. I'd completely forgotten Eloise's warning, but I would have never expected *this*.

The room itself is on the cozy side, with a vaulted ceiling. The windows along one wall are tall and arch, illuminating the space. The additions to the room are what take my breath away.

Shelves.

Shelves upon shelves custom built for the space in a beautiful warm wood with a number of display cases like I use in my workroom in my apartment. Each surface is decoratively carved like the rest of the manor.

Most of the shelves are empty save for one that has books lining it that I picked out with Alasdair. A few other books are unfamiliar.

The center of the room has a sitting area facing a contained woodless fireplace for reading. And there's a work desk in the corner of the room with the best light.

"We thought you would like your own workspace," Elliot says, his voice tight with anxiety. "From all of us. I picked the furniture, Broderick made the shelves of course, and Alasdair got some books to add to your collection. We wanted to make sure we had enough room for the collection you already have."

Alasdair grips the back of Elliot's neck. "Relax, my heart. Give her a minute to absorb it."

"This is—" I don't know what to say. My heart is too big for my chest, each beat lodging more and more emotions into my throat. "It's wonderful."

"Do you like it?" Broderick asks.

"I love it," I breathe, stunned. "But you guys shouldn't have—"

Alasdair makes a sound that cuts me off. "Grace Starling, we are courting you. We wanted to give you a place here of your own. We want to prove that we can make you happy. You're ours to spoil. If you let us."

I look into the faces of the gargoyles surrounding me, and tears fill my eyes.

"It's the most perfect thing that anyone has ever done for me," I croak.

It's more than the stuff. The stuff is lovely and thoughtful. The colors of the decor echo my own choices in my apartment. It's that they carved out a space for me in their home, their lives. And for a talent that has been scorned by other witches as being the wrong kind of magic. This is acceptance. This is family.

I sniff.

"Don't cry, sweet witch." Broderick pulls me into his arms, and I let him, wrapping my arms around him for a hug.

"I'm trying not to," I say. "I don't even know how you guys pulled off something like this while I've been here."

But I do. All those times one gargoyle would take me out. The closing up of the turret for winter that had been *hours* of construction sounds.

Elliot snorts. "It wasn't easy. We were going to save this for a little later in our courting, but we thought it might cheer you up."

My breath shudders out and Broderick holds me tighter before handing me over to Elliot.

I press my face into his neck. "You've accomplished that. It's—thank you."

Elliot kisses my forehead and passes me over to Alasdair, who pulls me into his arms. I'm shy at the press of his body, but my affection for all of them overflows past whatever awkwardness rises.

Alasdair's chest puffs up in pride. "Come and see the books I picked out for you."

And for the rest of the afternoon, I don't spare a single thought for the job I can't go to or to the stalker that won't leave me alone.

All my heart and mind are filled with are pages, a cozy fire, and the males that inspire the deepest sort of good ache in my soul.

CHAPTER 45
GRACE

"There you are! I don't know why I didn't just start here," Elliot exclaims.

I look up from my e-reader, snuggled in the corner of my favorite sofa that Elliot had picked out for my workroom. Something about having my own space in the house settles my spiral of anxiety. Now that I have a place to let my magic go and work, the manor feels more like home. I even let the guys convince me to start moving stuff from my apartment workroom here.

"Hello, you," I say with a smile. Elliot has been making an effort to leave his glamour off while he's at home. It's a slow process, but he seems happier without it. The tension he carried in his shoulders is absent now and I don't see him wince in discomfort nearly as much.

"You look like a treat," he says.

I snort. I'm in a pretty swing dress that is a favorite because of how comfortable it is with barely any makeup. I'm trying to embrace this vacation as a moment to relax. I don't know why Elliot is watching me like I'm the tastiest morsel he's ever seen.

"Can I join you?" he asks.

"It's your house," I say, gesturing to the sofa.

Elliot narrows his eyes. "Yes, but I thought we made it clear that this is your space. I don't want to intrude."

I hum, secretly pleased for the delineation.

Elliot sits on the sofa, sprawling in the way that I've come to be familiar with gargoyles. The seat is large to accommodate tails and wings, but the posture when seated is a shared trait.

"What are you reading?" he asks.

My lips twitch. "Do you really want to know?"

Elliot is not an avid reader like Alasdair, and I've caught him glazing over a time or two when I'd describe something about a book. It doesn't bother me, my book conversations with Alasdair make up for Elliot's need to be doing something active every moment of the day.

Elliot's smile is sly. "That depends if it's sexy or not."

I laugh. "This one could get sexy, but it's going to be a slow burn."

"Pah! That hardly works to get you hot and bothered for me."

I poke his side with my toe. "You, sir, are obsessed."

Elliot's smile widens. "Oh, I'm not the one you should be calling sir."

Just like that, my blush rages. He's talking about Alasdair. The gargoyle that exudes command and dominance. It's no secret that bed play with him will be of a different sort than with Elliot and Broderick. They are more playful with games of dominance and submission than Alasdair is.

They tease me with my delight in submitting. It's more of a give and take. With Alasdair it will be… somehow more.

But that hasn't happened.

I glance at the fireplace. "I don't know if I'll get to call anyone sir. I've tried seducing—"

"Oh, my star, you are adorable. Lingering glances and extended touches during those reading sessions of yours are not seduction attempts."

I narrow my eyes in annoyance.

Elliot raises his hands. "It's not your fault! You're so polite when it comes to facing Alasdair. Your submission is so absolute that you won't push him to act. You're not a brat."

My annoyance flees and I poke him again. "Like you."

"Like me," he says, beaming and wrapping a hand around my ankle. "I do know how to get things done."

The touch melts me. My body is so familiar with this gargoyle, he only needs to give me the lingering glance he teased me about and I soften and heat all at once. Elliot starts to massage my bare foot.

"Did you come find me for that? To get me all hot and bothered?" I ask, playful even as my body starts to respond.

"What? Oh, no. I was actually wondering if we should make a date for a session at the bathhouse?" Elliot asks.

"Oh!" Our arrangement with the Love Bathhouse slipped my mind.

"I figured you'd like to get out of the house… and our match is a successful one…" he trails off, almost as if he's waiting for me to correct him.

We were successfully matched, and then some. Even with the deception and all the craziness that happened after, our match has grown into a relationship.

A love match.

A mating.

I inhale and try to avoid the feelings surfacing. We're still courting, and no one has brought up mating other than in bed, which doesn't count.

But.

They gave me a library. Consider me seduced.

I nod. "Yes. I should have thought of that, but with everything else happening, I forgot."

Elliot digs his thumb into the arch of my foot and a small moan escapes my mouth.

His gaze raises to meet mine. "I think, and say no if you hate the idea, that we should all go together."

"Together?"

"You" —he tweaks my toe— "me, Broderick, and Alasdair. We should go as we intend to continue."

I bite my lip. "But Alasdair and I—"

"If he wants to take more time with you, he can sit this one out," Elliot says, unconcerned.

I press my thighs together at the thought of it. The light catches the smooth bite mark on the crook of Elliot's neck. Someday, I'm going to bear the marks of being mated too.

"Okay," I breathe.

"Okay?" He smiles like I've given him the biggest prize and pulls me closer to him by the ankle. The movement has my body sliding down the sofa and my skirt bunches up, exposing more of my legs.

I giggle and put my e-reader aside. "You're insatiable."

"And you're just so pretty. Who could blame me for wanting to put a little color in your cheeks?"

Elliot climbs over me and steals a kiss. He knows my body now, my tastes. He knows if he starts soft and playful, he can get me writhing and begging within a few breaths. Soon enough, his body presses against mine and he massages my breast with a hand until my hips rock into his.

Elliot makes a pleased sound and I know my arousal must be perfuming the air. I'm so wet between my legs. The flush of my skin tingles all over my body and tightens my nipples.

"Elliot," I beg, shifting my hips against his.

He smiles at me. "Grace."

Elliot slides a hand up my thigh and reaches the hem of my panties. "I miss the thigh highs."

Delight curls in my lower belly. "I'll have to wear them sometime."

Elliot drops a kiss to my chest, licking the skin as a tease.

"Show me your tits, my star."

I swallow but unbutton the dress front. Displaying the lace of one of my nicest bras. Elliot makes a low sound in his throat, a precursor to a growl.

His hand below tugs my panties down and I let him slide them from me, the fabric wet and leaving a streak of moisture on my inner thigh.

Elliot grins and slides the panties in the pocket of his kilt.

"I need those back," I say.

"You'll get them back. Trust me."

I narrow my eyes at Elliot but he's already reaching for my bra with his claw-tipped fingers.

I hold up a hand to stop him. "No you don't! This is one of my favorites. There will be no tearing or poking holes in it in any shape or form."

Elliot snickers. "I can be gentle."

"Tell that to my last pair of underwear," I say. The panties had been an old, cheap pair but the experience of having them ripped off had been half thrilling and half enraging until I'd remembered what pair it was. We'd all had a very detailed discussion on the destruction of clothing.

"Then take it off," he says, dragging one of his claws over my collarbone.

And I do. I wrestle my arms out of the dress sleeves and unclasp the bra before throwing it to a nearby chair. Elliot descends on my bared breasts with hunger, and I sink my fingers in his white hair.

Oh gods. The mouths and tongues on these gargoyles are intense. Elliot draws on my nipple and my core clenches around nothing. Syrupy heat flows through me like sticky honey.

A scrape of teeth and I arch into his mouth on a cry, my thighs squeezing around his torso. Elliot's hands snake under me and then he's picking me up from the sofa and settling me astride him.

My arms wrap around his neck at the change in orientation, but Elliot doesn't stop sucking on my skin and laving my nipples. My skirts get pushed higher and my bare pussy touches the skin of his corrugated core.

I lean back, releasing my grip on his neck. My hands fall to where our bodies near each other and I fiddle with the kilt garment until it opens and Elliot's cock surges in my hand, already weeping precum.

"Need you," I say and grind his length against my wet core.

"Then have me," Elliot growls out.

He slides in easy with how wet I am. The frequent number of times I've had either he or Broderick inside me and the salve helps me anticipate the fun kind of stretch from the too much kind of stretch. And Elliot's cock gliding inside me is a fun kind of stretch.

"Look how easy you take me," Elliot marvels.

I lift and drop myself a couple of times, pressing his knot against my opening each time I take him all the way in. I lose myself in the motion.

I ride Elliot, our moans in time with each other. The throb of his body inside mine makes my breath catch. The curls of climax start to stir in my belly.

"Oh, hello, Alasdair," Elliot says.

I squeak but Elliot squeezes my hips and thrusts in deeper to keep me from moving. I'm very exposed like this. My breasts are bare, with my dress around my waist and with the skirts bunched up, showing a good portion of my legs and ass cheeks.

The fact that Elliot is buried deep inside me could be missed from a distance.

Alasdair is in the library doorway, hand raised as if to knock on the doorjamb, eyes dark with the tantalizing lust I've caught sight of a few times before.

A seductive growl from the large gargoyle has my hips rolling to move Elliot's cock in and out without thought.

Alasdair inhales and takes a step back. "My mistake, I thought I was supposed to meet you here. I'll leave you two to your privacy."

"Don't go!" I say without meaning to.

Everyone freezes.

Supposed to meet you here.

I glare at Elliot. "You're scheming again."

"Sometimes you need a brat." Elliot shrugs but his cock kicks inside me and I gasp.

I turn my gaze back to Alasdair.

"I mean, you can stay, if you want…"

Alasdair's dark eyes make me want to shift away from his perception.

I swallow. "I-I'd like it if you stayed."

Alasdair surprises me by coming into the room and sitting on one of the large chairs turned to face the sofa. My cheeks burn with how we must look from that vantage point. How he must be able to see Elliot's cock sinking inside me.

"Do you want me to only watch, little witch?" Alasdair asks.

"… No," I whisper. "I want… I want to be with you too."

The room stills and the tension has my toes curling and Elliot moans as I squeeze around him.

"Elliot, show her to me."

I gasp at the tone in Alasdair's voice. It's one that brooks no arguments.

Elliot buries his face in my breasts, kissing them before sighing. "You're going to come so hard, my star. I can hardly wait."

I cry out as he pulls me off his cock and picks up a leg, turning me to face outward while still straddling him.

Alasdair is reclined in the chair, his eyes dark and scanning me.

"Remove the dress."

Elliot pulls up the dress and I clutch it to my barely covered front, nerves making me act out of reflex. Broderick and Elliot both love my body, will Alasdair?

The large gargoyle raises a brow. "I want to see all of you, little witch. Will you let me?"

I let my arms fall and drop my gaze, unable to keep eye contact as Elliot pulls the dress over my head. I'm completely bare. My pale breasts rise in my line of vision, the skin starting to redden with a blush.

Why isn't he saying anything?

Elliot's thighs are between my legs and his hands run over my hips in reassurance, but I start to shake.

My throat swells and I try to stuff the feelings of inadequacy down, but the pain is sharp. My blush isn't from arousal anymore and my eyes burn.

A shadow falls over my skin and Alasdair kneels in front of me.

"So beautiful," Alasdair says.

I gasp and it sounds like a sob.

Alasdair's brows crease. "What's wrong, Grace?"

I shake my head. "I-I thought—"

I can't continue though, the possibility that he'd decide against courting me after seeing *me* is too ugly to voice. Alasdair's eyes darken and somehow he knows what thoughts hold my body and emotions in a vise.

"Never, Grace. You're a feast for the eyes, I was only trying to compose myself. Seeing Elliot hold you like this is wrecking my self-control."

"Then don't control yourself," I whisper.

Alasdair smiles. "That isn't how this works. If you haven't noticed, I like to be in control. It fulfills something in my soul. It was poorly handled by me, letting you have a moment for doubt. I've just never been…"

Elliot's hands rise to cup my breasts and I jump at the contact. He kisses the back of my neck. "He's never been with a woman, star. You've blown our clan leader's mind."

"What? Never?" I ask.

Alasdair smiles. "I'm not casual in my intimacy. Your beauty makes my heart hurt, little witch. I want to do all sorts of things to you, have Elliot show me exactly how to bring you pleasure."

My breath catches as that statement sinks in.

"I'd like that," I say, and Elliot starts to pinch and pull on my nipples.

Alasdair's eyes fall to the action. "If you need to stop for any reason, just say so. Do you trust me?"

I nod.

"Is there anything you don't want? Any limits? I like inflicting a little humiliation, is there anything you don't want to be a part of this?" Alasdair asks.

Maybe before the naked pause I'd have answered differently, but now...

"I don't want you to say anything mean about my body. I still have a lot of bad feelings hanging around from the way I grew up." The confession is painful, but it's as if by bringing it to life, the burden of it lessens.

I duck my chin and Alasdair touches my face. It's the briefest of strokes, but my gaze snaps back to his. He looks angry on my behalf.

"You are gorgeous, Grace. Every day you take my breath away and now that I know what you look like out of clothing, I don't know how I'm going to keep from stripping you on sight."

My lips twitch. "That would make for a very cold winter."

Alasdair's eyes soften. "We'd keep you warm."

Elliot makes a sound in his throat.

"Is someone needy?" Alasdair asks.

"Yes." Elliot and I say in unison.

Alasdair raises a brow at Elliot. "I don't know if you deserve release, scheming like you have."

Elliot's hips shift under me. "*Fuck*."

I squeeze my thighs against Elliot's spread legs. "Alasdair…"

His gaze snaps back to me. "Let me explore you a moment. Elliot was just about to show me what you like."

Elliot does just that, continuing to pinch my nipples. "She likes these sucked."

I arch into his grip. When Alasdair leans in, Elliot moves his hands and Alasdair carefully strokes the skin of my breasts.

"So soft," he says before tweaking one.

"H-harder, please?" I breathe.

Alasdair's lips twitch and he applies more pressure. My eyelashes flutter closed as my hips rock up instinctually. Elliot's grip on me keeping my body balanced.

I cry out when Alasdair's hot mouth covers one breast.

"Fuck, you taste good," he says, his tongue stroking over my tender flesh.

He pulls away, his eyes glinting. "I've been remiss, little witch."

"What?" My wet nipple tightens in the cold air.

Alasdair's face approaches mine. "I haven't kissed you yet."

My lips part and he's there. The press of his mouth has me moaning. His tongue makes a teasing presence against mine and his taste floods my senses. He keeps kissing me, learning my every reaction to his nips and sucks.

My hips move on top of Elliot and somehow I hear his panting over the blood rushing in my ears as my ass grinds against his knot.

Alasdair breaks the kiss, leaning back. "Delicious."

"The taste of her cunt is heavenly," Elliot says. His head rolling against my shoulder.

I whimper. "I need…"

"Shh, Grace, we'll take care of what you need," Alasdair says. The dark lust that I've seen peeking out behind his caring eyes glimmers now. His hands grip my spread thighs and the squeeze of them has my eyes rolling.

"May I taste you, Grace?" Alasdair asks.

"Please."

"I like it when you beg."

Elliot makes a soft sound that heightens my anticipation. "He's going to be the end of both of us."

Elliot leans my body back and my thighs start to twinge in annoyance but the discomfort disappears when Alasdair's gaze lands on my wet pussy. Something feral surfaces for a moment before being tucked away under his calm mask.

Alasdair strokes the pad of his thumb up through my folds. I gasp as he hits my clit. He tilts his head and circles his thumb around it, making me squirm.

"Do you like this?" he asks.

I bite my lip, hesitant, but answer. "A little higher and bigger circles."

"I see," he says.

And he does because he softly strokes me until small needy sounds fall from my lips like the first snow, slow before forming a begging avalanche of pleas.

Alasdair's head dips and I cry out. His tongue strokes through my pussy. The growl that sounds in his chest is so deep and loud I can feel it throughout my whole body, as if I'm going to combust.

I come.

I shout to the gods and gush. The climax is a rush of a surprise, my body rebelling from being held in a high state of arousal for too long. The crash of pleasure is quick and subsides with my gasps.

My lips tremble and my eyes are wide on Alasdair.

"I-I'm sorry," I say.

Elliot shakes under me in a laugh.

Alasdair licks through my folds and I shiver. The action feeling good even with the sensitivity.

His smile is warm and devious. "Do you want to keep going?"

Keep going? My confusion must show on my face.

Alasdair's hand smooths up my thigh.

"Will you let me command you here, little witch? Accept my cock inside your cunt? Let us fuck you and give you the pleasure you deserve?"

Elliot sits us up again, lifting me higher, his hard cock pressing against my core again.

"Yes." My answer is quick and breathy.

"Yes…" He trails off as if needing me to answer this question, to pick a title for him.

I swallow. "Yes, alpha."

I don't know where the honorific comes from but as soon as I say it, it's obvious.

"Good girl." It comes out on a growl. "Now, fuck yourself on Elliot."

I make a sound that has me blushing, but I drop my hips and follow the order. Elliot and I moan as his cock slides in, my body welcoming it like it was meant to be there. The drag of Elliot inside me is almost too much now with Alasdair as witness.

I clench around Elliot. The wet sounds of us coming together make it even hotter.

All while Alasdair watches. His gaze hot on the place Elliot's body is forging into mine.

"Alasdair," Elliot whispers into my hair. "She feels so good. Can I come?"

Alasdair raises a brow. "Will you obey me even if I say no?"

Elliot curses. "You two were taking forever to do this on your own. You needed a little push."

Alasdair stands, undoing the kilt slung around his hips.

Oh, all gods above and below. Alasdair's cock is proportional to his size. The pattern of his skin darker here and ruddy, the head of him already wet with arousal and the bulge of his knot is intimidating. I must make a sound of alarm.

Alasdair lifts my chin to make eye contact. "Don't worry, little witch. We'll start slow."

My cheeks burn. "I don't know if that's going to matter," I mutter.

A dark lust glints in his eyes and his smile has my heart beating even faster. "You'll take it. I've seen that pretty pussy and know it can stretch."

Merciless heat spikes at his words.

Alasdair flicks his gaze over my shoulder to Elliot. "No, you can't come."

Elliot's grip tightens on my hips, trying to slow my motions.

"Noo," I whine, needing his body moving into mine.

Elliot whispers a string of curses. "Gods, Alasdair, please. If you let me come, I'll tell you something that will drive her crazy."

Alasdair tilts his head at that. His hand stroking down his considerable length. My hands itch to touch him. I don't know what Elliot is going to tell him, but it'll be true. He and Broderick have excavated things about me that had been revelations. Alasdair releases himself and his cock swings in front of me.

"Go ahead, little witch," Alasdair says to me. My hand comes around his girth and I let myself explore him. He's not much different from the others except in size. Maybe I can take him.

The thick cock is hard under my grip, and I stroke up the skin. The heat of him, the throb of it, has me tightening on the gargoyle filling my pussy. Elliot's hips buck into me, the press of his knot has me gasping.

Alasdair's cock jerks in my grip and more precum beads on the tip, but the large gargoyle remains unfazed. As if we're just sitting down to dinner. Something rebellious in my soul wants him to react. My mouth waters and I wet my lips. I lick the head of his cock, moaning and sucking the crown of him into my mouth when his heavy hand rest on my head.

Alasdair makes a low sound. "That's it, such a good girl. Take more of it."

I moan and more of his cock slides between my lips, my tongue licking the underside of him. The big gargoyle sucks in a breath.

Elliot moans, watching my actions.

"What were you saying, my heart?" Alasdair asks Elliot, sounding casual but there's a roughness to his words.

I try and fit more of Alasdair into my mouth as Elliot's cock continues to hit just the right angle inside me. Pleasure and pride making me bold.

Elliot's voice is tight, desperate. "She wants to be bred by us."

I gag.

I pull Alasdair's cock from my mouth, coughing in surprise. *That devious—*

"Is that true, little witch?" Alasdair asks and the tension in the room ramps up.

I wipe the saliva from my chin, compromised in almost every way. Alasdair fists my hair and tilts my head up to look at him.

"Do you want us to breed you?" he asks again.

My body tightens impossibly at the question in his low, rumbly voice, and Elliot curses viciously.

"Fuck, Alasdair, please. I need to come," he begs.

Alasdair ignores his mate's pleas, perhaps using that to punish him for his trickery, and focuses on me. Waiting.

My throat seizes. I can't say the words. I nod as much as the grip in my hair will allow.

Precum drips from Alasdair's cock and the dark look of satisfaction on his face makes me think this is an interest he's amenable to filling. He kneels in front of me, his hand sliding between where Elliot's and my body meet. The press of his knuckles against my pussy has me grinding down harder on his fist with a needy moan.

Elliot shouts as Alasdair squeezes his knot and I gasp at the hot gush of his release inside me.

"That's it, my heart. Fill her up with your release. It will make it easier for her to take me."

I make a sound at that, and Alasdair's intense blue eyes capture my own.

"Someday, little witch, you're going to take off the pretty necklace that stops you from getting pregnant and we're going to take turns filling this tiny pussy with seed until it takes. Can you imagine it? Overflowing with our cum and taking our knots until your belly rounds with our young."

I moan, overwhelmed at the visual and the sensation of smearing our combined fluids against Alasdair's fist. Elliot lifts my hips until his cock slides from me.

Elliot pants in my ear. "So good, Grace. You slay me."

Elliot wraps an arm around my middle and leans me back against him, unbending my legs until my feet are flat against the sofa cushion. My knees fall open like a present for the kneeling gargoyle before us, my body unbearably empty.

Alasdair moans. "Such a pretty pussy, leaking seed and ready to take me."

I gasp as Elliot grips the back of my knees and pulls back, exposing me. Alasdair's hand slides through my messy folds. The sound as obscene as I'm sure the view is. He pulls his large hand away and slicks Elliot's and my arousal down his shaft. It shines wetly on his long cock and I clench on nothing.

"Oh gods," I whisper as if to pray to whatever god hands out impossible tasks of fitting something so large into something much smaller. "Alasdair—"

He places the hot head of him against my pussy.

"Shh, little witch, you'll take my cock. It'll fill you and make you feel good. Do you want that?"

"Yes," I say, because I do. I want to feel the heat of him inside me even if my brain rebels at the logistics. Alasdair presses against me. It's a slow build of pressure and I circle my hips with a whimper.

The pressure increases and I pant, trying to relax. I bite my lip. It has to fit.

"Grace."

My attention snaps to Alasdair's tense face. I want to give. I want him to fill my body, to belong to him.

"Take me." Alasdair's voice is dark with the command and the head of his cock slides tightly inside of me.

"Oh gods!" I make a sharp sound with my words, but already, my body softens to take him even as my knuckles go white where I dig my short nails into his shoulders..

Alasdair's wings stretch and his grip on Elliot's thigh has the gargoyle holding me up for his mate, grunting.

Alasdair's groan reverberates down to my core. "So tight."

He clenches his jaw like all he wants to do is bury himself deeper inside me.

"Doesn't her pussy feel like magic?" Elliot asks. "Small pulses so she can get used to you."

I moan as Alasdair does as Elliot instructs. My toes curl. I'm the first woman Alasdair has ever done this with and I'm already losing my mind. Each touch spirals me closer and closer to the edge. Each dark look from him has shivers traveling through my body until the need is overwhelming.

What will it be like when he knows all my body's secrets?

"How is that, little witch?" he asks, as if he can't read the state of my soul from the clench of my flesh around his.

I bite my lip before making myself speak. "Hurts a little bit—"

Alasdair freezes.

"—but feels so good."

Alasdair makes a pleased sound and gives me more of his cock. I grunt and moan at the slide. His hand rests on my mons and lower belly as his thumb starts to stroke my clit in slow circles.

The stretch is immense, the sensation of my body cradling and accommodating his feels like an instinctual want. A primal need.

I need him moving deep inside me, rutting.

"Alasdair." I squirm.

Elliot's chuckle is dark. "Look at her getting all needy for you."

Alasdair's smile is more fangs than anything else. "What do you need, Grace?"

"More," I say.

Alasdair presses even deeper. The slide of his thickness into my body has me making pathetic sounds and begging until the swell of his knot presses against my pussy lips. The contact of that has my hands digging into his hair. Too overwhelmed to be shy about pulling.

I moan and gasp as he begins to thrust inside me, tilting my body this way and that until my sounds get louder. The tunneling of him inside me as he learns each way to make me dissolve pushes me higher and higher until I don't recognize the sounds I make.

Alasdair's forehead presses to mine. "That's it. Be a good girl and come all over my cock, little witch. I know you can."

I struggle in Elliot's grip. "I-I can't."

My body is strung too tight as it is.

Elliot releases my legs and starts to caress my breasts, tweaking my nipples. I gasp and squeeze around Alasdair, who grunts.

"Fuck, if you squeeze my knot like that, you'll throw me into rut."

His knot.

"I want it. I want your knot," I beg.

The snarl from Alasdair is feral, and he stops his thrusts to press his wide knot against me, all while circling my clit in a steady motion. The beginning of the bulge starts to stretch me and it's all too much.

I climax on a scream. Stars and colors blink behind my eyes and the gush of heat inside me has me crying out in unison with Alasdair's own shout. His fist presses against my opening, squeezing his own knot.

My head turns and someone kisses me hungrily.

"Fuck, Grace, you're so perfect," Elliot says as he drops more kisses to my lips, then my cheeks.

I turn my head toward Alasdair, whose chest is rising and falling with each breath. I can't quite identify the look on his face before it's chased away by a warm look as he begins massaging the muscles of my hips.

A small flame of pride lights in my heart at the sight of the fearsome gargoyle lax with release.

I look down and groan at the sight of my pussy stretched around his thickness. Excess cum oozing from me onto his knot. My cheeks heat and my brain starts to sluggishly catch up to how exposed I am. How filthy.

And how I failed.

"I didn't take your knot," I say without meaning to. My emotions riot, swinging from the pride and satisfaction to disappointment and embarrassment.

Alasdair makes a growly sound and lifts me from Elliot's hold before sitting on the couch with me on his lap. His cock starts to soften and as it does, more seed spills down his knot.

Elliot staggers up. "I'll get a rag."

Alasdair rubs my back. We're alone now and my inhale wavers.

"Grace," he says. "We don't need to rush. I want to take my time with you. If I wanted to knot you, I'd have done things differently. You are so small. I don't want to hurt you."

"Do you think I'll be able to take it?" I ask.

Alasdair's eyes soften. "Yes, it will happen when it happens."

The large gargoyle looks away in thought.

"What is it?"

"Knotting can influence your emotions on an instinctual level. It's not as big of an influence with Broderick or Elliot, but I'm clan leader…" he hesitates.

"I already like you, Alasdair."

His smile hides some underlying emotions that I can't parse, and I don't get any more opportunity to. I moan as he slides his cock from me and the aftermath of our joining drips on to him.

I blink, feeling emotionally drained and sleepy.

Alasdair pulls me into his arms, arranging my legs so I'm sitting on his lap instead of straddling him. His strong hands massage my muscles before they begin to tense up.

"Rest, Grace. Elliot will come and clean us both up."

As if he's given me a command, my eyes fall shut and I bask in the warmth of his large body against mine.

CHAPTER 46

ALASDAIR

I hold Grace's naked body curled on my lap; a fluffy blanket draped over us. She'd started to doze right after Elliot cleaned her up with a wink, as if he'd done good work with his trickery, seducing Grace and I into falling into bed together. I can't regret having Grace's body accept my own, but my heart aches.

I didn't want to seduce her. Grace reacts to my presence favorably; I knew we'd be compatible in bed. I wanted to have Grace love me first. I wanted to be the one that she shared slow kisses with as she comes down from climax.

Because I love her.

I love Grace Starling.

Every quiet evening together, every teasing smile, wrapped a ribbon around my heart, utterly tying me to this witch. The feeling is as fierce as my love for Elliot, but more fraught.

What if she never feels the same? My throat constricts.

What if I ruin this? Every time I've opened my mouth to talk about my feelings, I've messed it up. Broderick or Elliot can usually save me, but I want to connect with Grace through communication rather than sex.

Instead, I have a stack of letters no one will read and a track record of being a poor clan leader. What would Lachlan say if he knew how I've taken up the position he left vacant? I can't even verbalize my feelings to the witch in my arms or notice when Elliot began dating her in the first place.

I don't want to inadvertently influence her with my dominance or knot. With Elliot, I'm sure he'll push back when he's uncomfortable. But Grace submits so beautifully, in a different way than Elliot.

Grace stirs in my arms and blinks up at me. I'm struck again by how pretty she is. The light makes her hair and skin glow and the blush on her cheeks reminds me of her pink pussy enveloping me as if I belonged there.

Utter perfection.

"Hello," Grace says, tilting her chin down as if she's shy.

I scratch the ends of my talons softly over her scalp and she moans.

My heart swells in my chest and I pull away in indecision.

"Do you want to read something together before dinner?" she asks, the huskiness of her words should soothe the anxiety in my chest, but it doesn't. Every moment longer that we spend together is just another moment for me to misstep.

I should tell her I love her, but what if that makes her uncomfortable? What if it ruins the bonds she's building with Elliot and Broderick?

I need space. I need to think. Emotions threaten to overwhelm me.

I lift Grace from me and place her on the sofa, grabbing my kilt and wrapping it around me. "Actually, I need to head back into the office."

"Oh?" Grace's tone sounds off.

I glance at her, unable to help myself. Her hair cascades in soft, sexy waves. The blanket wrapped around her may cover her nakedness, but her face is all vulnerable hurt.

I've hurt her feelings. Despite my best intentions.

I need to go before I blunder anything else.

"I'm glad you're here, Grace." *You're everything Elliot predicted and more. You soothe my soul and bring out all my protective instincts.*

I love you.

But the words won't come.

"I-I'm glad to be here." Her brow furrows in confusion.

I squeeze my hand into a fist and keep from reaching out for her.

My heart lodges in my throat and I flee.

CHAPTER 47
GRACE

I've stolen Alasdair's textbook out of the family library and moved it to mine. It sits on my desk, staring at me as accusingly as an object can. The compulsion to feel the swell of loyalty and love left on its pages from him has moved from hopeful and addicting to painful.

It's been two days since the liaison in this workroom. Two days since Elliot spread me open for Alasdair to take. The ache from his cock left an imprint on my soul. I'd been tempted not to use the healing salve just to keep that little bit of him longer.

Because I haven't seen him since that night.

I'd gone from having his company in the form of lingering looks and secret smiles to not at all once he'd gotten a taste of me.

The others try to say it's something to do with their business, and maybe it is, but… it's starting to feel like he's avoiding me.

And it hurts.

I've sent a few text messages. Messages that he responds promptly to. Short answers that don't prolong the conversation.

I don't have my job to take my mind off whatever is going on with the Bramblewick clan leader and my fingers itch to pick up what I can from him from the textbook like a stalker. But each time I let myself bask in those emotions, reminds me that they aren't emotions he feels for me.

If he doesn't want me, I'll need to get over that.

And if he doesn't want me for a mate, can I stay here? I don't know.

I may not have been here long, but it already feels like home. I love my gargoyles. It's a confession that I've only told the shadows of my mind. My heart is so invested in being a part of this family that the mere suggestion of Alasdair getting sick of me is like a poisonous weed.

"Hey, sweet witch, we were starting to miss you." Broderick's voice startles me. "Did you get sucked into a project?"

Broderick and Elliot saunter into my workroom as if they've come to rescue me from my spiral of doubt.

I swallow and slide the textbook in a drawer. "Not really."

"You seem sad," Broderick purrs.

I shrug. "I've been thinking... and I think that I should go back to work."

"But Bradshaw—" Elliot starts.

"We haven't heard anything from him since he vandalized my car." I say. "Maybe he's given up. Mace said the Council hasn't been able to find him, so it's a real possibility that he's gone into hiding from the people he owes and the Council."

They don't respond, but my arguments are valid.

"We wanted to have a more definitive solution, but we might not get that. I can't just stay here under watch and guard forever."

Elliot smiles, teasing. "I wouldn't mind keeping you here forever."

I narrow my eyes at him. "You know what I mean. I have a career and I'm not going to give that up just because an entitled asshole owes money."

Broderick nods and pulls me into his arms. "I understand. We just worry about you."

His gaze is filled with warmth and affection. "We care about you and want you in our lives however much you want to be here. We love you, Grace."

The plain statement steals the air from my lungs and a tidal wave of relief washes away the anxiety I hadn't noticed behind my emotions.

"I love you," I say, and Broderick's shoulders drop in relief. I turn to Elliot, who is trying to slide up next to us, no doubt to steal me away from Broderick's hold. "And I love you."

Elliot's face breaks into a grin and he pulls me from Broderick's arms with a twirl.

"We've been holding back the words for weeks, my star. You've made me so happy," Elliot says, a look passes over his face. "What about Alasdair?"

My throat constricts as I realize how far I've stumbled into this.

CHAPTER 48

ALASDAIR

"And what about Alasdair?"

I hold my breath. I shouldn't listen, but the cracked door on my way from the turret had been too great a temptation. I wanted to sneak a glimpse of the woman plaguing my emotions.

The room falls silent, and it cuts through me. Wondering if Grace is as invested as I am in our relationship and having it confirmed that she isn't tears the soft spaces in my soul to shreds.

What did I expect? I've avoided her for days.

Days that I've tried to figure out how to express my emotions. How to court Grace without jeopardizing everything.

I've never had to verbally woo someone. Elliot had done the social lifting, had expressed his interest in no uncertain terms. With Grace, I worry I can't do things in a way that will let her know how I feel.

There have been many letters written. Many words I've tried to voice. In the end, I visited Lachlan. The face of my adopted father settled some of my angst.

There's a smack, and Elliot makes a noise.

"Don't pressure her," Broderick says. "If Grace wants to communicate her feelings about Alasdair, she will."

"I just—I'm not there yet." It's not the words Grace says, but her tone that is like another stab to the heart.

Vulnerability echoes clearly from her.

She's there with Elliot and Broderick and not me. It isn't something that should come as a surprise to me.

I pull myself away from the doorway. I need to fix this.

Or figure out a way to let her go. To let her be happy.

CHAPTER 49
GRACE

Alasdair doesn't come home for dinner. We're all gathered around the table. Eloise complimenting the spread I'd helped with when Alasdair texts Elliot.

The table stills at the announcement.

My phone starts to vibrate with a call from an unknown number and I press the ignore button with annoyance.

"Where is he?" I ask.

Just an hour ago, his absence was a painful squeeze on my heart. Now, now that I'm sure about my place with Elliot and Broderick, a different emotion rises.

If he doesn't want to be around me, he needs to tell me.

He can't just disappear after sharing what we shared without a word.

I have a place here, a home, and I'm going to fight for it.

"Uh, well, he's at work. He said to start without him." Elliot frowns and Broderick looks concerned.

"Is he at the office or a building site?" I ask, standing after just sitting down.

Elliot frowns at me. "Um, probably the office."

"Then that's where we're going. I am done letting him set the pace. He may be clan leader, but someone needs to tell him when he's being an idiot."

Graham grunts, pleased. "There always needs to be someone in a clan to do that." He kisses Eloise's hand.

The frown falls from Elliot's face and his eyes light up.

"You're right," Elliot says. "We're going to bring him home."

Broderick stands and my phone begins to vibrate again.

I frown at the caller ID and answer it.

"Ms. Rivera?" I ask.

Emilia's mother sounds distressed. "Thank goodness you picked up. It's about Emilia."

CHAPTER 50

GRACE

Fear and panicked disbelief constrict my breath.

"What's happened?" I ask.

"She hasn't come home yet, and I received this terrible call from a man saying that if I want her to stay alive, I should tell you to pick up the call, whatever that means. This has to be a prank, right? Emilia probably stayed late at work and isn't answering her phone." Ms. Rivera breaks off to inhale. "This is just that awful man who's been causing all the issues for you, playing a bad joke to get your attention."

My ears start to ring.

"Right, Grace?"

"I—" I clear my throat. "I don't know, Ms. Rivera. I'm going to answer the next call I get, and I'll call you back when I know more."

"Please," she whispers.

I hang up. The entire room is watching me in silence.

This can't be happening. Involving a human would be such a messy move for Theo. Ms. Rivera is probably right, that this is a manipulation to get me to answer the phone. Emilia is probably zoned out in her lab.

"Emilia could be in trouble," I say to the room. "Her mom thinks it could be Bradshaw."

I try and keep my breathing even. "Do you think we should call the Council?"

"*Fuck.* The Council isn't going to do shit for a missing human," Elliot says.

"But they want Bradshaw," I say. "They could send people."

The phone vibrates in my hand with the unknown number again and I pick up.

"Hello, Grace, nice of you to answer my call. If I'd known all I had to do is take a human to get your attention, I wouldn't have bothered with the gifts." Theodore Bradshaw III's voice is familiar to me, but sounds different. There's a singsong tilt that could be from desperation or sadism.

"You call vandalizing my car a gift?" I ask so the room knows who I'm talking to.

Elliot's eyes narrow, there's a deadly look on his face that I've never seen before.

My harasser chuckles. "Ah, well, I regret that a bit. You can't imagine how jealous I was. I have such great plans for us, but we can get to those later."

"You don't have my friend," I say, and can hear the tang of desperation in my words.

"Oh, I'd never bluff about that," he says, and Emilia's voice kills my last hope that she is okay.

"Grace, he's crazy. You've got to call the cops! Him and his friends keep doing stupid illusions and he thinks you're all witches—"

Her voice fades in the background as the phone is pulled away from her.

My heart feels like it's going to burst. "Emilia!"

Theo tuts over the phone. "I'll never understand why you chose to socialize with a human. They are so tiring."

I blink my tears away.

"What do you want?" I ask.

"I want you to show up and do what you're supposed to." Now Theo's voice is dark, angry.

"What I'm supposed to?"

"Yes." The word is a snarl. "You'll show up, and I'll let your precious human friend go once you marry me."

"Marriage? What, do you have a priest on hand or something?"

Elliot curses and I try to block out the people in the room sharing looks.

"Or something." The singsong nature of Theo's voice returns. "If you'd rather leave her with me, she is quite pretty. I'm sure I could sell her to the right fae. It'd be years before you'd be able to track her down. Who knows what condition she'll even be in by then?"

My stomach sinks at even as bile rises in my throat.

"Don't. Where do you want me to go?" I ask.

Broderick holds back whatever words he's going to say and Elliot's tail lashes behind him.

"Go to that burger place on Main Street and Seventh. Text this number once you get there. Leave your monsters at home."

I shake my head. Adrenaline making it hard to understand his words. "My monsters?"

Elliot stiffens, stopping who ever he's texting, and I regret asking.

"The gargoyles," Theo spits. "If I see one flick of a tail, the human will be the next reanimated body you deal with."

Fear and rage fight for dominance with a healthy dose of helplessness.

"I'm on my way."

"See you soon, future wife,"Theo says and hangs up.

I look at the phone in my hand and want to vomit.

"You're not going," Broderick says.

"Yes, I am. I need to call her mom." How can I explain what's going on?

"Give me her number," Eloise says softly. "Graham and I will handle it."

I nod and give Eloise the number. She grips my hand after. "Please be careful."

Elliot frowns at me. "Grace, you can't."

"I have to!" I'm already heading to get my coat. I don't think I have time to change into something more useful, like pants. "He needs me. He doesn't need Emilia."

"You're not going—" a rumbly voice starts.

"Yes, I am!" My head snaps up, Alasdair stands in the entryway.

Alasdair nods. "I know. I was saying that you're not going alone."

The tension falls from my shoulders. "He said he'd kill Emilia if you guys come with."

"Then he won't know," Alasdair responds.

"It's too much risk to her!"

"And we won't risk losing you. I am clan leader, you are clan."

It's on the tip of my tongue to deny that, but I can't. I am clan. Whether he decides to mate with me or not, Alasdair is my clan leader.

Alasdair dips his head when I don't refute him. "We won't abandon your friend, but we will rescue her together."

A man pops into being right next to us, startling the room.

Everyone curses, but Mace smiles and rubs his hands together. "I hear we have ourselves a rescue mission."

"I thought you were an informant?" I ask. *An informant who can teleport. That's a valuable skill.*

Mace sniffs. "I take on a variety of jobs and Elliot said we have a damsel in distress. Abductions are a pet peeve of mine."

I turn back to my clan leader.

"You won't be doing this alone," Alasdair says to me.

"Okay," I breathe, taking stock of the people around me and the situation roaring in my ears. I need help. No carefully planned agenda is going to keep Emilia safe. I need my clan. "What's the plan?"

Everyone starts talking at once.

CHAPTER 51
GRACE

"Are you ready?" Mace asks.

"No, but we need to get her out," I say.

"Good. That's ready enough."

We left the burger place for the unfamiliar address listed in the text we'd received. The text included a time limit. I glance at the clock for the millionth time. It wasn't explicitly stated, but the time limit is how long we are being given to get there. Any longer and any sign of noncompliance would be bad for Emilia.

"Are you ready?" I ask. The GPS tells us we're almost there.

"Oh yes, this isn't my first rodeo," he says.

I'd argued against Mace coming with me at first, but it was a stipulation Alasdair wouldn't budge on. The informant had been incredibly helpful with the execution of this.

I turn and we're driving up an old drive. The hedges on either side overgrown. An old mansion comes into view, and I squeeze the steering wheel. It would look abandoned if not for the light spilling out into the night from the various boarded-up windows. The building looks like it's ready to crumble under a strong breeze.

I put the car into park and the door opens. An unfamiliar man stands there, bored, a fire spell hovering over his hand, crackling in warning.

"Showtime," Mace says.

We get out of the car.

"You were told to come alone," the fire-spell wielder says.

I lift my chin. "I was told not to bring gargoyles. He's not a gargoyle."

The witch at the door doesn't seem to care and Theo walks out, an ugly look on his face.

"Who the fuck is this?"

"I've employed him to take the human away once you get what you want," I say.

Theo narrows his eyes, but nods to the mercenary. "Search them."

Another man comes out of the shadows and pats the both of us down, lingering a touch too long on my breasts before winking at me and stepping away.

"They're clean. No magic on them either."

I keep from sighing in relief. He didn't find the gift from Mace. It isn't much, but the lipstick stun gun is better than nothing. *This is a last resort. It won't kill them, but it can buy you time,* he'd said.

Theo sneers. "Good. Let's get this over with."

Let's.

The wood boards beneath us creak with every step as we're led into the mansion. The moon is bright through the dirty windows but it isn't until we're led into a large room that Theo's team bothered using any light spells.

"Emilia," I breathe.

My friend is gagged and restrained by one man while another stands nearby looking at his nails. Emilia's eyes are red as if she's been crying.

I look around but only see the four hired men.

"I'm surprised you've hired so many people with your lack of funds," I say.

"Shut up!" Theo shouts and my heart skips a beat, but he smooths back his hair as if calming himself. "That's something that's going to be fixed very soon."

The comment about his state of finances has the man restraining Emilia exchanging looks with the fire-spell wielder.

"You're lucky I'm still interested in marrying you after you've been shacked up with those monsters. As if your looks and embarrassing lack of magic isn't dissuading enough."

The sting of his dismissal doesn't make it past the fear I'm trying to stifle.

I try and hide the nerves pulling at my stomach. "And you're delusional if you think my parents are going to pay you a dime."

Theo only smiles. "I have a contract. Now let's not draw this out. Come here, Grace."

"And we'll get married? That will hardly hold up." I don't want to make him angry when Emilia is at his mercy, but what is his plan?

Theo's glee is ugly. "Married in a way. Soul bonds are still considered a substitutional union by law."

Mace stiffens beside me and ice pumps in my veins.

"That seems extreme," I say, instead of screaming in horror.

The idea of being connected soul deep to this man sickens me. Bonds are notoriously hard to sever.

Theo's eyes glint with madness. "You pushed me to this. All I wanted was to bring my family back to the status they deserve. Restore what we lost in the human market and provide for our next generation." He casts his arms out at the rotting floorboards and aged wallpaper.

"Witches like you want nothing more than a gaggle of children. Your hips will make childbearing easy enough." He sniffs, disgruntled. "Maybe not the child making, but that should only be once per kid. I'm sure I can rise to the occasion."

I clench my jaw. Theo is past logical thought if he thinks that's ever going to happen. I'd scratch his face off first.

But he has me backed into a corner and he knows it.

"Come here, Grace," he says. Pointing next to him and whatever the creature is that he's paid to bond us. I want to wipe the satisfied smile off his face, but cast a look over at Emilia.

"I'll let your human go with your employee as soon as you do as I've asked. I really can be quite reasonable."

I look to Mace, and he nods. He'll get Emilia out as soon as he can.

My clan will take over from there.

I hope they aren't too late.

I lift my chin and approach the man who has harassed me and attempted to terrify me, to bend me to his will.

"Your hand in mine, dearest," Theo says.

I look over to where Emilia is.

"She can go after our bond." Theo's words are cajoling and don't help the horror fueling my every move.

I inhale and place my hand in Theo's, my skin crawling at the contact with his.

At the first tug in my chest, the world devolves into chaos.

CHAPTER 52

ALASDAIR

"Do you think this will work?" Elliot's question comes through the earpiece clearly against the sound of the roaring wind. We fly high, invisible by glamour, following Grace's car as she drives deeper into the countryside.

"It has to," I say.

We will not lose Grace now that we've found her.

The car turns down a driveway. "That's it," I say, the chill of the air helping with the adrenaline from knowing our Grace is in danger.

The old mansion looks condemned.

"Elliot, approach from the grounds. See if you can get a visual through a window. Broderick, go from the roof. I'll go through the front door. Stay in position until my say."

We hover until Grace and Mace are led inside. Our dive is silent.

The Council should be on their way. Mace called a contact of his that could get some enforcers out to apprehend Bradshaw, but when they'll get here… is unknown. Waiting for the enforcers isn't an option, with Grace's friend in danger.

Once Mace gets Emilia out of harm's way, we can neutralize the rest of the group until enforcers do make an appearance.

Our only goal is to protect Grace. I will do whatever is necessary to bring Elliot and Broderick's new mate back unharmed. I will protect my clan.

Grace is ours.

We switch our earpieces to Mace's channel to listen to the conversation.

"I can see them," Elliot says. "They are in the ballroom on the left side of the house. He has four others with him. One has Emilia."

"We wait until Mace can get her away," I say. "The longer we wait, the more likely the enforcers will show up." That would be the simplest way to settle this. Even if Bradshaw is only wanted for hexing a car in sight of the public.

For gargoyles to accost a witch, even a wanted witch, would cause issues for the clan if not worse.

The Council isn't kind to vigilante justice.

I settle at the entrance of the mansion, my coloring camouflaging me. I approach as carefully as I can. The wood floor looks in terrible condition, but only creaks slightly.

The conversation of our enemy in my ear has fury building. The rage stalls out when the male witch gets to his plan.

"…Soul bonds are still considered a substitutional union by law."

Elliot's panicked voice muffles the conversation. "We can't let that happen, Alasdair!"

I keep my voice soft. "Does Mace have a clear way to get to Emilia?"

"...Not yet," Elliot answers.

"We wait." Our witch wouldn't forgive us for putting her friend in danger, even if it were to save her from a life of being connected to the cretin monologuing.

Broderick snarls through the earpiece when Bradshaw maligns Grace's body, and I don't blame him. My primal side wants nothing more than to tear the man's throat out.

"Your hand in mine, dearest. She can go after our bond," Bradshaw says.

There will be no waiting for reinforcements. Grace may never forgive us if Emilia is hurt, but her safety supersedes that.

"Mace," I say. "Get Emilia out if you can. We move now."

CHAPTER 53
GRACE

"Hey!" Theo snarls.

The tug on my heart stops as Mace appears next to Emilia and grabs a hold of her and the guy restraining her. They disappear as he teleports them away.

Glass shatters and I try and pull my hand away from Theo, but he doesn't let me, whipping me around so my back is pressed against his front like a human shield. An arm around my throat, cutting off my oxygen.

A roar fills the air and my eyes blur at the sight of Alasdair coming toward us. Elliot throws the fire-spell wielder against a wall. The being who had been about to complete the soul bond stumbles back as Broderick advances toward him before he turns tail and runs out a doorway. Alasdair grabs ahold of the minion who groped me and throws him to Elliot.

"Fucking animals," Theo says.

I struggle against his arm even as he squeezes my throat harder and black dots bloom in my sight.

Alasdair's voice booms. "Let her go and we'll let you live."

The gargoyles prowl closer, but I'm held hostage and I can see the concern in their eyes. They don't want me hurt.

"Leave and I won't have you arrested for trespassing," Bradshaw says.

He's deranged. I gasp for breath and slide my hand into my pocket to the stun gun. The movement of my numb fingers clumsy.

"We won't go without her," Broderick growls.

"She's my wife!" Bradshaw spits.

I uncap and manage to turn the device on when Theo begins an incantation that I'm unfamiliar with but raises the hairs on my body. The sensation of death fills the air and shadows gather around his hand, waiting for him to target the spell.

It'll kill them. This spell will kill my mates, no matter how resistant their skin is to magic.

I can't let that happen.

I jam the stun gun into Theo's chest and press. The snapping sound and blue light accompany my captor's spasms. He cries out and throws me to the ground.

"You bitch!" The rage on Theo's faced is deadly, and he draws the dark spell in his hand back and throws it straight at me.

It's too late to dodge.

The roar is otherworldly, shaking my soul and heart as a big shape covers me. The shadows hit him and dance over his skin. Parts of his marbled coloring changing color, changing to stone.

"Alasdair!" I cry.

Time slows, and Alasdair strokes a finger down my face as if I'm the most precious thing he's seen.

"It's my time, Grace."

No, no no no.

A fierce look passes over his face, and he turns from me. The transition of his skin to stone spreads over his back and up his wings, but his movements don't slow.

A crunch sounds through the air and Theo's body collapses to the ground, neck sitting at an odd angle. I scramble up and Alasdair turns to me. I run my hands over his chest as if I can wipe away the death the curse is inflicting on him, but cold stone takes the place of warm skin, the spread increasing.

"J-just hold on. We'll get a healer."

There has to be a way to heal him. It can't be too late.

"Shh, little witch, they'll take care of you."

He cups my cheek and tears blur my vision and I press my eyes closed as if that will stop anything.

The pads of his fingers freeze and harden against my cheek. I open my eyes and Alasdair stands before me, entirely stone.

I scream.

CHAPTER 54
❦BRODERICK

I pull Grace into my arms after checking that the scene is safe. Her anguished sobs rend through my soul as if it's tear-soaked paper.

Grace's scream and Alasdair's stillness spreads pain through me. I'm no stranger to loss. Lachlan, my parents, but to lose Alasdair is to see our future crumble before our eyes. It's too much to consider at this moment. I suppress the pain to tend to my mates.

Our clan must be cared for. All hope isn't lost yet.

"Calm yourself, Grace. He'll come back to us," I say. There is no telling when he'll come back. The likelihood of this sleep being a permanent rest increases the longer it goes on, but those are all details that aren't important right now.

I turn to my other mate, and Elliot's eyes are vacant, glazed-over hopelessness. He knows the details. I lift my arm to him, and he looks at me as if nothing will ever be okay again.

Dammit, Alasdair, you better come back!

I make a guttural sound that has Elliot coming to me, wrapping his arms and wings around us. Grace's sobs go on unchanged, and I rub her back.

"He's… resting, star." Elliot's voice thickens as he speaks, and he buries his face in her hair. "Please breathe. Please stop crying. If you cry, I'll cry. We need to figure this out. *Please*."

Grace's sobs get quieter, and she tries to breathe.

A man teleports into the room and I tense before identifying Mace.

"The human is safe," he says. "And that last man is restrained. Your elder helped me. What's—oh no."

The demon's face falls when he catches sight of Alasdair.

He looks to me. "Is it…"

Permanent. I'm glad he trails off instead of speaking it aloud.

"We don't know," I whisper. "Can you teleport his statue back to our home?"

"Yes, but we have other things to worry about."

"Like what?" My pain morphs into frustration.

"The enforcers have arrived."

CHAPTER 55
GRACE

Broderick's grunt vibrates against my cheek, and I raise my head with a sniff. Elliot wipes the tears from his eyes.

I can't look at the statue of Alasdair right now.

The Council enforcers have arrived.

Three men stride into the room. Two have the air of witches and the third's size makes me think shifter. The witches break off and head to where Elliot had stacked the unconscious mercenaries Theo had hired.

"You're late," Mace says.

The shifter frowns. "If you had only waited—"

I cut in. "Then my friend would have been worse off than she is."

The shifter's frown is a fierce thing that seems to be the standard expression on his face.

"You won't be considered responsible for her finding out about our world."

"I don't care about that!" I say.

The shifter shakes his head. Probably discounting me as hysterical. He does a slow circle of the scene and his eyes land on Theo's body.

"This is a mess," the shifter says, his voice gruff. "You've killed a witch in his home."

I grit my teeth. "A witch who abducted my friend."

"Humans aren't under our jurisdiction," he says. His tone isn't smug or snide. He's only recounting facts.

"Are you saying that Alasdair could face charges from the Council for protecting me?" I ask.

The shifter hesitates. "I'm saying, a gargoyle killing a witch—"

"He's my mate," I say. Elliot and Broderick still.

The shifter stops talking and raises his brows. Mates have special protections under Council law. Figures, with shifters being such a big part of the paranormal population.

"You're mated to him?"

I lift my chin. "Yes."

"And you're under full knowledge that as soon as I put this in my report, that matehood is binding?" he asks.

I sense Elliot and Broderick exchanging looks, but I know what I want. I want Alasdair. He's mine and I'm going to claim him.

"Yes."

The shifter rocks on his heels. "Okay."

He turns back to his coworkers. "Looks like we missed the action. Let's clean this up. The hired help probably have warrants out."

I breathe out in relief and let my eyes fall to Alasdair, Elliot's and Broderick's words working their way through my grief.

He'll come back. He's resting.

And now, he's my mate.

CHAPTER 56
ELLIOT

My heart thuds hollowly in my chest, and Broderick drags his claws through my hair. We're in Alasdair's bed, surrounded faintly by his scent, while he's in the turret next to Lachlan. A statue. To wake or not wake, only time will tell.

Bramblewick manor had been solemn on our return. Even Emilia and her mother hadn't demanded answers from us. Miraculously, they'd decided to stay the night, saying that gargoyles are terrifying but at least they know that we're on their side. Eloise set them up in a guest room.

We'll answer their questions tomorrow. We'll do everything we need to tomorrow. Tonight, I let the grief inside me pool. Tonight, I miss the presence of my clan leader and mate while surrounded by the scent of him.

Grace had started to cry again once we were all alone in his room. Her grief taking physical form. She's never seen a gargoyle become stone. She isn't taking it well. Hell, I'm not taking it well either.

I glance at her soft face. The tear tracks dry on her cheeks. She'd cried herself to sleep, and we let her. Tonight had been a rough one for her.

Alasdair saved her life.

"He'll wake up, won't he?" I can't help but ask.

Broderick sighs, his eyes sad. "If he gets a choice, he'll wake up. He won't leave us. He won't leave both the mates he has now."

The crook of my smile is almost painful with the heaviness of my heart. "She claimed him."

"Are you really surprised?" Broderick asks.

I think about it a moment, remembering the soft exchanges between Alasdair and Grace.

"I guess not. I didn't want to hope for it too much," I say. "He has to wake up."

Broderick kisses my forehead.

I snuggle deeper into him, the itch to wrap myself in the safety blanket of my glamour is there, but my greater need is to be fully present with my mates. I need the comfort that comes from the skin to skin of my true form and to give what the comfort that I can to those I love.

"He can't leave us," I say.

All that's left is making sure Alasdair has a whole clan to come back to.

CHAPTER 57

GRACE

For this silent, awkward moment, I'm numb. Numb is better than sobbing. I don't think I'll be numb when I finally go up to the turret to see him.

But he won't wake yet.

I try and muster something, some feeling over the loud ugly emotions of my fear and grief, but all I have is guilt. I look down into the steaming mug of tea that Eloise had prepared.

"You're probably angry at me," I whisper hoarsely.

"Yep," Emilia says. Emotions flicker across her face in combination. Hurt, anger, concern. "But… I can't yell at you when you're like this."

Eloise had already handled explaining the basics about our world to Emilia and her mother. That the world is much bigger than humans are aware.

Emilia turns her gaze to the garden and her breath puffs out white in the chilly air.

"You'd yell?" I ask. I don't think I've ever heard Emilia raise her voice.

Her eyes snap to me and now the emotion on her face is pure frustration.

"I was abducted, Grace! I thought they were all lunatics that watched too many television magicians while growing up! Then *gargoyles* turn up to save the day. And I found out my best friend has been lying to me for the entire time we've known each other. Yeah, I'd yell."

"I should have told you," I say. Some of the numbness receding as guilt wells in my heart. "I was planning to tell you—"

"When?"

I inhale. "If you'd believe it, when I came back to work."

Emilia glares at me. "That's convenient. Why now when you've spent years leaving me in the dark?"

I squeeze the hot mug. She deserves honesty.

"I've always told myself that exposing you to this world would be uncomfortable for you. I didn't know any humans who knew about this world. Finding out there are gargoyles and shifters, let alone magic and witches, when you're a human… I didn't want you to live in fear. But that was a stupid excuse."

My eyes water. *Don't cry, don't cry.* "Being around Eloise, I realized that you'd be fine. Humans can adapt and you could prefer knowing about all this. I realized my real reason was more selfish… I-I didn't want you to stop being my friend."

"Why the *fuck* would I stop being your friend?" Emilia gets as close to yelling as I've ever heard her.

"I don't know." My voice raises too. "It's not logical. It's just… I didn't want you to reject me. You were the only person who cared about me for *years*. I didn't want to risk that."

Emilia sits back and shakes her head. "You are absolutely ridiculous."

"I know," I say.

We both fall silent. A bird sings a trill, and the world is suddenly lighter. Emilia knows and I never need to lie to her again.

"You're right about one thing." Emilia's eyes shine, her words a whisper. "I'm so damn scared. What do I do, Grace? The bogeyman is real. I restore books! I don't have any defensive skills against magic things."

I sniff. "That's where you're wrong. You have me. Your place is already protected, there are some charms you can carry. I can teach you all you need to know because I also don't have any flashy powers that protect me either. We'll take it one step at a time."

Emilia inhales and nods. She picks up a cookie on the table in a nervous fidget.

"How's your mom doing?" I ask.

Emilia snorts and shakes her head. "Good, actually. Probably going to pray twice as hard now."

That makes me smile. "It's not all bad."

Emilia lifts her brows.

"Think of all the old books there are," I say.

There. There's a light of hope in Emilia's eyes. "There are old books?"

I grin. "Oodles of them. Some of them needing to still be used. The director will probably be thrilled to have your restoration skills on tap for magical assets."

Emilia blushes. "If there are books, then it can't be that bad… I'm still hurt, you know."

"I know," I say.

"How is… your guy? Is he going to be okay?"

I blink rapidly, but it doesn't stop the sudden tears. As the sadness rushes back.

"I don't know," I croak.

And like the good friend she is, Emilia holds my hand and has me start telling her every single thing about this new world to keep my mind off everything.

CHAPTER 58
GRACE

Alasdair's face is even more intimidating in stone. In stone, he's the dark brooding gargoyle I first met. His heavy brows and sharp features are as dissuading as any carved statue in a cathedral, the personification of judgment and warning. In stone, his mouth doesn't curl with a teasing comment and his eyes don't heat with dark lust.

Alasdair is frozen in time, his hand reaching out just how he'd done when he'd cupped my cheek. When he assured me that Elliot and Broderick would take care of me. When he said it was his time. They tell me that he's coming back, but I don't know if it's something he's planning to do.

I sniff. My nose is red from the cold of the turret, even though the space isn't open to the night air anymore.

It's been a day since Alasdair began his sleep. Elliot said that a healing sleep could last a day, two days, or even a week, but his eyes had been dark with concern.

I snuck up here alone. I don't know if seeing Alasdair this way would have me breaking down again and I don't want to burden Elliot and Broderick with my tears.

I needed to see him. And now that I have, I hate it. I hate how final it feels, how hopeless it all is.

The hope in the face of such pain is its own kind of hurt.

"Please don't leave us," I whisper. *Wake up!* I want to shout it from the rooftops.

Alasdair is my clan leader, my reading partner, my protector, and my mate. Whether he wanted to be or not.

"Grace."

I spin at Elliot's voice.

This gargoyle's eyes are warm and soft, even if he's wearing his glamour. He'd had to make some errands for the business and wouldn't let anyone else tell him to leave it for another time. *Alasdair will return and I will not let our business or clan be in a worse state than he left it,* he'd said.

"Sorry," I say.

"What for?"

I don't know exactly what for, and then it comes to me.

"He's your mate. I shouldn't be going on and on as if my feelings are as important."

Elliot shakes his head. "Don't be ridiculous, my star. We're both his mates."

"You're the mate he chose." Now that the words have started, they won't stop. "What if he wakes up and is angry that I claimed him? He had no choice in all of this." I make a vague hand gesture. "Before everything happened, he was avoiding me."

Elliot wraps his arms around me. "Hush. Alasdair isn't the best at expressing his feelings."

"What if he doesn't really like me?" The pain of the possibility stabs me.

Elliot pulls back. "Hey, stop it. He wants to be your mate. He'll be thrilled you claimed him."

"How can you possibly know that?"

A guilty look crosses over Elliot's face and he shrugs before reaching in his inside coat pocket. "I know, because he wrote it all down."

Elliot pulls out a bundle of folded papers, thick with corners bent and secured by a rubber band. He holds the bundle out to me.

"What are those?" I ask.

"See for yourself."

My fingers brush over the texture of the paper and waves of clashing emotions have me pulling my hand away. *Alasdair.* Each fiber of paper is heavy with my mate's emotions. Flavors of worry, desire, and affection mix on my tongue.

Elliot doesn't move, letting me take my time. I breathe in, preparing myself, before I take the bundle. The waves of emotions are still there, but I can focus on one impression at a time. I sit on the stone bench and remove the elastic.

The papers are all folded in thirds, as if they are letters. Letters that were never sent. Slowly I unfold them one by one, placing the precious pages on the stone bench as if they are a collection I'm cataloging.

They are all dated over the time frame that my gargoyles have been courting me and each page gives a mixture of feelings. Each page flavored different. They are all addressed to me in some way. The first page starts with the words:

To the witch who has entranced my mate,

And is tight with stress and hesitation before splashes of humor wash the feelings away with heavy doses of frustration and hope. I don't even look at the contents of the letter yet. The emotions flowing would take hours to fully catalog. But this isn't an Archive project. These are the innermost thoughts of the gargoyle I love.

I move over each item and let the impressions flow over me, sweetening with time and practice and something else. *Love.*

I touch the last one and gasp, wrenching my hand away at the pain. The rejection and despair are almost too much to bear.

I glance at Elliot who looks away, his brow furrowed in pain even though he doesn't feel it from touching the paper. I lift the letter to read.

Little witch,

Today you confessed your love for Elliot and Broderick. The joy I feel that you have found your place in our clan is only outpaced by my own guilt and pain. Guilt because I'm jealous of the people I'm closest to and pain because I do not hold a place in your heart.

Jealousy has no place in our lives, but it's there. I want to be happy that you're happy, but I ache for your love, Grace.

Because I love you.

I don't know the exact moment it happened, but it did, and I haven't been able to express it in a way that didn't feel as if I were pressuring you or opening me up for heartbreak.

My pain that you don't return my feelings is ridiculous. It's not your fault that I've struggled with my hesitation since our night in your workroom, stalling because I don't know how to secure your affections.

I'm not smooth like Broderick or witty like Elliot. What can I offer one that shines as brightly as you?

In my indecision, I visited Lachlan, it's how I overheard your confessions. It's only now that I'm sitting and writing this letter that you'll never read that I remember one of the most important lessons he imparted to me.

Because my inability to express emotions and vulnerability isn't a new thing, merely an old mechanism that rushes to the surface at the most ill of moments.

When I first came to the Bramblewicks, I'd done everything I thought a young gargoyle should do when being accepted into a family that wasn't his. Anything to keep Lachlan, Eloise, and Graham from changing their minds. I studied and cleaned and listened to all of Graham's stories from his younger days.

But it felt wrong, and I was still plagued with the feeling that I didn't belong. It got worse and worse until I was a tangle of emotions that hardly made sense. I felt unworthy of the clan.

I left.

Luckily, I was young and dumb, and Lachlan found me. It hadn't occurred to me that he'd come looking.

No one had come looking for me before.

When he found me, he only asked me why I'd left, and it came out in words in a way that I have seldom voiced since. He listened to my worries that I would never belong, that I'd never be good enough to be a Bramblewick.

After I'd thrown out every single ugly feeling at his feet, my clan leader spoke. He told me to listen to him and to never doubt his words because he is my clan leader and knows what is best for me.

It wasn't that what I was doing was wrong, it was my motivations. I wasn't working at being myself and contributing my uniqueness to the clan. I was so worried that they'd see the things that made me who I am and throw me out like my father had done.

"That's not going to happen. Alasdair, you have to stop trying to do things the way you think everyone wants you to do them. You are Alasdair Bramblewick. You are singular and will express and do things differently. It does not make them wrong."

So I must find my own way of telling you of my love. I must trust that either you'll accept it and return it because you feel the same, or that you'll tell me that our mating is not to be.

I will respect either decision because you are needed here. And I will stop hiding. I am Alasdair Bramblewick, and a clan leader does not let old wounds stop him from doing what is best for his clan.

I am late for family dinner.

Love,

Alasdair

I set the letter in my lap, the sob building in my chest. In the end, he did find his own way of telling me.

CHAPTER 59
GRACE

"What's going on?" I ask.

Broderick and Elliot turn from the wall that's between my guest room and Broderick's room. "We're trying to figure out logistics for when Alasdair wakes. His bed is large, but we'll need a bigger one if we're going to fit all four of us."

When Alasdair wakes. Spoken as if it's inevitable rather than a possibility that decreases as the days go on. Alasdair has been sleeping for four days. Bramblewick manor oscillates between letting the grief steep through the walls and into our tasks and times like now. Times full of hope and planning for the future, as if it isn't possible for Alasdair to remain stone.

I'd gone back to work today, needing to be distracted Emilia and I are working out our new normal and there's a pang of sorrow in my heart for what we've lost, but how we are now is more honest and she deserves that.

"And what does that have to do with the wall?" I ask.

"Well, a larger bed means we need a larger room. We're trying to figure out a way to have that and for everyone to have their own rooms should they need them."

"What about the guest bedroom on the next floor?" I ask. "The one with the tiny bedroom next to it."

"And the nursery on the other side! Yes, that would work fantastic," Broderick says. "We can knock down the wall and then we'd be close…"

Broderick's face falls. Not even he, the most optimistic and cheerful of us, can talk about future children in our unknown situation with Alasdair.

I nod, sadness beginning to well.

Elliot moves toward me.

"Come on, Grace." Elliot wraps me in his arms. "Let's go and bother Eloise about how she's making the pot roast. I'm sure she'll love us intruding in her kitchen."

I let him pull me into another distraction.

***

Neither gargoyle wakes as I slip from the bed. The absence of Alasdair from our unit is too much for me to drift off. The sheets have stopped smelling of him.

I put on my usual robe and creep out of the room. Bramblewick manor remains silent tonight. The love that reverberates through the walls echoes with a loneliness. Sorrow hangs in the air, soaking into the very manor.

I climb the stairs and pass my workshop, heading to the turret.

I do this every night, hoping that this moment will be the one that our clan leader returns to us. The others do the same at different times than I. I've caught them both talking to him as if he can respond, telling him about the business or my return to work. No one knows if he can really hear them, but talking must make them feel better.

Other than my first plea, I have a harder time talking to him. But tonight…

Something about the dark shadows stabs deep at my heart. Maybe it's the discussions earlier, the mention of a bedroom next to the nursery with hope in the eyes of my mates, no matter that none of us have the heart to play intimate games past cuddling.

We're dysfunctional. The way we move is out of sync. We're missing an integral piece and without it…

I strike a long match from the boxes kept here and light the candles placed in front of Alasdair and Lachlan. The light dances over their faces. Each waver of the flame gives them the illusion of life.

I come to stand right in front of my mate. Grief and something new and inappropriate forming in my chest. Anger.

I part my lips and my confession falls from it.

"You don't get to stay like this," I whisper, and my voice cracks. "It's not fair. You all are everything on my stupid list."

The words echo in the sacred space.

"This is supposed to be when we start our life together. You made me trust you guys. Trust that if I fell for you, if I went along with Elliot's strategy, that you'd catch me. And I wouldn't have to be so alone anymore."

I hate these selfish feelings, but they are almost easier to take than the grief. The grief is never ending.

"And now I'm here, and it's everything you promised except you're missing, and nothing is okay."

I hiccup.

"Fate or whatever gods don't get to take you from me. I need *you*."

I press my cheek into his stone palm, knowing it's wet from the stupid tears I can't help shedding. My next words are vehement and honest.

"I love you, Alasdair Bramblewick, so you better wake up."

The hand on my cheek roughens in texture and cracking sounds through the air. I stumble back as stone Alasdair shatters with a mighty roar.

CHAPTER 60

ALASDAIR

I stretch, groaning as my muscles pull. I'm alive. It's as much of a surprise to me as the words wavering in my memory. Words that must have been a dream.

I love you, Alasdair Bramblewick, so you better wake up.

A feminine gasp has me looking down into wide eyes. The tear tracks on Grace's cheeks shine in the candlelight. I still at the sight of her in that short robe that teases her supple thighs.

"Grace," I start, my voice full of awe. "Oof—"

She throws herself at me, wrapping her arms around my neck. "You're alive!"

Her words are thick with emotion. The warmth of her body against mine and the smell of roses in her hair settles a rightness in my chest. Something clicks as the grogginess of waking fades.

"You love me?" I ask.

She freezes and pulls away enough to look up at me. Her pretty face determined.

"I love you. You don't need to say it back or—"

I press my palm to her face, my thumb stroking her lower lip. The tangle of emotion in my chest unwinds at the confession.

"I love you too, Grace."

"Oh." She blinks. "I thought you had a problem saying the words…"

I frown in confusion and a hot blush overtakes her cheeks.

"I read your letters. I thought we lost you…" The blush darkens.

"What letters?" I ask, then I remember the incoherent outpouring of my feelings on paper and my eyes widen. "How?"

"Um, Elliot—"

I curse, my hand falling from her face. Of course Elliot would find the letters. Anything even slightly hidden is game for snooping to him.

"They weren't meant for you," I say.

Grace's face falls in despair and I quickly correct myself.

"I wrote them for you, but I never planned on sending them." I swallow, my cheeks hot in embarrassment. "I was trying to figure out what to say."

"Oh." Her lips part.

"You can have them back." Grace's voice is small and hesitant. "They helped me while you slept. I didn't know if you were going to ever wake. The impressions on them felt like the last thing of yours I'd have."

Impressions. She could feel the emotions that I'd been struggling with in those letters and she's still here, telling me she loves me.

She's here for me.

I wrap my arms around her and lift her from the ground to kiss my witch. She responds quickly, opening herself to me, chasing my taste with her lips.

Grace moans before she pushes back against me, breaking our kiss, panting. "Are you okay—you're injured!"

"Not anymore, though this isn't the place for this. I want to see the others, reassure them that I've woken, but give me this moment with you."

I press my forehead to hers and my throat swells.

"I want you to be my mate," I say.

Grace freezes in my arms.

"Um, about that—"

"Alasdair! You're awake!" Elliot cries out and rushes us, throwing his arms around the both of us before gripping my face and kissing me. The kiss goes on and on until Grace squirms against me and her arousal blooms in the air.

I break the kiss with a grin. "I'm glad to see I was missed."

"You don't know the half of it." Elliot's voice is tight, and I think my scheming mate may be holding back tears.

Broderick comes next, somehow fitting in. Waves of relief flow from my friend, and he presses his head against mine. "I'm so glad you're back."

"You would have been an excellent clan leader in my place," I whisper, and Broderick taps me upside the head in annoyance.

I press Grace's body against mine. The rejuvenating effects of my sleep and hunger to feel my mate and the woman I'm courting makes me eager.

"I need you." I kiss Grace's forehead. "And you." I kiss Elliot's. "And I suppose a helping hand would be welcome."

Broderick's grin is wide. "Sounds like a claiming."

It does indeed sound like a claiming. Right now, I want to embrace what I have. Later I'll let myself panic about almost losing it all.

Grace starts to pull away in my arms as we exit the turret and descend the stairs.

"Let me carry you. I'm trying to convince you to be my mate, after all."

Elliot's brows go up and Grace ducks her face and mumbles into my chest.

"What was that?" I ask.

"You are my mate," she says. "I claimed you in the eyes of the Council."

There's a hitch in my step.

Grace continues. "They were going to put you on trial for killing Theo!"

She protected me.

"Oh?" Surprise is my first response; concern is my next. "You didn't feel pressured, did you?"

Broderick rolls his eyes at me and Grace glares. "I claimed you because I wanted to. No one told me to do it, and that it protected you was sugar on top."

My lips twitch. "Alright, little witch. You are fearsome and have claimed me. I see how it is."

Grace and I are mates. We'll still do a ceremony and party as tradition for our kind, but this witch is officially mine. All the worries I've had of courting disappear on a wave of relief.

We get to my bedroom, and I inhale, pleased. They've been sleeping here while I rested. The combination of scents is a homecoming.

"Are you okay with being my mate?" Grace asks.

"I'm ecstatic." I nuzzle her hair. Gratitude and love have me squeezing her hips and moving her against where I'm hard and ready through my kilt.

Grace gasps and rocks her hips against me, mewling in disappointment when I pull her away to set her on the sheets. Elliot pulls our bodies together by his grip on my kilt and kisses me as he starts untying it with a growl of his own.

Our kiss breaks, and my kilt falls to the floor.

"Alasdair…" The look on Elliot's face is pained.

I caress his face. "Shh, I'm here."

"I love you." His intake of breath sounds like a sob. "I was so worried that because I'd brought trouble to our door—"

"Hush. If anything had happened, it wouldn't have been your fault, just as it wouldn't have been Grace's fault. Our clan is whole and when there is danger, we all must rise to meet it." I kiss his forehead and feel the tension drain from him.

Grace's moan has us both looking over as a bare Broderick removes her clothing. Her robe is gone, revealing a frilly nightdress, the fabric so thin that the dark of her nipples and the warmth of her skin shows. Broderick slowly pushes the hem of the dress up, chasing it with kisses and nips, leaving pink marks on her pale skin.

Grace digs her fingers into Broderick's curly hair as he starts to lick her pussy. I want to feel her tight around me. I want to claim her and make our clan whole, but I look back to the mate I've been with for years. I need to care for Elliot.

I untie his kilt until it falls from his lithe body, and he steps from it.

"What do you need?" I ask.

Elliot's eyes are dark and complex even as they shine with happiness.

"I want us to take her. I want to claim her and watch you claim her."

"Are you sure? I don't want you to feel neglected," I tease. Usually, Elliot would be the one that I'd spend hours spoiling and claiming.

He bites his lip. "In my darkest moments, I thought I deserved to lose you for what I did. Like karma or fate was coming back to bite me, even if I don't believe in it."

"My heart…" I hold Elliot to me, our bodies swaying. I have no words for that. I can only be grateful that my rest was not final.

Elliot inhales. "It's hard to believe that this is real. Our clan is complete, you're okay, and I just… I want to appreciate it."

Grace cries out as Broderick kisses up her soft stomach to where he's plucking her nipples.

"Then let's appreciate. Let's claim our witch," I say and turn to the bed. "Broderick."

The order is unspoken but clear.

Broderick sighs. "I know, she's just so tasty and hot for us."

He pulls the dress all the way off. Grace falls back on her hands, her tits jiggle with the force of Broderick's undressing and the arch of her back lifts them as if for our mouths.

I step before her. Grace's eyes go wide at my bare, aroused body.

"Little witch, are you ready to be all of our mates? Take our seed and add to our family?" I ask and tap a claw on her contraceptive necklace. Her breath catches at the reminder.

"One day, little witch," I say. My voice thrums with promise and her eyes lid in desire.

"Today," she says.

We all stiffen at that. My gut tightens in surprise and heat. Grace twists the necklace chain.

"Is that okay?" she asks, as if interpreting our posture as anything other than primal need. We are beasts, after all. The thought of a fertile female offering herself hits our senses on an instinctual level.

I clear my throat. "It's more than okay."

I look at my clanmates in question, and they both nod. The movement a hungry one. Our inner predators rising.

I look back into her big eyes. "Are you sure, Grace? You don't want to take any time to plan this out?"

"You almost died, Alasdair. I'm done waiting for everything to fit my plan perfectly. I want this with you all. I've never been surer in my life." She holds the thin chain between her fingers, as if waiting for one of us to object.

We won't.

"Take it off, little witch," I say. "We have a promise to fulfill."

CHAPTER 61
GRACE

My breath catches in my throat. The promise Alasdair made about filling me full of seed and knots.

I can't wait.

Just like I can't wait to start our lives together. This is us. This is the right time.

My fingers are eager as I undo the clasp of the necklace. The chain of the charm drags against my skin and Broderick catches it on a claw, moving it to the bedside table for me.

The tension in the air is drugging. Alasdair's claw traces up my throat and under my chin. The prick of it has shivers traveling over my skin.

"You'll take my knot tonight," Alasdair says.

A spike of fear and thrill has my heart pounding. "Yes, alpha."

The hungry growl from Alasdair has euphoria singing in my blood.

"We're going to fill you up, stretching you to the point that you can take my knot," Alasdair says.

They move as if choreographed, all the gargoyles on the same page. Broderick slides behind me, pulling me up on his lap as Elliot takes position between my legs. He kisses me with long and heady pulls. When he presses his body against mine, it grinds my ass against Broderick's hard cock.

Broderick moans in my ear. "You're so *fucking* beautiful, Grace. We're going to take good care of your greedy little cunt. Elliot's cock is the easiest to take. He's going to get you sloppy wet and hot for this until your body is begging to swallow our knots."

I moan and Elliot's hot cock slides through my soaked folds. Elliot smiles at me, his eyes glittering in a tease. "I wonder who is going to be the one who sires our first child. I am the first. I could fill you to the brim and get the job done before these two even get their cocks out."

Alasdair growls, hand fisting in Elliot's white hair, but it doesn't stop the gargoyle on top of me from sliding home inside my body. I gasp. His girth stretches me around him and the places he hits in my body increase the throb of pleasure. I want to be filled up so full.

"We won't fight over Grace's pussy. We aren't quite that primitive," Alasdair says. The tightness of his body belies his words.

"She likes it." Elliot says with a moan. "Gets so tight. So perfect."

Elliot starts to rut into me, his knot pressing against me with each thrust.

"Oh yes," I whisper, each move hits a spot inside me that has my toes curling.

Broderick's hands cup my breasts and massage them in a way that has my whole body tensing in want. His cock slides with precum between my ass cheeks and up my back. His shaft and knot pressing teasingly against my asshole each time.

"Someday, sweet witch, I'm going to take your ass while Elliot ruts into you. Wouldn't you like that?"

"Yes, yes, yes," I say, and Broderick slides one of his hands down my body, slipping to where Elliot's and my body meet, rubbing slow circles around my clit. The pleasure is overwhelming. I move, my feelings and sensations too much to keep still, but Broderick holds me tight, making me take the stimulation and each slide of Elliot's cock.

I grunt and twist until the climax racing toward me hits and I arch my back with a cry. Elliot groans and presses his knot against my opening as my pussy flutters around his cock. I yelp as my body yields to his and all I can focus on is the stretch of my body as his knot slides into me.

Elliot's hips jerk against mine, the muscles of his core tight. Heat fills me and I whimper at the pressure.

"That's it, Grace, take it all," Elliot moans, rocking his body with each throb of his cock.

We pant and my body clamps on the knot inside me, the place where it swells against my internal walls throbbing against my G-spot.

"I could stay like this all night now that I have you under me." Elliot teases the other hungry gargoyles in the room. "I think I can fill you up at least one more time."

My lips twitch. "Elliot—"

Alasdair growls a deep sound that has Elliot and I gasping as his knot slips from me. Elliot blinks, stunned as his seed drips. He stumbles back against Alasdair, a combination of our releases streaking his front.

"Well, isn't that a nifty trick?" He looks back at his mate.

Alasdair blushes. "I didn't know that was possible. It just came out of me."

The cool air hits the sweat and arousal between my legs and I shiver, Broderick's grip around me and stroking fingers the only thing keeping me warm.

"Makes sense with reproduction." Broderick shrugs. "If there is a stronger alpha around, having a knot stuck in place would make a female inaccessible. We've just never done something like this before."

I squirm as Broderick muses about gargoyle dynamics and keeps circling my clit, gasping when more seed leaves me on a gush.

"You definitely feel wet enough. Are you ready for me, Grace?" Broderick purrs.

I nod without thought as I watch Alasdair slide his hand over Elliot's slicked front. Applying it to his own cock before Elliot hungrily drops to his knees and laps at it. The move has heat building in my cheeks.

Broderick's grip around me comes to life and suddenly I'm on all fours. He presses the head of his cock against my pussy, and I gasp as my body gives to him.

I groan as he sinks the rest of his shaft inside me, slowly. My pussy acts as hungry as they teased me about, accepting more and more of the larger gargoyle until his knot is flush with me. As if my body knows what we're doing, knows that I need to be claimed.

Broderick snaps his hips and my breath leaves on a sound at the impact of his knot.

"I told you I'd claim you like this. Like the beast inside me wants." He grips my shoulder and holds me in place. "My beautiful witch, take me."

Each move of his body into mine defies polite description and is tinged with utter need.

He *fucks* me.

And I take it. It's intense and ramps up something desperate in me. Something different than the slow building of need and climax of before. Pleas fall from my lips, unintelligible and slurring together with each impact.

My hands clutch the sheets and instinct has my chest sinking to the bed. Each thrust sinks Broderick deeper into my body, imprinting on me so that I'll never be free of him.

"Broderick," I beg, needing the release that is calling my name.

Broderick groans and curses. His fangs drag over the shoulder he isn't holding, and he sinks his teeth in. He grips my hips with both hands now and snarls as he forces his knot in.

I scream, dropping my face into the sheets as my climax takes me. Each spurt of his release pushes my release higher with the ache of pressure and heat. The orgasm goes on and on until I can only gasp in air.

Broderick releases my shoulder, the spot burns but he licks away the blood and I shiver. He turns us on the bed, spooning as I pant. *Gods, my brain is gone.*

"You take my knot beautifully, sweet witch." Broderick runs his hands over my body. The warmth of them over chilled skin relaxing me. The swell of his knot still large inside me but he doesn't rock or try to prolong our connection.

"You bit me." My words lack heat. The sensation of feeling claimed wraps around my heart. I'd forgotten about bites.

"Should I have bitten her?" Elliot asks, claws combing my long hair away from my face.

Alasdair's voice is a rumble. "If you have to ask, then no. The instinct is either there or it isn't."

The sound of Alasdair wakes my body up some. As if it knows I'm not done. The clan leader will be the last to claim me. I'm his and no deep ache is going to stop me from accepting all of him.

My breathing starts to return to normal and Broderick kisses the sensitive parts of my neck. I hum in pleasure and the bed dips. I blink and Elliot lies there, head propped up on his elbow as he starts to add to the soothing touches.

He winks at me and the touches stop being soothing. He tweaks a nipple and slides his body down. I moan at the hot lick of his tongue on my stretched pussy. Broderick hissing as the tongue wraps around him.

"Elliot, don't. If you keep that up, my knot will never go down—" Broderick moans.

"Brat." Alasdair smacks Elliot's ass. "He likes it when I growl."

"Maybe I need to learn how to growl at him." Broderick says and Elliot's eyelashes lower before he sucks on my clit.

I gasp and Broderick curses as I tighten on him. Alasdair strokes his hand over his cock, his eyes dark in anticipation.

"Elliot." Alasdair's low growl hits me in my gut again and Broderick breathes a sigh of relief as he slides free of me.

Elliot pulls away and winks at me. "It's hot. As is seeing the seed dripping out of you."

My cheeks burn.

Elliot turns back to Alasdair. "I think she's wet enough to take you. Are you ready to be bred, Grace?"

"Oh gods," I say. My core and pussy already heavy with arousal, achy with the way I've already been stretched.

"Come on, troublemaker." Broderick grips Elliot by the hair and pulls him in for a kiss before lifting him into his arms. Leaving me on the damp sheets, facing a hungry clan leader. Alasdair looks even bigger.

I pull myself into a sitting position, gasping at the gush of wetness between my thighs, even after Elliot's tongue bathing.

I look up at my clan leader, my mate. His nostrils flare. "Will you claim me?" I ask.

Alasdair's eyes darken and he nods. My breath escapes on a relieved shiver.

"Lie back for me. Spread your legs wide."

I do, my nerves lodging in my throat, my lips trembling. He places his large hand on my thigh and pulls it even wider. I whimper, feeling the combined releases flowing from me and dripping over my asshole. Alasdair watches the procession, his tail wrapping around my other knee to keep me wide as he places his hand on my pussy. He brushes his knuckle over the sensitive skin before pressing it against my asshole.

I draw in a breath in alarm, and Alasdair smiles.

"That isn't going to happen tonight. Someday though, for now, just enjoy the sensation."

He massages his knuckle against the ring of muscle and my eyes close at the foreign sensation. It inspires a different coil of arousal that sparks my curiosity. I moan, relaxing into the touches. His hand pulls away and my eyes open at the feel of his cock pressing against my pussy.

The size difference is… substantial. If I wasn't so lust drunk, I'd be more hesitant about this, but my body knows what it can take, what I've already taken. And my body wants to be claimed by Alasdair. I want to be his.

I rock my hips up and Alasdair lifts them. My back sinks deeper into the sheets and he pushes his cock against me. I moan at the stretch of his girth and the head of his cock notches in.

"Oh gods," I whimper.

Alasdair grabs my hand and kisses my palm while he rocks his hips gently. The action is sweet and my heart melts. He starts kissing down my delicate wrist until getting to the soft part of my forearm. He sinks his teeth in.

"Ouch!" I yelp and then moan as his shaft sinks inside me, deep and hot.

"How does that feel, little witch?" Alasdair asks, licking the bite until the sting turns to a dull throb similar to the heavy ache of his cock inside me.

I shift my hips in his grip and the internal slide, making me groan. "Like you bit me."

Alasdair's chest shakes with a laugh. "It was an effective distraction, and my mark looks so pretty on your skin."

I pull my arm away from Alasdair and inspect his work. The bite mark does look pretty. Red against the white of my skin. It'll leave a delicate scar to trace.

A symbol of my belonging. I'm a Bramblewick. I'm their mate.

Alasdair drags his cock out of my body.

"So tight it's like you're trying to keep me inside you," he says.

When he slowly thrusts inside me, I throw my head back. The pressure is intense.

"So full," I murmur.

"Yes, you are. You're full of me, and full of the seed of our clan."

I know I'm full of seed because every thrust in is wet, the sounds are embarrassing and erotic all at once.

"I want yours," I say.

"You'll get mine, little witch, but you'll need to work for it. You'll need to take my knot." Alasdair presses the bulge of flesh against my opening on his next thrust in and I gasp at the added thickness, barely able to take any of it.

"*Gods*," I curse.

"Relax, Grace. It'll happen."

I nod my head and jump at the tickle of something stroking against my clit, groaning as Alasdair's tail massages it.

"I don't know if I can do this." Tears spring to my eyes and Alasdair's touch becomes soft, his face warm.

"I love you, whether you take my knot or not."

I wrinkle my nose at the words.

"But," he says, his eyes dark. "You can take me, and you will take me if you want to be filled with my cum."

My breath out is a silent keen. I need exactly that.

"Yes, alpha," I say.

He grunts at my soft words, and I hear Elliot moan. I turn my head and see Broderick's body moving against Elliot's, his hand wrapped around his throat. Elliot's eyes are on Alasdair and I, his cheeks a darker gray.

"They can't handle watching us and not touching each other," Alasdair says. "You spread wide, taking my cock is too hot for them to sit and twiddle their thumbs."

I gasp a laugh. "So they're twiddling something else?"

"The sight of you is arresting, little witch. How can they resist watching you be claimed by me?"

"Give it to me, Alasdair. Make me take you," I say.

The first sharp thrust inside me. The jolt of heat at the slap of his knot against me has me ready for the next. Alasdair doesn't disappoint. His body moves into mine, stretching and hitting the spots inside me I didn't know I needed filled.

My body accepts Alasdair as its alpha. Each thrust brings whispers of pleasure singing through my veins and I submit. I give. I yield.

I don't know how Alasdair knows that it's time, maybe it's the way my moans sound or how my body squeezes him, but when he presses his knot against me this time, I take it.

My back arches. My groan is guttural at the deep stretch and surrender of my mind as his knot slides inside and expands, locking us together as the hot rush of his release fills me. I cry out and push against his chest, almost in panic at the rush of pleasure and pressure. My body tightening on his in anticipation of peaking.

"It's too much," I gasp.

Alasdair's body is tense, and he growls, motionless except for the clenching of his core muscles to keep his body from rutting inside me. More heat fills me, overflowing even as I squeeze harder around his knot.

"Breathe, Grace, you're doing great." Broderick strokes my face.

Elliot caresses my breast, his voice filled with awe. "Look at you, my star. You've done it."

My body starts to relax until the tightness of our fit isn't all consuming. I moan at the beautiful ache of cradling Alasdair in my most intimate place.

Alasdair's mask of concentration breaks into a curve of his lips. A low, pleased sound reverberates through his chest.

"You stole my sanity there," Alasdair says, rocking his hips softly. "Is this okay, now?"

I hum. "Yes."

The tug of him inside my body starts to build pleasure in my core.

Alasdair's body moves against mine. "It's time to reward our witch."

Elliot continues to play with my nipples and Broderick grasps my hair, pulling it just hard enough to amp me up. Alasdair's tail rapidly strokes my clit until I start to struggle against the clasp of our bodies.

It's all too much, as if my senses are in a tug-of-war and each pull leads to collapse.

"That's it, little witch. Squeeze my knot," Alasdair growls, using the pad of his thumb to rub my arousal over my clit. I thrash and writhe until finally my orgasm crashes over me as Alasdair's mouth meets mine, taking my scream for his own. Taking my body and my love and giving me everything I ever wanted in return.

It's sometime later, after the cleanup and a proper shower, that we're cozy in bed together. The larger bed is a little cramped for three gargoyles and a woman, but I lay on top, in the groove between Alasdair and Elliot.

I trace my fingers over Alasdair's unique color patterns in a dazed way, letting my mind start to slip into the world of dreams. Dreams are second best to what our life is now.

Alasdair grips my hand in his and kisses my head. His words have tears of happiness springing to my eyes and a glow of love in my chest that will not be suppressed.

"Welcome home, Grace."

EPILOGUE
GRACE

I laugh and snap my mouth shut; my teeth and tongue icy from the frigid wind. The city lights from below illuminate all of us. Me in Elliot's arms, bundled up in my thick long coat, hat, and mittens. Broderick and Alasdair fly in front of us.

I'm glad my mates demanded I dress in layers because this night flight is *freezing*. My nose is probably bright red, but I wouldn't trade this for being warm at home tonight.

The world from above is dazzling. The wisps of clouds trail over and under us. Illuminated by the full moon above and the lights below until they look like dusky cotton candy.

"Having fun?" Elliot asks loudly in my ear.

"This is fantastic!" I call back.

Elliot smiles. "I'm glad."

I'd reminded Elliot about his promise of taking me flying sometime and he said he'd remedy that if I didn't mind the cold. I didn't realize he'd meant to do it *tonight*. I'd needed to take an extra ten minutes to revise my clothes and in the end had still gone with a dress.

I have plans hidden under this dress.

Even with the delay, we are going to be right on time. Alasdair ushered us out the door. He's scaled back on the business, trying to find a balance now that he's investing more time in being clan leader. He's been happier lately but is still very punctual about appointments.

"There it is!" Broderick yells back, pointing to a building roof that has a door open. The light from the inside casts a cheerful brightness over the snow on the roof.

"It's good that we're planning to stay the night," Elliot says. The white flakes start melting against my skin and coming down in swirls.

We land on the roof and a figure approaches us from the doorway.

"Rose!" I hug the matchmaker, and she laughs.

"I'm glad your trip here went smoothly. Let me show you to your group's room," Rose says, narrowing her eyes at Elliot. She's probably still annoyed about him being able to lie to her, apparently part of her gift is picking up on dishonesty.

Unfortunately for her, my gargoyle is skilled in that arena.

***

We openly marvel at the room once Rose leaves us. The space is luxurious, with a medium-size bathing pool sunk into the ground on one side and a large padded area with bedding on the other. The entire room is done in mosaic designs of pink roses with gold accents.

Alasdair prowls around the space, ever our protector.

The hands of my other two mates grab at me, taking my coverings and coat first.

I laugh as Elliot helps me pull off the snow boots as Broderick removes my dress with efficient tugs. I fall into a chair that is more pillow than support in a slip that is just short enough to give Elliot the eyeful he wants. He stills, and his gaze meets mine.

"Is it my birthday?" Elliot asks, his hand holding my stocking-clad foot.

"Sure," I tease.

Broderick trills a purr and I press my thighs together. The black stockings decorate my thighs with lace against my sensitive skin. The garter belt can be seen through the thin fabric of the slip.

"Fuck me, little mate. You look like a gift," Broderick says.

Elliot is still stunned. His hands sliding up the stockings, careful of his claws. He traces where the lace stretches around my thigh, and I shift my hips.

"Like a sex goddess," Elliot says.

"Elliot." We all jump at Alasdair's rumble. "Perhaps you should give our little witch a thank you gift rather than stare."

Elliot lets out a growl and dives in. I cry out as his dexterous tongue licks me through my panties before he slides it inside them and me.

I gasp as Broderick's tail wraps around one leg, pulling it a part to present me better to Elliot.

The slip is gone in my next breath and Broderick carefully removes my bra.

Elliot's tongue strokes in and out of my pussy and my thighs pull against Broderick's grip and tail.

"C-candles!" I say. "We have to start the ritual."

Elliot gives a long lick up through my slit and pulls away playfully. "Why didn't you say anything?"

We stumble over to the altar with teasing spanks and laughs.

Alasdair's mouth twitches. "Heathens. I can't take you to a hedonistic bathhouse without you misbehaving."

I slide my arm around him. My bite mark brushes against his back, healed.

"You like us misbehaving," I whisper.

"I like benefiting from your misbehavior," he rumbles.

There are pillar candles set on the altar. After our revelations to Rose, the bathhouse accommodated for my extra mates easily. We are hardly the only poly mating they've had.

There are five candles lined up. We each light one candle with a long match, and, with some maneuvering, light the middle candle together. Our bodies huddle close as we all grip the match together. As soon as the wick of the candle takes, the air ripples with an unearthly static charge.

"That should be it—" I end on a screech as Elliot picks me up and dashes for the large, padded area meant just for this purpose. I'm giggling as he gently lays me on the bedding.

"I wasn't done," he says and slides back down my body. My giggles turn into moans when his mouth lands back on me. Elliot unsnaps my garters and pulls my panties off, leaving me completely bare before my mates except for the lacy tights.

Broderick pulls some items from the bag he brought, giving them to Elliot.

Elliot makes a happy sound and picks up the item. My gasp echoes off the tiled walls when I see the butt plug. Elliot's eyes glint and his smile widens.

"Are you excited, my star?"

I pant and clench on emptiness that won't be there much longer. Soon I'll be filled to the brim.

"Yes," I whisper.

"Good girl," Alasdair says, and I bite my lip to keep from begging.

Elliot lubes up the butt plug and flips me onto my hands and knees, one of my mates puts a large pillow under me to grip. Big hands, that I suspect are Alasdair's, pull the cheeks of my ass apart and the lube hits my asshole in a drizzle.

Elliot massages the cold plug against my pucker and I try and relax the nerves that tighten my body with anticipation.

"So hot watching your ass stretch for the toy. We're going to make you feel so good tonight."

I whimper and Elliot pushes the rounded tip of the plug in and out.

We've done anal play a few times and even worked in Broderick's cock once. Tonight isn't going to be only anal though.

"I get your marvelous ass tonight." Broderick says, reaching under me and caressing my breasts in a way that makes my body feel even more empty. "You'll take me for every single time you've bent over in front of me, taunting me."

I shiver at that. The plug feels large against my ass, but it'll fit.

Elliot sighs. "You get so wet when we play with your ass."

"Feels good," I murmur.

In the corner of my vision, I see Alasdair grab another item from the bag.

"Get that plug in place, my heart, so you can get yours," Alasdair says.

Elliot rocks against me and pushes harder on the plug. I moan, trying to relax.

"You've got this, Gracie." Broderick coaxes. "Just like before. Bear down—"

I cry out when the plug slides in and all of my mates moan. I wiggle my ass, getting used to the pressure.

"Is that okay?" Elliot asks.

"Yes." My cheeks hot. "Your turn."

I turn over to enjoy the show of Elliot bending over and Alasdair starts working the butt plug inside him. Not as gently as Elliot had done for me.

Broderick drapes his body over mine. He kisses me and I moan in delight, pulling him in. My lips are still cold from our night flight despite the heat and humidity in the bathhouse.

Broderick hums. "You're cold. Do you want to take a soak?"

I bite my lip. The steam rising off the water calls to all my cold bits. "It won't ruin the moment?"

Broderick purrs. "Never. It will be good to leave the plug for longer."

My blush fights with the chill of my skin.

"We have all night," Broderick says, sliding off my tights before picking me up like he usually does. I've gotten used to the surprise bridal carries. I make a sound as the position changes the way the plug feels and I clench around it.

"A quick soak. Like, enough to get my nose to stop feeling cold," I say, squirming at the sensation of being filled there.

Broderick wades into the pool until we're both submerged. I moan with total abandon, my body going lax once it hits the water. The heat is perfect and sinks into my skin.

Broderick laughs. "You were saying?"

"Maybe a little longer than a quick soak," I say.

Broderick lets me sink more in the water and my feet touch the bottom. His hands run over the skin of my back, and he starts to massage me.

I sigh, my head falling back. "Careful, or I'll fall asleep before the fun part."

Smack!

Elliot's responding cry has me snapping to attention. Elliot's face is contorted in pleasure-pain, the gray of his skin making it impossible to see the imprint of the hand on his ass. Alasdair steps away and the end of the butt plug is right where it's supposed to be.

Elliot's tail is curled all the way up and he's rocking his hips back. "Please, Alasdair."

Alasdair's laugh has a cruel edge to it that has my whole body tensing in delight. "If you want something after how bratty you've been, you'll need to get me hard."

Elliot crawls toward Alasdair, licking the larger gargoyle's already hard cock.

"Fuck, they're hot," Broderick whispers in my ear.

"Mmhmm," I say.

Broderick's hands come around and he plays with my breasts. Each touch and squeeze has me clenching around the butt plug.

My ass presses against my gargoyle, his cock hard and ready.

"Broderick," I whisper.

He purrs. "All nice and toasty, Gracie?"

"Yes." My voice sounds needy.

"One thing." Broderick turns me and steps on a higher ledge. He presses my breasts together on the surface of the water and pushes his slick cock between them.

The sight of the head of him thrusting through my breasts has me biting my lip. Broderick groans and pinches my nipples.

"Please, Broderick." My voice is reedy from need. "It's going to be harder to fit you if I come."

Broderick releases my breasts with a reluctant sigh. He pulls me out of the pool and kisses me as the water runs down our bodies.

"You're such a gift, Gracie."

I nip his lip. "Then give me what I asked for."

"Broderick," Alasdair says.

Broderick dries me off and carries me back to the bedding. I fall to my knees where Alasdair is reclining on the pillows, Elliot's head bobbing over his cock. I crawl over and slide my hand over his chest. Alasdair grips my hair and kisses me.

"Little witch," he says, his voice striking a chord in my body like always.

"Alpha."

"Are you ready to get fucked?"

I shiver and nod.

An arm wraps around my waist, pulling me back against the scent of cedar. Broderick starts moving the plug in and out of my ass, and I moan.

"Spread your pretty thighs for your alpha, Gracie. I'm sure he'd love to see how wet you are from being all plugged up. I wonder, how much will you gush when I fuck your greedy ass?"

My face burns as Alasdair inspects the arousal coating my thighs. Elliot releases Alasdair's cock with a pop. His eyes dark and a growl escaping him at the sight of my pussy on display.

Broderick pulls the plug from me, and I cry out. He kisses my shoulder, the spot marked with his bite. "You're doing so well."

Broderick's wings fluff some pillows, and he pulls me into a spooning position, the pad of his finger circling my clit and the head of his cock sliding between my ass cheeks.

He leans away and I hear the click of the bottle of lube. When he presses back to me again, his cock returns on a glide of lube, pressing against my asshole.

"You're ready for me, aren't you?" Broderick asks.

I'm desperate for him. "Please, Broderick."

I gasp as Broderick starts to press against me, relaxing enough that my body gives to the head of his cock. I make a sharp sound at the stretch of it, and everyone freezes. I take deep breaths, trying to adjust to the burning stretch of my body around his cock.

"Do you want to help distract our mate, my heart?" Alasdair asks Elliot.

Elliot's fangs flash with how wide his grin is. "Of course."

Alasdair and Elliot move toward us. Elliot trails his long tongue down my body before sliding it between my legs with a groan as if he licks ambrosia rather than my wet pussy.

Alasdair leans down and kisses me. "You've got this little witch. Let Broderick inside you so we can stuff you full."

Precum beads on his cock and I lick my lips. "Can I taste you?"

Alasdair's rumbly growl has my body tightening. "Of course you can."

He doesn't make me beg for it. I grip the shaft and suck on the head of him. I can't take him as deep as Elliot can, but I flick my tongue over him and suck down his taste, reveling in the praise.

"Such a good girl, you're our pretty mate that just wants all of your holes filled," Alasdair says, combing my hair out of my face.

Broderick's purr is low, and my body reacts, relaxing. Broderick slides deeper in my ass. I moan around Alasdair's cock and bask in his pleasured growl.

The throb of Broderick's cock and the slide of Elliot's tongue whip the sensations surging through my body to greater heights.

Elliot starts kissing up my body and sucking on my nipples as Broderick moves his cock in and out of my tight ass. My body adapts and the heavy stroke of him against my insides makes my pussy achy and empty.

Alasdair pulls his cock from my mouth and I make a sound in dismay.

"It's time to fill you up, little witch. Spread your legs for Elliot."

Elliot releases my nipple and slides up my body, taking my face in his hands and kissing the taste of Alasdair from my mouth.

I widen my legs and Elliot slides his weeping cock against me.

"Ready, my star?" he asks.

I try to suppress the urge to whine. The anticipation has me wanting to be filled.

"Just take me already," I say.

Elliot's eyes glitter and he pulls my hair so we're making eye contact. He notches the head of his cock in my pussy and thrusts forward. I gasp when the pressure gives and the smug look on his face transforms into a pained awe as his thickness slides inside me.

"Fuck, you're so tight," Elliot says. His voice as tight and desperate as I feel. Elliot presses his forehead against mine and pants. "I can feel Broderick inside you."

Alasdair positions himself behind Elliot. Elliot cries out as Alasdair removes the plug and pushes his thick cock into him without preamble or warning.

The push presses Elliot's knot against me but it won't go in. There's no room for it, no more give.

Our sighs and moans build as our bodies move together. Broderick and Elliot pushing deep before dragging out. Every thrust of Alasdair pushes Elliot inside me.

We're so connected I could cry.

Each move sets off a chain reaction of sensation and heated bliss.

Broderick circles my clit in a steady rhythm. When he scrapes his teeth over my shoulder, I'm done for.

I come on a shout and Elliot growls, his body thrusting into mine harder until Alasdair reaches around and grips his knot and the hot flood of Elliot's release fills me up. Elliot cries out as Alasdair's hips push hard against his, sending Elliot deeper into me.

Broderick's purr breaks on a snarl and his fist brushes against my stretched ass before his heat fills me there.

Our gasping breaths are the only sound in the room.

"Fuck me," Elliot says.

"I think that's been covered, for all of us," I say.

"Well, if you only *think* it, perhaps we should move on to knotting," Broderick purrs, but his voice is teasing enough that I'm pretty sure he's joking.

Alasdair takes my hand and our fingers interweave.

Even without knots, we stay joined. The way I can feel my mates' breathing and heartbeats in tandem with the touch of our bodies makes my heart swell in my chest. I sigh in bliss, unwilling to break our connection. Broderick's and Elliot's hands run over my body, soft touches as the sweat cools on my skin.

Alasdair kisses my palm.

"Was it all you wished for?" Alasdair asks.

My smile is content and fuzzy. "This is all I could ever want."

Alasdair chuffs. He knows I'm not talking about the sex.

Elliot kisses me softly. "Together."

Broderick kisses my shoulder.

"Ours."

Theirs.

EXTENDED EPILOGUE
EMILIA

I unlock my office and I frown at a small crate sitting in front of the door. That's strange. The crate has shipping stamps on it and looks like a crate that Grace would get.

She's been introducing me to more and more of what she handles, using the lure of old books to soothe the ruffled feathers and fear caused by discovering her lies. Lies that revealed that the world is just as dangerous of a place as my anxious paranoia has been trying to tell me for years.

Usually, the crates are shipped directly to her lab, so I don't know why it's here. Maybe it's been sent to her office by mistake? I sigh and pick it up. It's lighter than I figured and my blood rushes to my head as I straighten too quickly.

I shake my head and place the crate on Grace's desk for when she gets in. That won't be for another couple of hours. I hadn't been able to sleep, what with worrying that there may be a monster in my closet or down the street or at my favorite food place.

So many people everywhere I turn that could overpower me with laughable ease.

Stop thinking about it!

My social anxiety had been bad enough without knowing that I could get hexed for looking at a witch the wrong way. If I'm not going to sleep, I might as well get some work done.

There's an email from the director that shows up first in my inbox titled: Crate Delivered to Office. It details that the crate contains a damaged book that Grace needs to catalog and that I need to evaluate how much of it can be restored. I roll my eyes. How kind of the director to ask whether my current workload would allow for me to accept this project.

Asshole.

Attractive asshole, but an asshole all the same. Not that I've ever spoken a full sentence to the man, but his curt emails and the way he looks down his nose at me until I turn tail and run leaves much to be desired.

A hum of excitement sings through my blood. I love old books. I narrow my eyes at the crate. I have a crowbar around here somewhere. Grace won't be in for hours, and it would be easier when blocking out my time for the week to just evaluate the book now.

There's no reason I can't look at it.

What harm can a book do?

THE END

Note from the Author

Hello Dear Reader!

Thank you for reading Deceived by the Gargoyles!

This book… when Stalked by the Kraken received more love than I ever anticipated, I knew that my next monster romance had to be my first monster crush, the Gargoyles cartoon from the 90's. I adored that show and will probably be a Goliath fan girl for life.

I started this project with utter excitement, which overflowed in every aspect of book creation. I blew past my deadlines repeatedly. The Bramblewicks demanded more time, and I gave it. I enjoyed being in this world so much. I just want to curl up on an over large couch and stay at Bramblewick Manor forever, but the story had to end so that I could share it with the world.

And Grace and the Bramblewicks deserved to get their happy cuddly ending.

A thank you to Cat Giraldo for (rapidly) beta reading this book! Your insight allowed me to tell this story with the care and respect it deserves.

As always, thank you, Dear Reader, for reading my book. It's always a marvelous thing that people read the books that I create and I'm grateful for you.

L. Lark

About the Author

Lillian Lark was born and raised in the saltiest of cities in Utah. Lillian is an avid reader, cat mom to three demons, and loves writing sexy stories that twist you up inside.

More information about Lillian can be found on her website at LillianLark.com